LAWLESS

HARROW CREEK HAWKS
BOOK 3

TRACY LORRAINE

AUTHOR NOTE

Dear reader,

Lawless is the third book in the Harrow Creek Hawks series. It is a dark captive why choose romance. This means our lucky lady gets to enjoy three guys and doesn't have to choose.

If you're not okay with that, or any of the warnings below, you might want to pass this one by!

Dub con, non con, rape and coerced sex (not on page, but implied from past), self harm, bullying, violence, child sexual abuse (in flashbacks), child abuse (in flashbacks), captivity, knife play, breath play, sociopathy, physical abuse, kidnapping, confinement, nightmares, PTSD, detainment, obsession, narcissism, verbal abuse, torture, blackmail, slut shaming, scars, sibling loss, infertility, loss of the ability to conceive via trauma.

If, like me, you're now internally screaming *give it to me*, after reading that, then let's go.

Enjoy the ride!

T xo

1

ALANA

Silently, Mav opens the front door and tugs me through it, out into the night.

Cool fall air rushes over my face and a shiver races down my spine. Although I don't think that has anything to do with the temperature, and everything to do with what's happening.

With my hand locked in his, Mav takes off into the darkness.

I want to look back, to see if either of them are watching us but I can't, he's going too fast, forcing me to run to keep up with him.

It's no secret that the manor house that Reid and JD have made theirs is massive. It can be seen up here on its hill from almost every part of Harrow Creek. But it isn't until now that I fully appreciate the vastness of the grounds.

My lungs burn and my leg muscles scream as Mav continues forward, as if the hounds of hell are snapping at our feet.

"Slow down," I beg, my body quickly giving up on me.

I knew things were bad after my time down in the

basement, but my lack of exercise over the past couple of weeks is now blindingly obvious.

"We're almost there," he whisper-shouts back.

His grip on my hand tightens and he keeps up his pace. I want to cry and demand that he stops, but I don't. Whatever is going on is serious. He wouldn't be doing all this if it weren't.

My legs are trembling, my chest heaving when he finally slows to a stop under the cover of trees on the perimeter of Reid's land.

The second my legs stop moving, I bend over, resting my hands on my knees, and try to catch my breath.

Unwilling to stop touching me, Mav's hand lands on my lower back. His presence, his support and his love are unrelenting.

Finally, I get the chance to do what I wanted to do when we first left the house.

Standing up straight, my chest continues to heave as my eyes find the building in the distance.

All the air rushes from my lungs as I discover exactly why I'm so exhausted. The imposing house looks like it's miles away. Okay, so that's a bit of an exaggeration. But still...

Strong, warm arms wrap around me from behind before Mav rests his chin on my shoulder. My hair tickles around my face, getting caught up in the light breeze before I shiver again.

Leaning back into him, soaking up his strength, my eyes dart from window to window before my heart sinks.

They're not there.

They're not watching.

"What are we doing right now?" I whisper, my voice getting carried away in the breeze.

"What is necessary," he replies cryptically. "Come on, we need to get out of here."

My lips part to argue, to demand answers, but they quickly close again. Despite desperately wanting to know everything, I also know that now is not the time for that conversation.

Mav releases me, leaving me cold, and I gasp the second lightning illuminates the sky on the other side of town.

The bolt ominously crackles through the air before a rumble of thunder makes the ground shake beneath us.

"We need to move," Mav says, taking my hand again and tugging me from my spot. Thankfully, though, this time, there is no running.

I didn't pay all that much attention to my surroundings when Kane brought me here; I was too lost in my own head to see the direction he drove to access Reid's manor, or to see the hidden gates that we're now walking toward.

Quickly, I scan the wall surrounding the vast property, my eyes locking on the lethal razor wire that runs across the top.

I swallow nervously, worried that Mav is going to expect me to somehow climb over that without being ripped to shreds.

"It's okay," he says softly. "I have the access code."

My eyes dart to his, narrowing in suspicion.

"Babe, don't give me that look. You know I'm more than just a pretty face."

Shaking my head at his smug grin, I stand by his side as he punches the code in, and only a second later, the locks in the pedestrian gate disengage and it swings open.

Mav takes a step forward, but my feet don't move.

It wasn't so long ago that the only thing I could think

about was getting away from this house and the men inside and back to Mav.

But now, as I stand on the threshold of freedom, I'm second-guessing myself.

Back in that manor house, despite Reid's cruel intentions, I was safe, protected. Victor, Razor, my father... none of them could hurt me while I was under Reid's roof. It gave me a sense of freedom I'm not sure I've ever felt. Especially in the last few days after Mav joined us.

Reid might not like me very much but something tells me that he'd fight just as hard as Mav and JD if someone came for me, or even threatened to do so.

"Doll?" Mav whispers when he gets a few feet ahead and realizes that I'm not with him.

I hold his eyes for a beat before turning and looking back over my shoulder.

His heat burns down my side when he steps up to me.

Threading his fingers through the hair at the base of my neck, he gives me little choice but to turn my attention back to him.

His eyes bounce between mine as he reads my thoughts.

I hate that he knows exactly why I'm lingering, and I hate even more that it puts a darkness in his own eyes.

He wants to be the only one for me.

He's my husband. He should be my one and only.

I mean, he is. Ultimately, he is the one I want. The one who owns my heart.

But there's another man in that house who has made my heart beat a little faster over the past two weeks.

I knew it wasn't anything serious. I knew that it was just a bit of fun between captive and captor. It was nothing but

Stockholm Syndrome. But that doesn't stop me from grieving the connection we found.

It was fucked up.

But... it was us.

I let out a sigh, my warm breath racing over Mav's face. His brow wrinkles as he waits for me to pull myself together.

Sliding my hands up his chest, I stretch up on my tiptoes and give him the truth.

"I trust you, Maverick. And more than that, I love you. I want to be wherever you are. Whatever this is, I'm with you one hundred percent."

Releasing my hair, his hand slides down until he's cupping my jaw.

For the briefest moment, he rests his brow against mine and closes his eyes.

"You know that I'd lay down my life to protect you, right?" he asks before his lids lift again, leaving his dark eyes boring into my lighter ones.

"Mav." I sigh.

"I mean it. You are the single most important thing in my life."

Tears flood my eyes and a lump the size of a basketball clogs my throat.

"Come on, we need to get out of here," he says before I manage to find any words in reply.

He releases my face, leaving me cold without his touch. Grabbing my hand, he drags me behind the tall wall that conceals the mansion behind us.

He treks through the undergrowth as if he's done it a million times before. Pushing aside any feelings about leaving Reid's manor, I follow my husband.

He might tell me that he'd lay down his life for me, well,

in return, I'd walk right into hell for him. Some might say that I already have. But there is nothing in this life I could do to repay him for everything he's given me.

I might have fucked up on the loyalty part of our marriage, but I want to show him that I didn't do it lightly, and that not once did I forget about him.

"Just up there," he says when we've been walking for a good twenty minutes.

Thunder and lightning still rumble around us, illuminating our way through the trees.

It's probably not the undercover escape he'd planned, but it's too late to go back now.

"Is that a car?" I ask when another bolt of lightning illuminates the air around us, the brightness flashing off the windows.

"Our getaway driver," Mav says, glancing at me with a knowing look.

He planned this. I guess that explains why he was so quiet last night.

"You've really planned this, huh?" I mutter as we close in on the black Chevy.

Mav doesn't reply; he's focused on our escape.

The second he steps up to the car, he pulls the back door open and gestures for me to climb inside.

As my foot leaves the uneven ground beneath us, there's another loud crack of thunder before the sound of heavy raindrops surrounds us.

"Quick," Mav says, his hands wrapping around my waist and lifting me up.

"Good evening, young lady. Long time no see."

The familiar voice gives me pause as I scoot across the back seat to give Mav space to join me.

Looking up, my eyes collide with a pair of soft, kind ones I know all too well.

"Sheila," I cry, both relieved and mortified to see her.

I've no doubt that she already knows everything. She might not be Mav's biological grandmother but that has never stopped her from stepping into the role. Over the years, there haven't been many secrets between them, especially after Daisy came along and Ivy died. Mav has been there for them without question, supporting both of them in a way he would have if Ivy were still here.

"Nice hair. Didn't think I'd ever see you cut it."

Pain cuts through my chest as I think about my new look and that old promise I made to Kristie.

"Thanks," I mutter, my voice twinged with sadness.

While I try not to drown in unwanted memories from my time in Reid's basement, she studies me.

"Can we just go?" Mav suggests. "I didn't drag you into this so you could spend the night interrogating Alana."

"Not interrogating, Maverick," she chastises. "I'm just concerned. For both of you."

Finally, she spins back around and brings the engine to life.

I don't think Sheila dislikes me. She's never been rude or horrible or even judged us. But she's skeptical, curious. She desperately wants to understand the true dynamic between us. And I'm sure my sudden disappearance, followed by Mav's, hasn't helped things.

Silence fills the space around us as she puts the car into drive and pulls out from under the tree cover and out onto a path.

Reaching over, Mav captures my hand, holding it tight in his as his concerned stare burns the side of my face.

He might have questions, but right now, I have more,

and I think they're a little more pressing than how I truly feel about leaving that house and the men inside behind.

"How's Daisy?" I ask, leaning forward to focus on Sheila as she takes a turn that will lead us away from Harrow Creek.

"Oh, you know," Sheila says fondly. "A whirlwind like always."

I can't help but smile as I think of the dark-haired little terror. She reminds me so much of Kristie when she was little it hurts. She's incredible though. Strong-willed, independent, opinionated, almost four-year-old. All the things that I hope will serve her well in a place like Harrow Creek.

But it also terrifies me. I've experienced firsthand what life can be like here for young, innocent girls. The thought of Daisy experiencing anything like I have, like her mom did; well, it sends ice racing through my veins.

Mav's offered to help relocate both of them so that Daisy can grow up somewhere nicer, but despite knowing that it's probably best for her, Sheila can't do it.

I get it. As much as I want to leave, the thought of leaving memories of Kristie behind rips me to shreds. But living in the past doesn't help anyone. If we want to experience the best of life, we need to look forward, to plan for a better tomorrow instead of drowning in what's already gone.

Maybe one day Sheila will find the strength to walk away from the memories of everything this town has stolen from her. Maybe she won't. But one thing is for sure, Mav and I will do whatever it takes to protect that little girl. I will do anything I can to ensure she doesn't experience even a hint of what I am. And something tells me that even though we've just left them behind, Reid and JD will do the exact same thing, and not just for Daisy, but for every little girl and young woman in this town. Every single one of them deserves to live a life without fearing every man they pass on the street, and risking having their innocence stolen too young.

"You okay?" Mav whispers, feeling my hand trembling with both fear and determination to do the right thing.

"Honestly?" I ask, turning to look at him, "I've no idea."

MAVERICK

My stomach knots and Alana's brow furrows in confusion as she stares back at me.

"Sorry for waking you and doing this in the middle of the night," I whisper, although I've no doubt Sheila is eavesdropping on my every word.

Alana shakes her head, rebutting my apology.

Part of me expected her to argue. When I went up to bed earlier and didn't find her waiting for me, my heart sank. It would have been so much easier if she were there. I could have waited until the house was silent, woke her and done this without risking waking JD.

Seeing her curled up in his bed with him... it hurt. I could deal when I was there too. But knowing she'd turned her back on me and so obviously chose him, well... ouch.

On some level, I get it. Since the moment I saw Victor appear on the screen before us, I shut down. The shutters lowered the second his arrival was announced, and as the minutes went by, it only got worse.

As a kid, I idolized both Victor and Dad. I thought they were these larger-than-life gangsters, the kind you watch in movies. But as I got older and realization dawned, things changed fast for me.

I could have walked away. Maybe I should have when I first started getting suspicious of their activities. But then the first time I looked into her eyes after figuring it all out, I knew I couldn't do it.

The girl who made it all look easy. The girl I'm pretty sure we were all jealous of because she didn't have the kind of responsibility on her shoulders that we did, was suffering more than any of us.

All I had to do was figure out a way to get her out of there without risking her life, and my own in the process.

The only thing worse than leaving her in the hands of those men, would be getting her safe, and then dying, leaving her unprotected for them to come for her again.

A violent shudder rips down my spine. Alana feels it, her hand gripping mine tighter before she slides across the seat and tucks herself into my side.

She shivers against me. I've no idea if it's from the fresh fall night air or due to fear, but either way, I wrap my arm around her and hold her tight.

"I love you," I whisper, just in case she needs a reminder.

It's not until she slides her hand under the hem of my long-sleeved black top, the coolness of her skin hitting mine that I realize I was holding my breath.

Holding her tighter still, I press my nose against the top of her head and breathe her in.

My need for her is at an all-time high right now. Despite the current situation and the fear for her safety, desire thrums just beneath my skin.

I used to think it was bad before, but now I've had a

taste of her, and watched her in action with JD... well, it's borderline obsessive.

Sheila drives like a bat out of hell toward our first stop. It's not necessary, I'm pretty confident we got out unseen, and the roads are deserted, but it seems she enjoys pulling on her Penelope Pitstop mask and putting the pedal to the metal.

Before long, the bright yellow sign for the motel I agreed to let her out at looms ahead. With a sigh of what I can only assume is disappointment, she slows the car and turns into the entrance.

"We're staying here?" Alana asks, nervously looking out the window. "Isn't it... a little close?"

I guess she understands that we're running then. Not that the black clothing and midnight dash covered that up very well.

"We're just letting the getaway driver out," I say lightly as Sheila pulls into a space and kills the engine.

"Oh," Alana breathes. I can't tell if she's relieved or disappointed.

"And lucky for me, I've got a friend waiting in room number nine," Sheila teases with a wide grin on her face.

I just shake my head, more than aware of what she's like while Alana blurts, "What?"

Sheila's eyes meet my wife's in the rearview mirror before she states, "I've got a child-free night, dear. You didn't think I was going to make myself a hot cocoa and go to bed early, did you?"

Alana's mouth opens and closes. She knows Sheila pretty well, but clearly, not this well.

"Is that what you would do?" Sheila taunts, fully aware of what Alana has been up to behind my back.

My stomach knots as the reality of all that hits me full force.

But my anger, my jealousy over it all is pointless.

The only person she's slept with willingly has been JD, and as much as that betrayal stings, I also understand it.

Maybe if I hadn't seen them together, I wouldn't. But for some fucked-up reason, I get it. The way she needed him while she was kept as their prisoner. Hell, even the way she's needed him since.

It's just proven to me that I was a stupid fucking asshole for the way I've kept her at arm's length all this time.

I thought I was protecting her, stopping her from having to endure all the pain of the past by holding back. Keeping myself from being just another one of those men in her eyes.

But seeing her with him, hell, even with me over the past few days, I've learned things about my wife I never knew. Things that make my dick swell in my pants despite our present company and the air of uncertainty around our lives right now.

"Uhh..." Alana starts but Sheila tuts, shaking her head. "I know you well enough to know that's not what you'd do, missy."

"Now," she starts. "The two of you get the hell out of here and get yourselves safe. We all need you alive, you hear me?"

I nod, feeling like a child being chastised by my grandmother while Alana agrees.

"I'll look forward to hearing the good news and finding you at my door in a few days."

"Might be a little optimistic," I mutter, dread sitting heavy in my gut.

"Well, you know me," she says, forcing a smile.

"Go and have your fun," I encourage.

"Oh, I will. Christian does this thing where he—"

"Go, please," I beg while Alana's body trembles with silent laughter.

"Pfft, you can't use the trick if you don't know about it," Sheila teases.

"I think I'll be fine."

"Whatever," Sheila scoffs lightheartedly. "Seriously, though. Look after each other and come back safe."

After promising her again that we will, she climbs out of the car, taking her heavy ass purse with her. I've no idea what she keeps in that thing, although something tells me that she's probably packing.

No, scratch that. Sheila is a badass, her late husband taught her well, it's why she'll never leave Harrow Creek. She is definitely packing.

"Everything you asked for is either in the glove box or in the trunk," she says before giving both of us a firm look in the eyes and slamming the door.

Nothing but the echo of the slam can be heard for a few seconds as we watch her close in on the motel until the very far door opens and a shadowed man steps out to greet her.

"Is she really having a booty call?" Alana asks, finally breaking the silence.

"I think..." I start, amusement beginning to bubble up. "I really think she is. Maybe the two of you aren't all that different after all," I muse, making Alana tense.

Sheila and Alana might appear to get on, but I'm not sure either really trusts the other. They've been brought together because of me. And while I'd love for them to fully get along, I'm happy that at least they can put their feelings aside and spend time together. And for Daisy. That girl needs all the people in her corner she can get.

"I think I might have underestimated her," she mutters, deciding to ignore my comment.

"Shall we get out of here?"

"Yes," she breathes. "Where are we going?"

"If I tell you, I'd have to kill you," I tease, reaching for the door so I can take Sheila's place in the driver's seat.

"It better be decent."

"Babe, have I ever taken you anywhere that wasn't?" I ask, dropping back inside the car and watching as she decides against the door in favor of climbing between the front seats.

"Remember that one time you took me camping?" she asks, turning to me with a raised brow.

"It wasn't camping. It was glamping."

"Mav." She sighs, making me smile because I know what's coming next. That weekend I'd planned not long after she finished high school was a fucking disaster. "There was nothing glamorous about it. We had to basically shit in buckets."

Laughter bubbles up as I think back.

"Yeah, but admit it," I say, starting the car and backing out of the space Sheila had pulled into. "Nowhere else you've been has been as memorable."

"Our pod had cockroaches."

"Exactly." I laugh. "Memorable."

Shaking her head, she reaches for the radio and finds a country station. However, it soon becomes clear that she doesn't actually want to listen to it when she curls her legs beneath her and turns to me.

"What is happening here, Mav?"

My grip on the wheel tightens.

"I think Victor knows that we were at Reid's," I confess, the words turning my blood to ice.

All the air rushes out of Alana's lungs, her arms tightening around her middle as if she's holding herself together.

"The dishes," she whispers. "I knew he—"

"The thing he picked up in the hallway... it was your hair tie."

She gasps, but doesn't say anything for long, agonizing seconds.

"It could have been anyone's. Reid and JD could have brought any gir—"

"They don't take women to the house, Doll. The only other female who's been there recently has been Letty."

"So it could be hers," she argues.

"Yeah, it could," I agree. "But are you willing to risk it?"

Her head falls back against the headrest and her eyes close.

It's hard to keep my attention on the road ahead when all I want to do is comfort her. To pull her into my arms and assure her that everything is going to be okay. But I can't, and not just because I'm driving.

"So what? We're running away?"

My chin drops but no words spill free.

"Yes and no."

Her attention burns the side of my face as she waits for me to explain.

"You made me promise, Doll. Our future over their demise."

The weight of that promise, of her demand for me to agree, sits heavy on my shoulders, and something tells me that I'm not the only one feeling it.

"Yeah," she agrees.

Glancing over, I find her chewing on her nails in concern.

Reaching out, I tug her hand free and twist her fingers with mine.

"I know you want them gone, Doll. Trust me, I know. But if we have to walk away and leave Reid to do the heavy lifting, then I'm willing to let that happen."

Her grip tightens and she swallows nervously.

"I do want them gone," she agrees. "Everything used to be so clear. Kill them all and embark on our future. But all of this... everything that's happened in the last few months. Hell, even days. It's muddled everything."

My chest constricts at the thought of her falling for JD.

They have a connection, that much was obvious from the first time I saw them together. But how deep does it run? And is she already regretting forcing me to make her that promise about our future?

Dropping my head into my hands, I let out a pained sigh.

"You're going to need to give me more than that," I complain.

"I'm aware," Aubrey mutters, the bottle in her hand clanking against the glass tumbler she's pouring the amber liquid into. "If this job were easy, you wouldn't have called me."

"Shit. I know," I say, slouching on the couch in her fancy-ass hotel room—that I'm paying for, I might add.

Letting my head fall back, I close my eyes and suck in a handful of deep, calming breaths.

It does fuck all to chill me out. Unease continues to trip through my veins while dread knots up my stomach.

Aubrey stays silent as the slosh of scotch fills the air before she puts the bottle back on the side and then swallows it down in one go.

"You seem to have forgotten mine," I point out bitterly.

"And you seem to have forgotten that you drove here,"

Aubrey teases. "You might be bankrolling this, but I don't have a spare bed for you to warm."

Lifting my head, I glare at her as she pours herself another drink.

"I can handle one." I scoff. "I'm no lightweight."

She smirks at me before grabbing a second tumbler and pouring me a drink, although it's nowhere near the amount I need right now.

Carrying them both over, she places them on the coffee table before curling her legs beneath her and getting comfortable on the couch opposite mine.

"So..." she starts after taking a sip from her drip, "I feel like there's more to all of this than you're letting on."

Reaching for my drink, I rest my elbows on my knees, swirling the contents of the glass around between them as I try to decide how much to confess to.

"I know you want him dead. That's no secret. But up until now, you're been clear-headed and fully focused. Something is different. I've never seen this..." She waves her hand up and down in front of me. "Side of you. You're agitated and nervous. It's not a good look," she adds to further piss me off.

"Sorry, I'm not quite as emotionally stunted as you, Aubs." The grin I give her is nothing but insincere.

She snarls at me, baring her teeth, but there's no fire behind it. She continues studying me as if the answer is written all over my face.

Suddenly she stills, as if whatever she's trying to figure out has just slapped her across the face.

"There's a woman, isn't there?" she suddenly asks.

"What? No. Don't be crazy," I argue, finally lifting the glass to my lips and throwing the contents back.

It burns, but not as much as I need it to.

"Oh, there so is."

Aubrey grins, her eyes alight with excitement as she waits for me to spill the goods. She looks so... normal like this, it's hard to remember who she really is and what she does for a living. Right now, with her hair pulled back into a messy bun and her face clear of makeup, she looks like a normal young woman. It's easy to see why she's so good at her job. She manages to get even the most astute men to fall at her feet with that innocent doe-eyed look. It's exactly why I'm paying her so handsomely for her skills.

"There's not," I state, needing to change the subject.

It's not that I don't trust her to know about Alana and Mav. Quite honestly, what's happened with them is child's play compared to what she already knows about my plan with Victor. But still, the confession never leaves my lips.

"What about you? Any men on the scene."

She scoffs. "If you're going to try to deflect, Harris, at least make it a question worthy of our time."

"Gotta be better than asking if my old man has put out yet," I mutter, revulsion rolling through me at just the thought.

"I mean, if you want to talk sex lives, I'm an open book." The evil glint in her eye makes me shake my head at her.

"I'm good. Thanks."

"Dude, you're just jealous because I'm getting more action than you."

"I highly doubt it. Don't you know who I am?"

"The arrogant, egotistical prodigal son of the great Victor Harris. Every motherfucker in this town knows who you are." She grins before taking another sip of her drink. "Doesn't mean you're seeing any action though, does it? So... back to my original question... who is she?"

"She's no one."

Aubrey's eyes light up. "Ooooh... married? Older? Wait... does JD have a sister because that would be a story." My teeth grind so hard I'm surprised one doesn't crack. "No, wait... I've got it. Stepsister. We all know Victor has fucked almost every pussy in this town; I bet you've got siblings of all varieties all over the place.

"You still reading those trashy books?" I tease.

"My books are not trashy, thank you very much. They are very stimulating literature."

"Stimulating, sure." I laugh.

"Joke all you like, but if you were to read one, you might learn a thing or two about how to win this woman over, because it seems to me that she's got you all twisted up in knots right now. She giving you the runaround? Poor baby Harris," she coos as if she's talking to an actual baby. "I bet it isn't very often that people say no to you, is it?"

"Remind me why you're here again?" I deadpan.

"Because, apparently, I'm one of those who can't say no to you," she confesses.

"You're not exactly getting me results though, are you?" I scoff.

"Oh, tone it down. It's been a couple of days. You always knew getting answers out of that stone would take a while."

"Well, you need to up the ante. Things are progressing faster than I anticipated and I need to know what he's thinking."

"I'll get you what you need, don't you worry about that."

"Good," I state before pulling my cell from my pocket and checking the time. "I need to go. And you need your beauty sleep."

"What are you trying to say?" She faux gasps.

"You've got a corrupt son of a bitch to manipulate, you

need to be in top form," I say, abandoning my glass on the coffee table and pushing to my feet.

"I've got this," she assures me, following me to the door of her suite. "I'll be in touch," she promises. "And if you need any tips where your girl is concerned, you know where I am."

"I'm good, but thanks."

"Oh, I'm sure you are." She winks.

"Why did I come here?" I ask.

"Because you love my charm and delicate touch."

"Delicate, my ass. Watch your back, yeah?" I say before taking off down the hallway.

"You don't need to worry about me, Harris," she retorts. "The devil wants me in hell just as much as he wants you."

I'm still shaking my head as I step into the elevator to leave.

In another life, Aubrey could probably be my perfect woman. She's got as much blood on her hands—if not more —than I have, and I know that I'd never shock her with any of the shit I'm involved in.

But my life is never that easy.

———

The house is steeped in darkness when I step inside. Not that I'm surprised, it's almost two in the morning.

Aubrey's hotel might be out of town, but I took a detour in the hope of clearing my head.

But every time I try, all I can see is my father holding his hand out and placing that hair tie with strands of Alana's blonde locks into my palm and my heart plummets all over again.

There's a chance he doesn't know. Of course there is. It could have been anyone's.

But my father knows me better than I'd like him to. He sees things. More than others. And I know he's suspicious as fuck right now.

He didn't say anything, didn't give any kind of hint that he knew, but deep down, I know he does.

And what's even more terrifying is that I've no idea what he's going to do about it.

He might not have appeared to care that Alana was gone. But we'd all be naïve to believe that. She was working for him, so he must have a need for her. Surely he wasn't just employing her to piss off Mav.

But does he care that she's gone? Or, has he just pulled another girl in off the street as a replacement?

Is she completely disposable like almost everyone is to Victor Harris, or does he secretly need her back?

And what about Mav? Victor openly said while he was sitting on my couch that he'd happily replace Mav if he didn't fulfill his role within the organization. Did he mean that?

A million and one questions spin around my head as I make my way up the stairs. The steps creak and crack in a way I'm all too familiar with as I approach the top. It's just another feature of this old house that I love.

Pausing at two closed doors, I look between them, my need to check in almost too much to bear.

I bailed earlier. After my brief, yet heated conversation with Mav, I was out the door.

I didn't know what else to do. Hanging around wasn't going to fix anything.

If Victor knew, then it was too late.

We had to act. And we had to do something fast.

If he finds out everything I've been doing before I'm ready, all of us are as good as dead.

I just need all the pieces I've been carving to fall into place at just the right time, and I'll finally get to discover if it was all enough.

Or if all this planning, all this hope, was for nothing.

Forcing my legs to keep moving, I walk into my bedroom and immediately strip my clothes off, and step into the shower.

As the water rains down on me, I lift my hand, studying the healing cuts that Alana cleaned for me a few days ago.

My heart begins to race as I think about her gentle touch that day despite her anger.

Most others would probably have let me bleed to death after everything I'd done.

But she didn't.

She forced me to sit there and tortured me with her proximity and sweet scent.

To be fair, that was probably exactly why she did it.

She knew the effect she had on me down in my office. There wasn't exactly anything discreet about the way my dick was trying to bust out of my pants as I pinned her against the wall.

I should have been stronger. I should have pushed her away when she came to find me.

A humorless laugh tumbles from my lips.

That one moment of weakness is the least of the things I shouldn't have done since I locked Alana up in my basement.

Ignoring my semi that's been woken up by memories of those few minutes in my office, I clean up before falling into my bed, my skin still a little damp.

I'm exhausted, but I already know I'm not going to fall

asleep. My body might need the rest, but my head is spinning.

There are too many moving parts in this whole plan. I'm putting too much trust in untrustworthy cunts. Any of them could be double-crossing me. Promising me that they're with me, all the while promising their allegiance to my father.

I knew the risks when I first embarked on this takeover plan. But I decided they were worth it.

Someone has to do something about my father's reign of terror. And I'm pretty sure there isn't anyone else out there with the skills or allies—hopefully—to make it happen.

The only positive about it all failing is that I won't be here to witness it.

I lie there tossing and turning, listening to the sounds of the house that usually send me to sleep, my head full of plans, fears, and what-ifs. All the things I refuse to allow anyone else to see. JD is the closest person in the world to me, and even he doesn't know the truth about how nervous I am about all this. I won't let him see it either. He might appear strong to the outside world. Most of the time he is. But he has these moments. These brief moments where I see the broken boy of the past and it fucking terrifies me that he'll go back there.

I know he doesn't take his meds, claiming that he needs to feel something, even if it does hurt. He refuses to accept that the medication he has now has been vastly improved from that of his childhood. He doesn't want to go back there. And I understand that, but I'm more scared about what happens when it all goes wrong than I am of his emotions being a little dulled.

It's the reason I need to talk to him the second he's awake. Another reason why I'm nowhere near drifting off.

I can't risk him waking up and not hearing instantly.

We need to talk. And it needs to happen sooner rather than later.

I'm still staring up at the ceiling an hour or so later when my cell starts ringing on my nightstand.

With a groan, I reach over and grab it.

The screen lights up before me, making me wince, but it's the unknown number that has me sitting up and my heart beating a little fast.

Usually, I'd probably ignore it. But there is too much shit up in the air right now.

Swiping my finger across the screen, I bring it to my ear.

"Hello?"

"Reid Harris?" a deep, accented voice says, making my hackles rise.

"Yes. Who is this?"

"Ms. Rivera requests your presence in person to discuss some urgent matters. You have been booked on a flight at six a.m., someone will collect you at arrivals and take you to her."

"Six a.m. this morning?" I bark.

"Yes, I suggest you make your way to the airport as soon as possible."

My lips part to respond, but the line goes dead, leaving me with nothing but my increased breaths.

"Fuck. Fuck," I sneer, combing my fingers through my hair and pulling until it hurts.

I've been fucking waiting for this. Trust the fucking cartel to choose the most inconvenient time.

My cell buzzes in my hand, and when I glance down, I find my flight details staring at me.

With a groan, I throw the sheets off and march toward

my closet because when the cartel calls, you fucking answer.

As quietly as I can, I slip into JD's room, and using only the flashlight on my cell, I find a piece of paper on his desk and scrawl out a note for him to let him know where I'm going and to call me the moment he wakes.

Dread settles heavy in my gut that I'll probably be flying. But I can't wake him now and tell him everything I need to; I'll miss the fucking flight. And this might be my one and only chance to find out what Luciana knows about this trafficking ring.

I stare at my rushed handwriting and sigh.

There isn't any other choice.

With a final glance at my sleeping best friend, I back out of his room and silently close the door behind me.

In only four minutes, I'm back in my car and heading toward the airport, praying that I'm making the right fucking decision here.

4

ALANA

Something tickling against my cheek brings me to, and I groan as reality begins to come back to me. But it's not long before it's overridden by my aching back and neck from the way I'm curled up.

"Morning, Doll," a quiet yet raspy voice says beside me.

I groan again and force my eyes to open.

I have every intention of looking over at Mav, but the second my vision clears and the view before me emerges, everything flies out the window.

"Where are we?" I ask on a gasp.

"Heaven?" Mav suggests lightly before the car falls silent.

I stare ahead, my gaze glued to the beautiful yellow and orange sunrise. The colors are reflected in the still ocean before it turns a stunning, welcoming blue.

"Yeah," I whisper, unable to speak any louder in case it ruins it.

It's not until the heat of Mav's fingers warms my ear as he tucks a stray lock of my hair behind it that I remember everything.

"Where are we?" I ask again, finally ripping my eyes from the sunrise and focusing on my husband.

He looks exhausted. His eyes are bloodshot and ringed with dark circles.

"It doesn't matter. All you need to know is that we're safe," he assures me, reaching out his other hand and cupping my jaw.

My heart swells as I stare into his dark eyes.

Instantly, I believe him.

I know that no matter what, he'll protect me.

Things might be weird between us, but when I'm with him, I know I'm safe. I'm home.

"Have you driven all night?" I ask. Stupid question really, but it spills from my lips regardless.

"Yeah, and thankfully you fell asleep so you couldn't tell me off for speeding to get here so that you could see this."

"You're too good to me," I confess.

A humorless laugh bubbles from his lips, as his eyes drop to mine for a moment.

"I think we both know that's not true."

He leans forward, making his intentions well known. But just before our lips touch, he pauses. Everything that used to hold him back floods his eyes and he starts second-guessing himself.

"Is my breath that bad?" I joke, trying to make light of the situation.

"Doll." He sighs, his minty breath rushing over my face.

The scent makes me cringe because I know for a fact that mine is nowhere near as fresh.

"Nothing has changed, Mav. I still want you. Just because we've left them behind it doesn't mean—"

His lips collide with mine a beat before his tongue pushes inside in search of mine.

A moan rips up my throat as his fingers slide into my hair, allowing him to angle me exactly as he wants me.

Heat floods through my body, ensuring every inch of me is fully awake.

Reaching out, I wrap one hand around the back of his neck, anchoring myself to him as the other slides up his denim-covered thigh.

His muscles bunch as I get higher. I expect him to stop me. Hell knows he has every other time we've gotten this far.

But to my utter delight, he doesn't, and only two seconds later, my hand brushes over his dick, straining against his pants.

Fire races through my veins and I let myself indulge in the one thing that gets me out of my own head.

A deep growl rumbles in the back of his throat as I continue to tease him.

Knowing he's enjoying it, that he's allowing me to do it, sends heat rushing between my legs.

I kiss him harder, deeper, my nails dragging across his scalp with my need for him to be closer. And he matches me move for move. His own desperation oozing from every glide of his tongue against mine.

"Mav." I moan, rubbing my thighs together in the hope of finding some friction. "I need—"

Dragging his lip away, he rests his brow against mine and whispers, "To stop."

"N-no," I stutter, barely able to find the words. "That's the opposite of what I need right now.

"I know, babe. But if we don't, I'm going to do

something I'll really regret," he says flatly before finally pulling fully away and pushing the door open.

"Oh." I breathe, my body cooling faster than I thought possible, as the old unwelcome feelings of not being good enough churn inside me.

But before he climbs out, he reaches over and takes my chin in his grasp.

His grip is firm and holds a promise of all the things I so desperately want from him.

"Do not take that the wrong way, Doll. You cannot possibly imagine how many times I've fantasized about fucking you over the last few years," he confesses, his dark eyes boring into mine. "It's literally the only thing I dream about. But as much as I want it, I'm not doing it for the first time in the front seat of someone else's car."

The kiss he places on the tip of my nose at the end of that confession makes my eyes burn with emotion. Thankfully, he doesn't see it because he turns his attention to the glove box.

"Here." He growls, his voice rough with desire before dropping something heavy into my lap. "Take it everywhere you go. No exceptions."

I glance down, and my eyes widen.

"Uh..."

"It's loaded with a full clip. Don't overthink it. If something seems off, just point and fire. Everything I've taught you will come back, I promise."

He glances up at me as he takes his own gun and tucks it in the back of his pants before climbing from the car.

I stare down at the weapon.

It's not that I'm not used to seeing them or being around them.

Mav has multiple guns in different places in our house. He's spent hours teaching me to use one properly and hone my skills. But he's never handed me one to keep before. Sure, he's always told me that if anyone breaks in or comes to threaten me—namely Victor or our fathers—then I shouldn't hesitate to use it, that he'd protect me from the fallout. But it never felt quite as real, quite as dangerous as this.

He pops the trunk behind me, forcing me into action.

Stuffing the gun into the pocket of my hoodie, I push the door open and join him at the back of the car.

"What's in there?" I ask as he pulls the strap of a duffel bag over his shoulder.

"Everything we need." After locking the car, he snags my hand and tugs me toward a track that I assume leads us to where we're staying.

We're engulfed by tree cover in seconds, and with the sound of the ocean filling my ears, I can't help but think back to the conversation in the basement with JD about the places we dream about going.

I said the beach and he said the mountains. This has a little bit of both.

I wonder if he'd love it as much as I do already.

Thoughts of what—or who—we've left behind make my heart ache. Thankfully, Mav guides me around a corner and everything I was just thinking about is forgotten.

"Oh my God," I gasp, finding the most incredible log cabin nestled into the trees. "That's—"

"Unbelievable," Mav finishes for me.

"How did you find this place?" I ask, in total amazement.

He's been locked up in that house just as much as I have. When did he get a chance to do all this?

He chuckles lightly. "I'm not just a pretty face, remember."

Slapping his arm lightly, I allow him to tug me closer.

"Want to check out the inside?"

"Hell yes," I cry, practically running up the stairs to the deck.

He keys a code in to give us access and then swings the door open for me.

I take off like a toddler in a sweet shop, discovering everything this place has to offer.

Downstairs is a huge open-plan kitchen, dining, living area with floor-to-ceiling windows that lead out to a massive deck that showcases the stunning view of the ocean.

It reminds me a little of Reid's kitchen that overlooks Harrow Creek, but I shove that thought down as quickly as it emerges.

Upstairs, there are two impressive bedrooms with attached bathrooms most people back home could only dream of.

I quickly choose my favorite—the one with the ocean view, obviously—but when I step out, my eyes catch on the other bedroom and I freeze.

It wasn't so long ago that Mav and I were living in our house and occupying separate bedrooms. It's only in the last few days that we've shared a bed.

Now we're alone, will we go back to that? Or is that kiss out in the car a sign of things to come? Is this finally the start of us?

Excitement and anticipation collide in my belly along with all the other emotions I'm battling from our midnight getaway.

Sucking in a deep breath, I roll my neck in hopes of working out the kinks and make my way back downstairs.

I've barely made it halfway when the scent of coffee hits me, making my mouth water and my stomach growl.

My legs move faster with my need and when I spill into the kitchen, I find two steaming mugs on the counter while Mav dives through the bag he carried in.

"What's all that?" I ask as he begins laying it all out.

"Burners, more guns, ammo, enough clothes for a week for both of us."

"Jesus, Mav. How did you do all—"

"Sheila has had this stuff for a while," he confesses while placing our clothes into separate piles. "I knew this would happen one day."

"You knew we'd end up running?" I ask, making sure I'm following.

"Yeah. It was inevitable that things would blow up in our faces at some point. Don't you think?"

My lips part to argue, but then I think of everything we've gone through to get here, and the words fall away.

"So you've had this place for a while then?" I ask, my heart skipping a beat at the thought of it being his.

"I wish." He scoffs. "This was a surprise for both of us."

"Oh," I say, hopping up onto a stool at the island and looking around. "Pretty epic one. Where exactly are we?"

"Off-grid. You're safe here."

I nod, unable to feel anything but safe while we're in the middle of nowhere.

Grabbing one of the mugs, I lift it to my nose and inhale the rich scent while Mav pulls out a handful of my panties.

I watch him for a moment, trying to untangle them, and add them to my pile, but he fails.

"You enjoying yourself there?" I tease.

He pauses and for a moment, I think he's going to drop them and try to pretend nothing happened. But then a smirk curls at the corners of his lips and he glances up at me through his long, thick lashes.

My stomach somersaults as he lifts the tangled mess to his nose and inhales deeply.

Oh my fucking God.

Heat pools between my thighs as his eyes hold mine, the tension between us crackling like wildfire.

"Umm," he rumbles. "Washing powder."

His eyes crinkle at the side with amusement before a laugh erupts from my chest.

"You're such an idiot," I cry as he laughs alongside me.

Abandoning my panties, he moves closer, spins me around, and the second I spread my thighs, he steps between them.

Holding my face in his large hands, he dips his head and drags his nose across my cheek before nuzzling my hair.

"The real thing smells so much better," he confesses before twisting his fingers in my locks and pulling my head back so sharply it startles me. But the shock only lasts a second before overwhelming joy takes over. For so long I've wanted Mav to throw me around like I'm nothing more than a rag doll. I began to wonder if he was capable of it, but I'm starting to experience signs that he might just be the kind of man I always hoped he would be.

His grip on my hair stings, but it's so welcome and even more so when he plunges his tongue between my lips and continues the kiss we started in the car.

5

MAVERICK

Forcing myself to move, I rip my lips from Alana's and take a huge step back.

Dragging my eyes open, I stare at the incredible woman sitting before me.

She's dressed head to toe in black because I told her what to wear when I woke her in the middle of the night. She barely even questioned me.

I don't deserve her. I really fucking don't. But she's here, and despite everything I've told myself over the past five years, my resolve is going to shatter.

Some might say it already has.

I've had her lips wrapped around my dick. I've come down her throat for fuck's sake. That is not the delicate, gentlemanly way I always told myself I'd treat her.

But she wants it, a little voice points out in my head.

She's fucking begging for it.

As much as I hated it, hearing and seeing her with JD, it broke through something I refused to acknowledge, something she told me time and time again she needed, but I point-blank refused to accept.

Alana might be my wife, the only woman I've ever loved. But she isn't some delicate flower that's likely to break at any given moment. She's strong. So fucking strong. And she knows what she wants. I'm just the stupid motherfucker who's refused to give it to her because I think she deserves more.

What if she deserves exactly what she's got?

What if I do too?

I shake my head, unable to process all of that while she's sitting before me with swollen lips from our kiss, and desire darkening her eyes.

"Come back," she begs, reaching for me with little grabby hands.

"Have you seen outside?" I ask, turning away from her and shoving my hand into my pants for the second time since I got out of the car to fix the fact my dick is trying to bust out.

"Uh... no, not yet," she says as I open the sliding doors and step out into the morning sun.

Only a second later, the sound of her small feet against the deck hits my ears and she steps beside me at the railing, passing me my forgotten coffee.

"It's really incredible," she muses quietly.

Turning to look at her, I watch as she takes a sip of her coffee, her eyes locked on the sun as it rises over the ocean.

"Yeah," I whisper. "You are."

"W-what?" she stutters.

"Look, it's got a hot tub."

"Oh my God," she cries, forgetting all about my previous comment in her excitement. "I hope you packed my swimsuit."

Something explodes in my belly before making a beeline to my dick as I consider my answer to that.

"I packed for a quick getaway, Doll. Not a vacation."

She shrugs. "Oh well, I've nothing to hide. You?" she asks, turning those sparkling blue eyes on me.

To an outsider, it would be easy to think that she's dealing with this. But I know my wife better than that. Her favorite coping mechanism is pretending that everything is okay, all the while crumbling behind the façade.

"I think you already know the answer to that, don't you, Doll?"

Her eyes drop to my crotch and her tongue sneaks out, licking across her full bottom lip.

I've learned something else about her in the last few days too. She uses sex as a distraction from real life, from dealing with the pain that comes with it.

I can't say I'm surprised. After the childhood she had, it makes sense that she uses sex as more than pleasure.

I can also understand why JD caved to it too. Saying no to my wife is really fucking hard.

I should know, I've been doing it for five years.

Hard. As. Fuck.

She saunters closer, her intentions written all over her face.

"Doll," I warn before she closes the final inches between us.

She looks up, biting her bottom lip temptingly.

Reaching out, I cup her jaw, my thumb stroking across her satin skin.

"You don't need to do this. Not with me," I tell her.

Her brows pinch in confusion.

"Do what? Want you?"

"No, you can do that all you like," I say, in complete contrast to everything I've said previously. "You don't need to hide behind it or pretend that everything is okay. I know you, Alana, I know that leaving isn't as easy as you're making out."

Her eyes shutter and her breath catches, proving my words right.

"It shouldn't though," she whispers without looking me in the eye.

"Maybe, maybe not. I think we're long past worrying about what should be right and wrong, don't you?"

One of her shoulders lifts in the smallest shrug I've ever seen. "I shouldn't have liked being there," she confesses.

Stroking her cheek again, I tilt her face so she has little choice but to look up at me.

"To start with, I didn't. All I wanted was you. I had these dreams about you bursting through the door to rescue me."

"If I knew where you were, I would have," I tell her honestly. Hell, I kinda fucking did. I just so happened to find her passed out in the kitchen instead of in the basement.

"I know." She sighs.

Releasing her cheek, I grab her hand and lead her over to an outside swing seat. Darting back inside, I grab the blanket I spotted over the back of the couch.

Throwing it over her, I drop down beside her and tuck her into my side.

"I know how I reacted to begin with, but I need you to know that I'm not mad about it all."

"Mav, you don't—"

"Please, let me just speak a minute, yeah?" She nods, taking a sip of her coffee instead of responding. "Do I like that you've been working for Victor and spending time with his... associates?" She tenses beside me, preparing for my answer. "No, not one fucking bit. But also, I understand it. I know that he wouldn't have given you any other choice."

"He threatened you, Mav. I'd do anything he asked of me to protect you," she blurts before I shut her down.

Guilt eats at me, just like it did the first time she told me that all of this was because of me.

Deep down, I knew it would happen. I took away their little toy; they were always going to do something to hurt me. To punish me. The beating I received after we announced our wedding and they discovered what I did was nowhere near enough punishment.

"And everything that happened under that roof, I understand that too. I might not know the details about you and JD, but I could see that he was important to you. That he helped you get through all of that in a way you desperately needed."

"That's not an excuse."

"You don't need an excuse, Doll. All I've ever done is try to be the perfect man for you, but one look at the two of you together, and I understood that I was never going to achieve that. Not while I was holding back something you craved so badly."

"I'm fucked up," she confesses quietly.

"No," I state firmly. "You're perfect."

"Mav."

"No arguing. I love you, Doll. I always have. It's unconditional."

"Same," she agrees, making my heart seize in my chest.

Lifting my mug to my lips, she does the same, and we fall into a comfortable silence as we stare out at the ocean.

There are still so many things to say, so many questions to answer, and things to figure out. But for a moment, we're just us.

Just a man and a woman. A husband and wife enjoying their morning coffee.

"What happens now, Mav? Where do we go from here?"

Well, if there was ever a loaded question...

"With us or—"

"This situation with Victor," she finishes for me. "I'm kinda hoping after what you just said that we're good, at least on some level."

"Yeah, babe. We're good. Wouldn't be here right now fulfilling my promise to you if we weren't."

"Good. That's good. But—"

"Honestly, I don't know," I confess. "My biggest priority right now is keeping you out of harm's way. I know Reid's plan, but I don't know when everything is going to play out."

"But if Victor knows that we were there then—"

"Yeah, it's probably going to be sooner than later."

"It's going to be messy, isn't it?" she asks hesitantly.

"It's the Hawks, of course it's going to be messy. We just have to hope that the ones spilling the blood are the right ones."

"You're on Reid's side." She smirks. "Who'd have thunk it?"

"If I knew then what I know now, things could have been very different, Doll."

"Aw, you made friends," she teases.

I can't help but scoff. "That might be pushing it a bit."

"You spent days under the same roof and didn't kill each other."

"There's a bigger enemy at play than Reid. And..." I start before swallowing roughly. "Maybe he isn't quite as bad as I always convinced myself he was."

Alana's body trembles with a laugh.

"You two are as bad as each other. So we're just hanging out in paradise until we think it might be safe to return?"

"Something like that," I agree.

"How will we know when it's safe?" she asks, looking up at me with her large blue eyes that always draw me in and hold me captive.

"You want to go back?" I ask. Honestly, I assumed she would. Despite all our plans to put an end to Victor and the men who hurt her and then run away into the sunset. Everything has changed in the past two weeks.

"Do you?"

"Doll," I sigh, abandoning our mugs on the decking and repositioning us so we're lying across the swing seat, "I want whatever you want."

"Then I guess we'll figure it out together, yeah?"

"Sounds perfect," I whisper, pressing a kiss to the side of her neck, sending goose bumps racing over her skin.

"This is nice."

"Yeah," I say, sliding my arm around her waist and tucking my hand beneath her hoodie, something I never would have done before all of this. "It really is."

"Just so you know," she says quietly. "I'm yours. And... I want everything with you. Everything."

It's not until I wake up with the fall sun burning my face that I realize she's gone.

My heart jumps into my throat as I frantically push myself up and call for her.

But there's no response.

"Fuck," I bark, pushing to my feet and looking around. "Doll?" I call again. "Alana?"

But there's nothing.

I run through the house, checking each room. My panic grows with each one I find empty.

She has to be here. She has to.

We're in the middle of fucking nowhere. We're safe here, we're sa—

My fears are suddenly halted when I run back outside to check the deck again when a figure appears down on the beach.

My steps slow as I approach the railing at the edge of our deck, my eyes locked on her.

She's still wearing the oversized hoodie I put her in before we left Reid's manor last night, but she's shed the leggings and boots so that she can walk through the shallow waves as they crash against the sand.

Fuck. She looks so perfect down there lost in her own head.

There is no one else, nothing else, for as far as the eye can see.

It's almost exactly what I pictured when we used to talk about our future after Harrow Creek.

I stand there for the longest time as she walks the entire length of the beach and then back. Nothing but the ocean and the birds flying overhead can be heard.

She looks so peaceful, so content.

If only that were the case.

6

JD

A happy noise rumbles in the back of my throat as I wake up, memories of the moments before I fell asleep coming back to me.

My dove.

Fuck. She's so fucking perfect.

Everything she does. How fucking strong she is, how she doesn't take any of our shit. How incredibly fucking filthy she is.

My morning wood jerks as I remember just how it felt to sink inside her. Tight, wet... Ecstasy. Fucking ecstasy.

If I could have that for the rest of my life, I wouldn't need any other kinds of highs, or distractions. She'd be enough.

She'd keep me level, balanced... happy.

A contented sigh spills from my lips and I roll over in search of her warm body. But as I reach my hand out, all I'm met with are cold sheets.

"Dove." I groan, already mourning the loss of her hot little body.

Shifting to her side of my bed, I bury my nose in her pillow, breathing in her scent and trying to ignore the little voice in my head asking when I gave Alana one-half of my bed.

I lie there listening, hoping that I might hear her in my bathroom. Even better if the water starts running. Not sure there's a better way to start a day than a nice round of shower sex.

With need for my girl growing, I throw the sheets off the bed with such vigor, that the paperwork strewn across my desk flutters, some sheets falling to the floor.

I catch a brief sight of the notebook I found and promised Alana that I'd write in.

Oh yeah, filthy shower sex with my dove sounds like the perfect way to start it off.

Wrapping my fingers around my shaft, I slowly stroke myself as I march toward the bathroom.

I'm so lost in my own head, my dirty fantasies, that it doesn't register that the door is half open, or that it's silent inside.

Pressing my free palm against the wood, I force it open with so much strength that it crashes back against the wall.

But I soon find that the only one it startles is me because the room is empty. There aren't even any signs that she's been here.

But she was. Last night, she was in my bed and wrapped in my arms. I know she was.

"Fuck," I bark, spinning on my heels to go in search of her, kicking all the fallen paper aside as I go. Just like everything else strewn across the floor and furniture in this room, I'll deal with it later.

Marching across the hallway, I twist the door handle

and swing another door open; it doesn't crash back against the wall this time, but that doesn't stop my heart from sinking when I find a fully made-up bed.

If Alana wasn't still with me, then I assumed she'd slinked back off to be with Mav in the middle of the night.

As much as that thought stings, it makes the most sense.

My hand falls away from my quickly deflating dick and I continue forward to check their bathroom. But I already know what I'll find. The room is in total silence. It's empty. And I don't just mean literally, it's like they've been completely wiped from it. As if they were never here.

"Shit," I hiss when I find exactly what I was expecting.

My fingers twitch at my sides, the tips of each digit beginning to itch with a very familiar feeling as reality begins to dawn on me.

With my heart in my throat, I take off again, running down the stairs, letting the creaks fill the air around me, praying that their voices will drown them out when I find them.

But there is nothing.

No scent of coffee, no evidence that there have been people here at all.

I stand in the middle of the room, as naked as the day I was born, as the ants begin to take over.

They explode from my fingers, marching up my arms and across my torso.

Lifting my hand, I scratch at my chest, the patch of skin right above my heart.

"No," I bark. "No, they have to be here. They just have to be," I mutter to myself as I move toward the slider that will lead me outside.

The sun is high in the perfectly clear blue sky; it would make sense that they're out—

Nothing.

Scrubbing my hand down my face, I stare at the table Alana and I were dancing on only the other night, then the swing seat where we had our heavy conversation and she showed a little too much insight into the issues I battle on a daily basis.

If she really knew, she wouldn't just leave...

The pool is still, the jacuzzi empty, as is the rest of the yard.

Fear and desperation drip through my veins like poison as the ants finally make it down to my toes. The need to claw my skin off is real. I fight to keep my head, to focus on the issue at hand.

Sure, they might have found a way to run, but Reid will find them.

He'll find them and he'll bring her back for me. I know he will.

Retracing my steps, I take the stairs three at a time in the hope I can leave the ants behind.

But they follow.

They always fucking follow once they get started.

I storm into Reid's room like a barely-contained tornado.

"Where is she?" I demand, giving zero shit about waking him. "I can't find her and I think—"

My words shrivel up and die when I find his bed empty. Although, unlike Mav's room, at least there is evidence that he's been in it.

"Reid?" I bellow, inviting myself into his bathroom.

But again, it's empty.

"What the fuck is going on?" I hiss.

The second I'm back in my room, I scan the mess for my

cell, desperately trying to remember where I might have abandoned it.

The notebook catches my eye again and I dive for my desk, erratically searching for the device.

There has to be a reason behind all this. Something sensible that doesn't need me to freak out.

But that's easier said than done when I don't know what the fuck it is or where everyone is.

I give up on my desk and spin around, searching for the pants I was wearing yesterday.

Shoving my hand into the pocket, I come up empty.

"For the love of God," I bark, frustrated at myself that I'm such a fucking disaster I can't even find my own goddamn cell phone.

I turn my room upside down, making it even more of a war zone. But still come up empty.

With my chest heaving and my brain running at a million miles a second with thoughts, I collapse onto my bed.

It still smells like her. But I've no idea if it's a good thing or not.

Burying my face into her pillow, I scream as loud as I can, hoping to scare the ants away, to make them disappear as fast as they emerge.

But they don't go anywhere. If anything, the itching only gets stronger.

Do something, Julian. Make it stop.

"FUCK," I bellow, before flipping over to stare at the ceiling, hoping it'll hold all the answers.

I kick my leg out and my foot collides with something under the sheet.

Sitting up, I shove my hand under and search it out.

"Yes," I hiss, although any excitement I might have felt

at finding it quickly dies when I find an angry red battery flashing at me.

I make quick work of plugging it in and wait for it to power up, confident that there will be something from Reid.

But when it eventually comes to life, there's nothing. Well, not nothing. There are a stream of memes and gifs from Devin and Ezra, a ton of bullshit spam emails, and a weird message from an unknown number asking for me to reply.

Ignoring it all, I open my contacts, find Reid's name, and hit call.

But nothing happens. It doesn't even take me to his voicemail.

"Fuck."

I try again, and again, but nothing.

My hand trembles as I pull my cell from my ear as I try to piece all this together.

I'm sure there's a very reasonable explanation for all of it. But that isn't exactly how my brain is wired.

Reid, I'm not overly concerned about. It's not the first, and probably won't be the last, time he's uncontactable. Doing the shit we do, sometimes you need to fall off the grid for a little bit.

Ellis could probably find him for me. But it's not his disappearance that's making my skin crawl.

It's Alana's.

I knew letting Mav out of the basement was a risk. Even more so leaving the doors unlocked.

There was every chance that they'd leave at the first opportunity. But with every hour that passed, the risk of that happening lessened.

Reid let Mav in and told him about the plan to take

down their fathers. Mav lowered his walls when it came to being intimate with Alana and pushed their relationship to the next level, or maybe even a few levels after what we all did together.

I guess, I just stopped thinking that it would come to an end, that she would leave me.

They always leave...

Abandoning my cell on the nightstand, I march through to my bathroom and turn the shower on, twisting the temperature dial as high as it'll go.

While I wait for steam to fill the room, I stand at the basin and force myself to look into my own eyes.

"She'll be back," I tell myself, trying not to notice the dark shadows in my eyes.

But the longer I stand there trying to convince myself of that fact, the less optimistic I feel.

Something is wrong. I feel it right to the very core of my being.

It's a feeling I've felt before, and one that I never wanted to feel again.

Loss. Grief.

Desperation.

Curling my fingers around the countertop, I tighten my grip until it hurts.

That little bit of pain shoots up my arm, banishing the ants.

But the relief is short-lived because the second I let go, they're back with a vengeance.

"FUCK," I roar, my deep voice bouncing off the walls around me before I spin around and plant my fist in the tiles.

The crack of the ceramic, and possible bone, echoes around me. But it doesn't stop me from doing it again, and again.

Blood covers the light gray tiles and drips to the floor from my knuckles.

But the pain is so good.

So. Fucking. Good.

I continue until I can barely breathe. My chest heaves, but my lungs don't seem to pull any air in.

Crashing forward, I rest my brow against my raised arm and stare at the mess I've made.

I should feel regret.

But only the need for more rages within me.

More blood, more pain.

More relief.

Always more fucking relief.

With one last look at the bloody, broken tile, I push from the wall and stumble into the shower, letting the water scald me, continuing to feed the need for pain.

"Yes," I hiss as the water washes away the ants, the itching draining from my body as my skin turns red and prickles in an entirely different way.

Hanging my head, I watch as blood drips from my knuckles landing at my feet before the evidence of what I've done swirls down the drain.

She's going to come back...

She's not coming back.

She doesn't want you.

She doesn't need you.

Not like she does him.

You're nothing.

No one.

A bit of fun to fill her time with.

It doesn't matter how hard you've fallen.

You never stood a chance.

Tipping my head back, my chin drops as I roar out my frustrations in the hope of drowning out the voice.

But it doesn't work.

It never fucking works.

7

ALANA

My skin burned with awareness the second Mav's eyes landed on me from up on our deck.

But I didn't turn to him and let him know I was so hyper-aware of him.

I always have been. I used to know when he walked into a room or came home without ever having to see him.

Our souls are just that entwined.

But since things have changed between us, I'm even more aware of him than ever.

Every glance, every touch—no matter how innocent—burns straight through me like a laser.

It's incredible yet overwhelmingly frustrating.

Especially when he allowed me teasing kisses like in the car and the kitchen when we first arrived, and then backed away.

I want to shake him and demand to know what's holding him back.

He wants it. God, does he want it.

Both times he was like steel in his pants.

Despite Reid's teasing down in the basement about my husband not being able to perform, I know for a fact that it is not the case.

His body is ready and raring to go. His head however...

With a sigh, I continue forward, letting the warm fall ocean water lap at my feet.

Being in a place like this... A place where the air is filled with nothing but the sound of crashing waves and birdsong, I should feel lighter. But being away from Harrow Creek is making the weight of everything seem even heavier.

I know the promise I forced Mav to make. And while I stand by the fact that our future together is more important to me than anything else, leaving that house and not being a part of what happens next isn't sitting right with me.

Somehow, without me even realizing it, I became part of that duo of misfits living under that dark roof.

I fit there. I found some kind of peace there.

But what happens now?

I sigh, reaching up to tuck a stray lock of hair behind my ear when it catches in the light breeze.

Do I really want to hide out here and wait for the signal that Victor is dead?

But what if that isn't how this whole thing plays out?

I force that thought from my head the second it emerges.

It has to be how it plays out. I can't consider the option that Victor is well... the victor in all this.

My heart knots up as I think about the two men living under that roof.

Yes, in some ways they're just mini versions of the men who brought us all up. But then, so is Mav.

Reid was right the day he accused me of hating on him because of his father.

My stomach rolls painfully, forcing me to wrap my arms around myself as I vividly remember the first time Victor came to the house for me.

My skin prickles with disgust as, even all these years on, I remember his touch. His calloused, cold hands against my skin.

Without warning, I retch, poison from my past filling my veins and flooding my stomach.

The only thing I've ever been able to do to dispel it is to take control.

Time and time again, men have tried to steal that ability away from me.

My father, Victor, Razor, all the others who seemed to rotate through our house like a revolving door to get their sick and twisted kicks.

I was nothing more than a zoo exhibit at times. A fucking petting zoo at that.

But while Reid and JD might have grown up under their command—one of them more so than the other—they are not them. Not even close.

The fire I've seen in Reid's eyes when he's talked about ridding his father and the others from this world was real. The potent hatred that oozed from him when I confessed my truths, confirming all his fears was overwhelming, so was his reaction to it afterward.

Just thinking about that moment being pinned to the wall by the enigma that is Reid Harris sends a rush of heat through my body so strong that it pushes away some of the disgust.

Lifting my hand, I wrap my fingers around my throat, attempting to recreate how it felt being completely at his mercy.

I may not have been in charge during that heated exchange, but I had control.

If I told him to stop, I've no doubt that he would. Not that I would have.

What I'd just told them... I needed it gone. And the best way to make that happen is to lose myself in pleasure. To use what had been forced on me almost my entire life and turn it around. To take pleasure out of it on my terms. And to trust the man I'm with not to take it too far.

I gasp, my hand falling from my throat as my other arm drops to my side.

A laugh tumbles from my lips as I realize what's happened.

I trust him. Reid 'The Devil' Harris.

Blowing out a slow calming breath, I stare out at the ocean and let its serenity wash over me.

We might be gone, but something tells me that we won't be forgotten.

Reid might be fighting his own battle against his father, but I also know that he's fighting for me too. For me, for Kristie, and all the other girls and women who have come both before and after us.

He's going to do it, and then somehow, we're going to dive into the whole trafficking ring and we're going to get the answers I crave about my sister.

I've no idea where I'll be once I know the truth, but at least I'll know. No matter how painful that might be.

I sense Mav's closeness long before the heat of his body burns my back and his hands land on my hips.

A whimper escapes my throat when he nuzzles at my neck, peppering kisses along the sensitive skin.

"You look so beautiful down here," he whispers, making the hairs on the back of my neck stand on end.

Leaning into him, I rest my head against his shoulder and close my eyes as his arms band around my waist.

"Kristie would have loved it here. The beach was her happy place."

He doesn't respond, but his arms tighten and he presses another kiss to the spot that turns me to mush beneath my ear.

It's everything.

We stand there together for the longest time with the shallow water lapping at our feet and the warm fall air blowing around us.

No words are said; they're not needed. I feel everything he wants me to in his strong embrace.

"I've got a surprise for you," he finally whispers. Goose bumps erupt as his breath dances across my skin.

"Oh yeah?" I whisper.

Excitement tingles inside me, but as much as I want to know what he's done, I also want this moment to stretch out into eternity.

Just the two of us surrounded by nothing but the wind.

I guess it's too perfect for us anyway.

It's a fight not to sob in disappointment when he releases me, but I put my trust in him and what he's done and allow him to guide me back up to the cabin.

The scent of the bubble bath hits me the second I turn the corner in the master bedroom, the one I fell in love with.

"Mav," I sigh the second my eyes land on the tub, "you found candles."

"I haven't got any champagne though."

I shake my head. "It's perfect. Thank you."

Spinning around, I rest my arms over his shoulders and stretch up on my toes to brush a sweet kiss over his lips.

"Take as long as you like. Relax. I know shit is weird, but there is nothing to do but chill out here. Make the most of it." *You've been through enough.*

He doesn't say those final words, but I read them in his eyes nonetheless.

Removing my arms from his shoulders, he lowers them to my sides and takes a step back.

My fingers twitch with my need to reach for him, but I stop myself.

As much as I might need him, I'm also aware of how much he's been pushed out of his comfort zone recently.

I'm not the only one who needs a little peace and quiet to try and get everything straight in my head.

So without saying a word, I let him back out of the room and close the door behind him.

The second I'm confident he can't hear me, I let out a pained sigh before stripping out of my hoodie and underwear and stepping into the bath.

The temperature is perfect, despite how long we were standing down on the beach.

A satisfied groan spills from my lips as I sink under the mass of bubbles, my muscles relaxing more with every second that passes.

Resting my head back, I close my eyes and allow my thoughts to drift to nicer things, the future where Mav and I could have a life together like this. No danger, no fear, no stress.

I don't fall asleep. At least I don't think I do. Instead, I just linger on the edge of consciousness. It's a place I like, a place where I can control my thoughts, stopping them from going to dark and twisted places that will leave me fighting to breathe and drowning in my own fear.

When I come back to myself, the bath is cold and the bubbles have all but vanished.

Pushing myself up, I lift my hands from the water and find my fingertips pruned.

I climb from the bath, wrap myself up in a huge, white fluffy towel and wring the water from my short locks with another.

Rummaging through the vanity, my eyes narrow in suspicion when I find some of my products.

I can't help but smile at Mav's thoughtfulness as I cleanse and tone my face, and then slather on some vanilla moisturizer.

Do I miss the cherry scent JD got me? Yeah, if I'm being honest, I do a little.

By the time I'm ready to walk out the door to find something to wear, I feel a little stronger than when I first walked in here.

Yes, things are still a mess. But while I've got my husband by my side, how bad can things really get?

"Oh my God." I gasp the second I pull the bathroom door open and discover what's waiting for me. "Mav, this is..." My words trail off as I take in the darkened room and flickering candlelight. He stands right in the middle of it, wearing only a pair of tight black boxer briefs, his hair and skin still damp from a shower.

I'm not sure I've ever seen anything quite so tempting in all my life.

"Is it... shit," he says, lifting his arm and combing his fingers through his hair. His muscles ripple, the ink covering his tanned skin almost dancing as he moves. "It's romantic, right? I wanted it to be—"

"Perfect." I sigh, my heart aching in the best possible way. "It's incredible. You're incredible."

At my words, his face relaxes, an almost smile twitching at his lips.

"Yeah?" he asks shyly.

He probably hates how unsure he is right now, but I can say for a fact that he looks fucking adorable.

There's something to be said for bringing a dangerous gangster to his knees like this.

It's addictive. And I pray it never gets old.

Moving closer to him, I press my hands against his chest and slide them up until they're gripping the back of his neck.

"Yeah."

I brush my lips against his. The kiss is everything and nothing all at the same time.

I want more. I need more.

But also, I want time to stop so we can just have this perfect moment together.

As I stretch up on my tiptoes in the hope of deepening the kiss, his hands land on my hips before gliding up. He traces the dip of my waist before both hands slide to my back, crushing us together.

There are so many things I want to say, so many questions I want to ask.

Mostly, why now?

Why, after so many years, is now the moment he's chosen for us to take this step? Assuming that's what this is.

No man does the whole candle thing for any other reason... right?

8

MAVERICK

My hands tremble so violently against her back, there's no chance she can't feel it.

The second her tongue brushes against my bottom lip, my mouth opens, eagerly inviting her in.

Kissing Alana is one of the best things in the world.

The first time she did it, the day I proposed, I didn't think I'd ever be able to live my life without having her lips against mine every single second of the day.

I knew my self-restraint was good back then. I'd lived with her for eighteen months at that point. Watched her walking around teasing me, tempting me in any way that she could.

But that one short taste of her... It threatened to undo everything I'd told myself I'd hold back when it came to her.

She was sweet like candy, but there was also something else. It wasn't bitter, or salty, or anything bad. But there was an edge. An edge that reminded me just how dangerous she was. I don't mean in the way I am, or Reid, or any other member of the Hawks we've both been forced to endure our entire lives. Dangerous in a way that she held the power to completely consume me.

And that was bad.

I wanted it. I wanted it so badly. But I had a job to do, I had promises to deliver before I even considered allowing myself something like I have right now.

Those promises still might be outstanding. The men who hurt her, as far as I know, are still alive and kicking, but we've made progress. We have a small army of people fighting with us now—fighting for us.

As much as I might not like it, Reid is gunning for the same goal as us. And while he has his sights set on Victor, it goes without saying that JD, his brothers, and anyone else close to them will be right by his side.

It's sure more than I've ever had.

It hasn't always been that way. As a kid, I had plenty of friends, even more so when I was initiated into the Hawks. I was like a god then to all the others who hadn't succeeded.

But as I learned more about the ongoings behind closed doors of our senior members, I started to back away.

Then it only got worse once Alana became a part of my life.

I couldn't risk anyone discovering where she was until I had a solid plan for how to protect her.

The idea of marrying her, making her untouchable, was always a niggling thought at the back of my mind.

I could have suggested it earlier. Honestly, there was no reason to wait until she was eighteen.

I was a fully-fledged member of the Harrow Creek Hawks; if I wanted to marry her, I'd have found a way to make it happen. Fake documents are easy to come by if you know the right people.

But I was too much of a pussy to bring it up.

What if she said no?

What if she was planning to run sooner than she let on?

What if she didn't feel about me the way I always hoped she might?

Alana's nails rake down my scalp, making a shiver of desire rip down my spine and successfully dragging me from my own head.

"Fuck." I groan when she does it again.

My dick aches, straining against the fabric containing it and digging into the softness of her stomach.

"Mav, please. We've waited long enough."

"Doll." I growl, sliding my hand down to her ass and effortlessly lifting her from the floor.

The second she wraps her legs around my waist, the heat of her pussy explodes against my dick and I very nearly come right there and then.

Gritting my teeth, I grip her ass harder, forcing her to stop moving against me.

After five long years of nothing, of borderline unbearable torture, I'm balancing on a knife's edge.

How I didn't blow the second she wrapped her pretty pink lips around me that day in Reid's kitchen, I don't know.

Somehow, I'd managed to grit my teeth and hold on for a few minutes, but pushing inside her after all this time is going to be another thing entirely.

"I need you so badly, I can't even think straight," she confesses as I lay her down on the bed.

Releasing her, I attempt to stand, but her legs remain locked around my waist, refusing to let me go.

"Doll." I growl.

I know what she wants. I watched her take charge with

JD, controlling the narrative to ensure she got exactly what she craved.

He might not have noticed that she was the one calling the shots while she was on her knees for him, but I certainly did.

I've learned a lot about my wife in the last few days.

She loves sex. Okay, so that's not exactly new. But she craves it, needs it in a way I never understood.

And it's not just any kind of sex she yearns for. It's the downright filthy kind.

She wants to be treated in all the ways I've tried to protect her from.

Our eyes lock as she refuses to release me, a silent battle of wills ensuing between us.

I know what she wants. She wants me to rip the towel off, flip her over, spank her ass and fuck her into oblivion.

Fuck.

Fuck.

I want that too.

I want it so fucking badly that just the thought has precum soaking my boxers.

But this can't be that.

After all this time, it just can't be.

Reaching behind me, I wrap my hands around her ankles and force her to release me.

Planting her feet on the sheet, I reach up and grip the towel.

My hands continue to tremble, but I'm not sure if it's with need, fear, self-restraint, or disbelief. Or possibly a little of all four.

Giving a short, sharp tug, the soft fabric is released from where she had it tucked around her chest, and I get to reveal the vision that is my naked wife beneath.

I am one lucky motherfucker.

The second I drop the towel, she makes quick work of tugging it from beneath her and throwing it over the side of the bed.

"The time for restraint is over, Mav. I respect the fuck out of everything you've done for me, all the ways you've held back because you thought it was the right thing to do.

"But I lie here right now, as your wife, as the woman who loves you more than her own life, begging you to finally make me yours.

"I need it, Mav. I need it so—"

My knees hit the mattress a beat before my palms land on either side of her head and my lips claim hers.

She groans into our kiss, her hands sliding up and down my back before she begins tugging at the fabric that's still covering me.

"Patience," I mumble.

"Five years, Mav. That's more patience than anyone should have."

Dropping to one elbow, I tuck the other hand beneath her neck and tilt her just so, allowing us to deepen the kiss.

It's everything and not enough all at the same time.

When her hands can no longer reach, her foot takes over, pushing and shoving at the fabric of my boxers.

"Anyone would think you're desperate for my dick, Doll."

"Anyone would be right." She gasps as I suck on the soft skin of her neck.

Her nails rake down my back, scratching me up in the most incredible way as I bruise her.

It's not entirely the soft and gentle lovemaking I had in mind, but I can only be so good.

Releasing her with a pop, I begin working my way down

her body, worshiping her like I've been fantasizing about for years.

I kiss, lick, and nip at her breasts, teasing her relentlessly. She cries out in desperation, her fingers tugging at my hair until it hurts, trying to force me where she wants me.

"Yes, yes," she pants when I get closer to her hardened nipple.

It's the prettiest pink, perfect, everything. And the addition of the jewelry. Fuck, yes.

"Oh my God," she cries when I finally wrap my lips around her peak and suck her deep into my mouth.

Her moans of pleasure echo around me, making my cock jerk and my balls ache with the need to feel something similar, to get some kind of release.

I switch to the other side, making the most of having her all to myself like this before I work my way down her stomach.

The thought of tasting her again makes my mouth water enough for me to sit here drooling.

By some kind of miracle, I manage to keep my cool—I think.

Pressing my hands to her inner thighs, I spread her open for me.

Her muscles tremble against my palms, and when I drop my eyes from hers in favor of her pussy, I find it slick and swollen.

"Alana," I breathe. "It's been so long since—"

"You were perfect," she cries impatiently. "Everything you did... do it again, please."

Not needing any more encouragement than that, I drop to my front and run my tongue up the length of her pussy, ass to clit.

She mewls and moans, screams and cries as I zero in on that little bundle of nerves and dig out every move that used to come so naturally back in the day.

With her fingers twisted up in my hair, she drags me closer, begging for more with actions as well as words.

I have to get her off. I have to. There is no other choice.

There is every chance that I'll go off the second I push inside her slick heat, and there is no way she's not getting hers first.

I might have turned into a two-pump chump, but there is no chance of me leaving her high and dry.

With her sweet taste flooding my mouth, I release one of her legs and push two fingers inside her.

She grips me like a vise the second I slide them in, and it makes my head spin with what's to come.

"Mav. Oh my God, Mav," she cries as I curl my fingers, searching for her G-spot. "Yes. Yes."

She gushes as I find it, her juices dripping down my fingers as I suck her clit into my mouth, laving it with my tongue.

"Shit. Oh, shit. Fuck. Mav. MAAAAV," she screams as I push her over the edge.

Her entire body locks up as pleasure slams into her. If it's possible, her cunt crushes my fingers even more as wave after wave of pleasure seeps through her. It's just as stunning and enthralling as it was the first time I saw it.

Pride rushes through my veins as I finally pull back, leaving her a sated, panting, beautiful mess in the middle of the bed.

I take her in from head to foot, memorizing every single inch of her sinful body and wondering just how I managed to hold back all these years.

She's incredible, perfect, and she wants me just as fiercely as I do her.

9

ALANA

y body burns, my skin tingles, my heart races, and my muscles twitch in the most satisfying way. But none of that compares to the way Mav gazes down at me.

I have never felt more beautiful, sexy, wanted, loved in my entire life.

Even without his touch, I'm flying higher than I ever have in my life.

This is what we needed.

This connection. This... realization that the universe brought us together for a reason. Yes, it was for us to protect each other—him looking after me more than the other way around, of course—but this right now... honestly, the rest of the world could explode around us and I wouldn't notice, or care.

I have everything I've yearned for in the past five years right here, and now all I need to do is get those damn boxer briefs off him and let him—

"Yes," I whisper when he finally tucks his thumbs into the fabric around his waist.

My mouth runs dry as he reveals those hidden inches of skin I'm so desperate for.

With one final shove, the fabric falls down his thighs, his hard length springing free.

My breath catches as I stare at it.

For so long I've imagined how he might look hard and ready for me. But never did he ever look this good in my head.

"Please," I whimper like a desperate whore.

Planting one knee then the other on the edge of the bed, I spread my legs, giving him enough space to shuffle between them.

"This isn't going to last long," Mav confesses with a grimace. "I'm already on a hair-trigger right now and I'm not even inside you."

His giant hands wrap around my waist, dragging me down the bed to meet him.

He's right, he's not even close to being inside me, but the heat of his body and the jerk of his dick against my inner thigh is the biggest tease I've ever experienced.

"I don't care, Mav. I just want you, whatever way I can get you."

"Fuck, Doll. I love you." He growls before falling over me and stealing my lips in a filthy kiss.

His tongue plunges into my mouth, seeking mine and I can't help but roll my hips, desperately searching for some friction.

"I know there is no rush," I confess as he peppers kisses along my jaw. "But I think I might die if I don't feel you inside me in the next few seconds."

Shifting his position, his hand pushes between us, grasping himself.

"Oh God." I moan as the head of his cock grazes my

over-sensitized clit before dipping lower. He coats himself in my juices before he comes to rest at my entrance.

My muscles clench around nothing, my body aching to feel him push inside me, stretching me open instead of teasing me with just the tip.

"Fuck." He groans, his neck rippling with a thick swallow as his eyes shutter.

"More," I beg. "Please, I need—"

My words are swallowed by a gasp as his hips thrust forward, his thickness stretching me wide and hitting me so deep, it makes my eyes roll back.

"Maverick." I gasp as my body fights to adjust to his sudden invasion.

His jaw ticks, his teeth grinding behind his pursed lips as he desperately tries to cling to his restraint.

"Fuck me, Mav. Take exactly what you need."

His eyes open, revealing two pools of dark liquid lust staring back at me.

"I have everything I could ever want right here," he confesses through clenched teeth, and my heart splits wide open.

"I love you," I whisper.

"Fuck, yeah. Shit, your pussy is fucking insane, Doll."

"It's yours," I blurt before he leans over me again and kisses me slowly and deeply. His hips move at the same time as his lips, fucking me in a way that makes tears burn the back of my eyes.

My body burns with my need for more, my heart crashing against my ribs as the intensity of the moment washes over me.

No one has ever treated me like this before. No one has ever touched me so gently, so passionately.

I've only ever been a toy for men to use. They treated

me however they felt fit and didn't give a shit what I wanted or what felt good.

But being with Mav is the complete opposite to that.

His hips roll again, his grip on my waist tightening as his dick pushes deeper, and I can't stop the emotional sob from ripping from my lips.

He stills before pulling his head up to look at me.

Abject horror covers his face.

"Shit. Am I hurting you?" he asks in a panic as a tear trickles from the corner of my eye, racing down my temple to soak into my hair.

I shake my head, the lump of emotion so huge in my throat I'm unable to force any words out.

"Doll?" he asks, softly, cupping my jaw and lowering back down to press his brow against mine.

His entire body trembles with restraint and the knowledge that he's doing all of this for me makes even more tears come.

It's not like it was with JD when I completely lost my shit. That was overwhelming and in an entirely different way.

This is... intense, incredible. Everything I've ever wanted.

"I love you," I blurt. "Everything is perfect."

His eyes shutter again as he tries to process my words.

"Please, don't stop. I want to feel you," I whisper, my voice rough with emotion.

"You sure?" he asks, his brows pitching inward in confusion.

"I've never been surer in my entire life."

Accepting my words, he slowly rolls his hips again.

My breath catches as the tip of his cock hits that magical

place inside me. Sinking my fingers into his hair, I drag his mouth back to mine.

My other hand slides down his back, loving the way his muscles ripple as he moves inside me until I grab his ass, trying to force him even deeper.

Maverick Murray burrowed his way into my heart a long time ago. It's now time for him to bury himself under every inch of my skin.

"Can't— Can't last." He gasps into our kiss, his cock swelling with his impending release.

His hand holding my hip, slips to my clit.

"Mav," I cry when he pinches me.

"Not going... without you," he grits out.

"Oh God." I moan when he plays me so perfectly.

"Fuck." He grunts, his head resting against mine again as he stares down into my eyes. I swear, he can see all the way down to my black and tarnished soul.

"Yes. I'm there. Right there." I gasp, my muscles clamping down around him, making him groan as if he's in pain. "Stop holding back," I beg, raking my nails down his back hard enough to draw blood until I grip his ass and wrap my legs around him.

"Fuck, Alana. Fuck. Fuck. Fuuuuuck." He growls, his eyelids lowering as pleasure rushes through his body and his cock jerks inside me. But he never breaks our eye contact. Not for one single second.

Watching him fall, feeling him coming inside me is the final push I need to fall over the edge with him. Pleasure explodes from my lower belly, shooting out and making every single one of my nerve endings tingle in delight.

My lids shutter automatically as I drown in the overpowering sensations.

"Eyes, Doll. We haven't waited this long for you to shut me out."

Instantly my eyes fly open.

"I need you to know it's me," he says, losing the demanding tone from his previous statement, allowing a little vulnerability to seep in.

"I know, Mav. I know it's you. I love you."

Dragging his face down to meet mine again, I kiss him hard and deep in the hope it can make up for all the years we didn't get to do this.

At some point, he pulls out of me, leaving me feeling empty and lonely. Which is ridiculous because he is right here, his arms are banded around me and his hot skin and taut muscles are pinned against mine.

"Can't get enough of you." He confesses before licking up the column of my neck.

"You don't have to. We can stay right here and do this until we die."

He chuckles at my words, the sound making all my hairs stand on end.

"No one has ever made love to me like that before," I confess, needing to give him more than just my body.

"You're mine," he states, before hooking my leg around his hip and opening me up for him. He's already hard again. "And I'm not them," he says so quietly I can only assume he wasn't meant to say the words aloud.

He reaches between us and pushes against my entrance. We both moan as he slides inside my slick pussy, but as overwhelming as the feeling is, it's not enough to forget what he just said.

Pressing my hand against his chest, I force him to still.

"That's what you were scared of?" I ask, needing to have this conversation before anything else happens.

My body complains, violently, if the way my pussy clenches around him is anything to go by, but I'm not giving in to her right now.

He sighs and closes his eyes.

"Mav." I sigh, shifting closer, not that it's really possible, but I try, nonetheless. "You never, ever could be like them." I cup his jaw, grazing my thumb over the roughness of his cheek. He hasn't shaven in a while, possibly since he was locked in Reid's basement. I know he's not a fan of it, but I think it looks good on him. Certainly felt good between my thighs.

Heat blooms between my legs, and I know he feels the rush of wetness around his cock because his fingers clench against my ass.

"You're not the only one who's never made love like that before, Doll," he confesses, his voice distant and slow. "Before you, I wasn't exactly..." He trails off, unable to find the right words.

"Maverick," I say lightly, a smile twitches at my lips, not that he can see. "Are you trying to tell me you like rough and dirty sex?"

He swallows, his fingers twitching again, but after a beat, his lashes flutter and he reveals his gorgeous dark eyes to me.

My breath catches at the torment I find swirling in them.

"Do you want to know a secret?" I ask.

"Doll," he warns, already predicting what I'm about to say.

Hooking my leg higher around his waist, I force his dick deeper before clenching my muscles around him.

"I love dirty, rough sex too."

"Babe, I—"

"I know I probably shouldn't," I say before he can interrupt me. "But I do. I need it, Mav. I'm like a fucking junkie. I need the pain, the feeling of being completely at a man's mercy. I want you to take control, to throw me around. I want you to take what you need and punish me until I've got tears rolling down my cheeks and I'm begging for relief."

His brow crinkles as he tries to process my words.

"I know it's fucked up. Trust me, I really know that. I spent years battling against my fantasies and desires. It's wrong. After everything I've been through, I shouldn't want any of it. But I do.

"But I also understand why you've done what you've done. And I know you're scared, I get your fears. But I promise you, there is nothing you could ever do to me that would make me ever consider that you're like them.

"I want whatever dark and dirty thoughts flicker through your head," I say, tracing his deepest frown line with my pinky finger. "Choke me, spank me, hurt me. Right here, right now, I'm giving you consent to do anything."

His eyes widen at my words and his lips part as if he's about to argue.

"Anything," I repeat, needing him to understand that nothing is off the table for me.

His lips close and he swallows, his eyes searching mine for a lie.

"You've just... Shit, Doll." His hand trembles against me and I swear he stopped breathing.

"All of it. I'm already fucked up; I promise you can't make me any worse."

It's meant to be a joke, but the way his eyes blaze with fire, I realize it missed its mark.

"One step at a time, yeah," he says, rolling onto his back and dragging me with him, letting me take my fill of him and ride him until we're both sweaty and falling into powerful releases.

The moment I walked out of arrivals, I clocked the man who was waiting for me.

He wasn't dressed up, or even obviously packing, but there was a glint in his eye as he casually scanned the steady flow of people who'd just walked through customs, granting them entry to Mexico. I doubt anyone else around me notices it. They're all either too excited to embark on their vacations or relieved to be home with loved ones.

Despite my need to sigh in frustration, I keep my expression hard and neutral as I walk toward him. My muscles ache and my jaw hurts from grinding my teeth in impatience during the flight.

I'm sure anyone else would have gotten some sleep. But there was no fucking chance of that happening. I had no idea who was around me; I wasn't giving any motherfucker the chance to get a jump on me when I was least expecting it.

His eyes lock with mine, and he gives me an almost

invisible nod before turning around and walking toward the exit.

I guess I'm following then...

The second we step out of the siding doors, I reach up and pull my aviators down over my eyes, scanning my surroundings, looking for the guy's friends. There is no way he came here alone. I know Griff said that he thought Luciana was working on her own with this little mission. But that doesn't mean she doesn't still have a small army around her like her husband, and other members of the Rivera, have shadowing their every move.

Suspicion trickles through me when I don't spot anyone who looks like they might be loitering in case something goes wrong as we approach a blacked-out town car.

The guy pulls the back door open and gestures for me to get in.

My arm twitches in a knee-jerk reaction to check for my gun, but I catch myself. Not just because it's not there but because I don't want him to think that his silent routine is intimidating me.

It's not.

The second I'm seated, the door slams shut behind me, leaving me with nothing but silence and the scent of new car.

It's not until his own car door is shut, ensuring our privacy that the man looks into the rearview mirror and catches my eyes.

"Good morning, Mr. Harris. I trust you had a relaxing journey," he says in a deep, heavily-accented voice.

"I did," I agree. How can I not? I had a first-class fucking ticket. It seems that I'm not the only one willing to splash the cash when it comes to getting the person I need right in front of me.

"Fantastic," he muses, giving me a tight smile before twisting in his seat and holding his hand out. "Cell phone, please. Turned off. And anything else you can be tracked with."

I stare at him in disbelief, but he doesn't budge an inch.

Understanding that this whole trip is going to be for nothing if I don't hand it over, I pull my cell from my pocket, swipe the screen, and power it down.

I'd called JD the second we'd landed, but there was no answer, and he still hasn't emerged out of his bed, it seems.

"Thank you," the guy says with an insincere smile before pocketing it. "I assume you didn't smuggle any weapons?"

There's a part of me that wants to make a snide comment about my fists. JD would if he were sitting. But instead, I shake my head.

"I might be reckless, but I'm not stupid." I scoff instead.

"Good to hear," he mutters, turning back around to start the car. "Just a short journey and you'll be able to clean up and relax before your meeting."

Curling my fists in my lap, I refrain from saying anything else.

I don't want to clean up and relax. I want to get this shit done and go home. But clearly, I'm not on my timeline now; I've got to fit into Luciana Rivera's schedule.

Tipping my head back, I allow my eyes to close for a beat as I just take a breath.

This is where I need to be right now. If I'm going to get to the bottom of what my father has been doing, if I'm going to give Alana the closure that she needs and help her discover what happened to Kristie, then I have to suck it up and do as I'm told.

All I can hope is that it's worth it. That Griff isn't

leading me down the wrong path while I need to be in Harrow Creek, protecting my future and those who are important to me.

If it were anyone other than my uncle, I might be questioning just how easily I hopped on a plane and left the country. But I trust him. I have to. He has questions that need answering just as much as I do.

It's almost an hour before the guy—who never actually introduced himself—pulls off the freeway and down an almost secluded track.

The terrain changes, leaving me bouncing around in the back of the car.

"It's not the front entrance," he explains.

"You don't say," I mutter, the car bouncing so hard over a pothole that I almost hit my head on the roof. "Did you want to slow down a little?"

He doesn't respond to my suggestion, nor does he slow down.

His decision. It's not my car he's fucking the suspension up on.

I breathe a sigh of relief when he finally brings the car to a stop and kills the engine.

Despite going into the hotel through the back entrance, it's instantly obvious that we're not in just any hotel.

Every surface is either marble or gold, and I'm pretty sure it's not the cheap kind either.

I'm led toward an elevator and the guy opens a hidden panel before tapping in a code, instructing it to rise through the building.

My reflection taunts me from every angle, reminding me that I haven't slept and that I look in no fit state to meet with Luciana. No wonder the guy suggested I rest.

The seconds tick by as the elevator continues to rise. By

the time the doors open, allowing us to exit, I'm surprised we're not on the roof.

Long, white hallways with thick dark gray carpets spread out before me. There are only a handful of doors in each direction, confirming my suspicions about the kind of room—or should I say suite—that can be found on a floor this high in the building.

The guy takes off and I diligently follow behind him, noticing, and not for the first time, that he is packing something I really don't want to be on the receiving end of.

Finally, at the far end of the hallway, he slows to a stop and pulls a card from his pocket.

After unlocking the door, he passes me the card.

"Someone will come and get you when she's ready," he informs me before taking a step back.

"At what time?" I ask.

"When she's ready," he repeats.

"I need to make a phone call," I state, thinking of JD at home.

"Then you'd better hope she doesn't keep you waiting," he says before retreating down the hallway.

"Brilliant." Thank God Alana wasn't that much of a diva when she was in my care. Or after, for that matter.

I whistle appreciatively as I walk deeper into the suite I've been given.

It's not exactly Harrow Creek.

Just like everywhere else, all the furniture is white, all adorned with gold embellishments. It's... a lot. And doesn't exactly fit with my lifestyle or upbringing.

Clearly, Luciana and I live very different lives.

After walking through the bedroom, I dump my backpack on the bed and stalk toward what I hope is a bathroom.

The second my eyes land on the huge walk-in shower, I strip down and step under the huge rainfall shower head.

The water runs warm instantly, hitting my shoulders with incredible power and helping my muscles to relax.

With an exhausted sigh, I tip my head back and let the water rush over my face.

A loud bang drags me from the depth of sleep.

I sit up, my heart lurching into my chest as I reach under my pillow for a weapon.

But there isn't one.

I'm not home.

I'm—

"Time to wake up, sleeping beauty," a smug motherfucker sings from the doorway.

"What time is it?" I ask, my voice raspy with sleep.

"Five o'clock."

"In the evening?" I blurt, glancing toward the windows.

"Yeah. Ms. Rivera will see you now," he informs me.

"Now?" I ask, looking down at what I'm not wearing.

"Well, I'm sure she'd rather wait two minutes so you don't walk into her suite in your underwear. But I should warn you, longer than two minutes and you might not get the meeting you're so desperate for."

His words make my hackles rise. "Who said I was desperate?" I bark, throwing my legs over the edge of the bed and pushing to stand.

He doesn't reply, and he also doesn't move.

"Take a photo, it'll last longer," I mutter as I shove my legs into the spare pair of jeans I stuffed into my bag before leaving the house a few hours ago.

Jesus. How is it still the same fucking day?

"Nah, a little too much cock for me," the guy deadpans. "Angel, by the way."

"Ah, you must be higher up the ranks than the last guy then."

Angel laughs, letting me know he's aware of who I'm talking about.

"Jose isn't a man of many words. If he didn't introduce himself, he clearly didn't deem you important enough to know it."

"Nice."

"Don't take it to heart. I didn't know his name for months. And I work with the miserable motherfucker."

"Right," I say, dragging my shirt over my head and shoving my feet into my boots.

"Ready?"

"Well, I was going to do my makeup, but if I don't have time then…"

"Don't be a smartass," he chides as I march past him.

I might have left JD behind, but in his absence, it's nice to keep his humor alive.

"Were you planning on leading the way, or am I meant to guess where I'm going?"

"Knew this was a bad idea," he mutters under his breath as he trails behind me, slipping out of the suite when I open the door for him.

He overtakes me before marching to the other end of the building.

Should have guessed that she'd be as far away from me as possible.

She might have invited me here, but I'd be an idiot to think it's because she trusts me or that I can actually be of any help.

The only thing I can hope is that my reputation precedes me better than hers does. All I remember of her is being her husband's pretty little shadow.

"They teach you manners in Harrow Creek, right?" Angel asks as he unlocks the door that I hope leads to his boss.

"Barely, but I'm sure I can manage."

Without waiting for him to go first, I surge forward, proving my previous statement wrong.

My rushed steps soon come to a stop when I find a woman standing in front of the floor-to-ceiling windows wearing a suit that's a white as the furnishings and fits like a glove. Her red hair shines in the evening sunlight, giving the look a softer feel. But don't be mistaken, she might have soft curves and delicately styled hair, but even from behind, she oozes power.

"Good evening, Ms. Rivera," I say, my voice cold as it echoes around the silent suite.

She doesn't react or let me know that she's heard a word until she suddenly spins on her killer heels and pins me with a look that would make most men cower.

I don't think I've ever learned anything so fast in my life, but I know right there and then that Luciana Rivera is not someone I want to mess with.

I also realize that she's just the person I need on our side for what's to come.

I just about managed to hold myself together until sunset.

But the second that ball of flames disappeared behind the hill that overlooks Harrow Creek, all the hope drained out of me.

When I stepped out of the shower earlier with skin prickling and red from the temperature of the water, I told myself that they'd all return. That I was freaking out for nothing.

Reid had a plan. A plan I trusted.

I knew the plan.

We'd been over even the tiny details of it over and over again. Even after Alana and Mav showed up, we went through it.

Mav might have thought he'd pushed me aside, but that wasn't the case at all. Reid found ways to ensure I was fully up -to-date. And none of those new up-to-date plans involved them disappearing on me.

Reid wouldn't allow it. That motherfucker is overprotective on a good day.

He hides the fucking knives from me, for fuck's sake.

He's not willingly going to leave me alone to...

I shut that thought down. The desire to do something has my hands trembling and sweat beading at my brow.

I'm not known for my self-restraint. It's probably how I managed to end up like this in the first place.

If I'd fought the darkness harder when I was a teenager then maybe falling into the darkness now wouldn't be so easy.

I crawl onto my bed with a bottle in one hand and that notebook in the other.

One of them excites me more, and it's not the one that promises a whole world of pain as I bleed out my thoughts through ink, letting them stain the paper before me as if they're real things.

But I promised Alana that I'd try. And right now, without her, I'm fucking desperate.

Settling back against my pillows, I look at my cell sitting on my nightstand.

I tried calling Reid more times than I'm willing to confess to. But the line just cuts. I've no idea what it means that it's not even going to voicemail, but it can't be good.

I've no way of contacting Alana and Mav. As far as I know their cells are—

The pen in my hand drops.

"In the safe."

Without a second thought, I race off the bed and down the stairs, storming into Reid's office with one single destination in mind.

Curling my hand around the bookcase that hides all our treasures—okay, Reid's treasures. I have fuck all to my name —I pull it open.

If you didn't know this one moved, then you would never guess.

I'm as gentle as I can be while my hands are trembling and my body is practically vibrating with the need to claw off my own skin. Thankfully, none of Reid's beloved special edition books take a tumble.

When—if—he returns and finds one of them damaged, my life wouldn't be worth living.

There aren't many physical objects that mean anything to Reid, but these books are well up there. I get it, and I respect it enough to keep my fucking distance for fear of even looking at one wrong. If people think that I'm one of only a few people who aren't scared of my best friend, then they need to think again. Even I have my moments when Reid really loses his shit.

The second the safe hiding behind the bookcase reveals itself, I step forward, trailing my fingers over the keypad, praying that he hasn't changed the number on me.

It wouldn't be the first time he's hidden all the sharp things inside and locked me out for my own good.

I already know it's not where he's hiding the knives. He thinks he's being all slick, putting them somewhere he doesn't think I'll look. But I know.

I could tell him. But secretly, I love that he tries to do whatever he can to keep me safe.

It's just another thing about my life now that makes me second-guess myself when things are getting bad.

I might not have much in life, but I have my best friend, and I know without a doubt that I always will.

He's my brother in all the ways that count, and I have complete trust that he'll never leave me behind. Not like everyone else.

So where is he? A little voice whispers in my ear as I key in the code and wait to see if he's locked me out.

The beep of victory fills the air as a green light appears, granting me access through that layer of security.

Opening the panel, I find the biometric scanner beneath and press my hand to it.

You didn't think Reid would be satisfied with just one layer of security, did you?

Again, it beeps, allowing me access to the safe.

Pulling the heavy door open, I find it almost empty.

There are a few bundles of cash, some guns, and knives. A grenade... interesting. And then what I've come for, a stash of cell phones. There's one in a pink diamond-encrusted case, and another beneath it in a plain black one.

Bingo.

Ignoring all the others, I pull them out and check to see if they've got battery.

Alana's is dead, but Mav's has ten percent. Swiping the screen, I wait for it to ask me for a code, but to my surprise, it just unlocks. I can only assume I have Reid to thank for that.

I can't imagine Mav would risk not having a passcode on here.

Without bothering to look at anything else, I open his camera roll.

The last few pictures are memes that I ignore in favor of one of a woman with blonde hair and killer curves.

Absently, I close the safe and put the bookcase back into place with a lot less care than I opened it with now that I've got access to my biggest addiction.

As I scroll up through his images, I quickly discover that I might not be the only one with an issue when it comes to his wife. I guess he's just got the authority to be this obsessed, seeing as he put a ring on it.

Making my way back upstairs, I fall onto my bed, completely lost in images of my little dove over the past five years.

When I get a critical battery alert, I plug it in and keep going, desperate to find the very first ones of her when Mav took her in.

The change in her is gradual as time passes between images. Anyone else might not notice the way the color of her skin pales or the lightness in her eyes darkens. But I do. After only a handful of days really, I feel like I know her better than almost everyone else in my life.

Seeing her pain, the way she'd clearly been suffering at the hands of her father and the others, makes something blindingly hot explode within me.

Looking back now, it's so obvious. Her beauty might be there, but any hint of happiness, of hope, has been snubbed out. Ruined. Totally fucking destroyed by how she'd been treated.

Pain lashes at my insides as I consider what her life had been like and the ants multiply with every second that passes.

I want to return to that time five years ago and be the one to save her.

Why didn't we see it?

She was miserable and hurting. It should have been obvious.

I could have been the one to bring her back to life.

Maybe if you weren't drowning yourself back then.

You couldn't look after yourself, let alone anyone else.

Closing my eyes for a beat, I let my own pain rush through my system.

It's almost unbearable. Painful knots of grief twist up my stomach, shooting down my limbs like electrical currents.

My mouth waters, and my skin itches, begging me to slice it open, desperate for the release.

With the first image Mav has of her on the screen, I rest against the headboard again and lift the bottle of vodka I snagged from downstairs to my lips.

My hand trembles so violently that it's hard to successfully pour the liquid into my mouth.

But the second I do and the alcohol burns down my throat, I get just a taste of that relief I so desperately need.

I swallow shot after shot, and every time I lower my head, my eyes lock on sixteen-year-old Alana curled up under a blanket on a couch reading a book.

Her eyes are on Mav; she knows he's taking the photo, but there isn't a hint of a smile.

Her complexion is gray; the shadows under her eyes are dark and her lips are dry and cracked.

I can only assume he took the photo to document how much her life was about to change. He certainly didn't take it to capture a moment of happiness.

Or was it?

Being with him, being safe... it must have been the best day she'd had in a long time.

With the vodka warming my belly and slowing the ants, I pick up the pen and rest the notebook on my knee.

I stare at the blank page for the longest time.

But then I glance at that photo again and the sight of her looking so vulnerable, so broken and yet so strong, all at the same time, opens up something inside me.

Dear diary...

I pause, my need to purge the poison from inside me colliding with my need to be a strong, unshakable member of the Hawks. Reid deserves to have a right-hand man he can actually rely on. He shouldn't be forced to hide the knives and anything sharp or potentially dangerous that he comes across in the house.

With a pained sigh, I grip the pen tighter again and try to force my hand to stop trembling so my writing is legible.

I knew what I was doing. But I was powerless to stop myself from falling.

The end was inevitable.

And here we are.

You're gone and I'm alone.

I guess history does repeat itself.

I want to say that this time, there is a chance that I'll get you back.

But honestly, I couldn't even blame you if you ran out of Harrow Creek and never looked back.

You deserve that.

You deserve to be happy.

So does Mav.

I just wish...

I just wish it could have been me holding

your hand, leading you toward a future full of happiness and laughter.

People always leave.

My father...

I guess he didn't leave. He just... never existed.

My mother, once she decided that I wasn't good enough to hold her attention. The drugs had a tighter hold on her than I ever did.

That's probably why I'm so fucked in the head.

I've no evidence that she was high, stoned, tripping, or whatever else while she was pregnant with me, but it sure would explain a few things if she were.

The foster parents who promised to give me the kind of family I deserved.

The group homes where the staff wore what appeared to be genuine smiles when I entered, only to turn into a version of the devil incarnate when the social worker's back was turned and the doors locked behind them.

School was my sanctuary. Spending time with Reid and Knox and a handful of others who had no idea about my life was the best it ever got for me.

Suddenly, I had a family of sorts.

I belonged.

People appeared to care.

The guys were the first people who didn't stab me in the back the second it was turned.

It was incredible.

I was happier than I'd ever been in my life.

Until I met you.

Maya.

I still remember the day you turned up at the group home. You looked like a bedraggled cat. I swear, to this day, you were the cutest thing I've ever seen.

Your red hair was sticking up in all directions. You even had leaves sticking out of it.

There was mud smeared on your face, your hands were bloody.

I was fucking obsessed the second my eyes landed on you.

There was no way that anyone as small or as pretty as you should have looked like you'd been fighting with a bear and won.

But you did, and you stole my heart.

From that day on, I was so fucking gone for you.

Everything you did amazed me. Every smile you sent my way made my stomach flip over.

And every time you touched me, my dick got so fucking hard it was painful.

You had no idea though.

All you wanted to do was leave.

I got it. I still get it.

That place was worse than hell.

But with you there, it was bearable.

No, it was better.

We had so much ahead of us. But you couldn't see past the next three years until we aged out of the system and could embark on our lives.

It was all I wanted.

You and me against the world.

We'd have been so fucking unstoppable.

Bonnie and fucking Clyde shit right there.

The pen stills as the trembling becomes too much to keep going.

I hang my head, barely able to sit still as the memories of the first woman who stole my heart rip through me.

I thought I'd dealt with it all, and came out the other side.

I've fucked so many women over the past few years. Not a single one of them has stirred any of the kinds of feelings I felt back then.

But Alana.

One look at her down in that basement and everything changed.

Maybe it was because she was trapped.

Or maybe it was something I'd been waiting for.

I guess I'll never know. But everything *she* made me feel when I was just fifteen came flooding back.

I loved it as much as I hated it.

I have such fond, incredible memories of our short time together.

But I also have such painful, haunting ones too.

It's not until something lands on the page before me that I realize I'm crying.

Well, maybe not crying. There's no noise or any of the heart-wracking sobs I remember from back then. But there are tears.

Reaching for the vodka, I down almost half of it in one go, needing something to get me through this.

I shouldn't have started.

This isn't cathartic. It's torture.

It's exactly why you've never taken this suggestion seriously. You knew it would lead you here…

Abandoning the bottle, I scratch my forearms, my eyes lingering on the dark, thick ink that hides so many of my past mistakes.

Evidence of the pain.

Of my attempt to escape it all.

To be with her.

It's been six years since you left.
That's more than six times longer than I knew you for.
Yet, right now, it hurts just as much as the day you left.
You broke me.

Do you know that?
You took the one precious thing in my life
and you fucked it up.
You fucked me up.

Grasping the bottle again, I try to finish what's left, but most of it spills down my face, runs down my chest, and soaks into my boxers.

"You fucked me up. And I've just let it happen all over again," I slur as if she's right here with me. "I fell again, and she left me. Just like you did. Only this time, I've no idea where she's gone.

"Help me. Tell me what to do?" I beg, the vodka drowning out any kind of rational thinking as I happily dive into the darkness that's been trying to drag me down all day.

All I can hope is that this time, the pain comes to an end.

12

MAVERICK

Alana's stomach growls loudly, interrupting the silence that surrounds us.

"I should probably feed you, huh?" I whisper, not wanting to ruin the tranquility.

It took us a long time, but we eventually made it out of bed in favor of stumbling into the huge walk-in shower to wash the sweat from our skin.

Can't say that we ever let each other go, though.

I've spent five years desperately trying to keep my hands to myself. And now that I've touched her, it's like a switch has been flipped and I can't let her go.

The warmth and softness of her skin is even more addictive than I feared it might be. And add in the little noises and loud cries she lets out when I thrust inside her and push her over the edge, well, safe to say that I've fallen in love with her all over again.

"I'm okay. I've got everything I need right here," she lies, tightening her grip on my arm.

After our shower, I grabbed the comforter and dragged Alana out to the balcony attached to our bedroom. While she was in the bath and I was pacing around the cabin nervously, I found an identical swing seat out here to the one we fell asleep on downstairs this morning.

"You haven't eaten for hours," I argue, ignoring the other reasons why I know she's not okay.

We're going to need to properly talk about the men we left behind us and how she feels about it, but now is not the time. We at least need to be clothed for that situation.

"Nor have you," she counters.

A satisfied smirk pulls at my lips as I think about exactly what I've eaten in the last couple of hours.

"I think you'll find I have." I growl into the crook of her neck, making her shudder with desire.

It doesn't matter how many times I've made her come—and I've done it a lot since she walked out of the bathroom earlier today—she still wants me.

She's utterly insatiable. And I love it almost as much as I love learning all these new things about my wife that I refused to see or acknowledge before.

Here I was thinking it was a miracle that I managed to restrain myself all this time, when really, she must have been the one having the hardest fight with her libido.

I know that Victor didn't give her a choice in what she ended up doing for him, but I can understand why she might have agreed, even if that wasn't the case.

She has needs. Needs I wasn't fulfilling.

A little of the self-hatred I felt back at Reid's manor drips through my veins.

It doesn't matter that I was trying to do what I thought was best, I still failed.

"Eating my pussy doesn't count, Mav." She laughs.

The soft sound wraps around me, making the hairs on the back of my neck lift and my cock harden against her ass.

"It really should." I groan. "It could be the only thing I eat for the rest of my life, and I'd die a very happy man."

"So I can tell," she whispers, grinding her ass back against me.

"Aren't you sore?" I ask when she shifts enough to allow me to nudge against her entrance.

"You were listening to my confession earlier, right?" Twisting around, she finds my eyes, letting me see the honesty in her words. "I love the pain," she says, temptingly biting down on her bottom lip. "It makes me feel alive."

"I promise you, Doll. You're very alive right now."

Unable to stop myself, I wrap my hand around her thigh, spread her open, and thrust my hips.

"Oh shit. Pretty sure you feel better every time."

"Good news for our future then." I groan between clenched teeth because she's right. It is better every time.

I know she wants rough and painful, but it's going to have to wait. Today is about us connecting, about us learning each other's bodies and what makes each other sing.

We've got plenty of time for all the other things she wants. I'd be lying if I said my imagination hasn't been on overdrive since she confessed what she really wanted earlier.

Some of the ideas scare me as much as they excite me. But I refuse to continue to be controlled by my fears.

It's time that I finally opened up and listened to what Alana wants, what she needs from me. And who am I to deny her anything she desires?

I trust her.

I trust her more than anyone else on this planet. I have to believe her when she says that no matter how dark and dirty we get, that she'll never see me like them.

It's going to take me a while to fully embrace it, no matter how much I want it. It won't happen today, and probably not tomorrow, but soon.

"How did I live this long without having your dick inside me?" she asks, although I'm pretty sure she's talking to herself more than she is me. "It's so fucking perfect. The way it hits me. Deep. So fucking deep even like this."

"Just think of all the time we have to make up for," I whisper before nipping along the shell of her ear, making her body shiver and her pussy clench.

"More days like this?" She gasps as I thrust a little more forcefully, making the seat rock back and forth faster.

"So many more days like this," I promise.

Pushing up on my elbow, I grasp her chin with my other hand and twist her around so I can claim her lips. And I don't release her until she's come on my dick again and I've filled her pussy full of cum, ensuring that she's going to feel me dripping out of her for the rest of the day.

Forcing myself to pull out of her, I climb over her body and stand on unsteady legs as she rocks back and forth on the swing.

"Doll." I laugh when I catch sight of the pout on her lips.

"I miss you," she whines.

"I'm standing right here," I say, holding my hands out from my sides, inviting her to take a good look—as if she hasn't already done that many times over today. That and so much more.

My cock twitches as I remember her trailing her tongue over some of my tattoos earlier. Fuck, that was good.

"Not good enough," she complains.

"Oh, Doll. Are you being a brat?"

She shrugs dismissively.

"Brats get punished. You know that, right?" I growl darkly.

Her chin drops and her eyes widen, the glittering blue darkening with interest.

"I don't care," she sasses, keeping up the act.

Pushing up to sit, the comforter falls around her waist, exposing her full breasts and pierced nipples.

"Jesus, you're perfect."

Sucking her bottom lip into her mouth, she drags it between her lips as her eyes appreciatively drop down my body.

"Not too bad yourself, Murray," she teases. "Now, either get me something to eat," she starts before pulling the comforter away from her completely and spreading her legs. My eyes drop instantly, zeroing in on where my cum is leaking out of her.

The desire to thump my fists against my chest and roar *mine* like a caveman has never been stronger.

This incredible, sexy, intelligent woman is mine. And right now, she's so full of me, it's dripping out of her.

My fingers twitch with my need to reach out and push it back inside her.

Deep down, I know it can't achieve anything. I know her dark secrets, but that doesn't stop me from wanting to keep her full of it.

"Or," she taunts, reminding me that she was saying something. "Get on your knees and have your next meal right here."

If it weren't for her stomach choosing that exact moment to growl angrily again, I might have just thrown caution to the wind and done it.

"After you've had food, I'll spend all night on my knees if you wish."

"I thought I was getting punished," she quips.

A smirk spreads across my face as I stare down at her, my dick swelling as this conversation continues. Who knew I still had this kind of recovery time?

"I never said you'd get to come."

Her face twists in displeasure before a smirk twitches at her lips and her eyes blaze with... is that pride?

"Oh Doll, we're going to have so much fun," I tease before turning my back on her and walking away.

"What? Mav, wait. Come back," she calls, but it's too late.

I have the world's quickest shower. I hate every second of washing her scent off me, but I have every confidence that I can rectify the situation very soon.

She still hasn't appeared when I stalk back into the room naked and drag a clean pair of boxers from the pile of clothes on the dresser. A pair of my own boxers. What a novelty.

It was a long time ago that I first packed an emergency bag for both of us.

Five years ago, to be exact.

I knew that at some point, someone was going to find out what I'd done, and we'd have to run.

The only other person I trusted, other than Alana, was Sheila. So she's had this bag that I've added to over the years, along with a burner she was never allowed to turn off or allow to die. She knew as well as I did that one day I'd call telling her that it was time. Turns out, that day was yesterday. And thank fuck she pulled through.

Thoughts of what might be happening at home threaten to dampen my mood, so I push them away.

It's not our issue anymore.

Alana played her part. She opened up about what

happened to both her and her sister. Would it be nice to be
there when Victor, my father and hers get taken down?
Absolutely. It would be fucking incredible. But it's not
necessary. The most important thing now is her, our future,
and keeping my promise.

I duck out of the room and head to the kitchen to
discover what we might have to eat.

There's enough food here to last a couple of days, and
then we're going to need to make a decision about what
comes next.

We could take off into the sunset and never look back
like we always planned. I can contact Sheila; she can get
into our house and grab anything we might need, and we
can disappear.

The thought of leaving her and Daisy tugs at my heart.
But Sheila has made her decision to remain in Harrow
Creek with her granddaughter very clear over the years, and
I have to respect her wishes.

Or we wait it out, wait for some kind of signal that
everything has settled and return home.

Staying in Harrow Creek was never part of the plan.

But something tells me that things have changed.

Mostly, the look in Alana's eyes when I dragged her
away from that house yesterday. Away from him.

Julian Dempsey.

Honestly, he's not a bad guy. I've never had the same
opinion of him as I have of Reid. He's just always seemed...
a little lost, I guess.

He's followed Reid around like a lost little puppy for as
long as I can remember. But he seems to be a great soldier, a
hard worker and a loyal friend. Any bad decisions he's made
are because of the leader he follows. And spending time
with him at Reid's place has only solidified those opinions.

Although I must admit, even as much as I hate it, he seemed less lost over the past few days, and I fear that might have something to do with the woman not so far away.

I'm hardly surprised; she does possess those kinds of magical powers. She sure sucked me in good and then refused to release me from her tight hold. She didn't even know she was doing it either.

Movement from deeper in the cabin hits my ears and I drag myself from my thoughts and tug the fridge open, surveying the contents for something for dinner.

I might not have skills like Reid does in the kitchen, but I'm more than capable of rustling up something edible that will hopefully give us some energy after all our... activities.

13

ALANA

My muscles are tight and my core aches in the most delicious way as I silently pad toward the kitchen where Mav is crashing around like he's destroying the place. He's always been a noisy and messy cook.

Memories of watching him in our kitchen at home bring a smile to my face, but it falls a little when that image suddenly morphs into someone else moving effortlessly and flawlessly around his own state-of-the-art kitchen.

Shaking him from my thoughts, I continue forward.

This right here is everything I ever wanted.

My husband all to myself—and not holding anything back—the beach, peace and quiet with the knowledge that the men of my past are being taken care of for us.

So why is it that I don't feel as relaxed or as content as I always thought I would when this time came?

Today has been all kinds of incredible. Having Mav finally shed his fear and open up to me, both mentally and physically, was everything I could have wished for, and it holds the promise of so much more.

I should be satisfied, complete.

But something within me is still as unsettled as ever, and dread sits heavy in my stomach.

We're safe here. I have no doubt about that. It's not fear of being found. Even if Victor knows that we were at Reid's, I really doubt he cares enough to embark on a wild goose chase to find where we've gone. He's got bigger issues with what his oldest son is attempting to do. And if he does know about our location, then he must be suspicious as hell about what Reid is up to.

Reid and Mav's rivalry is well known through the Hawks, add in my fucked-up situation with Victor and he's got to be coming up with all kinds of scenarios about how we ended up there.

I guess all we can hope is that Reid manages to pull off whatever he's planning, sooner rather than later, so we never have to worry about Victor's next move again.

For a moment, I try to imagine what it'll be like. The freedom, the lack of looking over my shoulder waiting for the next strike.

Will my nightmares die with them?

I guess that could be one wish too many. Something tells me that I'm going to be stuck with the horror of my past for the rest of my life.

But knowing we've protected numerous little girls and women from the lives that Kristie and I lived... A smile twitches at my lips.

I just want it to be over. To stop the pain and the abuse of those too young and innocent to understand what is going on around them.

Refusing to lose myself in my dark thoughts when everything around me is so good, I take another step forward and round the corner to find Mav putting the finishing touches to sandwiches.

The second he realizes I'm here, his head lifts and his eyes find mine. And the second they do, the widest most sincere smile I think I've ever seen spreads across his lips.

"Hey," I say, my stomach a riot of butterflies as the air crackles between us.

His pupils darken as he drops his gaze down my body, taking in what I'm wearing.

"That's my shirt," he states, almost sounding in awe.

"It is."

Sucking his bottom lip into his mouth, he drags it between his teeth as his eyes rake back up my body.

"Do you know how fucking badly I wanted to see you walking around in my shirt in that house instead of theirs?"

My smile widens as I step closer, my skin tingling with awareness and craving his touch.

"Feeling a little possessive, were you?" I tease.

"Doll," he warns, his jaw ticking.

"You loved it and you know it."

His eyes flash with heat and it makes me wonder what memory is playing out in his head right now.

"You're trouble." He growls before reaching out the second I'm in touching distance and pulling me into his body.

One of his arms bands around my back, pinning me in place while the other lifts, his fingers sinking into my wet hair and dragging my head back so he can kiss me.

It's perfect.

Everything I've ever wanted.

But before I can completely lose myself in him again, he pulls away.

"Eat, Doll. You need to eat."

Rolling my eyes like the brat he accused me of being upstairs, I hop up onto the stool as Mav slides one of the plates toward me.

"Soda?" he asks after watching me for a beat, ensuring my skin continues to prickle with his attention.

I nod before ripping my eyes away from him in favor of the sandwich. My stomach growls loudly, making him laugh as he emerges with drinks.

"Oh my God," I mumble when I take my first bite. It might only be a simple cheese and ham sandwich, but shit, I really needed this.

Mav moves closer and I gasp as the heat of his bare arm brushes against mine.

"Good?" he asks, his eyes dark and hungry.

Something tells me that he's not asking about his sandwich, but so much more than that.

I guess it's a good thing that my answer would be the same no matter what.

"So good," I assure him, reaching out to squeeze his thigh beneath the counter.

His muscles pull and twist beneath my palm and I squeeze tighter.

I don't move my hand as he starts on his own food. I can't. I need this connection to him. The reminder that this is real.

Silence stretches out between us as we eat; it's not uncomfortable, time with Mav never is, but it is full of unasked, loaded questions.

He finishes before me, pushing his plate away and draining his glass of soda long before I've made it even halfway through my sandwich.

His hand drops beneath the table and his fingers twist with mine.

"It's okay," I whisper, "You can ask."

"Doll." He sighs, hanging his head.

He wants to know everything, but at the same time, he's terrified.

I get it. I really do. I feel the same.

Everything about the last two weeks of my life has been a headfuck of emotions. Most bad, but some good. So freaking good.

"You... you care about him, don't you?" he asks hesitantly.

My heart knots and my chest tightens as I think about the man in question and everything we've been through. "Not as much as I care about you," I counter.

"Babe, that's not what I'm questioning," he assures me. "This," he says, lifting our joined hands and dropping a kiss on my knuckles, "Us. It's not in question."

The second my eyes find his, butterflies take flight in my belly.

'I love you,' I mouth.

"I love you too. But I need to know what happened back there. What really happened."

I nod. I knew that I wouldn't get away without giving him the dark and dirty details, but I was hoping to put it off as long as possible.

"Shall we sit somewhere a little more comfortable?" I suggest.

His eyes alight with mischief.

"What are you thinking, Maverick Murray?"

"Finish that and you'll find out."

Pushing my plate aside, I hop to my feet.

"I'm done."

"Alana," he warns, noticing that I've only eaten half my sandwich.

"I'm fine. Honestly."

His face twists in concern and when he looks down at my body hiding behind his shirt, I know it's because of the weight I've lost.

Reid might have fed me well once I emerged from the basement, but stress has stopped me from eating full portions. And right now is no different.

"I'll have something else later," I promise, hoping to squash the overprotective caveman I can see emerging.

"Okay, grab your drink," he says before pouring himself another and then leading me outside.

"Ah, I think I like this plan," I muse when he turns toward the hot tub. "But I don't have a suit."

He chuckles as he places our drinks on a small shelf. "What a shame. Arms up," he says before dragging his shirt up my body, leaving me bare for him. "Yeah," he muses before slapping me on the ass and urging me to get in. "Real fucking shame."

"Oh God." I moan as I step into the warm water, my muscles instantly relaxing, just like when I sank into that bath he ran for me this morning.

"Keep that shit up and there won't be much talking happening in here," he warns, before dropping his shorts and significantly improving my view, which is already pretty spectacular as the sun sinks toward the horizon over the ocean.

"I don't have a problem with that," I muse, my eyes locked on his rippling muscles and shifting ink as he lowers himself opposite me.

He's too far away for my liking, but only seconds later, his legs tangle with mine under the water, giving me the connection I need.

"So, where were we?" he prompts.

"So much for a nice relaxing soak," I mutter under my breath, making him smirk.

"Brat," he teases.

Resting my head back, I stare up at the darkening sky and let my mind wander back to my first few days as Reid's captive.

His favorite inmate, I think he referred to me as a time or two.

Blowing out a sigh, I allow myself to take a trip down memory lane.

"Reid was... well, he cut my hair and pierced my nipples," I say lightly. The former still hurts. Every time I look in the mirror, I remember that promise I made Kristie all those years ago. It's stupid. She's gone. Has been for a long time, but the big sister in me wants to keep any memory close and keep every promise I made to her. But the latter, I can almost look back at that fondly now. I quite like the pink bars through my nipples. And I know for a fact that I'm not the only one, evidenced by how Mav licks his bottom lip and swallows at just the mention of them.

"But JD, he was... well, JD. His idea of torture came in a very different form." A smile twitches at my lips.

I pause as my next words dance on the tip of my tongue. Mav isn't going to like them, but that doesn't stop them from being true.

"I'm a whore, Mav. And JD—"

"No," he barks, sitting forward so fast that water sloshes over the side of the tub. "You're not."

"I am though. Look at everything I've done. Victor may not have paid me but he—"

"Stop," Mav demands, dragging his hand down his face. "All you've ever done is what you felt you had to. That doesn't make you a..." He swallows the word.

"Doesn't it? What you just said, isn't that the case for every woman who finds herself in a similar situation? Just doing what they feel like they have to."

His jaw ticks with irritation, but he can't argue with me. He knows I'm right.

"Anyway, JD saw it. Reid wanted to scare the truth out of me, but JD... he knew there was a better way to do it.

"We had a connection from the very first time he came down to see me. I didn't know what it was to start with, but I think our dark childhoods might have helped us bond long before we dived into those nightmares." Not that I know much more than the basics of his past. "He drove me to the brink of insanity, Mav. It was insane. He intrinsically knew how to play me, how to make me weak, and he used it against me in the best kind of way."

Mav's shoulder and neck muscles pull taut. If he were to lift his hands, they'd be clenched tight.

"It was electric. When he put me out of my misery... well, I've never experienced anything like it.

"I broke, Mav. Completely fucking shattered. And he held me through it, wiped my tears and promised me that everything was going to be okay.

"He was there for me in a way I've only ever experienced from you. He cared. He does care. And..."

"And?" Mav prompts.

Lowering my head, I find his eyes.

"JD is fragile," I confess. "I don't know the details, but there is a darkness there. It lingers too deep for most to see, but he let me in and—" I swallow thickly, trying to force down the massive lump that's crawled up in my throat as I think about him curled up outside Reid's room that night I kicked him out.

"You're worried about him?"

"Yeah. I'm not sure that he'd handle this," I say gesturing between us and the place we're in. "Very well."

Mav's jaw pops again. It's the only sign I need to know that I'm not the only one who came away from our time in that house with a fondness for the joker with the lingering darkness.

14

REID

"I'm putting a lot of faith in you with that," Luciana says, nodding at the thumb drive she slid across the desk toward me a few minutes ago.

"I know. And I can assure you, everything you've found is in very safe hands."

"There are very few people on this planet that I trust, Reid. I hope you understand that."

My lips part to agree, but she continues before I manage to get a word out.

"I have a very, very select team working on this with me," she says, looking over her shoulder at Angel and Jose, who are standing guard behind her. "If the wrong people catch wind of us snooping where we're not wanted, the result will be death, and not the fun kind."

"I know what I'm doing," I assure her again.

Luciana Rivera has shown very little emotion during this meeting, but right now, her mask is slipping. This isn't just any mission she's tasked herself with. It's personal. I'd put everything I have on it.

"We will find out more and we will get the answers we need," I promise her.

Her eyes narrow at my words, but she doesn't respond to them.

"Angel has a phone for you. Do not give the number to anyone, and do not answer any call that doesn't come from one of the three of us."

"Understood."

"If you need us, if you find anything out, call us. Day or night."

"You got it."

She nods at me and I push to stand, sensing that our meeting is over.

"Well, thank you for this... unexpected meeting."

She stands and holds her hand out over the table.

"Hopefully next time we see each other, progress will have been made."

Our palms connect and I'm shocked by how cold hers is.

"We will take them down," I state confidently. "No matter how deep it runs, or where it takes us. We'll make it happen."

For the first time since I stepped into this room, a small smile spreads across Luciana's face.

"That's good to hear."

Pulling my hand free, I snatch the thumb drive from the desk and walk around the chair ready to make my exit. I need to get the hell home to make sure Harrow Creek hasn't burned to the ground in my absence. Honestly, it wouldn't be all that much of a bad thing, but a few of my favorite people are there, and I would set the world alight if my cunt of a father hurt them any more than he already has.

I sense one of Luciana's bodyguards behind me as I step up to the door, but I don't turn to look.

"We have you booked on a flight in a few hours. I suggest you get some rest before it's time to leave," Luciana says behind me.

A rush of air passes my lips as relief tugs at my tired muscles.

"Will do, thank you," I say before pulling the door open and stepping forward, ready to do as she just suggested.

"No, Reid," she says, the tone of her voice stopping me in my tracks. "Thank *you*."

"I'll be in touch," I promise her before walking out of the room and down the hallway in the direction of my room.

"Can I have my cell back now?" I demand when I get to my door, and turn to glare at whoever is following me.

Angel gives me an apologetic smile.

"Luciana's safety comes first," he says simply.

"I'm not going to—" I swallow my words when it becomes very clear by his expression alone that there is nothing I can say that will change his mind.

"What time is my flight?"

"5 a.m."

"Fantastic," I mutter, pulling the keycard from my pocket." I've no idea what the time is, but I do know it's not as close to 5 a.m. as I'd like.

"One of us will come and get you and drive you back to the airport."

"Great. Until then…" I march into my suite and let the door slam behind me.

I have no desire to humor these guys. Yes, they might be connected to some of the most dangerous drug dealers that exist, but I'm not exactly a cute fluffy bunny either.

If they wanted someone to cower and be scared, then they invited the wrong person here.

The second I walk into the living room, my eyes land on a giant clock that covers a big chunk of the wall.

"Brilliant," I mutter, seeing that I've got hours until I'll be able to get in contact with anyone.

Dropping onto the couch, I twist the thumb drive over and over in my hand, wishing I could see what was on it.

Luciana might have explained the contents, but it's not enough. I need to see it with my own eyes.

I need the locations she's already uncovered, where some of the girls and women have gone.

I need the names of the men she has discovered are involved. My father and his inner circle are some of them.

My need to tell JD about the intel I've uncovered burns through me.

It isn't very often that I do something like this and don't have him by my side. Or at least call him the second I'm done.

But it's not just him I want to tell.

I want to tell her.

I want to look into Alana's hopeful blue eyes and tell her that we might be a step closer to her finding out about Kristie. That I have a list of names literally in the palm of my hand that could help uncover so much more.

"Fuck," I hiss, unable to deal with any of the feelings that woman erupts inside me.

Irritation continues to build within me, making my knee bounce and my fists clench and unclench.

With my eyes on the clock, I swear time moves slower than it ever has in my life.

I have all this intel in my hand and no way to look at any of it. No way to get it to Ellis.

"ARGH," I bellow, losing my fight with sitting still and pushing to my feet to start pacing.

"Just answer your motherfucking phone," I spit, canceling the fifth call to JD since I got my cell back. The second Angel handed it over, I was gone without any kind of thanks. Asshole move? Probably. But I was long past giving any kind of shit after sitting—or pacing—in that suite alone for the past few hours.

He was chattier than Jose was on the way here, but not a lot, and he certainly didn't say anything worthwhile. Not that I expected him to, but it would have been a little easier to deal with instead of the bullshit small talk.

Everyone in front of me in the queue to get through security all turn around and sneer at me. I can only assume the people behind do the same, but I don't bother to look.

Trying again, JD's phone just rings and rings.

It's the middle of the night, he's probably asleep...

"Fuck." I growl.

He should be asleep. He probably is asleep. But that doesn't stop the ball of dread from growing impossibly large in my gut.

JD always answers his phone. Always.

Even mid-fuck if he knows it's me, he'll pick up. Much to the irritation of the woman he's screwing.

So the fact he isn't now sets off a million warning bells in my head.

Changing tactics, I find Dev's number and hit call.

"Hey, you're through to Dev. I'm too busy hustling to talk to you right now. You know what to do."

"Fucking asshole," I mutter, scrolling through my call log to find someone else. Although the chances that he'll be balls deep in some poor unsuspecting college chick is pretty fucking high.

Scrubbing my hand down my face, I call Ez.

If it were any other time, I'd go for Ellis, but I guarantee he's either asleep or up working on an assignment. Neither of which he'll want to be interrupted.

If Ez doesn't answer then...

"Fucking time do you call this, Bro." He groans, although something tells me that he's far from crawling into bed.

"Suck it up. I need you to do something for me."

"I'm working."

"Good, you should be." I growl. "Is Dev with you?"

"Yeah, he's somewhere. Although I'm not sure if he's working or playing."

"Go find him, tell him you're leaving and head to mine."

"Where the fuck are you?" he barks, thankfully sounding sober.

"Mexico."

"Why the fuck are you in Mexico?"

"Not important right now. I need you to go to my place and check on JD?"

"Check on... why? He sick or something?"

"I..." Lifting my hand, I comb my fingers through my hair and tug until it hurts.

"Sir, you need to hang up your phone," a security officer says when I finally get to the front.

"Shit," I hiss. "Look, just go over there and make sure he's—"

"Sir," the guy growls.

"I'll call you back in a bit."

Hanging up, I hold my hands up in defense, all the while glaring at the jerk before moving forward to dump my bag and boots into a tray along with my cell.

The second I have everything on the other side, I hit call again. When it connects, it's instantly obvious that he's driving.

"Where are you?"

"Won't be long," he says cryptically. "What's the fucking hurry."

I shrug, not that he can see it. "Just a hunch."

"You've got me racing across town in the middle of the night on a hunch?"

"Yeah, I fucking have. You got a problem with that?" I snap.

"Jesus. Who pissed in your shoes."

"Ez," I warn.

"Seriously, why are you in Mexico?"

"I'm standing in the middle of an airport; I can't discuss this right now."

"I just need to know that everything's okay at the house and it can't wait until I get back."

"Something has happened, hasn't it?"

"When hasn't it?" I mutter, finding the gate half empty as people eagerly board and drop into an empty row.

"Fair. But this sounds serious."

"Ez." I sigh, slumping low, my exhaustion getting the better of me. "There's so much more going on here than any of us realized."

"Shit. Mexico," he muses. "You have a meeting?"

"Yeah."

"Cartel?"

"Mm-hmm," I mumble, not willing to say a single word about it.

"Fuck. That is serious."

"Ez?"

"Yes?"

"Can you stop asking so many questions and focus on getting there faster?"

"Slave driver." He scoffs.

When I look up, I find I'm the only person still sitting here and the line is getting shorter.

"Bet you don't say that when you look at your bank account," I counter.

"Pfft. Someone's got to put the work in around here."

"You find Dev before you left?"

"Yep. He was working hard on two chicks."

"And I'm assuming that work wasn't getting a sale."

"Only if he was selling his dick."

I sigh and scrub the back of my neck as a call goes out for the final passengers to board.

"Pretty sure they'd already dropped some Molly, so he probably scored twice."

"Lucky him," I muse. When was the last fucking time I saw any action that wasn't my right hand, exactly?

Fuck. I can't even remember.

"Drought still hanging on, huh? You should just fuck Al—"

"Don't finish that sentence," I warn.

"Why the fuck aren't they checking on J?"

"Because I can't contact them. Their cells are in my safe and—"

Ez's laugh cuts off my explanation. "So you still don't trust them, then."

"That's not—"

"Final call for—"

Shit.

"I'm getting on a plane," I mutter, grabbing my bag and throwing it over my shoulder. "You're gonna need to—"

"Okay, I'm pulling through the gates now," he says, and I happily fall silent as I wait for what he's about to find.

"Everything is dark. That's good. Right?" I don't say anything. "Or not," he mutters.

My heart is in my throat as I hand over my boarding pass and wait for Ez to say something.

"It's quiet. He's probably asleep."

"Go check, please."

Ez falls silent as I make my way down the tunnel to the plane.

Glancing behind me, I notice that I'm the last to board, and when I step onto the plane, I see everyone is already seated and ready to go.

"Sir?" a flight attendant says, gesturing me toward the first-class seats. "We're ready to depart."

Following her orders, I find my seat and fall into it.

"You still there?" I growl.

"Yeah. Just heading up now."

The speakers on the plane crackle before the captain welcomes us onboard and runs through all the things I don't give a shit about.

The doors are closed, and out the window, I get my last glimpses of Mexico.

"Sir, you're going to need to hang up," the attendant says politely.

"Yeah, I will, I just... Ez, talk to me."

"Opening his door now."

"Sir, this is serious, you need to—" but her warning is drowned out by Ez's voice as it booms through my speaker.

"Oh fuck. JD," he bellows. "JD, shit. Talk to me."

My stomach bottoms out hearing the fear in my brother's voice.

"Ez, what's happening?" I yell, ensuring all attention turns on me.

"Shit. I don't know. There's blood. So much fucking blood. Julian," he snaps. "Open your eyes, man. Look at me."

"Is he alive? Fuck. Tell me he has a pulse." My voice is nothing but desperate as I squeeze my eyes closed and silently pray. Not that any god or deity would listen to a gangster like me.

"Sir, I'm sorry, but you really need to hang up." Ripping my eyes open, I glare at her.

She cowers a little, but she doesn't back away.

"Y-yeah, I think there is. But... fuck, you need to hurry, man."

The weight of the distance between us presses heavily on my shoulders.

I should have fucking woken him before I left. I should have told him everything.

"Call Doc. He'll fix everything," I shout before lowering my phone and cutting the call. A sharp pain cuts right through my heart as it goes dead. But what else am I meant to do? If I get thrown off this plane then...

My hand trembles in my lap as I put my cell on airplane mode, allowing the attendant to see.

"We'll get you back there as soon as we can," she says softly, her face wrought with concern over what she just overheard.

I nod, unable to speak through the panic and fear that's consuming me.

Last time, I got there just in time.

But will he be as lucky the second time around?

15

MAVERICK

"Oh yeah, I definitely found heaven," I murmur into Alana's neck as I push inside her from behind.

She chuckles lightly, making her pussy clamp down around me. My eyes roll back as pleasure like I can barely remember from my previous life floods through my system.

"Go on, argue with me and tell me that I'm wrong?"

Her entire body trembles as I slowly roll my hips, hitting her as deep as I can in this position.

We lie on our sides, her back to my front, exactly how we woke up.

The sun has only just started rising, casting the room in a beautiful orange hue.

I figure that once I've made her come, I can carry her out to the balcony and we can watch the sunrise, just like we watched it set last night.

Definitely heaven.

"Can't." Alana gasps as my grip on her hip tightens and I tug her tighter against me.

"You sore?" I whisper. No matter what she says, I'm

fully intending to take it slow, but I still need to know. I want to know every single thing about her body and what she's feeling.

"Yes, but in the best possible way. Don't you dare stop." Her voice is raspy from sleep, and even sexier than it usually is.

"There's no chance of that."

"Never hold back with me again." I'm pretty sure it's meant to be a warning. It starts that way, but when I grind my hips, it turns into nothing but a desperate plea.

"Never," I promise.

Sliding my hand to her thigh, I drag her leg over my hip, giving me better access as the other curls around her waist from underneath to reach for her clit.

The second I collide with her wet, burning cunt, she tenses and sucks me deeper.

"Yes," she hisses, rolling her hips in time with mine.

Confident she isn't going anywhere, I release her leg and skim my hand up her body, teasing her breasts with my pointer fingers, circling her nipples, and refusing to give her what she really needs.

"Mav." She moans when I flick one of her piercings. "Please."

"Greedy little doll," I muse, finally giving her what she's so desperate for and gently tugging on her piercings.

They're not fully healed, and I should probably leave them alone, but she makes it so fucking hard. Pun hugely intended.

She's so needy and pliant. I fucking love it.

Could have been doing this for years, a little voice pipes up in the back of my head. But being here with her now, experiencing everything I am, I find it hard to regret anything.

Maybe it was always meant to be this way.

Maybe we were meant to have those years together, the world's longest form of foreplay to really get to know who each other is before we embarked on this side of our relationship.

Alana might need this, crave this, but after the years of abuse she suffered, maybe she needed the time to figure out exactly what she wanted on her own terms.

"Stop thinking so hard," she demands.

"Sorry," I mumble.

"It's knocking you off your game."

"I'd hate to give you any less than you deserve, Doll."

"You're perfect."

A self-deprecating laugh tumbles from my lips. "I'm far from that, babe." Lifting my hand again, I wrap my fingers around her throat. Her body startles at the bold move and my cock swells just thinking about how we look right now.

My fingertips graze her soft skin before my grip tightens, making her gasp and her body tremble even more violently as her need for release grows.

Leaning around her the best I can, I brush my nose across the shell of her ear.

"Are you going to come for me like a good girl, or are you going to be a brat again?" I rasp. I'm so close to her, I see all the little hairs lift on her upper arm and her nipples harden even more than I thought possible.

"I'll be good," she whispers. "For now."

A growl rips from my throat as I think back to last night and the little brat/tamer role-play we had going on.

I've never experienced that before. All the women I was ever with prior to Alana just wanted to fuck a Hawk. They didn't care about games or making more of it than what it was. They were whores who wanted to brag about whose dick they'd been bouncing around on.

But last night opened up a whole new kink that I can definitely get on board with. Hell, I'll get on board with whatever she wants.

I want to be the man who gives her everything she desires and then some.

Will it push my boundaries? Because it's her, yeah. But I'm pretty confident that I can figure a way around it. Having her coming all over my cock will certainly help.

"Oh God, Mav." She gasps, barely able to breathe with my grip on her throat and her impending release. "More, I need more."

I have a moment of hesitation, but her next cry of desperation shatters it in a heartbeat and I tighten my grip a fraction more, cutting off her air.

The second I do, she falls headfirst into an intense release. Her body convulses violently against mine as her greedy pussy sucks me deeper. But even that doesn't seem enough as she screams through it.

The second she's done, I release her throat and allow her to suck the air she needs into her lungs.

"Fuck. Mav. That was..."

"Not it," I bark, lifting her slight body effortlessly until she's on all fours.

"Oh yes," she mutters, dropping to her elbows and sticking her ass up in an offering.

Pulling my arm back, I spank the flawless skin of her backside, watching in delight as it reddens for me.

"Mine." I growl. "You. Are. Fucking. Mine."

"Yes. Yes. Please." She pants, wiggling her hips. Her slick pussy glistening in the early morning sun, making my mouth water.

I spank her again, obsessed with my vivid handprint against her pale skin.

"You want more, babe?"

"Always," she confirms a beat before I slam into her from behind.

Her walls ripple around me, welcoming me home as I bottom out in her in a way I couldn't achieve when we were lying down.

"Ready?" I ask, my muscles pulled with my need to unleash on her.

"So ready. Make it hurt, Husband."

"Fuck," I bark before pulling out and slamming straight back in. That little reminder that she's mine, all fucking mine, makes my head spin and my balls ache in the most delicious way.

Being with her like this after so long, it's intoxicating. It makes me forget about ever having doubts and reservations about treating her the way I dreamed of.

In only seconds, the room is filled with the sounds of our skin slapping together and our heaving breaths. And it's not long until her moans, mewls and cries for more flood my ears.

Fuck. They're the best fucking sounds in the world.

I knew they were, I used to stand outside her slightly open door and listen to her get herself off. It was the most beautiful kind of torture. But knowing those sounds are because of me. It's a whole new level of pleasure I didn't know existed.

I didn't care about any of the women in my past, and I'm ashamed to say that their pleasure was never my priority. But with Alana... I could spend my days just watching and listening to her come and never need anything more. Okay, that's a big fat lie. I need her like I need my next breath.

Sweat beads at my brow as I continue taking her more roughly than I should, knowing she's sore. But I can't stop myself. I need more. Always fucking more.

When my desperation to see her becomes too much, I slide my hand up her back, the heel of my palm bumping over the notches of her spine until I'm able to wrap my fingers around her throat again.

But this time, I don't cut off her air supply; instead, I drag her up until her back is to my chest once again.

Her skin burns mine, my blood at boiling point with the softness of her skin against my ink and hard muscles.

I release her throat in favor of her jaw and twist her to face me so I can claim her lips.

"I'm fucking obsessed with you, Doll," I confess, our mouths pressed together before I plunge my tongue into her mouth, and tangling it with hers.

My free hand finds her clit and I play her until she's right on the edge. But I don't let her fall again. Not until I'm ready to unload in her.

"Please," she whimpers, ripping her lips from mine.

"Fuck, you're incredible." I pant before kissing her again. I need every inch of her touching me, anything less isn't enough.

This time when she starts whimpering, her pussy clamping around me as her release surges forward, I don't stop it.

"Alana," I bellow as my balls draw up and pleasure shoots through my body.

"Mav," she cries, suddenly going limp in my arms before we crash to the bed.

I only just manage to catch myself before I crush her beneath my much larger frame.

For long seconds we just lie there, our limbs intertwined, our skin slick with sweat and our chests heaving.

It's everything I've ever wanted and so much more than I could have dreamed of.

"Can't get enough of you," Alana murmurs, much to my delight, long minutes later.

"Same, Doll. Same." I chuckle, feeling like I could sleep again.

But just when I think I might close my eyes and give it a go, she expertly rolls from beneath me and hops to her feet as if she hasn't just been fucked within an inch of her life.

She smiles down at me with such excitement and life in her light blue eyes, butterflies flutter wildly in my belly.

"I've got an idea," she says, bouncing on the balls of her feet. "You with me?"

Pushing myself up so I'm sitting, I let my eyes roll down her body.

"Hell yeah, I'm always with you, Doll."

"Good." Before I know what's happening, she's out of the room, running along the hallway and down the stairs shouting, "Catch me if you can."

"Fuck," I hiss before jumping to my feet and taking up the chase. "Where are you going?" I call as my feet thump against the stairs.

I hit the ground floor as she pulls the slider open that leads to the deck. She darts through, her short, messy hair nothing but a flash of blonde in the sunlight.

With a smile spreading wider across my face, I continue my chase, although I do slow down, allowing her to get where she's going.

My eyes are locked on her bare body as she races down the steps that lead to the private beach beyond.

Once she's halfway down the beach and able to predict where this is going, I pick up the pace, more than ready to do this together.

The second I catch up to her, I snag her hand in mine and pull her toward the crashing waves.

"Ready?" I call, the water already splashing up our shins.

"Hell yeah, I'm ready," she cries into the tranquility around us.

Together, we run into the water, and it's not until we're over waist-high that we slow down. However, when I look back at Alana, I find her in up to her chest.

Placing my arms behind her, I sweep her off her feet, and with a squeal and a splash, I tug her into my body.

"Skinny-dipping on your bucket list, Doll?"

"Isn't it on everyone's?" She laughs before I lift her high and throw her into the deeper water.

Her scream is cut off the second she goes under, and when she comes up, frantically wiping water from her face, I can't help but laugh at her expression.

"You're going to regret that," she warns darkly.

My smirk grows. "Is that right?" I taunt, ready and willing to fight dirty.

"Oh, hell yeah."

She pounces faster than I was expecting, but my reflexes are pretty good—or at least they are when I'm not fighting Reid Harris—and I catch her mid-air.

We play around, splash each other, and laugh like little kids, but despite my happiness, the whole time my heart aches for the woman before me because she never got to experience these kinds of simple pleasures as a kid. I mean,

I'm not exactly swimming in heartwarming childhood memories myself, but I had good friends growing up and we had a lot of fun. Much more than Alana and Kristie ever did.

Catching my eyes and clearly able to read my dark thoughts, Alana muses, "She'd have loved this. We always talked about what a holiday at the beach might be like."

I cup her jaw, leaning in close, so my nose brushes hers. It doesn't matter that Harrow Creek is barely a few miles from the ocean, it was still a dream of those little girls.

My jaw ticks with irritation.

"It's okay," she soothes, mimicking my action.

"I want to give you it all," I promise quietly. "Every dream you ever had."

"You have, Mav. You've given me so much more than you could ever appreciate."

"I'm going to give you more."

"I can't wait," she says, jumping up and wrapping her arms and legs around me like a koala.

She kisses me until we're both breathless and the temptation to lay her out on the beach becomes too much. With the water lapping around her body, I push back inside her and fuck her until her screams are hoarse.

"We should probably go shower," I say, finally rolling off her and landing in the damp sand.

"I don't think I can walk."

A happy laugh tumbles from my lips.

"I don't think I've ever felt this good," I confess, rolling onto my side and sliding my hand across her belly. Unable not to touch her.

Twisting her head, her eyes find mine. And while I know she feels the same, there is still the lingering hole that JD has left in her.

I hate it. But right now, we can't risk doing anything about it.

It's another half an hour before we manage to pick ourselves up and head inside, leaving sandy puddles behind us.

"I have sand in places there should never be sand," Alana complains as she climbs the stairs in front of me, giving me an epic view of her ass.

"Worth it," I muse, unable to ignore my own uncomfortable sand-chafing issues.

"Will you rub cream into my sore bits?" she teases, swaying her hips back and forth.

"Any day of the week, babe."

Laughter follows us into the master bathroom and the massive walk-in shower.

Turning to face me, she throws her arms around my shoulders and reaches up on her toes.

"I love you, Maverick Murray," she whispers. "Thank you for being crazy with me."

"Anytime. I love you too."

We shower like we have all the time in the world, but while we might not stop touching each other, we don't take it any further. I think we're both in agreement that we probably need a rest. We're like horny teenagers now that the wall between us has been completely obliterated.

With her wearing one of my shirts, and me in nothing but a pair of boxers—at her request—we head toward the kitchen for some breakfast.

With Alana sitting at the island watching my every move with heated eyes, I grab everything I need and set about making us omelets.

I'm almost done when a loud knock rips through the cabin.

My heart jumps into my throat, and on instinct, my hand moves behind me for my gun. But it's not there.

Spinning around, I meet Alana's terrified eyes.

"Who's that?" she whispers as if she thinks they might be able to hear.

"Probably no one. Kids, maybe," I reason.

We're in the middle of nowhere, but I don't know for a fact that there aren't other cabins in walking distance.

"Mav?" she whispers again, climbing off the chair and coming around the counter to me.

"It's fine. I'll grab a gun and go—"

The knock comes again, this time harder and more demanding.

"Or we should go out the back?" she suggests.

"Babe," I say, taking both of her hands in mine. I search her eyes, desperately trying to dig up something reassuring to say. "No one knows we're here. There is no way to track us either. The car was untraceable, we have nothing on us."

What I really want to tell her is that if it's Victor, or any of his men, then they'll have the place surrounded. There will be no easy way to get out.

She nods, but I'm not sure she really believes a word of it.

"Ignore it?" she tries, but the knock comes again.

Whoever it is, they're not going away.

"It'll be fine."

Leaving her with her arms wrapped around herself protectively, I grab the gun I stashed in a unit by the front door. After releasing the safety, I hide it behind my back and reach for the handle, praying that I'm not about to face reality.

16

REID

By the time the flight attendant opened the doors to let us off, I was like a barely-restrained bull. They knew it too and allowed me off the plane before everyone else.

With my phone pinned to my ear, I raced through the airport.

But Ezra didn't answer.

The only time I was forced to lower it was through security, but then it was only for a split second while my ID was checked.

"Fuck. Fuck. Fuck," I bark as I close in on my car.

Logically, I know he's not ignoring me on purpose. Ez might be a bit of an idiot, but he's not cruel. He's not our father. None of us are.

Even our littlest brother has a couple of redeeming qualities if you look hard enough.

Every muscle in my body is pulled tight as I race toward home. I go through every light without stopping and break every speed limit. But I don't give a shit. I need to get there.

"Fucking finally," I bark when Ezra answers yet another call.

"Sorry, sorry, I left my cell downstairs while I—"

"Is he okay?" I bark, not giving a shit about what he's done with his fucking cell that stopped him from answering me.

"I... uh... Doc hasn't said much. I think he's waiting for you. J's lost a lot of blood. Doc has patched him up and sedated him."

That doesn't sound good.

My grip on the wheel tightens and I press the gas harder.

I need to be there.

I should have fucking been there.

Scrubbing my hand down my face, guilt lashes at my insides.

I played this wrong. So fucking wrong.

I knew he was struggling, and I just fucking left.

"I won't be long. I'm driving into the Creek now."

"We'll be waiting."

I nod, despite the fact he can't see me.

Silence falls between us and nothing but the crackle of the connected line fills my car.

"Where are Alana and Mav, Reid?" Ez asks.

Releasing my vise grip on the wheel, I slam my palm against it. The force of the hit makes it jerk to the left and the entire car follows, sending me into the other lane.

I barely react to the blaring horn that comes from behind me as I almost take his bumper off.

"FUCK," I bellow, my voice echoing around my car.

"What have you done?"

"Don't. Just fucking don't," I mutter. "Go and sit with JD and tell him I'm coming."

Ez blows out a pained breath. I feel the weight of it right to the depths of my black soul.

"Yeah, you got it. See you soon."

I hang up without another word. What else is there to fucking say.

Everything is falling apart around me.

All I need now is Victor to piss all over my plans and come for me and everything J and I have been working on for the past... too fucking long will be for nothing.

By the time I pull through the hidden gates that allow me entry to my property, the sun is high in the sky, casting one side of my home in an ominous dark shadow.

Swallowing down the giant lump of emotion that's clogging my throat at the thought of my best friend suffering in my absence, I pull up next to my brother's car and climb out.

As much as I'd like to sit out here pretending that all is right in my world, one of the most important people in it is inside my house suffering, may even be fighting for his life.

The front door crashes back against the wall as I burst inside and make a beeline toward the stairs, my backpack landing on the hardwood floor with a thud.

I take the stairs three at a time in my need to get to my best friend—my brother—and I crash through the door with my head spinning and my hands trembling.

I'm vaguely aware of both Doc and Ez in the room, but my eyes lock on the pale face that's lying in the middle of a very neat and un-JD-like bed.

"J," I breathe, rushing to his side and gently lowering my ass to the bed.

The arm closest to me has a cannula in it that's hooked up to a bag of blood hanging on a hook next to the bed. The other is resting on top of the sheets, his forearm covered with a fresh bandage, another cannula disappearing under his skin. Almost every inch of his exposed skin is stained red with dried blood.

Acid swirls in my stomach and burns up my throat as I take it all in.

"I'm so fucking sorry, man," I say softly, speaking solely to him.

I've no idea if he can hear me or not, but I need to fucking say it.

I search every inch of his insipid, gray skin as pain spears through my chest.

I promised myself the first time this happened that I would do anything in my power to stop it from happening again. For a lot of years, he hasn't shown any signs of coming close. But since Alana turned up, he's become more and more unstable.

I get it. I totally fucking get why.

It was falling in love that fucked him up the first time.

It's like watching history repeat itself.

Ripping my eyes from him, I hang my head in shame.

I put my need to gather information against my father before JD and I'll forever live with the regret of that.

I should have told Luciana no, or demanded an extra ticket and taken him with me.

Painful seconds pass with nothing but the sound of JD's shallow breaths filling my ears.

I startle when a warm hand lands on my shoulder.

"It's going to be okay, Bro," Ezra says, sounding uncharacteristically empathetic.

"Fuck, I hope so," I mutter.

Sucking in a deep breath, I lift my head, my eyes finding Doc who's resting against the opposite wall with his arms crossed over his chest, his previously pristine white shirt soaked with my best friend's blood.

"What's the verdict, Doc?" I ask, my voice hoarse with emotion. There are very, very few people in this world that would cause this reaction in me, but the man in the bed before me is right at the top of that short list. And I don't fucking care who knows it.

"He was very, very lucky. If Ezra called me even ten minutes later, I think we could have been having a very different conversation right now."

The sincerity those words are delivered with hits me like a punch to the gut.

I thought he was lucky last time, but this time... shit.

Lifting my hand, I rub the back of my neck, trying to ease the tension that's been there since my call with Ez earlier.

"Where do we go from here?" I ask, my eyes focused back on JD.

"I've stitched him up and sedated him. He was already unconscious by the time Ezra found him, so we've no idea what kind of state he was in."

I just about refrain from barking anything obvious at him about JD's mental state for him to have done something like this.

"We'll keep him under while we get some blood back into him, and then we can try reducing the sedation and see what happens. Do you have any idea what's triggered this? He's been stable for so long."

"Yes," I breathe, regretfully.

But I don't need to say anymore. Doc knows. This isn't our first rodeo after all.

"He fell in love, didn't he?"

My heavy sigh is the only confirmation I give.

"If you're okay from here on out, I need to go home and shower," he says, nodding to the state of his shirt. "But I'll be back later in a few hours to change the bag over and check on him."

"Whatever you need to do, Doc. You know the drill."

Nodding, he pushes from the wall and stalks closer.

"I don't know what is going on here, Reid. But this is the second near death this house has seen in as many weeks. Whatever you're doing, please tread carefully. You're all too young to succumb to the darkness of this town." He holds my eyes for a beat before glancing over my shoulder at Ezra.

This time, I'm the one to nod. I'm pretty sure that at this point, there's nothing I can say that wouldn't be a lie.

"I'll see you soon. May I suggest you try and get some sleep. With all due respect, you look like shit."

And with those words ringing in my ears, Doc marches out of the room, and not long after, the house.

"Fuck," I hiss, dropping my head into my hands.

"Bro, he's not wrong. Have you looked in the mirror?" Ez teases, trying to lighten the mood.

Twisting around, I take in his equally exhausted face and barely manage to rein in a cutting remark when I remember that he was the one to save J's life today.

Instead, I go with, "You hungry?"

"Yeah, fucking starving. What are you thinking?"

Pushing to my feet, I keep my eyes on JD.

"You gonna be okay here for a bit?"

"Yeah, Bro. I got it. Still got plenty of cleaning up to do," he says, gesturing to the trail of blood that runs from the bathroom and across the bedroom carpet.

The words are on the tip of my tongue to tell him to leave it and that I'll get someone in to do it.

But I swallow them down.

We can't trust anyone to be here, to know about this right now.

If Victor knows we're weak, then he might take his chance.

We need to keep face. As far as anyone outside of this house is concerned, everything is normal. Just me and J ruling from our castle on the hill.

Just me and J…

Why does that thought feel so fucking wrong now?

Refusing to allow reality outside of this situation to sneak in, I press my hands to my knees and stand up.

"I'll be back."

"Bring coffee," Ez demands.

"Bro, who the fuck do you think I am?"

I take off, thoughts of everything that's unravelling around me making each step harder than the last.

As I get to my kitchen and come to a stop in the middle, I realize just how empty and cold this place feels.

There are no mugs and plates littering the counter; there is no music, chatter or laughter filling the air.

It's not something I ever thought was missing. But apparently, all it took was a few days for everything to change.

Stepping up to the sink, I curl my fingers around the counter and stare out the window at the valley beyond, wishing I could predict what's going on down there, that I knew what moves Victor was planning.

He knows they were here; no words were needed when he passed me that hair tie.

That one simple move confirmed my worst fears. He's on to me.

And it's only a matter of time before he manages to turn the tables and have me at a disadvantage

I might have convinced even some of his closest allies to back me in my takeover mission, but I'd be a fool to think he couldn't buy their loyalty back just as easily.

Money talks. It's how I've managed to achieve what I have so far. But I learned from the best, and unfortunately, he is the fucking best.

With a roar of irritation, I push from the counter, spin around and rip the fridge door open.

Standing around doing nothing isn't going to help anyone.

We need food and rest, and then I'll try and figure out my next move. In the meantime, all I can hope is that Aubrey gets me some intel.

A shudder rips through me as I think about what I've sent her in to do. It's easy to forget that she's just a normal person when she's always in work mode. But seeing her in her hotel room with her messy bun and rumpled clothes, it was a harsh reminder that under it all, she's a human. And I'm sending her into the most toxic of situations.

Yes, it might be her job, but still. I already have enough blood and guilt to deal with. I don't need any more if this should all blow up in our faces.

With a tray loaded down with two plates of homemade waffles, scrambled eggs and bacon, and two steaming mugs of coffee, I make my way back upstairs.

Ezra has clearly given up on his cleaning mission and is

dozing in a chair that is usually covered in JD's dirty clothes.

"I have food," I say, making his eyes pop open.

"Love you, Bro," he says, his eyes widening at the sight of the amount of food I hold in front of him.

"Funny, you only ever say that when I have food."

"Coincidental," he mutters, grabbing the plate and immediately stuffing a piece of bacon into his mouth.

"Jerk," I hiss, resting my ass back against J's dresser, my eyes on him as I eat.

I barely taste it; I might as well be eating sand for how much I enjoy it. And I've barely made a dent in the massive portion before I give up and abandon it.

Placing it on the desk beside me, my eyes catch on the bloodstained notebook page that's covered in his messy scrawl.

I have to do a double-take at the words at the top of the page.

Dear diary...

A frown creases my brow as I stare at those two words.

I'm about to read more when my cell buzzes in my pocket.

Pulling it free, my blood runs cold at the name staring back at me.

Victor Harris.

Rolling my lips between my teeth, I blow out a slow, calming breath before straightening my spine and preparing for the worst.

Swiping the screen, I open the message and discover that I wasn't prepared at all for it.

Well-played.

But rest assured, the next round of hide and seek will be a much bigger challenge.

And if I thought that was bad, the photo that follows sends my world into a tailspin.

17

ALANA

My entire body vibrates with fear as Mav walks toward the front door in only a pair of boxer briefs and a loaded gun behind his back.

I want to believe the words he said about it being kids, being anyone other than the one man I never, ever want to see again.

A million and one questions race through my mind as each second stretches out like hours, but I can't latch onto any of them.

The fear coursing through my veins is too potent to focus on anything else.

My entire body jolts as I watch him wrap his fingers around the handle and push it down.

Unlike me, he shows no fear or hesitation as he pulls the door open, and I'm reminded exactly who the man I married is.

I stop breathing as he stands there staring at someone on the other side.

It feels like forever, but in reality, it's probably barely more than a second before someone speaks.

And when the voice hits my ears, my knees buckle, and I stumble back into the corner of the kitchen.

"Good morning, Maverick. Long time no see."

The loud crack of a gunshot rips through the air a beat before it's replaced with my scream as I race forward, expecting to see my husband on the floor, bleeding out.

Reid might have only grazed his shoulder, but I've no doubt that the owner of that voice wouldn't make such allowances.

But thankfully, when I get there, it's Mav's gun that fired, although the man I assume he aimed at doesn't seem to be dead. Frantically, Mav pulls the trigger on the gun, but nothing happens. It's not firing.

"Ah, Alana," he sneers. "How wonderful of you to join us. Your husband here just made a very grave mistake. I hope you're both ready to pay."

My heart pounds so hard, I can feel it in every single inch of my body as I stare into the cold eyes of one of the men who ruined my life.

"Mav," I whisper, reaching for his hand.

"Aw, this is cute. Although I must say, I'm surprised you're still interested in this whore, Mav. Especially now she's my son's sloppy seconds. I really thought you'd draw a line there."

An inhuman roar rips from Mav's lips as he flies toward Victor. The gun drops to the floor and I shriek as it fires, shooting a bullet across the room that, thankfully, lodges itself into a wall.

With his fist curled, Mav is about to throw a punch into the cunt's smug face when another deep, dangerous voice rumbles from behind us.

"I think you've already made enough mistakes, Son. Don't you?"

Mav pauses immediately at the sound of his father's voice.

I feel them before I see them, closing in on us from behind, proving that my idea of running earlier would have been pointless.

They've got us surrounded.

"Let us go. We're leaving. We're not going to do anything to any of you," Mav states confidently.

If I didn't know him as well as I do then I might believe he's totally unaffected by their arrival, but one look in his eyes and I see his fear is just as potent as mine. But something tells me that it's not for him. It's for me.

Bile burns up my throat that, even now, he'll put my life before his own.

"Maybe it's not you we're worried about. If you were going to take a strike at us, you'd have done it years ago. You're nothing but a pussy, and it makes me wonder if you truly are my son after all."

Mav barely reacts to his father's words, but I see the slight widening of his eyes. Mav would love nothing more to discover that he didn't share any DNA with that asshole. We're not that fucking lucky though.

"I'll give you anything you want," Mav offers. "Just let her go."

The man behind me moves closer. I already know who it is, the third fucking amigo. But the second his scent fills my nose, my stomach rolls and I fight not to retch as memories slam into me one after another.

Be a good little girl for Daddy, Alana.

I'm jerked back, my heart somersaults as my stomach revolts again when a strong set of arms band around me, pinning me back against a hard body.

"That's cute, Maverick. Real fucking cute," he taunts,

his hot breath rushing over my ear and down my neck, making my skin itch with disgust. "You always were trouble, weren't you, Alana? Nothing like your little obedient sister."

"Don't you dare talk about Kristie," I sneer. The sound of her name rolling off his lips forces me to find my fight, and I put into practice everything Mav has ever taught me in an attempt to break free.

"Doll," he shouts, lunging for me, but Razor and Victor are on him before he even gets close.

"Get your dirty fucking hands off of her," he demands. "She's mine. Not yours." Spittle flies from Mav's mouth as he glares pure death at my father. The man who single-handedly started this nightmare that is my life.

I fight like I've never fought before, but it's not enough. He's too strong for me. Well, that's what I decide to go with, the alternative of my body submitting to his after all the years of abuse is just too much to handle right now.

"That's enough, whore," Dad barks before I'm suddenly released from his grip, but the relief is so brief I almost immediately wonder if it even existed before his hand flies toward my face and he backhands me so hard, everything goes black.

Maverick

"NOOO," I roar, lunging forward in the hope I can break free of the hands holding me back.

One-on-one, I could take both of them without breaking a sweat, I've no doubt. They might be old, but they're still very much in shape. But two against one, they have the edge.

"You have no fucking right to touch her," I bellow,

staring in horror as a trickle of blood runs from her eyebrow.

An inferno rages inside me and just before I manage to slip free of them, Kurt pulls a gun from his waistband and aims at his daughter.

"Stop or I'll end it right now."

My blood runs cold as fear like I've never experienced turns my entire body to ice.

I fall deathly still, the only part of me that continues to move is my heaving chest as I hold Kurt's eyes.

"Let her go," I repeat. "Take me. I'll give you anything you need if you let her walk away."

All three of them laugh darkly as if what I just said was the funniest thing they've ever heard.

I look around at the place we'd found our solace the last few days. The place where we'd finally given ourselves to each other. But it's no longer the cabin that brought us peace and happiness. Now it's tainted with pain and nightmares, just like everything else in our lives.

"It's cute how much you love her, Son. Truly. It's admirable. Some might say it makes you a better man. But that isn't us.

"She makes you weak." He snarls, his fingers still digging into my upper arms.

"Just look at everything you've done because of her."

"You've betrayed us," Victor spits. "You've lied to us. You've colluded against us."

"You don't know anything," I scoff. "All we want is a new life. A fresh start as husband and wife away from here."

"And is that how you ended up with my son? Because you wanted to break free? A man you hate," Victor demands.

"The men I hate are standing right here in this room. You and any others who have hurt my wife."

"Reid hurt your wife, did he not?"

My teeth grind as I think of what he did to her. But none of it, not one single part of what Reid did even comes close to what they did to her. How they corrupted her. How they broke her.

"No?" Victor taunts. "Did he just use her up and spit her out like the whore she is."

I barely recognize the furious roar that bounces off the walls around us as my own. His words give me the final bit of strength I need to finally rip free of their grasps.

Instantly, I race toward where Alana is out cold on the floor, but before I drop to my knees beside her, the sound of multiple gun safeties being released rips through the air.

"Move and we'll shoot her," Victor says coldly. There is no emotion in his voice and it makes me wonder if he could be as heartless if one of his own children would be at the other end of that gun. Probably. That cunt cares about nothing but his own gain, whether it be money or power.

I pause standing right by her side. So close and yet so far away.

"We can do this the easy way or the hard way, Son. It's all up to you."

"I'm not your son," I snarl, finally saying words I've dreamed of hurling at him for years now. "I've no interest in being related to someone as sick as you."

"Well," he says, giving himself a moment to absorb my insult. "That's a real shame, boy. Because you're all mine."

"How do you know?" I taunt. "You only fuck whores. I could be anyone's." His jaw ticks in irritation.

I'm his oldest child, his very first offspring. But there are plenty more coming up behind me. Many of which I'm probably not even aware of.

"You're right. She was a whore, don't even remember her name," he says, carelessly. "Shit fuck too."

Shaking my head, I bare my teeth at him.

I know nothing of my mother. There are no photos, no nothing. All I've ever heard is shit like this. That she was so worthless that she couldn't even keep me.

"Didn't stop you, did it? However, from what I know, nothing ever does. You're disgusting. All of you," I spit, ripping my eyes from the man who brought me up to the others who are also pointing their guns at my wife.

"You're mine," Dad states.

"Razor," Victor spits. "We don't have time for this touching little father/son moment."

Replacing the safety on his gun, Dad tucks it away in his pants before moving closer.

"Are you going to choose the easy way to save that hot piece of ass down there?"

I glance at Alana, my heart bleeding for her.

I failed you again. I'm sorry.

Holding my arms out from my sides, I offer myself up. "I'll do as I'm told. Just... just don't hurt her."

"Yeah," Victor snarks. "We'll see. If I remember rightly, she's always loved a bit of pain."

Bile sloshes in my gut before burning up my throat at the thought of him ever laying a single finger on my wife. On my underage, innocent, precious wife.

If it weren't for the fact both he and Dad have guns pointed right at her, I'd be on them.

No one gets a free pass to talk about my wife like that.

"See," Dad taunts. "This is exactly what we mean. Victor is your leader, and just look at what she makes you want to do to him. She's turned you into a disrespectful little cunt."

"No," I argue, my voice as unsteady as my body. "You all did this. You all did this when you decided it was okay to treat her and others like nothing more than a toy. You're disgusting, all of you are—"

Dad slips around me while I'm focused on Victor and Kurt and wraps something around my head and between my lips.

"Motherfucker," I mumble, as I grapple with him, throwing punches that land every single time, helping to release some of the fury that's raging within me.

I spit the cloth to the floor.

"Mistake, old man." I growl darkly, but before I manage to land any more hits, a gun presses to the side of my head.

"Keep going, boy," Kurt taunts. "We'd love to have this party with your doll without you."

"Fuck you," I sneer. "You're not getting your hands on her again."

"You want to bet?"

With the barrel of the gun pressed to my temple, he forces me to turn to watch as Victor assesses the state of my wife.

"I do understand why my boys were so taken by her."

"Kane wasn't though, was he?" I bark, needing him to know that I have all Alana's secrets. There is nothing he can say that will turn me against my wife. Nothing.

"Oh, you are such a fool," he mutters, dropping to his haunches to get a better look.

I struggle to swallow through the giant lump of fear that's clogged in my throat. I want to fight, but Kurt's gun is ever-present digging into my skin.

I won't give them the satisfaction of taking me out like this.

They think they're going to taunt me until I break, but that is never going to happen.

I am stronger than them.

"She was mine first," he sneers, "never forget that."

My teeth grind, but it's the only visible reaction I give.

But then Victor reaches out and my entire body jolts with the need to do something.

"Careful, boy. She wouldn't look so pretty with your brain splattered all over her pretty skin."

Disgust rolls through me as he tucks his finger beneath the hem of my shirt she's wearing, exposing her.

"Oh, you really have been a lucky, lucky boy, huh, Maverick?"

"Get your fucking hands off her."

Allowing the fabric to drop back into place, he holds them up in surrender.

"I'm not touching. Not yet," he adds darkly, pushing to full height again.

As he turns to me, ready to spit some more venom, a quiet whimper comes from Alana.

"We need to get out of here," Dad says.

Silently Victor and Kurt agree.

"Back to my previous question," Dad says, turning his eyes on me. Eyes that are so fucking similar to mine it disproves everything I said earlier about him not being my father.

"How are you going to play this?"

Everything in me wants to fight, to take the hard route and see if I can come out on top. But one look at my wife and I know what my answer is going to be.

She needs me right now and there is no fucking way I'm fucking this up more than I already have.

"Do what you have to do," I offer. "Just... don't take her from me."

"Aw, don't worry, Mav. We'll make sure you have a front-row seat to everything we have planned."

"Ez," I bark, barely able to speak through the anger that surges through me like a tsunami.

"Yeah," he mutters around another mouthful.

"Call Ellis. Get him here right the fuck now."

Whatever he hears in my tone is concerning enough to force his attention away from his plate and to me.

"What happened?"

"Just get him here, yeah?"

I take off before he has a chance to answer and storm into JD's bathroom for a moment to myself, but I soon discover my mistake.

Blood.

There is blood fucking everywhere.

My stomach knots up painfully as I think about exactly what JD went through while I wasn't here. Stumbling forward, I collide with the counter and spin around, resting my ass against it as I take in the devastation.

He could have died here tonight.

If I didn't call Ez to get him to check, I'd have come home to find him dead. Right fucking here.

Emotion burns up the back of my throat, my eyes red hot in a way I haven't felt for a very, very long time.

"Fuck," I breathe, shoving my fingers through my hair and tugging.

JD's okay.

He's going to be okay.

But Mav and Alana...

The ball of dread in my gut grows and my anger multiplies until my entire body is taut with it and the need to go and burn the motherfucking world down.

"FUCK," I roar, louder this time in the hope of dispelling everything that's raging inside me.

Anger, pain, guilt, and the worst, fear. Fear for two people that I never would have given a second thought to only weeks ago.

Everything changed in this house the second Kane dragged Alana through my front door that night, but I never realized until this moment just how fucking colossal that change has really been.

My fingers grip the counter until they start to cramp, but I don't let go. I can't. I need to feel just an ounce of the pain those around me are feeling.

I promised Alana that I'd help with her mission to take down the men who hurt her. I thought I'd done what I needed to do to protect her—them. But all I've achieved is to hurt everyone.

The only man left standing right now is me.

I might have the power to take down Victor with an army behind me, but alone... I stand no chance.

"Bro, are you—"

"I'll be out in a bit," I mutter, dropping my arm and tilting my face to the ceiling.

Closing my eyes, I suck in a deep breath in the hope it'll help clear my thoughts.

JD has to be my priority.

I've let him down enough recently.

But the second the darkness consumes me, the only thing I see is the image on my phone.

It guts me all over again.

A roar rips from my throat, and I spin around and turn the cold faucet on to splash my face, but I freeze when my eyes land on the object in the sink.

My knife.

The knives I've been fucking hiding from him.

"T hought you'd climbed out the window in there or some shit," Ez deadpans, when I finally emerge having barely got a handle on my raging emotions.

One second I'm consumed with so much anger I'm not sure how I keep myself from storming out the house and finding that motherfucker. Then the next, I'm drowning in so much guilt I can barely move my legs and force myself forward.

"Is he coming?" I ask, my voice hoarse and broken.

A deep frown creases Ezra's brow as he watches me approach a still-unconscious JD.

"Y-yeah. He's on his way. Didn't want to ditch out of class early, but I told him it was serious."

Dropping my ass to the bed, I keep my eyes on my best friend.

The color of his skin and the dark shadows around his eyes make me feel sick. And knowing he did this with one of my knives.

I shake my head, wishing I knew what was going on in his head to make him do this.

Sure, I have a good clue from looking at that diary entry, but knowing JD, that'll only have been the half of it.

"What's going on, Reid? You're hiding shit and I don't like it."

"Get Dev here too. It's time we all talk."

His chin drops, but no words spill free for a second or two.

"Shit. This really is serious, isn't it?"

Scrubbing my hand down my face, I scratch the hair covering my jaw.

"More than I want to admit," I say the words so quietly he probably wouldn't hear them if the room wasn't so deathly quiet.

"Whatever it is, we've got your back," he promises me. "The Harris boys stick together, you know that."

A bitter laugh spills from my lips.

"You know, he's going to have to return at some point," Ez mutters, talking about our youngest, absent brother. "Maybe now could be the time."

"He's—"

"Bro, it's like... late and shit. Get your ass out of bed. You're needed at the house of terror," Ez barks into his cell, stopping me from saying anything more about our little brother.

"He's coming. Will probably smell like a fucking garbage can."

"What's new," I deadpan.

"You finished with this?" he asks, gesturing to my plate.

"Yeah. I can't stomach it."

Without another word, he takes what's left of my breakfast and leaves me alone with JD for the first time since I got back.

Long seconds pass after he closes the door behind him until I find some words.

"Fuck, J." I sigh. "I'm guessing you didn't see my note."

Silence.

"I should have woken you and explained. I just... I thought you'd see it and call me. I was going to explain everything. Fuck. I can't believe how badly I fucked this up. I'm so fucking sorry."

Getting up, I walk over to the window and stare out at Harrow Creek, disappointed that I don't find it engulfed in flames.

"I'm going to fix all of this, J," I promise. "I've no idea how. Everything is even more fucked than you know. But somehow... somehow, I'm going to give us all the lives we deserve."

The image on my cell taunts me.

"I'm not going to leave you again. You're my priority right now, J. I can't do the rest of it without you. Just like we always planned, we will take over this motherfucking town. You still with me?"

Silence.

Letting my head fall back, I send up a prayer. I've no idea if anyone up there listens to fucked-up motherfuckers like me, but right now, I'm willing to try anything to fix this. To fix him.

Falling into the chair Ezra was in not so long ago, I lean forward, resting my elbows on my knees and just watch him, waiting for any sign of life to prove that Doc's words were right. That he's going to get through this.

And before I know what I'm doing, I let another promise spill from my lips.

"I'll bring her back for you, J."

I swear his little finger twitches at my words.

"J?"

Nothing.

"Fuck," I sigh.

I've never felt so fucking torn in my entire life.

Pulling my cell from my pocket, I open the tracking app that shows where everyone is.

Ez is here. So is Ellis now it seems, and Dev is halfway between Maddison and Harrow Creek.

It's the other dots that I'm more concerned about, but it seems they haven't moved.

My grip on my cell tightens to the point I think I'm going to crack it before I open the photo again, not allowing my eyes to linger on the two figures and instead the background, desperately trying to search for signs. But there is very little to go on. I'm not surprised. My father is smarter than he looks, which is why I believe every single word of that message he sent me.

I've just got to hope he's not smart enough to be aware of some of the things I have in play right now.

Things that will hopefully lead me straight to wherever they are. And if they're in a better state than JD is right now then all the better.

"What's going down then, Boss?" Devin asks when I finally drag myself from JD's side to join them.

As much as I don't want to leave him, the last thing I

want is him waking to the things we're going to need to discuss.

"Clearly it isn't Alana because, according to this douche, she's gone," he continues, jerking his chin in Ez's direction.

"Ellis," I say, ignoring the other two momentarily. "Can you get up-to-date tracking? I don't think mine is right."

"You got it." Immediately he leans down and pulls his beloved laptop from his bag. The second he's flipped the lid, he becomes all business. Not that he wasn't the most serious of the three of them to begin with.

He begins tapping away, and I leave it to him in favor of the coffee that's sitting in front of my seat.

"J's... had an incident," I say gently. "He's going to be out of action for a bit."

Proving that he's still fully alert, Ellis's head pops up.

"That's really shitty timing, Bro."

"Trust me, I fucking know. I think... no, I know that Victor is aware that Alana and Mav were here."

There's a beat of silence before Devin sits forward in his seat—JD's seat.

"You really need to start talking, man. All this secretive shit and fucking about with our shipments has got to fucking give."

Sitting back, I stare at the three of them. The three men that I know for a fact would willingly walk headfirst into a war with me and J should the need occur.

Individually, we have more flaws than we can count. But together, we're fucking unstoppable. And that's exactly why I've always believed that we could do this.

Victor didn't raise weak sons. He raised us to take the helm when the time came. He gave us each a different role to ensure we were able to control every aspect of his business. He just wasn't aware that he was setting us up to take over long before he was ready, or that we were going to be the ones to bring his reign to an end.

I guess that's one of his biggest failures.

He thought we'd be just as hungry for power and control as him. He never banked on us getting any genes from our mother, who was his opposite in every way.

As a kid, I always wondered what drew our soft and caring mother to such a corrupt and sick bastard. But I understand it all now.

She was as much of a captive in her own life as Alana was when I first locked her up downstairs.

"We're taking over," I state. "Victor's time is done. I've spent the last few years collecting evidence against him and turning his allies to enemies."

"The shipments. You made it look like he was fucking up and turning him on us," Dev reasons. "You fucking threw us under a bus."

I glare at him.

"You can more than handle yourselves."

"Yeah, but you should have told us."

"Dev," I sigh, pushing my messy hair back. "There have been so many ways that all of this could have gone wrong. It still can. The last thing I needed was putting that weight onto your shoulders when you all had classes to think about on top of everything else.

"I never would have put any of you in danger. A few fucked-up deliveries is nothing in the grand scheme of things. Victor is still making a lot of money out of you all over there."

"Not the point," Dev sulks like he used to as a toddler.

"Does it really fucking matter now? What's done is done," Ezra reasons.

"I guess not," Dev mutters, clearly unhappy about being left in the dark. "So what now, and where are Alana and Mav? You offed them?"

"No, I haven't." I grunt, pissed off with all of this. I need to be back upstairs with J, not bickering with my little brothers. "When Kane brought Alana here, I thought I'd just teach her a lesson, let her confess what she was doing playing games and then send her on her way back to her husband."

Devin scoffs, but the second I raise a brow, he swallows whatever it is he wants to say.

"But I got much more than I expected from Alana Murray."

Devin's eye twitches with his need to make some lewd comment, and impressively, he actually manages it.

"I've been suspicious for a while that something even darker than we knew was going on, but I was never able to pinpoint anything other than a gut feeling."

"Ellis couldn't find anything. Griff and his boys neither. But it turns out, Alana was hiding all the secrets. They have the power to ruin Victor and his inner circle along with many, many others across the country."

"I was in Mexico yesterday meeting with Luciana Rivera."

"The fucking cartel are involved in this shit?" Dev barks, his eyes wide.

"No, not the cartel. Luciana. She's not working under orders, she's out on her own with this."

"Shit. What is it?"

Ellis is the one who speaks up, saving me the trouble.

"Dad and the others are involved in a human trafficking ring. They've been trading women and girls for years."

"T-trading..." Devin's voice trails off. "Fuck."

"Yeah, fuck," I agree. "They sold Alana's little sister when she was only thirteen." My lips part to spill more of Alana's dark past, but I quickly shut them again. They're her stories and they don't need to be exposed to anyone unless she decides to tell them herself. I've already taken enough from her. I should be thanking her for the intel, not fucking her life up anymore.

J needs her. Hell, Mav certainly needs her.

And I... am not fucking going there.

Ezra pushes to his feet, his fist curled tightly at his sides as his chest heaves.

"They're all going to fucking hell," he warns. "That is not how we do shit in Harrow Creek."

"It won't be soon. You're with me, right."

"Too fucking right, we are," Devin answers for all of them.

"They're still at the cabin," Ellis says. He doesn't need to agree, I already know he's fully invested. After all, he was the one who installed the trackers in Alana's nipple bars before I punched them through her skin.

ALANA

The first thing I notice when I come to is the pain.

My head is fucking throbbing, but I can't remember why.

Everything is hazy.

Moving my arm is possibly the hardest thing I've ever done, but after agonizing seconds, I manage to press my fingertips gingerly to my temple.

I hiss in a breath when I make contact and the pain multiplies to beyond unbearable.

I don't cry, but that doesn't stop fresh tears from leaking from my eyes as I desperately try to grasp what is happening.

Ripping my eyelids open is almost as hard as moving my arm, but once I manage it, I'm greeted with nothing but darkness.

My mouth is so dry it's almost impossible to swallow. If I didn't know better, I'd think that I'd swallowed a mouthful of the sand on the beach.

The beach...

I let out a soft sigh as I remember messing around in the ocean with Mav.

As we stood there splashing each other, I was able to laugh like I hadn't in a very long time.

I was no longer an adult with a life that was only fit for films and novels; I was young and carefree and on vacation with the most important man in my world.

It was everything I'd dreamed of.

Licking my lips, I muster up as much energy as I can manage.

"Mav." I wanted to shout it, but his name comes out as nothing more than a whisper.

My heart rate picks up when he doesn't answer. Not that I'm surprised, my voice was so quiet, I'm not sure it would be possible to hear.

I try and search for memories, but the only thing I can latch onto is the ocean.

My skin tingles as I remember how it felt as the warm fall water lapped at my body as Mav thrust inside me.

He's everything I ever wanted him to be and so much more.

He can be so gentle with me that it brings tears to my eyes, but his touch also promises so much more.

I know he's holding back, and I understand why. It took him five years to allow us to get to this point. This time, though, I have every confidence that we'll keep growing together, discovering new things.

I can't wait.

When my need for him becomes too much, I try speaking again.

"W-where are you?" This time even I don't hear the words.

I fight the darkness for another few seconds, but it's pointless, and it claims me all over again.

Repulsion rushes through me as multiple pairs of hands roam over my skin.

"No, please. Don't do this," I cry, although my voice doesn't sound like my own.

"You're going to have to try harder than that, princess," another says.

Bile erupts in my stomach, burning up my throat at the familiar voice.

"She wants it. We all know the fight is fake."

"She's nothing but a filthy whore who's been trained to want this. To crave us. She knows who gives her what she needs,"

"I bet she's wet for us already. Isn't that right?" the first voice says.

"Spread her thighs, let's find out."

Clenching my muscles as tight as I can, I fight against them.

"No," I cry. "I don't want you."

But my strength is no match for theirs and in embarrassingly short seconds, they have my legs spread for them.

Vomit fills my mouth, knowing where their attention is focused right now, and I'm forced to swallow it down.

I don't want them to see how they affect me. They'll only get a kick out of it.

"Fuck, I'm going to love finding out if your cunt is as good as it always was."

"Probably loose as fuck by now after what this asshole has had her doing."

"Nah, I only ever got good feedback. She's still the perfect whore we always knew her to be."

"Could have done so much better than that," a third familiar voice says.

"Yes, well. Maybe it's time you taught him a lesson he'll never forget. Sure seems that he has forgotten all the others," the first scoffs.

"If he didn't have intel that we need, he'd already be dead. Traitorous cunt."

"Noooooo," I wake up screaming.

My body is covered in a layer of cold sweat and I'm trembling from head to toe.

"Mav?" I cry. "Mav, please?"

I try to move, but something stops me. Something I didn't notice the last time I came too.

But then, my body was so weak and my head so fuzzy, I couldn't grasp anything.

Pushing my feet against something, I try to move it out of the way, but I can't.

I do the same with my hands, but all I find are bars that my fingers wrap around.

I pull and push, but nothing happens.

I'm trapped.

Oh God.

"MAV?" I scream, frantically trying to shift around, to break free from whatever it is. But I can't. "MAV?"

At first, his response is quiet, but it doesn't matter. I hear his rumbling voice loud and clear in my ears, and that's all I need to squash some of the panic.

"I'm here, Doll. I'm right here."

I blink against the darkness, desperate to see him, desperate to wake up from this nightmare.

But it's not a nightmare. I'm not asleep right now.

"I'm... I'm trapped."

"I know," he forces out. The crack in his voice rips

through my chest like a chainsaw.

"W-what's wrong?" Where are we?"

"I'm okay," he lies. "And I don't know."

I swallow thickly, racking my brain for a memory.

We were in the ocean, laughing, making lov—

A bang rips through the air and it dislodges something in my brain.

The door. The knock.

Mav going to answer it.

The sound of a single gunshot.

Victor Harris.

"Oh my God," I whimper, my eyes instantly flooding with red-hot tears that cascade down my cheeks.

"Shush, babe. You need to try and stay calm, okay." Mav's voice is stronger this time, and thankfully, I'm able to latch onto it like I have so many times before.

My fingers curl tighter around the bars I've found until I'm sure my knuckles are white. Not that I can see them. I can't see anything.

But he's here.

You're not alone.

Mav will fix this. He'll—

"I think I'm in some kind of cage," I blurt.

"Alana," he says calmly. "Do you remember what happened?"

I suck in a deep breath and close my eyes.

The images are clearer now.

"He came for us. Our fathers too."

"Everything is going to be okay," he assures me.

"How can you know that? Do you even know where we are?"

"No, but someone will," he states confidently.

I go still as his words float around me.

"Some— He knows," I whisper, terrified that we might be being listened to.

Silence greets me. It's all the confirmation I need.

There I was happily thinking that we'd given Reid the slip and were going to start our lives over where no one knew where we were. But all along he was still pulling the strings.

"So what now?" I hiss, annoyed with myself for being angry about something that I should be very relieved about right now.

If he knows where we are then he'll come for us.

Surely he'll fucking come for us, right?

Mav doesn't say anything else for the longest time. The only thing I can hear is his heaving, rattling breaths. They're enough to know that he's suffering.

I've no idea how.

He could be in his own cage somewhere in front of me, or it could be so much worse.

Men like Victor have no morals. They don't give a shit who they hurt. DNA means barely anything to them. Just look at what my father did to me and Kristie. He sure didn't give a shit that we were his little girls. The kindest thing he probably could have done back then would have been to kill us. But that would have been too kind and considerate for a monster like him.

When Mav does speak, even though it's whispered and full of unfiltered pain, it startles me.

"I'm sorry, Doll. I'm so fucking sorry."

Wrapping my arms around myself, I try to keep my sobs to myself. Wherever he is, he doesn't need to hear my pain as well as feel his own.

"I know." I whimper, barely able to force the words past the lump clogging my throat.

And I do. We've both fucked so much up recently, it would make me a massive hypocrite if I were to hold this against him.

He got me out. He gave me a piece of paradise that we apparently didn't deserve.

Our lives aren't beautiful sunrise walks on the beach, holding hands and sitting in a hot tub as the day comes to an end.

It's nothing but pain and heartache and mistakes.

"I love you, Maverick Murray. Always have. Always will."

"Doll." he sighs. I might not be able to see him, but in my head, I can perfectly picture his eyelids lowering and his head dipping as he tries to absorb those words. "I love you too. I'll get you out of this. One way or another."

"Not without you."

When his response doesn't immediately follow, my stomach knots up, aching almost as much as my cramped limbs.

"Mav?" I whisper after long agonizing seconds.

"Yeah, Doll?"

"You're hurt, aren't you?"

"Nothing I can't handle, babe."

His words don't settle any of the unease bubbling up inside me. But what the hell am I meant to do if I'm stuck in a fucking cage?

I drift in and out of a fitful sleep. Each time I come to, I wonder if the haziness is more than just the hit to the head I suffered at the hands of my father. He's strong, but I'm not sure he's strong enough to have this kind of lasting effect.

They drugged me. That's the only other option here.

My body shudders, losing its battle to stay warm when the room—or whatever we're in—is pumped full of cold air.

It's not all that different to being inside Reid's basement torture chamber. But at least there, I could move. The cot bed might have been hard and unforgiving as fuck, but I could get up and walk around, at least attempting to do something about the shivers that ripped through my body almost every second I was down there.

Right now, it's all I can do to wiggle my fingers and toes.

How the hell they managed to squeeze me in here, God only knows.

My nightmares come back to me and my skin prickles as I think about them touching me.

I was out of it, with no physical memory of what happened, but my subconscious knows, and it loves nothing more than taunting me with everything those men have done to me.

All I can hope is that they didn't do it in front of Mav.

It's one thing knowing that they abused me for years. He doesn't need to watch history repeat itself now that I'm an adult. Now that I'm his.

A loud sob rips through the air, and it's not until Mav whispers that everything is going to be okay again that I realize it came from me.

But this time, I can't fight it.

My body shuddering sobs rips through the air as I hold myself tighter.

I can't help it. Knowing they're close. That they've

touched me. That they're probably watching me break right now.

Mav continues to try to soothe me, but other than being wrapped in his strong, warm arms, nothing is going to help me.

I've no idea how long I cry for, but my eyes burn and my chest aches in a way I'd hoped I'd felt the last of.

But it doesn't matter how much time has passed, we're still in the dark. Even with my eyes adjusting to it, it's so dark that I can barely make out my hand in front of my face.

Wherever we are, we're not going to be easily found. And something tells me that Victor will have planned ahead.

Having us tracked is one thing, but there are plenty of ways to put a stop to that. More than I want to think about right now.

I have to believe that they'll come for us.

If Reid knew we left, if he was part of planning what I thought was our big escape, then he cares enough to come and rescue us... right?

A loud bang somewhere beyond the darkness rattles the floor beneath me, sending a rush of ice down my spine.

"Mav?" I whisper.

"Right here, Doll. Right here." He groans, sounding even worse than he did before.

There's another clank and then a rattle and only a second later, the room is flooding with blinding light.

My eyelids slam closed as I fight to adjust and heat almost instantly warms my body. It's not the sun, it's not that good, but it's such a relief after being so cold that I almost begin sobbing again.

But my tears are wiped away when I sense their presence.

Every hair on my body lifts and my skin prickles in a way I unfortunately remember all too well.

"Well, well, well look at that," Victor taunts. "Exactly where we left them."

Heavy footsteps move closer to us and fear makes me curl in on myself.

I might be in a cage—or at least assume that I am—but that won't stop them from hurting me. Nothing other than my death will stop them from hurting me.

Not wanting to be at a disadvantage, unable to see them, I risk cracking my eyes open.

The light is almost blinding, making my eyes stream with tears the second even a tiny bit gets in.

But any chance of taking this slow, of trying to lessen the pain, is ripped away when Mav suddenly cries out a second after the sound of what I can only describe as a whip cracks through the air.

My eyes fly open and the true reality of what we've managed to land ourselves in becomes clear.

My blood chills and my stomach bottoms out.

"No," I scream. "Mav. No, please don't hurt him," I beg, watching in horror as they do just that.

"Keep screaming, princess. And you'll be up there next," Victor warns as Razor continues.

"Oh no, we've got something so much better in mind for you, don't we, Vic?" my father taunts, darkly.

"Please, just let us go."

Dad laughs. Actually throws his head back and belts out a laugh.

"Ah, Alana. You never were the smartest, were you?"

"You sure you don't want to come?" Devin asks, lingering in the doorway that Ezra and Ellis just walked through.

"I'm not leaving him," I say, despite the fact that I'm fucking desperate to follow them and try and figure out what the fuck is going on.

I need to trust them to go and do this for me. They're more than capable of scoping out the place Mav and Alana ran to and looking for clues about where they went.

"Okay. We'll call you if we find anything," Dev promises.

"Thanks." He ducks out of the door, but I quickly call him back. "Be careful, yeah? They might have left—"

"Bro, we've got this. We're not fucking morons."

My lips twitch to point out there is more than enough evidence to convince him and Ez might just be, but now isn't the time for brotherly bickering.

"I know, Bro," I concede.

With a nod, he disappears again, leaving me with nothing but the sound of JD's steady breaths for company.

Slumping back in the chair, I keep my eyes on him, trying to remind myself that he's still here and that he's going to be okay.

I've no idea how long I stay exactly like that, but eventually, my eyes get too heavy to stay open and I drift off into an uncomfortable and fitful sleep.

I stir more than once, cracking my eye open to check on JD. But he never moves or does anything, and each time I eventually drift back off again.

When a door closing wakes me again, I fly out of the chair and pull my gun from my back.

I'm not even sure my eyes open, my body acting on instinct.

"Whoa, we're all friends here, young man," a familiar voice says as my vision begins to clear.

The sight of Doc standing before me with a deep V between his brows and his trusty case hanging from one arm relaxes me instantly.

"Sorry," I mutter, tucking my piece away and dropping back into the chair as my adrenaline wanes.

"Expecting someone else?" he asks, stalking over to JD and studying him closely.

"No, not really," I say honestly.

Victor won't come here, of that I'm pretty fucking confident.

Clearly, he wants to play games, not just have it out like normal people.

And I know why.

He's scared.

He raised me to be the person that I am now; he knows I'm better than him. Knows that if we went head-to-head, I'd beat him.

So the pussy is going to make me work for it. Hell, I do

want to work for it. I want to prove to everyone that I'm the right man for this. I want them to look at me and know that I went to war for them and that I'm going to do everything to make their lives better.

Honestly, it would be pretty fucking boring if he didn't. But still, there is a part of me that wishes it could all just be over and that we could get on with our lives, building a new future for this broken town.

"How's he been?" Doc asks, taking JD's vitals and tapping the results into a tablet.

"Fine. He's been out of it."

"As expected," he mutters as he continues. "I know he isn't going to like this, but he really needs to take his meds."

"I know," I mumble, my voice hollow with regret.

I should have been making him take them.

For a long time, I used to. We had a whole stupid morning routine where I used to make him take them in front of me. I used to fucking check he'd swallowed them too.

But as time's gone on and he's been more stable, I allowed him to convince me that he was coping, that he'd found other mechanisms to deal with the darkness that calls to him.

Everything was fine until her.

I want to be angry. Try and blame her for doing this to him.

But as much as I want to pass that guilt onto someone else, I know who it really falls on.

Me.

Yes, her presence might have been the biggest trigger, but she had no idea. Still doesn't.

JD can cover his issues like no one I've ever met before.

If he doesn't want you to know about his illness, then you never will.

My eyes dart toward the diary entry again.

Did she know?

Was she the one to encourage that? Or did she silently inspire him to try and get his thoughts into some kind of order?

I scrub my hand down my face as even more questions pile on top of the others already spinning around in my head.

"I've already put them into his IV," Doc continues reaching up to change the bag of blood that is now empty. "But when I take that out, he's going to need to—"

"He will," I confirm.

Doc raises a brow.

"This shouldn't have happened," I state. "And there is no fucking chance that it's ever happening again. I've nearly lost him twice now. I'm fucking done taking risks."

He still doesn't look convinced, but he drops the subject. After all, he's only got to write the script; I'm the one with the battle on my hands to ensure J takes them.

I blow out a pained breath as Doc starts working on replacing the dressing on J's arm.

I wince the second he pulls the wadding away and get my first look at the mess he's made of his forearm.

The tattoos he got after his cuts healed last time are wrecked, not that that's the biggest issue right now, but given what they represent when he wakes and sees, he's going to hate himself possibly even more than he did before taking that knife to his wrist.

Doc works meticulously, ensuring JD is patched up the best he can.

"This transfusion will run out in the middle of the night. He needs ano—"

"I've got it, Doc," I assure him.

"Reid." He sighs, looking as exhausted as I feel.

Those dark shadows lingering under his eyes only pile on a whole new load of guilt that I don't really need.

I've been putting Doc at risk for years. With every visit, he learns more about our lives and the things I'm planning.

Yet he still comes.

He still puts us back together as if he cares.

"It's okay, Doc. You've done enough already. You deserve to get a decent night's sleep."

He doesn't smile, but I see it in his eyes nonetheless.

"You'll call me if anything goes wrong?"

"Of course. But it won't," I assure him.

"I'll give him enough sedative to keep him out until at least tomorrow. Then once he has enough blood back inside him, we'll see how he is."

Nerves build inside me.

This was a cry for help, just like the last time.

Back then, he was drowning in grief, and he had no idea how to handle it. He might have said that he wanted to join her. But if that were true, he'd have used his gun.

Just like he would have done last night.

He's drowning and I just didn't see how close he was to going under.

Yes, I might have thought I was taking precautions by hiding the knives, but it was nowhere near enough.

With a pained sigh, I drop my head into my hands. The strength it takes to hold it up is suddenly too much to bear.

"He's going to make it through this," Doc says, his voice confident and unwavering. "It's just another bump in the road."

I know he's right. JD will get through this. But at what cost?

"Thank you, Doc. For everything."

"Anytime, you know that."

I give him the best smile I'm capable of and fall silent again as he finishes up.

After giving me very strict instructions about changing over the blood bag in a few hours, he gives my shoulder a supportive squeeze and heads toward the door.

"Call me if—"

"I know," I say, cutting him off. "I will."

"Things will look brighter tomorrow," he says positively.

Will they?

If Doc wants me to see him out, then he doesn't show it. Instead, he slips out of the room and thumps down the stairs. I wait until the front door has opened and closed before stepping up to JD's bed and studying the fresh bandage on his arm and the plastic tube disappearing into the skin on the back of his hand.

"What do you think, J? Will everything look more positive tomorrow?"

When a reply obviously doesn't come, I take another lingering look at his face before slipping into his bathroom.

I left a bucket of cleaning supplies in here earlier, but I didn't have the energy to embark on the challenge after talking to my brothers.

Now though... well, I still don't have the energy, but if Doc is talking about letting J wake up tomorrow, then it all needs to be gone.

He can't see this.

Stripping down to my boxers, I fill the bucket with hot water, and set to work.

There have been many, many times in my life that I've been covered in other people's blood, but none of them hit me as hard as this.

The second I look down and find J's blood smeared over my legs, I swear my entire world crashes down around me.

———

After cleaning up every inch of what happened inside that bathroom, I threw myself into his shower before starting on the carpet he'd fucked up as he must have tried to get to the bed.

By the time I fall back into the chair, the man in the bed is the only remaining evidence of what happened here recently.

If only that was as easy to fix.

"Where the fuck are you?" I growl when I wake up my cell and find nothing from any of my brothers.

Opening up the tracking app, I find that they're almost at the cabin.

It felt like I was cleaning for hours, but apparently, not.

Assuming Dev is driving, I find my chat with Ez.

> Reid: Anything?

My heart pounds as I wait for it to show as read, and the second it does, I sit forward.

> Ezra: Patience, big brother.

> Reid: Ez…

> Ezra: We're approaching the cabin via the trees. Trying to keep alert.

My teeth grind and my grip on my cell tightens, but I understand his jibe and don't reply.

Trust them to do their job...

My cell goes to sleep, leaving the room in darkness apart from the light I left on in the bathroom.

Every minute feels like an hour as I wait for news.

Why the fuck I didn't send them with comms, fuck only knows.

By the time the screen finally lights up with Devin's smug fucking face and his middle finger raised—a photo he stored for himself on my cell—I'm pretty sure I've ground a few of my teeth down.

"Are they there?" I bark the second the line connects.

"No," he says simply.

My entire body deflates.

"But you know where they are, right?"

"Also no."

"FUCK," I roar, barely holding myself back from launching my cell across the room.

"You seem to care a lot for someone who isn't meant to care, Bro."

"Shut the fuck up, asshole. I want that place scoured for clues. I need them found. Now."

"Ez and Ellis are already on it. If there is anything here, we'll find it."

"Fucking hell," I mutter, tugging at my hair in frustration. "Wherever they are, he's hurting them to get to me."

"Seems like it's working," Devin mutters like the helpful prick that he is.

"I will not give him the satisfaction of beating me—beating us. No matter what it takes, his time is done."

"I'm with you, Bro. One hundred percent. We're taking this motherfucker down."

He hangs up long before I'm ready, leaving me with nothing but silence and desperation.

With only one other person I trust to give me intel, I find Aubrey's contact and lift my cell again.

"Where is Victor?" I demand as a way of a greeting.

"Hi, Reid. How are you? It's so lovely to hear from you," she taunts.

"Aubs, this is serious." I growl.

"I don't know. Been nothing but radio silence for a few days."

"What the fuck am I paying you for exactly?" I bark, irritation exploding within me.

"I'll find him. Anything else you need to know."

"He has..." I hesitate, unable to find the words I need to explain who Alana and Mav are to me.

Enemies?

Allies?

Fuck. Everything is so fucking blurred, the line that was previously drawn between us all has been obliterated and I've no idea where that leaves any of us.

MAVERICK

Pain slices through me, but I'm long past the point of crying out.

It doesn't stop anything. All it does is cause Alana more pain. And she's already experienced enough of that.

Her cries and pleas for them to stop ring in my ears, making the agony in my chest far worse than what they're inflicting on my body.

If it means they keep their hands off her, I'll allow them to continue this as much as they like. But something tells me that this is just the start.

Another strike lashes across my back. Blood floods my mouth as I bite down on the inside of my cheek as the unforgiving leather whip burns across my flesh.

"No, please. Stop, stop." Alana sobs. "Hurt me instead."

"NO," I roar, finding my voice again. "Don't you dare fucking touch her."

I don't care what they do to me. I can take it as long as they don't lay a finger on her.

Another strike comes, dragging a scream from Alana's lips.

I can't see her; they've turned me around so that my back is to her, letting her get the full effect of their punishment.

I want to say it's the first time I've felt it. But I'd be lying. Just like I have been to her since it happened.

It was barely a month after we announced our wedding.

I told her that I'd been sent on a job out of town because I knew what was coming. I could see the promise of pain in the eyes of the three men standing behind me now.

As far as they were concerned, I betrayed them.

I guess I did.

I took their beloved little human toy and I locked her away and kept her safe. Then I made her mine.

If I weren't so determined to keep her safe and help her to rid the world of their toxicity, I might have revelled in the success.

They had no idea.

No fucking clue where she'd gone.

Until I unveiled my new wife to Harrow Creek and turned their evil eyes on us.

I knew what was coming. But I was also willing to take it.

I'd take anything if it meant she was okay.

I also knew that my punishment for betraying them was going to hurt.

So with her safe at home, I loyally followed orders to make it look like I was still on their side, that my sudden marriage to Alana had nothing to do with them and their treatment of her.

They knew, though. From the first moment I turned up at the warehouse they'd directed me to, I knew they knew.

We've danced the same dance for the past five years. Them knowing that I know everything and waiting to see what I'm going to do about it.

To start with, they watched me like... well, hawks. But as time went on and nothing happened, I can only assume they started believing that I was still on their side.

Fuck knows what they thought. I didn't really give a fuck so long as they stayed away from my wife and I got to keep my position in the hope of getting intel to help her find Kristie.

It never happened though. They kept those secrets locked up tighter than Fort Knox.

If I knew that Reid was going to be the one to help unravel all of this, then maybe I'd have put my hatred of him aside in my quest for vengeance for Alana.

They strike me again. It's so hard my feet slip on the blood-soaked floor when my back arches.

"Stop," Alana cries, barely able to speak through her sobs.

I want to assure her that I'm okay, that I can handle this. But I can't find any words.

Managing to find my footing again, I squeeze my eyes closed in an attempt to get myself together.

I can't lose my shit yet. This is only the beginning.

But despite being ready for it, another strike never comes.

Instead, there is only silence. Well, a silence that is filled with my wife's whimpers.

"You never were a fast learner, were you, boy?" Dad taunts from behind me. "We should have ended you the first time you were in this position."

Alana gasps, the words hitting the mark my father intended.

"We knew you were up to something then. We just wanted to see what it was and watch you hang yourself. And if that happened in front of your pretty little wife then all the better. We all know that she needs teaching a lesson." He tsks and all I want to do is run over to Alana and pull her into my arms, promising her that I won't let them touch her.

But I can't. I'm hanging from the fucking ceiling of whatever building they've brought us to.

They'll come.

Reid and JD will come...

Probably not for me. But they'll come for her.

JD won't let her suffer, and Reid needs her.

They'll come and then we'll end this.

Once and for all.

A cell ringing rips through the air.

"Afternoon, precious," Victor says, his voice lighter than I'm used to. It sends a wave of revulsion rushing through me to think that he's ever used it on Alana. "Oh, you are a needy little thing, aren't you?"

Bile swirls in my gut as we're all forced to listen to him speak to what I can only hope isn't a young girl.

Swallowing is almost as painful as my back when I try to force the acid back down.

I've no idea how long we've been here. But I'm dying for a drink, for food. For my arms to be lower than my head.

It's been a long time since I felt my fingers, and I can only imagine how deep the lacerations around my wrists go. I've had blood trickling down my forearms for hours.

I might not have been able to see it as we were forced to be here in the dark, but I felt it. I felt the unforgivable metal cutting into my skin, causing what I can only assume will be lasting damage to my muscles and nerves.

Fighting as hard as I can, I try to curl my fists, to know that I've still got some kind of control of my fingers. But I don't think anything happens.

"Oh, I'm more than interested in that. Name the time and the place, precious." Victor falls silent for a few seconds, giving us a little reprieve from the vomit-inducing show he's putting on. "You got it. I'll be ready."

"She got a friend?" Dad asks when Victor must have hung up.

He chuckles. "Not that I'm aware of. And anyway, she's too fucking good for the likes of you."

"She must be special if Vicious isn't willing to share," Kurt adds. "She's obviously better than you, eh, kid? He never had an issue sharing you."

"ENOUGH," I roar, able to find my voice when my girl needs it.

Kurt laughs darkly.

"She really has you wrapped around her little finger, doesn't she? She was good, sure, but never that good."

Putting every bit of strength I have into it, I try ripping my bindings from the hook they have me hanging from.

But unsurprisingly, all I achieve is more pain while the three cunts behind me get off on my pathetic attempt to free myself.

"Come on now, Mav. Your wife needs a real man, not a pussy who can't even look after himself."

"Fuck you," I roar, spittle flying from my lips as my body trembles, my fight or flight response on overdrive.

"We're not really interested in you, Mav. Your wife though..." Victor says darkly.

Sucking in a deep breath, I try not to allow his words to affect me. But it's impossible.

"We're going to fucking kill you," I seethe. "All of you. The last faces you'll see will be ours, and you're going to feel every second of the pain you've unleashed on us since the days we were unlucky enough to be born to corrupt, sick bastards like you."

I expect some kind of heated reply. But all I get is laughter.

Full on, funniest thing you've heard all week kind of laughter.

"Sure you are," Dad finally says. "Is that before or after you figure out how to create magic and get yourself out of that situation?"

"It's going to happen," I warn. "Mark my fucking words."

Victor tuts and it makes the hairs on the back of my neck rise. "He thinks his new friend is coming for him," he taunts.

"Ah," Kurt says. "The mighty Reid Harris. That's what everyone thinks, isn't it?"

"He is only what I made him." Victor scoffs.

"He's not coming for you," Dad adds. "He doesn't care about you."

"And your wife is only a pussy for him to fuck. To share with his trusty sidekick."

I half expect Alana to say something the second JD is mentioned, but she remains silent.

"Sure. You keep thinking that. I'd be looking over my shoulder though, if I were you."

No one replies and I imagine them looking at each other and shaking their massive egotistical heads.

They think they're so untouchable.

They might have been up until this point.

But their reign is coming to an end, whether they want to believe it or not.

I might not be the one to do it. Hell, right now I'm not even sure if I'll be around to tell the tale, but I have every confidence in Reid.

He will overpower these cunts and he will take control. I never thought I'd say it, but I can't fucking wait.

"How are you doing in there, princess?" Dad asks, turning his attention to Alana.

She snarls at him.

"Bit cramped, I'd imagine," Kurt muses. "Would you like us to let you out?"

"Get the hell away from her," I bark.

"So touchy, your husband," Victor taunts before his cell starts ringing again. "Ah, that is our time up, gentlemen," he says, commanding his minions. "Don't worry, though, kids. We'll be back soon. Try not to miss us too much."

With a few more taunts aimed to rile me up enough to cause myself more damage, they finally make their way out, ensuring the door slams loud enough that it echoes ominously for long seconds after they've left.

"Mav," Alana cries the second she's confident we're alone.

Hanging my head, I finally let myself fully experience the pain they've inflicted on my body.

My back is ruined. I don't need to see it to know that my skin is ripped to shreds and I'm losing enough blood to have the floor beneath my feet slick.

"I'm okay," I say after sucking in a deep breath, which I regret instantly. The pain only intensifies as my ribs inflate.

Keeping my eyes closed, I fight my need to spin around and look at her.

As much as I don't want her to focus on my back, I'm not sure I can handle seeing her in that cage.

Watching them put her passed-out body in there was bad enough. They ensured I watched every second they had their hands on her.

I was terrified they were going to take it further, but thankfully, they didn't. I don't believe that's because they have any kind of morals though. They're biding their time. Building up the punishment.

They'll start with my body before they turn on my head.

Unable to keep myself from her, I gingerly spin around, wincing with every movement.

Despite knowing exactly what I'm about to find, the sight of her all curled up and behind bars still takes my breath away.

A sob rips from her throat the second our eyes collide.

"I'm so sorry," she whimpers.

"Not your fault, Doll."

"I never should have said yes; I never should have stayed and put you at risk like I have."

Tears continue to cascade down her cheeks as she stares up at me, her bottom lip trembling.

"It doesn't matter because I never would have let you go."

And with that truth lingering around us, the lights go out, plummeting us into darkness once again.

"I love you," she whispers. The words hit me with the strength of one of Dad's strikes.

"I love you too, Doll. Stay strong for me, yeah. No matter what happens next. I need you to be strong."

"Don't talk like that," she warns weakly. "We're going to walk out of this together. Just like we always planned."

"What do you mean you don't know?" Reid growls in his scariest gangster voice.

Unfortunately for him, the person on the other end of the phone doesn't seem overly concerned by it.

"That isn't good enough. I need that intel, Aubs."

Aubs?

My brows pull together as I try to place that name.

But fuck, it's hard.

I might be hearing the words Reid is saying, but they just rattle around my head, the meaning of them not registering in my fuzzy brain.

Where am I?

"You need to get back there and find out more."

There's a voice on the other end of the line. A much softer voice that confuses me even more.

Surely he's not barking orders at a woman.

We don't work with women.

Not because we're sexist. Totally the fucking opposite. Women are fucking great at everything they set their mind to. And I've no reason to believe they also wouldn't be kickass gangsters if they so desired.

Victor is the old-fashioned cunt who thinks women's roles need to be very different to the men's.

I'm sure Alana would be fucking epic walking into meetings with this state's scariest motherfuckers and wrapping them around her little finger.

Pain like I haven't felt in a very long time slices straight through my chest as I think of her.

Fuck.

Lifting my hand in the hope of rubbing away the pain, something pinches my skin.

"What the—"

"Shit. JD. I gotta go," Reid says in a rush before whatever I'm lying on dips beside me. A bed, I guess.

"J?" he asks, sounding a hell of a lot softer and more concerned than he did on the phone only seconds ago. "J? Are you awake?"

It's not the first time I've heard his voice recently. But it's the first time I've managed to hear more than a handful of random words.

Not that it mattered, while my body was immobile and my head felt like it was stuffed full of cotton, I knew he was here. Even when he was angry and shouting. He was here. Wherever here is.

Parting my lips, I attempt more words, but despite moving my tongue and wanting to say them, nothing comes out.

"Shit," he hisses, clearly frustrated.

I want to open my eyes. I want to see him and let him see that I'm here, that I'm awake, but they don't comply with my brain. Nor does the rest of my body, it seems, when I try to move again.

It must have been a fluke before.

Every inch of me now feels like it's been filled with concrete.

"Do you need a drink?" he asks, a beat before a straw presses against my lips.

Somehow, I manage to find the strength to take a sip.

It feels like heaven as the cool water slides down my parched throat, easing the pain there.

But I never find the strength to look at him, and instead, the darkness pulls me under again. But before I go, I don't miss the warmth of his hand wrap around mine. He says something, but the words are nothing more than a deep growl.

They're enough.

He's here.

E verything is a little clearer again when I come to next time, although there is no one barking orders on the phone, there is... well, nothing. And that alone is enough for my eyes to pop open.

The curtains might be closed, but the sun hiding behind them still burns my eyes.

I've been out of it a while, that much is obvious, but everything else is fuzzy.

There is pain, so much pain, both physically and mentally, but for some reason, I can't grasp the edges hard enough to drag them to the present.

"R-Reid?" I stutter, my eyes focused on the ceiling.

"J?" His voice washes through me like silk over the most delicate of skin.

Alana.

But again, before memories clear, he's there, sitting on the edge of the bed and looming over me like the imposing Hulk that he is.

"Hey," he says softly. So fucking softly, it makes something tickle at the back of my nose.

What the fuck is that?

It's just Reid. Why the fuck am I getting all emotional?

"Fuck, it's good to see those eyes, J," he comments, staring right into them.

The tickle intensifies until my eyes begin to burn.

"How are you feeling?" he asks, his eyes darting between mine as if he's searching for something.

It takes me a moment to formulate a reply.

"Confused."

"You've been sedated for two days, J. That's to be expected."

My brow crinkles with a frown.

"Sedated? Two days. What?" Lifting my hand, I stare at the cannula stuffed into the back of it before my eyes trail up the tube to a clear bag hanging from a hook.

But it's not either of those things that make my head spin, causing acid to erupt in my stomach. That would be the bandage on my arm.

I recognize that bandage.

Déjà vu hits me so hard, I barely have time to warn Reid that I'm about to puke in his lap.

"Oh shit," he barks, jumping up a beat before I barf.

He darts from the room, and before I know what's happening, he's back with a bucket.

My stomach screams for relief, but my body won't allow it as it continues trying to purge me of the knowledge of what I've done.

By the time I fall back against the pillows behind me,

my body is covered in a layer of cold sweat and I'm trembling from head to toe.

Reid hovers beside me, holding the bucket and looking all kinds of awkward. If I didn't feel like I was dying, I might laugh at the expression on his face.

It isn't very often that he looks out of his depth, but right now is definitely one of those times.

Reid Harris might be a lot of things, but he was not designed to be a nurse.

"I'm okay," I force out, giving him permission to dump the bucket of stomach acid he's currently holding at a distance.

With a sigh of relief, he runs into my bathroom and disposes of it.

The second he's back, he looks down at the state of the sheets covering me and reaches for them muttering, "It's a good thing I love you, J."

Any humor I might have found in those words is soon eradicated when he tugs the sheets away, and I get a look at the painful evidence beneath me of what I did.

The previously light gray sheet is almost black with dried blood.

"Shit," Reid hisses, his eyes also locked on the massive stain.

"It's okay," I whisper, although it's a bold-faced lie. Nothing about this is fucking okay.

"J," he breathes, seemingly unable to find the right words to say.

"I'm sorry," I whisper, forcing the words past the messy lump of emotion clogging my throat.

"No," Reid says, shaking his head. "I'm sorry. I fucking left. I did this. I shouldn't have—"

"Stop, please," I beg, my voice cracking as it all gets too much.

His eyes hold mine, concern swimming in the dark depths.

"Let's get this cleaned up," he finally mutters, turning his attention to something physical.

It takes a bit of shuffling, but eventually, he manages to get a fresh sheet beneath me before covering me with another.

"Tell me what you need?" he asks, hovering by the bed and looking totally out of place in his own home.

Closing my eyes, I suck in a deep breath, trying to focus on what I need the most.

Sleep?

Food?

"Alana," I blurt. Her name spills from my lips before I even realize I've thought of her.

"J," he says again. The pain and hopelessness in his voice make my stomach knot and my chest hurt.

Memories slam into me. Waking up alone, going to find her.

The notebook.

The memories.

The pain.

Bleeding out all over the pages before everything became too much and the need to bleed out in a more visceral way became too much to bear.

Dragging my eyes away from Reid's pained ones, I glance around my room, looking for the notebook.

But everything is tidy. The desk is clear, and all the paperwork is gone.

Did he find it? Did he read it?

Not that it matters. Reid knows everything there is to

know about me, my life is an open book where he's concerned. But something uncomfortable still twists inside me at the thought of him reading those words.

My face burns with his stare as I focus on the desk.

Seconds tick by, but all they achieve is allowing me to remember more and more. Slowly, the pain returns, although the ants never appear.

I'm not sure if I'm relieved or terrified that they're not there.

It's a relief, sure. But they've been a constant in my life for a long time. In a fucked-up way, when shit is bad, they're a reminder that I'm still here. That I'm still living and there is a chance everything will get better.

What am I—who am I—without them?

It takes the longest time for everything to settle around me, but when it does, one thing becomes very clear.

"She's gone, isn't she?"

I glance back at Reid just in time to see him swallow nervously.

Fuck. This is Reid Harris sitting here before me. He doesn't get nervous. Ever.

So the fact he's looking at me with those cautious dark eyes fills my entire body with dread.

His lips part to say something, but no words spill free.

His hesitation doesn't make me feel any better.

"You'll get her back," he finally forces out.

I hold his eyes, desperate to feel the confidence behind that promise, but it's just not there.

I don't feel anything.

"You're lying," I state flatly.

"Fuck, J." He sighs, pushing to his feet. He starts pacing back and forth, and it puts me even more on edge.

Suddenly, he pauses and pulls his cell from his pocket.

Without looking at me, he swipes the screen and places it to his ear.

"Yeah," he agrees roughly to whatever the deep voice says down the line. "Yeah, okay. Yes. Just keep fucking digging."

When he hangs up, he's standing at the window looking out over his town.

His shoulders are pulled tight and his fists are curled tightly at his sides.

"Everything is a mess right now, J. We always knew that this was going to be the most challenging thing we've ever done. We knew we'd have to make sacrifices to get the result we wanted. I never promised you that it would be easy or without pain."

"The fuck are you talking about?" I bark, unwilling to be talked in circles in the hope he doesn't have to tell me the hard shit.

"Victor knows, J. He knows what we've been planning, and it's on. Now. It's happening right. Fucking. Now."

My heart, my lungs, my stomach... all of them plummet at the cold delivery of his words.

"Now?"

"Now," he confirms, his voice harsh and determined.

This time, there is no mistaking the confidence in his tone. He might have been trying to pacify me before, but this is real.

Everything we've been working toward over the past few years is about to come to a head. And here I am lying in a bed with fucking cannulas stuffed into the back of my hand.

Could I fuck any of this up anymore?

Slumping back, I stare up at the ceiling. The weight of

the stupid decisions I've made press down on me, but still, I struggle to really feel it.

"He's put me back on my medication, hasn't he?" I ask. There's no emotion in my voice, no nothing.

I don't even know why I'm asking. The answer is obvious. I can literally feel it in my blood.

"You nearly died, J. Again. I was summoned to Mexico to meet with Luciana, I left you a note," he says, spinning around and gesturing to my desk. "You were meant to ring me. I was going to explain everything."

I don't look at him. I can't.

Regret and shame burn through me like wildfire.

But it's too late now. I can't take it back.

I just have to try and take the look of disappointment and desperation in his eyes like a man.

23

REID

I pace back and forth in my office with Devin and Ezra watching my every move.

Ellis has left to go to class, but unsurprisingly, these two didn't need an excuse to skip.

Just like Dev said on the phone when they were at the cabin, there was no evidence to help point us in the direction Victor and his goons have taken Alana and Mav.

Aubrey has yet to come up with anything useful so we're still here floundering while they're suffering.

Every time I so much as blink, all I see is the image of them Victor sent. Alana curled up and locked in what I can only assume is a heavy-duty dog crate and Mav hanging from a chain from the ceiling. But while that looked bad, it was clear that it was only the beginning. Fuck knows what state both of them might be in now.

That photo came through days ago.

They're not dead. I'm confident of that fact. Victor wouldn't have anything over me if he killed them.

He wants us all to suffer as much and for as long as possible.

"What do we do now?" Ezra asks, his fingers drumming against this thigh nervously. "Surely we can't just sit and wait for him to make a move."

"That's what he wants," Dev says.

"Which is why we're not going to give it to him," I mutter. "I'm done playing by his rules."

"And how do you propose we do that when we have no intel?" Ezra asks.

"Something will come up," I say, sounding a lot more confident than I feel.

It has to.

Despite the past and everything I've thought of Alana and Mav, I can't leave them out there for Victor, Razor and Kurt to play with.

Not only would JD fucking kill me for doing so, but because they don't deserve it.

"Have you spoken to Aubrey today?" Dev asks.

"Not yet."

"If she's as good as you say she is, she'll find something," he assures me.

She's going to have to because we've exhausted all other avenues.

Ellis has done everything he can to try and get through the barriers Victor has put in place to stop us from tracking them. Griff has had his IT guys on it as well, but as of yet, nothing has been uncovered. His signal blockers are too good.

It's literally like they've fallen off the face of the Earth.

As far as we can tell, none of them have turned back up in the Creek to allow us to follow or track their cars.

There's nothing. And it's driving me fucking insane.

With every hour that passes, the fear that he's going to beat me only increases.

But I refuse to give up. I can't.

I've got to do this for J. For Alana and Mav. For my brothers. For this entire fucking town who needs that cunt out of their lives.

They might not know it, but they're all relying on me to see this through and come out as the winner.

There is no other option.

"I'm going upstairs. Call me if you hear anything," I bark before blowing out of the room and running up the stairs as if it'll help.

I stop beside JD's door to take a moment to calm down.

The last thing he needs is to see what a fucking mess I am over all of this.

I need to be strong for him. He needs my support and my strength.

Once I'm confident that I can walk into his room with my head held high, I take a step forward and push the door open.

"Hey, how are you doing?" I ask, thankful that my voice comes out strong and unwavering.

"Fantastic," he deadpans.

It's been just over twenty-four hours since he properly woke, and he seems to be getting stronger with every hour that passes. Thank fuck.

Doc swung by yesterday, changed his dressing, and removed the tubes delivering him blood and medication now that he's fully awake. That means the responsibility to ensure he takes his meds is now fully on my shoulders.

I could relax while it was automatically dripping into his veins. But now...

"What's wrong?" he asks, reading something on my face that I didn't want him to see. "What's Victor done?"

"J," I say, dropping into the chair and focusing on the view from the window instead of looking at him.

"Don't bullshit me. I might be down, but I'm not fucking stupid."

"I know you're not. I never said you were."

"Then stop lying to me. You think I haven't been able to see that something has been wrong since the moment I woke up?"

"My best fucking friend in this whole fucking world tried offing himself," I blurt without thinking. "Yeah, something is fucking wrong."

The second I turn to look at him, the weight of what I just said hits me full force.

"Fuck. I'm sorry. I didn't mean—"

"It's okay," he says, his voice cracking with emotion.

"No, it's not. Nothing is fucking okay right now," I hiss, combing my fingers through my hair and then dragging my hands down my face.

"Talk to me," he begs. "You're shutting me out and—"

"And you're surprised?" I ask. "Look at you," I say, gesturing toward where he's sitting in his bed.

Yes, he's up and functioning now. He's even managed a shower after we wrapped his bandage, but that doesn't mean he's ready for the brutal truth of what's happening right now.

"I fucked up. I know I fucked up. Everyone vanished, and I got all up in my head. She left, Reid. Rolled out of my bed and walked away without a second glance. I didn't even know our last fuck was a goodbye fuck. She didn't care, did she?"

I stare at him as he rants. My lips open and close as I debate what he wants and needs to hear in return, but fuck knows if I have the answer to that.

I'm not the person anyone needs while they're having emotional relationship issues, no matter how fucked up that relationship might be.

Will telling him that I thought Alana cared about him help? Or does he need me to say the opposite?

Hell, how do I know what is even true?

JD has fallen hard for her, that is the only fact I'm aware of right now.

"She cared," I eventually say, hoping it's the right way to go. It's the truth after all, and I owe him at least a little bit of that.

"You don't need to pacify me," he snaps, gently rubbing at the bandage wrapped around his arm.

"I'm not," I argue.

His eyes hold mine for a beat before he drops his head and stares down at his arm.

"For all the good it did. Fuck," he hisses, slumping lower in the bed and resting his head back against the wall. "I knew this would happen. I fucking knew it, even when she was down in the basement, yet I still continued."

"You shouldn't have made that bet."

He stills for a moment.

"This has fuck all to do with that bet, Reid. I'd have had her no matter what."

Ain't that the fucking truth.

"I just didn't expect for her to..." His words die off as he lifts his hand to rub at his chest.

I feel his pain almost as if it's my own, my chest aching right along with his.

Tell him, a little voice begs as I watch JD suffer.

But despite knowing that he needs the truth, the thought of the pain it'll cause him.

Her leaving is one thing, but knowing that Victor has her.

Fuck.

Lifting my hand, I rub the back of my neck as I try to figure out the best thing to do here.

It's going to fucking rip him apart if he knows she is at the mercy of him, Kurt, and Razor once again.

He'll be out of that bed and then the house before I'm able to stop him and end up doing something really stupid.

"I think I love her," he confesses, making the ache in my chest intensify.

"I know, man," I say softly.

"And she's gone. With her husband."

My lips part, but he beats me to it.

"I knew she'd choose him. I just didn't think she'd leave like that. I thought I meant at least something to her."

"You did."

He blows out a pained breath.

"It doesn't matter now though, does it? They've gone off together to embark on the future they always should have had. I gave him the push he needed, and now she's going to get everything she's ever wanted from the man she loves."

A sad smile pulls at his lips.

"I'm happy for her. For them, I really am."

He falls silent and I continue to fail to fill the void.

Eventually, he turns his eyes back on me.

"Did you tell me that you went to Mexico to meet Luciana?" he asks with a deep frown, as if he doesn't believe the words that are passing his lips.

"Yeah, I did."

He nods, seemingly happy that he's not imagining things.

"What happened? Did she give you anything useful?"

I give him a quick rundown of my meeting with the formidable Luciana Rivera before turning my attention to the thumb drive I left with.

"Ellis has been working his way through the files. But we have names and locations to dig further into."

JD's eyes light up for the first time since he came to.

"You think you might find Kristie?"

"Maybe," I say, although my voice doesn't hold much hope. I think he knows as well as I do that the chances of finding Alana's sister now is slim to none. If she is alive then she could be anywhere in the world. From what Ellis has found, this stretches far wider than just our little corrupt town.

It's huge. And if we handle this right, we're on the verge of uncovering something massive. The number of lives we could save by blowing this to pieces is beyond belief.

Just thinking about it makes my head spin.

"We have to tell her. If there's even a chance that it could lead to answers then she needs to know."

"I know. And we will."

"How? Do you know where she is?" he asks, hope filling his eyes.

"J." I sigh. "Somehow, we'll get her back for you." Even if it's just so you can say goodbye properly.

It's not a lie. I just wish I knew where she was so I could make it happen easier.

He studies me, searching for more. He's always been one of the only people who's ever been able to get a read on me and right now, he knows I'm hiding shit.

It's for his own good though.

Sliding lower in the bed, he closes his eyes, but he doesn't relax. His body is still strung tight with tension as one of his fingers nervously drums against his thigh.

"Talk to me, J. Let me in on what is going through your head."

He remains silent. His chest steadily lifts up and down as he loses himself in his thoughts.

"I read what you wrote." He startles at my confession but doesn't say anything. "They're not the same, you know that, right?" I ask, studying him closely.

I remember all too well how he reacted when Maya died.

It broke him. Completely shattered him.

I can't let him go through that again. I can't allow him to suffer like that.

We have to find her. Find them.

I've no idea what happens once we do. But I will not allow anyone, even my father, to take away anything else my best friend loves.

24

ALANA

I never thought it would happen, but as I lie curled up in my cage with my limbs cramping, all I want is to be back in Reid's basement.

Yes, I was cold, and it was uncomfortable. But compared to this, it was like a five-star hotel.

I had a bed, of sorts. A toilet. They provided me with food occasionally.

Here.

We have nothing.

Nothing other than pain.

Everything was so perfect.

The cabin. The beach. The sound of the crashing waves and the birds singing.

Mav.

He was so perfect.

Squeezing my eyes tight, I take myself back there with him. Trying to focus on the softness of his touch as he kissed me. The way his lips gently brushed mine before he gave himself permission to take.

And then when those touches turned rougher, harder... fuck.

For five years I've been dreaming of the way Mav would handle me.

I knew gentle would be his go-to. All he's ever tried to do is protect me. But I knew there was more to him than that.

I've heard the stories about his past; I knew what he was capable of. I was just never able to find a way to make him turn it on me.

Until our time in that cabin.

It held the promise of so much. Of a future filled with everything I'd hoped we could be together. Until it was cut short by the monsters who are set on ruining my life.

I often used to wonder why they didn't just kill me when I was younger. I always thought they'd want me dead to keep their secrets, instead of risking me being out in the wild. Turns out, killing me would have been too easy.

Where's the fun in chasing a dead girl when you can torture one who is very much alive?

"Mav?" I whimper, having successfully pulled myself out of any happy memories.

"Yeah," he croaks. It's all I need to know that he's in agony.

A sob rips from my throat as I remember them taunting him with it not being the first time. And all because of me.

I wasn't naïve. I knew when we announced our marriage and my sudden appearance that he was putting himself at risk.

Victor and my father weren't going to take it lying down, of that I was sure. But as far as I was aware, nothing came of it.

Apparently, I was very, very wrong.

"I'm okay," he croaks.

"I wish I could see you," I whisper, although the second the words are out of my lips, I regret them. If I could see the extent of his injuries, then the chances are I would be worrying about him even more than I am now.

"We're going to get out of this," he promises.

"I know," I say weakly, unsure if I actually believe him.

If he's right and Reid can track us, then why isn't he here?

Why aren't those sick pricks dead and why aren't we on our way back to his house where we'll be safe?

Wrapping my aching arms tighter around myself, I try to imagine it's one of their arms—all of their arms—holding me, protecting me, promising me that everything is going to be okay.

A pained sigh spills from my lips as the silence presses in on me.

"I love you," he whispers, making my sobs worse.

I've no idea how much time passes, or even how long we've been here. The cold, dark minutes are endless.

Every time there's any kind of noise, my entire body startles in fright that they're going to come back and hurt me, or worse, hurt Mav more than they already have.

If it means saving him, I'll offer up anything I have.

I'd do anything for him after what he's done for me.

The violent shivers ripping through my body never cease and the empty pit in my stomach only grows.

My mouth is dry, my need for water is unbearable.

If they don't bring us something soon, I'm pretty sure we're going to be verging on dangerous levels of dehydration.

And then there is Mav's blood loss.

I've no idea how he's even still awake with the amount

of it that was running down his body and dripping on the floor when the lights were on. I can't imagine those vicious wounds have healed all that quickly.

Nothing but hopeless desperation floods through me as I lie here, listening to nothing but Mav's deep breaths.

I want to keep talking to him, to make sure he's still with me. But at the same time, I want him to rest.

If he's right and we're going to be rescued, then he needs whatever strength he can get.

I dip in and out of sleep. In and out of nightmares of the men who are behind this. Every time I come to, my heart is racing with fear, I listen for Mav's breathing, and I don't relax until I hear it.

"Look at you," Victor taunts, his dark, evil eyes dropping down the length of my body.

My entire body quakes with fear as I stare up at him and the two men standing behind him.

A game of cat and mouse. And the mouse lost.

Isn't it always that way?

I'm wearing the white t-shirt I slept in last night. But unlike then, it was now covered in mud.

I knew today was going to be bad the first moment Dad looked at me this morning. There was something haunting in his eyes and it sent a shiver of fear skittering down my spine.

It's a look I'm very familiar with. It's a look that promises a whole world of pain the second Kristie leaves the house for school.

And I was right because no sooner had I waved her off from the living room window, his large body darkened the doorway leading from the kitchen.

"I'm feeling generous," he taunted, making my blood run cold and all the hairs on my body lift. "I'll give you thirty seconds head start." All the air rushed from my lungs. "Go."

Without another word from him, I took off, racing through the house and out through the back door.

Really, it didn't matter which way I went, he—they'd—catch me. It's how it always is.

If I didn't think it would hurt more to just stay still, I wouldn't put myself through the charade, but I have first-hand experience that doing so would be a bad idea.

Without shoes on, I ran over the deck and down onto our grass before attempting to disappear into the trees beyond as my father's voice boomed his countdown from behind me.

The numbers he barked hit me like a bat to the chest.

I wanted to wish that this time would be the last. That I wouldn't survive another onslaught but I couldn't. I couldn't let Kristie arrive home from school in a few hours and find me gone. I wouldn't put her at risk like that.

So, instead, I picked up my sore feet and moved faster.

His voice got farther away with every step I took.

I really should have predicted what happened next, but I didn't and the second a masked man jumped from behind a tree, I shrieked and attempted to dart in the opposite direction.

But it was pointless.

It always was.

They would always overpower me and take what they wanted. It was just how this worked.

They're the kings, and I'm merely the servant.

The slave.

In seconds, my arms were bound to my body and I was being frog-marched deeper into the trees.

The sun might be out, but with the thick cover of leaves above us, there was hardly any light getting through.

It was also the perfect cover for my screams.

No one would hear me out here. They were free to do as they pleased.

Not that it would stop them. Nothing ever seemed to.

When we got to the clearing, I was suddenly shoved forward.

Stumbling on the uneven ground, I crashed to my knees.

Pain shot up my thighs a beat before the rest of my body plummeted toward the ground.

I braced for impact, already trying to come up with a story to explain to Kristie why I've got a bruised face when I was suddenly stopped.

Pain exploded at the back of my skull as I was dragged up by my hair and thrown down on my ass.

I scrambled back in a pathetic attempt to get away, but it was pointless.

The man who caught me loomed in front of me, but he was no longer alone.

Two more masked figures closed in behind him.

I knew who they were. The masks were pointless. Just another part of their sick and twisted games.

Holding the man's eyes, dark eyes that I'd recognized anywhere, I attempted to look strong. Like I was able to endure anything they forced on me.

"I was promised a treat today, and it looks like your old man is going to deliver," he taunted, making my stomach somersault with fear.

Reaching up, he ripped his mask from his face, allowing me to see the evil snarl he was wearing beneath.

The two men behind did the same, no longer feeling the need to hide their identity as they moved closer.

I continued trying to back away, but the second Victor reached out and snagged my ankles, I'm hauled exactly where he wanted me.

My dirty shirt hitched up around my waist, exposing my white cotton panties.

"Cute," he taunted before pulling a switchblade from his pocket and flicking it open. "But totally fucking pointless for what we have in mind, princess."

My eyes fly open and in a heartbeat, I discover that the warmth around my ankles isn't just a visceral part of my dream.

It's reality.

The bright strip lights are illuminated above me, making my eyes water, and dark figures stand around me as I move.

"NO," I scream, attempting to kick out and remove the two hands that are locked tight around my limbs, but it's pointless.

I've been locked up in this cage for too long. My head might tell my body to fight, but my movements are sluggish and pathetic.

Everything hurts. Just having my legs stretched out as I'm dragged across the floor is agony.

A muffled cry hits my ears from the other side of the room and I throw my head back to find Mav.

His eyes are wide as he watches in horror as I'm dragged farther away from him. My heart drops when I find the gag between his lips, stopping him from crying out, from demanding they stop.

He might no longer be hanging from the ceiling, but he's still bound in place with chains around his wrists and ankles, forcing him to lie on his front in an attempt to protect his back.

The second I'm free of the cage, large hands wrap around my waist, and I'm hauled from the floor.

I scream, kick, and punch but none of my hits make an impact. If anything, they just amuse the men holding me.

"Come on, princess. Try and look like you don't want it. Don't you want your darling husband to at least think you're trying to fight it."

"I don't want any of this," I cry, trying and failing to put more effort in to breaking free.

A grunt rips from my lips when I'm thrown onto a tabletop on the other side of the room.

My cheek collides with the wood sending pain shooting down my neck.

Another cry comes from Mav as the chains holding him clank and rattle, but there isn't anything he can do to make this any better.

There is nothing either of us can do at this point.

We're too weak.

Too broken.

They're going to win.

Something cold wraps around my wrists before my arms are pulled tight over the table, leaving my chest pressed against the unforgiving wood and my ass in the air.

Crack.

I cry out, my eyes stinging with tears as the slap one of them just delivered to my bare ass burns down my legs.

Twisting my head around, I find Mav on the floor in the corner and hold his eyes.

It's okay, I tell him silently, hoping like hell he can read it in my eyes.

I can handle this.

He shakes his head, refusing to accept my plea.

But he's going to have to.

There is nothing he can do right now.

I swallow thickly as someone kicks my ankles apart. The sound of the shirt I was wearing being ripped down the back fills the air and Mav roars again.

With my ankles bound and my legs spread, I'm totally at the mercy of the three men holding us captive.

The only thing left to do is pray that Mav is right and that Reid and JD are coming because now would be a really good fucking time for that to happen.

"Been waiting a long time for this, princess," Victor taunts.

I scream when one of them spanks me again, but this time, I keep my eyes on Mav.

I'm sorry.

I'm so fucking sorry.

For the first time since I woke to find cannulas in the backs of my hands and a taunting bandage on my arm, I'm alone.

Unease trickles through me.

Something is going on. I can sense it every time I've looked at Reid.

He's holding things back from me because he doesn't think I can deal.

There's a chance he's right. A very big chance. It's my own fault. I'm more than aware of that. But being in the dark is worse than anything he could tell me.

It leaves me here wondering, and my mind loves nothing more than to come up with the worst possible scenarios.

Pushing myself so I'm sitting in bed, I lean forward and rest my elbows on my knees as I look around.

My room doesn't look like mine.

It's tidy.

I can see the floor and all the surfaces. The clothes that

are still out are folded neatly and everything else has been put away.

It's wrong. It doesn't feel like my space.

But then my body doesn't exactly feel like my own either.

Everything is wrong.

My movements are slower than I'd like, but my willpower to do something is stronger than my desire to remain sitting in bed, allowing my mind to spin.

Too much thinking is how I ended up in this mess in the first place.

I need a distraction. Something else to think about other than the person I really want next to me not being here.

I pause, the pain in my chest as sharp as ever as I think about her slipping out of my bed and disappearing in the middle of the night without a second thought about what she was leaving behind.

My legs are weak, my muscles pulling with the effort it takes to walk to my closet to find some sweats, but I don't allow my exhaustion to win.

I've done nothing but sleep and drown in my own thoughts since I woke up. It's time for something else. For a different view. To find out what exactly is going on.

Reid said that Victor knows and that we're about to find out if everything we've been planning is going to be enough to wipe him and his little fucked-up posse from the face of the Earth. But that's all I know. And it's nowhere near enough.

Pulling my sweats up my legs takes more effort that it should, and by the time I'm at the door, ready to make my escape from the room that has been nothing but a prison cell for the past few days, my chest is heaving with exertion, and I've got a bead of sweat on my brow.

I'm not exactly in the kind of state I'd like to embark on a war, but I guess it's too late to worry about that now.

The house is silent as I slowly descend the stairs, but I know that Reid isn't far away.

It's been impossible to miss the guilt swimming in his eyes every time he's looked at me since I woke up.

He thinks all of this is his fault, that if he'd have woken me and explained then it would have stopped me.

Would it have?

Honestly, I'm not sure.

She's still not here and he's still keeping secrets.

The only difference is that I haven't had a choice in taking my meds.

With a pained sigh, I scratch at the bandage wrapped around my arm as I take the last few steps.

I've only made it a couple more when the deep rumble of voices floats through the air.

Diverting away from the kitchen, I move closer to Reid's office.

Lifting my hand, I'm about to push the door open to announce my presence when the sound of my best friend's angry voice, quickly followed by a loud bang, gives me pause.

"This is fucking bullshit."

There's another bang before a loud sigh and the familiar creek of his chair.

"Someone will find something," Ezra soothes, making my brows pinch together.

I know everything is up in the air right now but that isn't the kind of tone I usually hear from any of the Harris brothers.

"And what if they fucking don't? Then what the hell am I meant to do?" Reid snaps, making my hackles rise.

"You really are the cup-half-empty type, huh?" Ezra deadpans.

"What the fuck else am I meant to be right now? I've no fucking idea where they are or what's happening to them."

Those few words alone make my heart drop into my feet and I'm moving long before I've registered the thought.

The door slams back against the wall, making both of the Harrises sitting inside this office startle and twist around in my direction.

"You don't know what's happening to them?" I bark, holding my best friend's eyes steady, letting him see exactly how serious I am about learning everything he's hiding from me.

"J." He sighs, sitting up higher in his chair and resting his elbows on the desk.

"Don't fucking J me. You're hiding shit. Shit I need to know."

His lips press into a thin line as I try to remain calm.

"For a good reason. There is nothing you can do to help right now so—"

"So?" I bellow. "You don't know where they are or what's happening," I repeat again. My blood runs cold as the realization hits me. "Victor has them, doesn't he?"

My knees wobble, threatening to give out on me, forcing me to reach for the wall.

"For fuck's sake, sit down," Ezra says, jumping to his feet as if he's about to help me walk.

"Not until I hear the truth. And I swear to God, if this motherfucker has sold them out then I'm going to turn around and walk straight out of this house without so much as looking back," I warn darkly.

I'm pretty sure they're as aware as I am that there's a

very good chance I'm nowhere near capable of doing that right now; I'll give it a damn good go, though.

Reid might be my best friend, but if he's willingly done this... if he's willingly given her back to the men who—

My blood runs cold, even without allowing myself to finish that sentence, and acid burns up my throat.

A large hand wraps around my upper arm and I startle at the contact.

"Sit down," Ezra demands, sounding very unlike himself.

He's usually a cocky playboy, just like Devin. It's bizarre to hear a concerned edge to his voice.

I'm so confused by everything that he's able to tug me over to my seat and gently shove me down into it.

No one says anything as he retakes the other chair, but the tension in the room, along with Reid's heated stare, is oppressive and unavoidable.

"Tell me what's going on," I force out as my fingers curl around the arm of the chair.

Reid's jaw ticks as he battles with his conscience— proving that he has one—as he tries to decide how much I can cope with.

"All of it, Harris. Don't you dare sugarcoat any of it."

"Fine." He sighs, falling back in his seat as if all the energy was just stolen from his body.

"Victor knows they were here."

My teeth grind and my nostrils flare, hearing him confirm what we assumed after his visit a few days ago.

"And?"

Reid hangs his head in a rare show of regret.

"I sent them away."

I'm on my feet in a heartbeat, my hands trembling with anger.

"You sent them away?" I boom, taking a warning step closer. Although, quite frankly, I'm not entirely sure what I'm going to do.

The room spins around me as fear, desperation, and disbelief war with the anger coursing through my veins.

"How could you? How could you send her back to—"

"I was trying to protect them," he bellows back. His chair collides with the wall behind where he is sitting as he presses his palms on the desk and stares me down.

His pose, his size, might be intimidating to many, but not to me.

I don't cower or show any kind of sign that I am going to back down.

"Bullshit," I spit. "You wanted her gone because you can't cope with how you really feel about her."

His brows pinch. "W-what?" he stutters, clearly not expecting my response.

"You want her and you can't deal so you've done what you always do and got rid of what you think the problem is. But allow me to let you in on a secret. It's you. You are the problem here. Not her."

"Alright, Taylor Swift," Ezra teases. "Shall we all calm down a little?"

"Fuck you," I sneer, shaking his hand off my arm when he tries to manhandle me again.

"I helped organize to get them somewhere safe where no one would find them."

Falling back into the chair, I drop my head into my hands and take a moment to try and process all of this.

"I didn't sell them out, J. I wouldn't. We need her. We promised her that we'd help."

Closing my eyes, I replay his words over and over, but

despite his reassurance that he hasn't done this. The anger and desperation don't lessen.

"And how has that worked out for you?" I hiss. "You're meant to be protecting her and you don't know where the fuck she is."

"That wasn't part of the fucking plan, J. I thought we'd covered all bases. They were un-trackable to anyone but us."

"So fucking track her," I bark, my stomach twists painfully, my ribs contracting around my lungs as I try not to think about what might be happening to her—to them—if all of this has failed.

"We're trying."

Silence falls between us, but the tension never stops crackling.

"If they'd have run, we'd be able to find them but—"

"They've gone off-grid," I finish for him, acid burning up my throat again at the thought of Victor getting his hands on her. Her father. Razor.

I retch as my short nails dig into my palms with so much force, I'm surprised the skin doesn't break.

"You sent them away and now they're locked up somewhere by your cunt of a father and we have no fucking idea how to get them back."

Pushing to stand, the chair behind me topples over and crashes to the floor as I stand there barely able to catch my breath.

No fucking wonder he didn't tell me this when I first woke up.

Reid holds my glare strong as I stare at him.

"If he has hurt her in any fucking way, I will never forgive you for his," I warn, my voice so broken and full of pain, it barely sounds like it belongs to me.

"J," Ez soothes, "we're doing everything we can here. Reid didn't anticipate—"

"I don't give a shit," I roar. "He should have considered this was a possibility and locked them back up downstairs or something. I need her, Ez," I plead desperately before turning to look back at Reid. "I fucking need her and they have her."

No one replies, but their sympathy is palpable.

It's just a shame they don't understand. Not really.

Yes, Reid might want her. But it's not the same.

And Ez. He has no clue about what me and my little dove had—have. How could he?

I'm at the door when Reid's cell starts buzzing on his desk, and my steps falter.

"Yes," he barks the second it connects.

My heart pounds as I wait for something. Anything to give me a little hope that all of this wasn't for fucking nothing.

That once again, Alana has fallen into the clutches of men who want nothing more than to hurt her.

"Yeah. Got it. We're on our way."

Spinning around, I find that he's already hung up and pulling guns from his drawers.

"Reid?" I whisper.

He pauses. "Aubrey found them."

M y cell buzzes in my pocket as I tuck a gun into my pants. But before I grab it, I pass another to Ez along with a knife.

"Where the fuck is mine?" JD whines from his position in the doorway.

"Don't do this," I warn, slipping my own knife into my boot.

A bitter laugh spills from JD's lips as he stares at me in disbelief.

"You are not leaving me here. That is not fucking happening."

My eyes drop to the bandage on his wrist and my insides knot up.

He's not ready for this. Not strong enough to deal with whatever we find at the location that is sitting on my cell.

"We've no idea what we're about to walk into. I'm not about to—"

"Fuck that, Reid. Fuck that. Alana is at the other end of this, that means I need to be there," he argues.

"You're not ready to fight."

His teeth grind and his jaw pops in irritation.

"Says fucking who? You? You might want to be in charge of this town but that doesn't give you the authority to tell me what to do, Reid."

I stare at him, knowing deep down that he's right but terrified that taking him with us is the worst possible thing I can do for him right now.

I swore to myself that I would make him my first priority.

Leading him headfirst into this war is not doing that.

Leaving him here and keeping him safe is.

"I don't give a shit what we're about to walk into. If she's there, if she needs me, that's where I'm going to fucking be."

"You've been sedated for two days, J. You've had a fucking blood transfusion."

"Yeah, and your fucking father has my girl," he roars back, his chest heaving and his muscles pulled tight with determination.

"What do we know?" Ez asks, attempting to break the tension as the two of us stand off against each other.

"Not a lot. She's going to call back. But we need to move."

"Then let's fucking go," JD announces before spinning on his heels and rushing from the room.

His heavy footsteps thunder up the stairs a second later as I assume he goes to get dressed.

"Fuck," I breathe, combing my fingers through my hair.

"He needs to stay here," Ezra says helpfully.

Looking over, our eyes lock and hold for a beat.

His lips part, but no words spill free. Instead, he nods.

He knows as well as I do that aside from locking him in the basement, we're not going to stop him right now.

"Call the others, tell them to drop whatever they're doing and get to the location I send them."

"On it, boss," Ez agrees before pulling his cell out. "Are we calling anyone else?"

"I don't fucking trust anyone else," I seethe.

"No, I know. But..." His argument trails off when I continue to glare at him. "We got this," he finally agrees before marching out of my office with his phone pinned to his ear. "Get your fucking ass out of bed, Bro. Reid's found them."

Something explodes within me at his words.

I want it to be relief, but there is nothing but dread.

JD is right. We've no idea what we're about to find at the other end of this. But if that photo Victor sent is anything to go by, then it's not going to be pretty.

Admitting defeat, I grab a bag and stuff as many weapons in as I can, including JD's preferred piece, and throw it over my shoulder.

By the time I join Ez in the hallway, JD is rushing back down the stairs.

He looks fucking awful.

He's pale, with dark circles around his haunted eyes. His hair is a mess, sticking up in all directions, and his shirt is wrinkled. He looks nothing like the Hawks' foot soldier that he is. He doesn't look deadly, or scary, someone that our enemies or customers should be intimidated by. He looks like he needs them to give him a hug.

"You don't have to do this," I assure him, trying to push aside the growing concern within me for what's happening to Alana and Mav to focus on him.

"I do and you know it," he says, his voice unwavering.

Stepping up to me, he reaches for the gun that's hanging

from my fingers—his gun—and quickly tucks it into his pants.

"What the fuck are we waiting for?" he barks before racing toward the front door.

Ez catches my eye as JD steps out into the sunlight.

He doesn't say a word, but I can read every single one he wants to say in his eyes.

"What's the alternative?" I mutter. "Leaving him here?"

Without waiting for a response, I surge forward and into the fall afternoon sun. But it does little to warm the icy cold dread that's running through my veins.

JD is already sitting in the passenger seat of my Charger waiting for me when I drop behind the wheel.

"Talk to me," he demands. "I need to know everything."

A pained sigh spills from my lips as Ezra pulls open the back door and joins us. But this time, instead of keeping JD in the dark, I tell him everything I know as we make our way to the location Aubrey gave me.

"He sent you a photo?" JD barks at my confession. "And it's taken you until now to find her."

"We've been trying," Ezra pipes up from behind. "He's taken them off-grid."

"He thinks he's winning," I murmur.

"Fuck that," JD snaps. "There is no fucking way we're letting that cunt win anything."

Silence follows his statement. None of us need to say the words; we all know just how vehemently we agree with them.

"He's put her in a fucking cage," JD fumes, his fists clenching and unclenching in his lap as he tries to process all of this.

"We'll get her," I promise before Ezra leans between the seats and grips his shoulder. "We've got this, J."

The rest of the journey is silent and tense. JD is practically vibrating with anger by the time I take the turn that leads to the location on the very outskirts of Harrow Creek that Aubrey sent me.

"You trust this chick, right?" Ezra asks as the car bounces around over the rough terrain.

My heart lurches in my chest as I hear his insinuation loud and clear.

But that's not what this is.

"Almost as much as I trust the two of you," I say honestly.

"And how come I've never met her?" Ez asks, leaning through the seats again.

"Because you'll probably try to fuck her."

"She's female, right?"

My teeth grind in irritation.

"Stay the fuck away from Aubrey. She'd eat you alive."

"Pfft, I really doubt that," Ezra mutters, pissed off by my lack of confidence in his skills.

"Where the fuck is she?" JD barks impatiently as I pull into a clearing and bring the car to a stop.

"She'll be here," I confirm, scanning the tree line for a hint of her. "Come on," I say, killing the engine and stepping out so she can see us.

No sooner have the three of us rounded the front of the car, when another one comes bouncing around the track behind us.

"Bet Ellis is loving that," Ezra teases as Devin's truck practically leaves the ground when he hits another pothole.

Shaking my head at them, I step up to J.

"Don't even think about questioning me," he hisses.

Holding my hands up in defense, I search his eyes, trying to find the answer for myself.

"I'll be okay when we have them back."

I nod. What else can I fucking do?

I'm still trying to come up with something to say when movement through the trees catches my eye.

My fingers twitch as I reach for the gun tucked into my waistband.

Okay, so maybe I lied earlier about how much I actually trust Aubrey.

I'm about to pull it free when she finally emerges from the shadows.

The second she steps into the sun, her dark hair practically glows and Devin and Ezra immediately stop talking.

I don't need to look back to know that their jaws just hit the ground.

Aubrey really is that beautiful. It's part of the reason she is so good at her job.

Her full, red lips part to say something, but I beat her to it. I'm not here for a nice little chit-chat like the other night at her hotel room.

"What's going on? Where are they?"

"I'll get to that in a minute," she promises before looking each of us in the eyes. Her attention lingers a little on JD, concern for him obvious in her usually cold and emotionless eyes. "You are all aware of what's going to happen once you storm in there, right?"

"Aubs," I hiss.

"Okay, okay. I'm just making sure. I wouldn't be your friend if I didn't at least give you a warning."

"We need her back," JD pleads. "Please, just tell us where she is."

Aubrey looks at J again before focusing back on me. A very small smile twitches at the corner of her lips as she connects the dots.

"Very well," she agrees. "I had a booty call with your delightful father earlier today and—"

Someone behind me gags before Devin mutters, "Spare us the details of that, please."

"Trust me, no one needs the details of that. I managed to follow him when he left."

"And he didn't see you?" Devin asks.

"I'm not an amateur." She scoffs, offended by his question. "He led me to an abandoned air base, and straight to an old hangar."

"Where?" JD barks impatiently.

Pulling her cell from her pocket, she taps at the screen, and a second later, mine buzzes.

"There."

"Is there protection?" I ask.

"Not that I could see. Just three cars. No security. Arrogant motherfuckers think they're untouchable."

"Half their problem," Ezra mutters.

"Do you know where they're hiding out themselves?" Ellis asks.

"No. I couldn't trail them when they left. It was too obvious. But I'm going to work on it."

"The second we get into this hangar, they're going to go even deeper underground," Devin warns.

"I'll find them."

"Your pussy that good, huh?" he taunts.

Aubrey smiles at him, but there is nothing friendly in it. In fact, it would probably make most men's balls shrivel up in an instant.

"As I said before," she sneers. "I'm good at my job. There isn't anything else for you to worry about."

"Fuck. I think I'm in love," Devin announces, making

Aubrey roll her eyes as her top lip peels back.

"Cute. But I'm not into little boys who like to play with guns."

"Jesus, can we just fucking get to the point here. You've got the location, let's just fucking go already," JD announces, marching toward the car, ready to get his girl back.

I turn to follow him, agreeing with his sentiment, but the second Aubrey speaks again, I pause.

"I've sorted you out a place to go after."

"A place?" JD asks, having also stopped.

"They'll come for you. All of you," she says, looking around us again. "I get that you want to do this as a team, but you need to think carefully about how you go about this."

Nothing but the squawk of a bird flying overhead fills the air as her words settle in my head.

"You three go home," I demand, staring at my younger brothers.

"Nah, Bro," Ezra argues, stepping forward. "We're in this fight with you."

"What he said," Devin agrees.

My eyes find Ellis's in the hope he's on the same wavelength as me.

"Reid's right," he agrees.

"But—"

"If Aubrey says the hangar is clear, then Reid and JD won't have any issues getting in and getting them out."

"But what if—" Ezra continues to try and argue.

"If Victor finds out we're all in on this, then we're all going to be in hiding. Reid needs us to be living our normal lives. Right, Bro?"

"Right," I agree, rubbing the back of my neck as I

silently thank Ellis for understanding. "We're going to need you, but now isn't the time."

With a nod, I spin around toward my car.

"We'll be in touch," I promise before dropping into the driver's seat, JD only a second behind me.

"I'll be in touch," Aubrey promises before disappearing back into the trees.

Bringing the engine to life, I throw the car into drive and floor it out of the clearing.

"I really hope you're ready for this," I warn, part of me still wishing we'd left JD at home. The next few hours could make him or break him for good.

I just fucking pray it's not the latter.

MAVERICK

She tries to fight it, to save me from the agony of hearing her sobs and whimpers, but she can't hold them in.

Each one hurts worse than any lashing from Victor's whip or anything else they could do to me.

For as long as I can remember, Alana has been my ultimate weakness. Hurt her and it fucking kills me.

All three of them know it too.

And watching as they threw her onto that table and tied her up was the worst thing I've ever experienced.

The way they looked at her. The way the three of them silently colluded about how the next few minutes were going to play out.

It was fucking agony like I've never felt before.

She's mine.

My fucking wife.

And yet, they had her.

They've already stolen so much from her.

She didn't deserve to go through it all again.

And all the while I was chained up and unable to do

anything but watch in abject horror as they prepared to destroy her.

Because that was what I was on the verge of witnessing.

Alana is strong. So fucking strong. I've always been in awe of her ability to hold her head high and put one foot in front of the other despite what she's been through. But enduring this all over again, the pain from her childhood, it had the power to finally tear her apart.

I thought it was going to happen.

Despite my demands they stop and her pleas for mercy, they had every intention of going through with it. Until Victor's cell interrupted them.

At first, he looked like he was going to ignore it and continue. But when it started ringing for the third time, he pulled it from his pocket, cursed and answered it.

Only minutes later, the three of them walked out, leaving Alana in exactly the same position they'd put her in, ready to—

I retch, acid burning up my throat as I think about what I came so close to witnessing.

Unable to hide my reaction, Alana's sobs get louder.

"It's okay, Doll," I force out, my throat burning.

I've no idea how long we've been here, but they haven't so much as given us water. We're not going to last much longer.

My vision is already fucked. I've got black spots floating around, and they're only getting worse with every second that passes.

My body is wrecked, my muscles too weak to move, even if I could.

Time is running out.

If I'm wrong and Reid and JD aren't coming, then we're fucked.

I've never really feared dying before. But fuck, the thought of going before her and leaving her alone with these monsters is fucking terrifying.

"They're not coming." She whimpers.

Squeezing my eyes closed, I pray that she's wrong.

For all we know, they could be outside right this second just waiting to storm the place.

It's either that or we die here.

There is no third option.

"No," I state as strongly as I can, refusing to let her see that my hope is waning. "They are." They have to be.

I lie there with my cheek pressed against the unforgiving, cold concrete beneath me, watching her.

Even now, she's the most beautiful woman I've ever laid eyes on. Her strength shines through, putting her above any other person on the planet.

Tears continue to leak from her eyes despite the fact her whimpering has stopped.

She's uncomfortable, that much is more than obvious.

She's gone from being cramped up in the cage on the other side of the room to being stretched out across a table.

I keep my eyes on her as long as I can, grateful that they haven't plunged us into darkness this time.

For as much as I hate seeing her suffer, being able to look at her helps me get through each second.

The unforgiving restraints on my wrists and ankles continue to cut into my skin, ensuring the wounds only get deeper with every minute that passes.

I don't look at the floor beneath me, but I know it's stained with my blood.

At some point, I must give up the fight with my exhaustion because when a loud bang echoes through the space around us, my eyes fly open.

They immediately stream with water as the harsh strip lighting above us seers into them.

Instantly, I find her.

She's exactly where they left her, her body trembling from the cold.

"What was that?"

Something akin to hope flutters in my belly. I'm aware that it's probably pointless, that at any second, the three of them are going to return and continue where they left off, forcing me to lie here and watch as they destroy my wife, but I can't help it.

"Are they back?" she asks, her voice cracking with fear.

"I don't know," I whisper, my eyes locked on the huge sliding doors on the other side of the space where it sounded like the bang came from.

Hope and dread riot inside me, both battling to take precedence as the doors rattle.

"Mav?" Alana whimpers. "Is it them?"

My heart races and my head spins.

If it were Victor and our fathers, they'd have just strolled right in like they have every other time. Unless they're trying to scare us.

But if it's Reid and JD...

My hands tremble, but this time, it's not just from the cold, it's anticipation.

If they've come for us then they'll free Alana. Even if they don't get a chance to free me, that'll be enough.

To know she's safe and away from their clutches. I could die right there happy knowing that Reid and JD would protect her.

I almost laugh at the insanity of it all.

Not so long ago, Reid would have been up there with quite a long list of men I wouldn't trust with my wife.

But now... I can't think of anyone I'd want on her side more than him.

A loud screech of metal on metal rips through the air, making me wince as bright sunlight from outside floods the space.

I blink, barely able to make out what's happening on the other side of the vast room as the sun blinds me.

Everything fades to nothing as two dark figures emerge in the brightness.

Alana's loud sob is the last thing I hear.

You can stop fighting now.

They came for her.

Alana

The sound that rips from my throat as my vision clears isn't human.

The relief I feel rushing through my system is beyond anything I've ever felt before.

"You came," I breathe. It's so quiet they'll never hear it all the way over there, but it doesn't matter.

They're here. They came for us, just like Mav promised they would.

"Mav," I call, desperate to hear his voice.

I want to turn around, to see the relief on his face, but I can't rip my eyes away from Reid and JD.

They're here.

They came.

It's over.

"Mav?" I call again when he doesn't respond.

"Dove," JD calls before he takes off running toward me. "Fuck, baby." His voice is rough, thick with emotion as he runs his eyes over me.

Shame threatens to burn through me at the position I'm in, but the relief is too strong.

"I'm okay," I whimper. "I'm okay. Go to Mav, he—"

"Holy fuck," Reid barks, clearly finding my husband chained up like an unwanted dog in the corner of the room.

"Go to him, please," I beg. "Please." The word is swallowed by a loud sob.

"It's okay, Dove. We're here. We're going to get you both out."

Without missing a beat, he begins tugging at the ropes that are binding my hands and feet to the table.

My muscles scream with every movement and the second my arms are freed, my legs give out and I collapse to the floor.

"Oh fuck," JD barks, rushing around the table to me.

Everything is a blur as warm arms sweep under my body and lift me up.

"I've got you, Dove. I've got you and I'm never letting you go again."

Staring up at him, I'm barely able to make out his features through the tears.

My body trembles as I continue to fight against the cold.

"Reid?" JD calls. "We need to go."

A deep grunt fills the air, forcing me to rip my stare from JD in favor of where Reid and Mav are.

"I'm going to need a little help here," Reid confesses.

The moment my eyes drop to the man at his feet, my entire world falls from beneath me.

"MAV," I scream. "MAV." But he doesn't move. He doesn't do anything. "Help him. Please, Reid. Do something."

"I-I—" JD stutters, holding me tightly to his chest.

"Put her in the car then come back and help me," Reid demands.

"I can't just leave—"

"Please," I whimper. "I need him. Please."

"Fuck. Fuck," he barks before spinning us around and practically running from the building.

The second we emerge from the building, the heat of the sun licks my skin and I crumble once more.

JD's hold tightens to the point it hurts, but I can't stop him. It feels too good. His strength, his warmth.

It's everything.

Long before I'm ready to let him go, JD's arms loosen and I'm lowered to a seat.

"Here," he says, dragging his long-sleeved shirt from his body and tugging it over my head. "I'll be right back." His warm palm cups my cheek before he lowers down, pressing his brow to mine. "Everything is going to be okay. I p-promise." The way his voice cracks on that final word sends panic rushing through me.

"Help him, Julian. Please. I can't lose him."

"You won't, baby. You won't."

He presses a kiss to my forehead and then backs away from me.

I reach out, but I can't get to him.

He's too far away. Just like every time someone tries to rescue me from one of my nightmares.

I get the taste of relief, only for it to be snatched away.

It's cruel.

So fucking cruel.

The image that emerged before us the second we pulled open those huge sliding doors that led us into the aircraft hangar is one I will never, ever forget. Closely followed by the scent.

I've smelled death a time or two in my past. But never has it smelled as potent or as toxic as it did when we stepped inside.

Everything I've been through, all my pain vanished in a puff of smoke the second my eyes focused on Alana.

Every inch of her was trembling. I had no idea if it was from the cold or fear, or what those motherfuckers had done to her, but it ripped me to pieces.

Bile swirled in my stomach as we moved closer.

Her position...

Fuck.

There's only one thing those sick cunts could have been doing with her naked and tied to the table like that. And they're all going to die very slow and painful deaths because of it.

I'm suddenly thrown to the right, my grip on the woman

on my lap tightening to stop her from colliding with the door.

By the time Reid and I got back to the car with an unconscious Mav between us, she had also passed out. Although, not in quite the same terrifying way Mav had.

His wounds are horrific. I can't even imagine how much pain he must be in. It's hardly a surprise he was unconscious when we found him.

"Careful," I whisper-hiss.

"We need to get them to safety."

"I'm aware, but Alana doesn't need a concussion on top of everything else."

Accepting my words, Reid eases off the gas a little, slowing his Charger down as we follow directions to where Aubrey's safe house is located.

Usually, I'd be on edge driving into Hazard Grove. But right now, it feels like a safer option than being in Harrow Creek.

Reid might not have made much progress getting Sidney Hyde on our side, but if what Mav has said is true, then he might just have an in with his stepson Malakai. That might be enough to help keep us safe while we're here. Should they discover we're even here, that is.

Glancing back, I take in the mess of the man in Reid's back seat.

Getting him in there on a normal day would be a challenge. But being unable to lay him on his ruined back made it even harder.

He looks uncomfortable as fuck. It's probably a good thing that he's out of it.

"You need to call Doc," I whisper.

"We can't, J."

"But—"

"I know," he hisses, cutting off my argument. "Aubrey is sorting it."

"You trust her medic more than Doc."

"No," he says fiercely. "But we can't risk it."

My teeth grind with my need to argue.

But I can't because he's right.

No matter how much Alana and Mav need him right now, we can't risk the fact he might be followed out of Harrow Creek.

Doc might be on our side, but we know all too well that Victor likes to play dirty. And the second he discovers we've taken his prisoners back, he's going to lose his shit.

"When is—"

"Aubrey is meeting us there. I don't know about her medic."

I glance back at Mav again.

"He's going to be okay," Reid assures me. He looks over, feeling my stare before following it up with, "there isn't any other option."

There's a part of me that wants to tease him about going from enemies to best friends, but I swallow it down. Things are too tragic right now for even me to start cracking jokes.

Reaching out, I lower the sun visor, cutting off the fall sun as it sinks toward the horizon.

Any other time, I might enjoy watching the sunset, especially with my girl in my arms. Resting my head back, I close my eyes and try to picture something different. I think about the secluded cabin in the woods I always picture when I need an escape. I think of brisk air, open fires and bubbling, steaming hot tubs.

I lose myself in thoughts of being cuddled up wearing nothing but a soft blanket in front of the fire with my girl.

We'd have a thick rug beneath us and I'd make love to her right then and there with the flame warming our skin.

It would be perfect.

I'm dragged from the fantasy when a deep groan comes from behind me.

"We've got you, Mav," I say, needing to reassure him that everything is okay. "We've got Alana too. You're safe now."

He doesn't say anything or give us any kind of sign that he heard me. But at least we know he's alive.

"We're nearly there," Reid confirms.

By the time he pulls up to a big house in the middle of nowhere in Hazard Grove territory, the sun has set, leaving us with only the Charger's headlights and the moon to guide our way.

"Go take her in first then we'll come back for Mav."

Nodding, I throw the door open and put everything I have into standing with Alana in my arms.

Reid was right to be concerned about me doing this earlier. Although, it's not my mental health that's suffering, not yet at least, the adrenaline that's pumping through my veins is keeping that at bay right now, but the effects of my stupid actions are making me slow and weak.

I need to be better for Alana and Mav. They deserve to have me fully fit and fighting for them right now.

My muscles ache and my legs tremble as I climb the porch steps that will lead me to the front door.

I'm almost there when it opens, making my heart jump into my throat.

"The fuck?" I hiss when a tall, slim body emerges. "Do you get a kick out of jumping out of dark shadows?"

Aubrey smirks at me. It's all the answer I need.

"Brilliant. Did you want to get out of the way?"

Rolling her eyes at me, she steps aside, pointing toward the living room, so I can put Alana down.

She hasn't so much as moved since I returned to the car and lifted her onto my lap just over an hour ago, so it startles me when she whispers, "No," and wraps her arms around my neck, refusing to let me go.

It breaks my already tattered heart.

"Dove," I breathe. "Trust me, I don't want to let go, but I need to help Mav."

A quiet whimper spills from her lips the second I mention Mav and she reluctantly drops her arms.

"I'll be right back, I promise."

Kissing the tip of her nose, I rush out of the room.

Proving that she's more than she appears, Aubrey has hold of Mav's legs as Reid attempts to heave the rest of him out of the car.

"Heavy motherfucker." He grunts.

"This is going to hurt like a bitch when he wakes up," I say, my eyes tracking every open wound across his back.

Reid stops moving, his own eyes landing on what his father has done, and I look up just in time to see his jaw ticking with anger.

"It's okay for you to admit that you're friends now."

Reid scoffs.

"We're all on the same team."

"And you all want the same girl," Aubrey pipes up, assessing the situation correctly.

"Are you still here?" Reid barks as he jumps back into action.

We manage to get Mav out of the car, and thankfully, he remains unconscious. I can't even imagine how much it would hurt otherwise.

"The master bedroom is right at the top of the stairs. Bed is massive so you won't have any issues."

Choosing to assume she means for treating Mav's wounds, I keep my mouth shut and keep moving.

As much as I might have missed Alana, and maybe even the asshole in my arms, I'm not sure we're going to be having any fun anytime soon.

When we hit the top of the stairs, we pass a couch that sits overlooking a set of double-height windows that look out over the forest beyond. It's so close to my fantasy in the car it sends a chill down my spine. We might not be in the mountains, but I'm happy to take whatever I can get right now.

Aubrey rushes ahead and opens the door. The room is fucking massive, but I pay it all little mind as we make a beeline for the bed and as gently as we can, lie Mav on his front.

"That's nasty," Aubrey observes.

Lifting my hand, I rub the back of my neck as I study Mav's back.

"When is your medic getting here?" Reid asks.

"Any minute," she confirms after checking her watch.

"I'm going to bring Alana up here. She'll want to be with him," Reid muses

He catches my eyes before he marches past me and shakes his head, stopping me from commenting. Not that I would. He's right. She's going to want to be where he is.

The thought hurts, but not as much as it could.

What they've just been through... fuck. I can't even begin to understand what it might have been like or what either of them need in the hope of moving past it.

"Sit down," he says, jerking his chin toward the couch.

His eyes hold a warning that I can't ignore and I stumble back, falling into the soft velour cushions.

It's light pink. Not exactly the kind of thing I'm used to living in Reid's dark manor of horror. Something tells me that Alana will like it though. I might have only seen a snapshot of their house, but it was comfortable, soft, a home.

My skin prickles with attention, letting me know exactly what—or who—Aubrey's eyes are on.

"What's the deal with the bandage then?"

I look up, narrowing my eyes at her.

I've met her a few times over the years, but we've never formed a friendship like her and Reid did the first time they met.

I know why too, I'm just too chicken shit to admit it.

Something hot and ugly bubbles just under my skin as I study her.

She's beautiful. Her long dark hair hangs to her waist. She has large almond-shaped eyes that are almost as dark as her locks.

I always thought of her as Reid's perfect woman. Was convinced that one day he'd realize it too and then he'd be gone, chasing her across the country on whatever job she was on and leaving me behind.

It never happened though.

And as the man in question steps into the room with a certain blonde draped over his arms, I start to understand why he never did.

Maybe she isn't his perfect woman after all...

Without saying a word, he lowers Alana onto my lap and takes a step back.

Our eyes collide and a silent conversation passes between us.

I promised you I'd get her back for you.

Shifting her, I wrap my arm around her and press my lips to her temple.

"You're safe now, baby. We've got you."

My heart shatters as she nuzzles against my chest, curling into me and allowing me to protect her.

"You three are in for a world of fucking pain with this situation, you do know that, right?"

"Do you have any kind of filter?" I snap back, aware that I never answered her question about my bandage earlier.

"No. I'd rather just get the answer I want. Oh, Jude is here," she says after checking her watch.

With a flounce that is way girlier than I was expecting, she disappears from the room and then runs down the stairs.

"Be nice," Reid warns.

"What?" I ask innocently. "I'm always nice. She just—"

"Doesn't beat around the bush?"

"Something like that."

When Reid first came up with the idea of dragging Aubrey into this mess, I thought he'd lost his mind. After years of thinking he was secretly hot for her, I really didn't see him willingly putting her in a position to have to fuck Victor. But then I saw him with Alana and I discovered my mistake.

He never wanted Aubrey.

I guess on paper they might appear to be the perfect couple. But life isn't that easy. And let's be honest. They're both cold-blooded murderers. There's no way they'd survive a relationship.

In only minutes, she's back, a nerdy-looking guy trailing behind her.

If I didn't know better, I'd expect him to pull out a

laptop and start tapping away like Ellis, but when he lifts his arm, I find a bag not all that different from Doc's hanging from his fingers.

"Jude, this is Reid Harris, Julian Dempsey." Her eyes narrow on mine as my jaw ticks with annoyance. She knows full well that I don't introduce myself to anyone with my full name. "Maverick Murray and his wife," she adds, digging that knife a little deeper as she nods at the woman curled up on my lap. "Alana. As far as we know, this is the extent of Maverick's wounds. Alana seems better, but we think there might be some hidden trauma."

Jude nods and stalks closer to Mav.

"Has he been conscious at all?" he asks, studying his wounds.

"He grunted in the car on the way here but nothing else," I supply.

Jude nods. "I'm going to give him some strong pain relief that will keep him under. Probably for the best because this is going to hurt."

"I'm going to leave you to it. Everyone want coffee?" Aubrey offers, giving Jude some space and peace to work.

"I'll help," Reid offers before the two of them disappear.

Silence falls over the room as their voices disappear.

"Who is she?" Alana whispers, startling me.

Looking down, I find her staring up at me with tear-filled eyes. There is so much pain in them it makes my chest contract as fire for vengeance on the men who hurt her fills my veins.

"Reid's friend," I say softly, unsure how I feel about the jealousy that's swirling in her eyes. "She's the reason we found you, Dove."

Lowering her eyelids, she breaks our connection.

"Hey, don't do that," I say, gently cupping her cheek and lifting her head until she has no choice but to look up at me.

"I'm sorry," she whispers, her voice so broken it slices right through my heart.

"Baby, you have nothing to apologize for."

Together we sit and watch as Jude cleans up Mav's back. Every time he makes contact with Mav's wounds, Alana jumps as if she can feel his pain.

She doesn't say anything, and I don't force her to. When she's ready to talk, I'll be here, more than willing to listen to anything she has to say.

29

ALANA

I wake with a start. My heart is racing and my skin is burning up as the image of Mav taking another strike from Victor's whip plays out over and over in my mind.

Staring up at the white ceiling, I take a few seconds to calm down and remind myself that we're safe.

Everything that happened yesterday felt like a dream. Like I was watching it all play out before me through some kind of cloud.

Honestly, it still doesn't all feel real.

Mav said that they would come.

I wanted to believe him.

But aside from Mav, no one has ever cared enough to rescue me. And on the face of it, Reid should have been the last person to stick his neck on the line and come for us.

But he did.

Forcing the image of Mav being tortured by the men he's meant to look up to from my mind, I think back to the moment those huge sliding doors opened and two dark figures stepped inside.

I'm not sure anyone has ever described Reid Harris and Julian Dempsey as their saviors before but fuck... that's exactly what they were.

A light snore comes from the other side of the room, and I look up to find JD stretched out on a couch not too far away.

He's still shirtless, exposing his ink and muscles and his arm is hanging over the edge with—

My breath catches at the sight of the bandage wrapped around his wrist and my brows pinch together.

But then there is another noise beside me and my attention is stolen by Mav, who shifts in his sleep.

The size of JD's bandage is put into perspective when I take in my husband's back.

Reaching out, I wrap my hand around his arm and squeeze gently.

He's out of it. I remember the medic saying that the painkillers would keep him out, but still, my need to reassure him that I'm here, that we're safe is too much to deny.

Tears burn my eyes as I continue to watch him.

I came so close to losing him. I know I did.

If Reid and JD didn't turn up when they did then...

Voices float through the air from the other side of the bedroom door, stealing my attention.

Glancing at the two men who are here with me, I gently —and very, very slowly—slip out from under the covers.

My legs are bare and dirty thanks to that cage they locked me inside, but the sight of JD's shirt hanging from my shoulders gives me comfort.

Lifting the fabric to my nose, I inhale a deep hit of the man who brought me so much solace back in Reid's basement.

But when I open my eyes, reality slams into me with the force of an eighteen-wheeler.

The light gray fabric is smeared with blood.

Mav's blood.

Acid burns up my throat as I vividly remember his brutal attack and the way Victor's whip cut through his skin like butter.

My head spins when I push to my feet, my legs trembling under my weight.

Reid reappeared at some point before I passed out with water and crackers. I remember guzzling down the water, but I have no memory of eating anything.

From the emptiness and pain in the pit of my stomach, I'd guess that I didn't.

With my hand on the foot of the bed, I shuffle my feet across the thick carpet and toward the sound of the voices.

Silently, I pull the door open and look out into the hallway.

My eyes widen when I take in the size of the hallway. It's not exactly what I was expecting.

Taking another step, I discover the reason for the space.

At the very end are large windows that showcase the view of trees beyond. The moon is sitting high in the sky, shining through the trees and creating a mass of eerie shadows.

It's hauntingly beautiful, and I can help think that it's fitting for the situation we're currently in.

But while the view might be impressive, it's the two people sitting on the couch before the windows that really steal my attention.

Reid looks as dangerous and as commanding as usual, even while trying to relax. He's got one ankle resting on the other knee and his arms stretched across the back of the cushions. But his body is anything but relaxed. His muscles are pulled tight, and his jaw is taut as he listens to the woman talk beside him.

I'm close enough to hear her words now, but I can't latch onto any of them. Instead, all I hear is the soft pitch of her voice as something uncomfortable prickles at my skin as I watch them together.

Reid might be tense, but his familiarity with this woman shines bright in the way he watches her.

My stomach knots as my temperature rises.

I don't realize I'm moving closer to them until something makes them both turn toward me, and I discover just how far away from the door I am.

"Shit." Reid gasps, sounding very unlike him, before he jumps to his feet and rushes over.

"I'm okay," I croak as the warmth of his giant hands burns through JD's shirt to my upper arms.

He looms over me, his presence huge and unforgiving, and the second I look up, my eyes locking in his dark and deadly ones, my knees give out.

"Alana." He growls, catching me long before I hit the floor.

Scooping me up into his strong arms, he holds me close against his chest.

His masculine scent fills my nose and I'm powerless but to rest my head against his shoulder as he stands there frozen.

"You should take her back to bed," the woman suggests.

Despite the effect her presence has on me, her voice is soft and caring.

It confuses the hell out of me.

Who is she?

There's a niggle of awareness in the depths of my brain like I already know the answer, but I can't grasp it.

"No," I whimper, the word falling from my lips before my brain has registered the thought.

"You should be sleeping," Reid warns, his voice is quiet, but I feel the vibration of it through his chest.

"Please," I whisper, although I've no idea what I'm asking for.

He hesitates but after a couple of seconds, he walks back to the couch and sits down.

The whole time, the other woman watches us with wide, curious eyes.

"Would you like anything to eat or drink?" she asks.

I part my lips to respond, but Reid beats me to it. "Water, coffee, and crackers. She didn't eat any before."

"You got it, Boss," the woman teases, saluting him before spinning on her heels and descending the stairs with a little more flounce than I'd like to see when I can barely stand.

I keep my eyes on her glossy dark hair until she disappears from my sight, but I still don't look away.

"Who is she?" I ask, unable to mask how I feel about having another woman here.

I've never been a jealous person.

Or more so... I didn't realize I was one.

The only man I've ever wanted was Mav, and he never, ever gave me a reason to question his loyalty.

Reid though... sitting here in his arms now, I realize that I don't really know him.

Unlike JD, he's held himself back from day one.

Yes, there might have been a couple of chinks in his armor, mainly that day in the gym when his resolve not to touch me cracked, or the night in the hallway when I tried to outrun my nightmares but other than that, he's been a rock.

I never stopped to think that the reason might be another woman.

"Oh, Pet," he muses, shifting beneath me to get comfortable. "I think I like this look on you."

A deep frown mars my brow.

"What look?"

His deep chuckle irritates me, but I don't have the energy to do anything about it.

"You sure you don't want me to take you back to bed?" he asks, although he doesn't so much as attempt to move.

Snuggling deeper into his warmth and scent, I shake my head.

"Will you... will you just... hold me?" I ask hesitantly.

He stills, sucking in a breath that he never releases.

Seconds tick by as I wait for a response, or to be thrown on the floor for even suggesting it.

But when his answer comes, it's not what I'm expecting.

"Whatever you need," he says quietly, his lips so close to the top of my head his warm breath sends a wave of warmth surging down my body.

His hold on me tightens and he finally releases his breath.

Silence falls between us, but it's not uncomfortable. The opposite in fact.

I know he's looking at me. My skin tingles with awareness, but at no point do I return his attention or let him know that I sense his stare. Instead, I keep my eyes on the trees outside, watching as they sway in the wind.

Noise comes from downstairs as the woman must crash

around in the kitchen, but he still never explains who she is or why she's here.

He trusts her, that much is obvious. Reid doesn't just let anyone into his inner circle. So the fact she's here and his brothers don't seem to be speaks volumes.

Eventually, the sound of delicate footsteps can be heard and in only seconds, we're rejoined by the beautiful woman who had all of Reid's attention not so long ago.

If she's shocked that I'm still sitting on his lap, wrapped in his arms, then she doesn't show it, well, not with anything more than a curious look at the two of us.

"One coffee, as hot as the sun," she says, shooting Reid an amused look before placing the tray in her hands on the coffee table. "A second more normal one, water, and crackers."

"Thanks." Reid growls.

She studies the two of us again, before tucking a lock of her hair behind her ear.

The way it shines even under the soft lighting makes me cringe.

I haven't had the chance to look in a mirror yet, but I can only imagine how bad I look.

"If none of you need anything else, I'm going to head out. I've got some vermin to chase."

Reid shifts beneath me.

"I think we're good for now. Just gonna hang tight. Heal."

"You got it. I've spoken to a few guys, they'll be here as soon as they can."

"Appreciate it."

"Okay, well. I'll be in touch," she promises, backing away. "I'll bring supplies," she adds before disappearing down the stairs again. Only a minute or so later, what I can only assume is the front door slams closed, plunging the house into silence.

Reid makes no move to get his coffee, which I know must be killing him.

Hating myself for doing it, I begin to climb off his lap, so he can indulge in his favorite treat. But the second my ass slides from his thigh, his grip on me tightens and I'm hauled back onto his lap.

"What are you doing?" He warns.

"Giving you space to drink."

"I have space," he argues before leaning around me and grabbing the bottle of water and crackers and placing them on my lap.

Happy that I have what I need, he leans again and snags his coffee.

"What?" he asks when I just stare at him in disbelief.

I blink for a few seconds, unable to find my voice.

"Do you want me here?" I ask

"We're safe here, Pet. They won't find you this time, I fucking swear."

My eyes bounce between his tired ones and the jealousy I felt at seeing him with whoever she is finally ebbs away.

He's sitting here with you in his lap, not chasing her.

The faintest smile twitches at my lips.

"That wasn't what I meant," I whisper.

His lips part and his brows pinch, but reality hits him before he can question me.

"Pet," he breathes, still ignoring his precious coffee in favor of looking into my eyes, "I'm so fucking sorry."

My breath catches at the sincerity in those four words.

There can't be many people in the world who've heard that tone from the notorious son of Victor Harris.

"I thought that you'd be safe there."

My brows dip in confusion.

"You knew?" I whisper. "You knew where we were?"

"Pet," he breathes.

"It was your cabin, wasn't it?"

His eyes drop from mine.

"You organized for us to leave in the middle of the night. You were trying to protect us."

His throat ripples on a thick swallow.

"For the good it did," he mutters under his breath.

"We're okay," I whisper.

His head snaps up, his eyes blazing with fire.

"He had you in a cage, Alana. Mav, he—"

Regret darkens his eyes before he looks away again, focusing on his coffee.

He takes a sip, not so much as wincing as the still-steaming liquid hits his lips.

Following his move, I lift the bottle of water and swallow down a huge mouthful, letting it soothe my raw throat.

My stomach growls, and on instinct, I reach for a cracker, nibbling the corner.

These two men have had a rivalry that has lasted their entire lives. The way Mav used to talk about Reid made me think that it wasn't something that would ever change.

He might never have been able to explain the reason why he hated Reid. It was all face-value things that stemmed from childhood. But I never got the impression that it was something that Mav would get over easily.

But seeing them together at Reid's place. Watching them find some kind of even footing, it's been quite incredible.

I'm not stupid, I know that they're not going to go from

enemies to BFFs in the blink of an eye. But having the same enemy. One so much more powerful than their hatred of each other, well... it might just be the start of something beautiful.

Or I might just be crazy.

Seeing that hatred, that anger in Reid's eyes now though. Feeling the tension that's locking up his body. I'd hazard a guess that he's hurting over what Mav has suffered just like I am.

I'm not sure when exactly we joined the same team. Maybe it was the moment I finally confessed everything, or maybe it was before that. Maybe it was from the moment I was first thrown into Reid's cell. But that's exactly what this feels like. It's not something I've ever really experienced before.

Sure, I had Kristie. But she was never fully aware of what our lives were really like. And then I had Mav. We were a team. Both of us focused on the end goal of shedding some corrupt Hawk blood and then running off into the sunset. But it was just the two of us, and as nice as the dream was, I realize now that that's exactly what it was.

We couldn't go up against the mighty Victor Harris and win. It was never going to matter what intel the two of us managed to dig up.

But now... I've got not one, but three fierce and deadly Hawks behind me. Fighting both with me and for me.

A true team.

That thought makes butterflies flutter wildly in my belly and a warmth spread from my chest.

"I swear to you, I tried to protect you." He clears his throat before looking up and holding my eyes. "Both of you."

"I believe you. Thank you for coming for us."

"I'd have been there days ago if I could find you."

I try to smile, I really do. I appreciate the shit out of what he's saying, but I just can't manage it.

"You want another cracker?" he asks when he notices that I've nibbled through a whole one. "Or your coffee?"

I think for a moment, trying to decide if my stomach can handle either of those suggestions.

Shaking my head, I take another sip of my water.

"Tell me what you need, Pet. Anything. I'll make it happen," he promises fiercely.

My eyes burn and my nose itches with emotion.

Who knew this cold, twisted gangster actually possessed a heart under all his layers of impenetrable armor?

Ripping my eyes from him, I glance down at myself, wincing at the state of both JD's shirt and my dirty legs.

Suddenly, the memory of their hands on my body makes me want to claw my own skin off.

"I need a bath," I blurt. "A really hot one."

Leaning over, he abandons his mug before shifting me slightly.

"Now that is something I can do."

In seconds, I'm in his arms again and we're walking through a door to my right.

The second we're engulfed by darkness, I panic and cling tighter to him. Hating those memories from our time in that aircraft hangar consumes me so violently.

Alana's body trembles violently in my arms. For a moment, I've no idea what causes the sudden fear to rip through her. But then I find the light switch and illuminate the room. She noticeably relaxes, but I don't.

My muscles that are already aching from being so tense only lock up tighter as realization dawns.

I can't say I'm surprised. It's not a secret that I learned quite a few of my tricks from our father. And light torture was always one of his favorites. It just seems he went for the blackout version this time.

I can only imagine the effect it had on both Alana and Mav, knowing that each other was close, suffering but not being able to see them.

"It's okay, Pet. I've got you," I assure her, cradling her slim body against my chest.

It should feel alien, looking after someone like this, but I find it weirdly easy.

Usually, I'm doing everything I can to make people

hurt, to force them to bend to my will. To break them down and get whatever I need from them.

But right now, I'm trying to keep her together.

The only person I've ever tried to hold together before is JD. And I think we all know how successful I've been with that.

My regret over everything that's happened multiplies again.

Everyone around me has been hurt because of me.

All of this is my fault. My unrelenting need to ruin my father and take over this town has done this.

JD nearly died. Again.

Mav has been tortured and punished for trying to protect someone he loves.

And Alana has been forced to revisit her nightmares, as if it isn't bad enough she can't escape them whenever she closes her eyes. She's just had days of experiencing them firsthand again.

"Are you going to be okay here?" I ask, hating how rough my voice is as I lower her to the counter.

But then she looks up at me with watery, terrified eyes, and I'm instantly flooded with relief that she can see it.

I've always prided myself in being a cold-hearted monster who can do whatever it takes to get the job done.

I don't regret that. I've achieved almost everything I've ever wanted by being that ruthless bastard.

But it's not all I am. Not really. And right now, I think Alana needs to see that more than anything.

She nods and I take a step back.

The whimper that spills from her lips as I remove my touch from her is quiet. If the house weren't so silent then I might miss it. But I don't. Instead, it wraps around my chest and makes it hard to breathe.

Cupping her face in my hands, I stare into her eyes.

"I'm not leaving. Not unless you want me to."

She shakes her head. The movement is so slight that I wouldn't know she'd done it if I couldn't feel it.

"I'm going to run you a bath, okay?" She nods. "We're going to fix this, Pet. All of it."

Her eyes fill with tears as she stares back at me. But this time she doesn't respond.

As I take a step back and turn toward the huge tub that has been positioned to make the most of the view beyond the huge windows, I can't help but wonder if it's because she doesn't believe me.

But then, why should she?

All I've done is hurt her. Even when I was trying not to. She ended up locked up in a cage and subjected to whatever our fathers deemed a worthy punishment.

My hand trembles as I reach for the faucet. Clenching my fist, I try to stop it so she doesn't see just how affected I am by all of this.

She needs one of us to be strong. And right now, I don't have a choice. That person has to be me.

The rush of water fills the air and I reach for a bottle of bubble bath that is sitting on the side of the tub.

Twisting the top, I tip the bottle and allow more than half of the contents to mix with the water, immediately filling the room with the scent of flowers.

After checking the temperature, I turn back to Alana.

She's sitting exactly where I left her, but instead of watching me, her gaze is locked on her hands that are resting in her lap.

They're dirty like the rest of her, showing just a hint of what she's been through in the past few days.

Under her nails is black, and I can't help hoping that it's

dried blood, that she managed to take a strike at at least one of them and leave a permanent reminder that she's not the weak little girl they can bend to their will.

The image of her laid out and tied up over that table when we stormed in fills my mind and acid rushes up my throat.

I've no idea how far they took it. Her body is covered in bruises that could be evidence of a whole host of things. But the position she was in doesn't paint any kind of picture I want to look at and it explains the black, empty look that's been in her eyes since the moment we found her.

I'd already planned a hundred and one painful ways to make our fathers pay for what they've done to all of us. But seeing that, experiencing firsthand what they'd been doing to her all those years.

Fuck.

It unleashed something so potent inside me. My need for vengeance is burning a whole new kind of hot, and there is no fucking way any of those motherfuckers is going to get away with it.

We're going to regroup and heal. And then we are going to take them down.

We're going to make them hurt in ways they've only ever imagined, and we're going to enjoy every fucking second of it.

They might be sick, but they need to remember the kinds of kids they raised.

"Are you ready?" I ask, stuffing all my hate and bloodlust back inside the box it needs to remain in for now as I step back up to her.

Lifting her eyes from her lap, they find mine. The look in them guts me and leaves me speechless.

It would be easy to promise her again that I'll make all of this right.

But that isn't going to be enough.

I'm pretty sure nothing ever will be after everything she's endured.

I guess all I can do from here on out is try and make up for the pain I've caused.

"Are you sure you want me to be doing this? I could go and wake JD and—"

"No," she says in a rush. "It needs to be you."

Her words and the trust she openly gives me despite everything slams into me like a truck, stealing my air and any response I might have.

Why me? Why after everything you have endured because of me do you want me to do this now?

And I'm not even talking about the last few weeks. If I'd have seen what Mav had all those years ago, then I could have done something about all of this back then. Or at least, I could have tried to.

My eyes shutter, unable to focus on the amount of hurt and suffering I can see in the depths of her blue eyes as I reach for the bottom of JD's shirt.

My knuckles brush her thighs and she gasps at the contact.

I know exactly why. I feel it, too.

She might feel a little broken right now, hell, she has every right to, but her fire is still there. It lights up a little extra hope inside me that she's going to be okay. That she's going to get through this.

As slowly and as gently as I possibly can, I peel the fabric up her body.

It's not the first time I've seen her naked, and it's not the first time she's taken my breath away, but this time, it's for an entirely different reason.

The bruising I saw littering her skin yesterday has darkened. They cover her shoulders, upper arms, ribs, hips, and thighs.

I stare at each one, some more than obviously finger marks, with poison spilling through my veins.

"Please, don't hate me," she whispers, curling in on herself in an attempt to hide.

"W-what?" I stutter unable to comprehend why she'd even say that.

"Their handprints, they'll fade and—"

Dropping the shirt to the floor, I take her face in my hands again.

If I thought it would be the right thing to do, I'd kiss her.

Hell, I'd do anything to show that she's still the same woman who snuck out of my house with Mav with so much passion and determination for taking those motherfuckers down. This is only a blip.

We all have to believe that.

"You don't owe me any kind of explanation, Pet. What I can see only makes me hate them more, not you."

Her breath catches as she continues to hold my eyes.

"You're a survivor, Alana. A fighter. Your strength is incredible."

She shakes her head, or at least tries to. "No, I'm not—"

"You are," I cut her off fiercely. "I might not know what happened with them, but I do know that you'll have fought as hard as you could. And you'd have done it for Mav, not for yourself. You'd have done it for JD too."

I don't mention myself, because I think we both know that she has every reason to hate me.

Her eyelids lower, refusing to accept my words.

"I've never met anyone like you, Pet. You're one of a kind."

The smallest of smiles twitches at her lips, sending a tsunami of relief rushing through me.

She's going to get through this.

"Come on," I say softly. "Let's get you cleaned up."

I lift her from the counter as gently as I can. I don't want to cause her any more pain than she's already in, nor do I want to add to the bruises.

I might have had thoughts about leaving marks on her, hell, the bars through her nipples are proof enough that I want her to remember that she's been at my mercy.

But not like this.

Lowering her feet to the floor in front of the sink, I reach for one of the new toothbrushes and load it up with toothpaste, all the while keeping my arms around her to help hold her up.

"I can stand," she argues.

"I know," I agree without moving an inch.

Dropping my hands to her hips, I continue to hold her as she brushes her teeth, then I sweep her off her feet again and lower her into the almost full tub of bubbles.

The sigh that spills from her lips makes goose bumps erupt over my entire body.

The second she's submerged, she curls herself into a ball and just stares ahead.

She looks so small, so vulnerable. It makes my chest ache.

I stand awkwardly, not really knowing what to do now that I've done as she asked.

Reaching up, I rub the back of my neck. The need to do

more burns through me, but I have no idea what that looks like.

"D-do you want me to go?" I ask, taking a step back from the bathtub.

"No," she cries, water sloshing everywhere as she turns toward me. Blood drains from her face, leaving her pale and terrified. "Please. Don't."

Her voice is so weak and broken, I've no choice but to move closer again.

She relaxes instantly, although not as much as she needs to.

With her eyes still locked on mine, she slides forward in the water, leaving a space behind her.

"Pet," I warn, my mind spinning with her silent suggestion. "I really don't think..." My words trail off when her eyes fill with tears, one spilling from the side and rushing down her cheek.

Fuck.

"Shit. Are you sure?" I ask, suddenly second-guessing my offer of giving her anything.

She nods before resting her chin on her knees and gazing up at me, looking so incredibly lost.

Shaking my head in disbelief, I reach behind me and drag my shirt off.

Her eyes glaze as she watches me with blank eyes, it's as if she's staring straight through me. It's a look I never want to see on her again.

I want her to look at me like she has in the past. I want the fire, the desire, the unfiltered need in her eyes as I expose myself to her.

I hesitate with my fingers on the waistband of my jeans, waiting for her to stop me, to tell me that I should go and get JD instead. But she never does.

She just waits for me to man the fuck up and do as I promised.

Closing my eyes for a beat, I toe off my boots and shove my jeans and boxers down my legs. Her gaze never leaves me, and I hate that her attention makes my blood heat and my cock stirs. I should be thinking about her and taking care of her instead of being the selfish asshole I usually am.

Finally, she moves, and her eyes focus. Her attention makes my skin prickle as she takes in my body before finding my face.

"Last chance to change your mind," I say, although my offer is weak at best.

Now I'm naked, all I can think about is stepping in behind her, pulling her into my arms, and doing whatever I can to put her back together.

I've never bathed with someone else before. Hell, I barely ever step into a bathtub alone. Don't have time to lie about in my own dirt. But suddenly, the thought of doing so is more than appealing.

When she thankfully doesn't say anything, I move closer and step in behind her.

I suck in a breath through my teeth as the heat of the water scalds my skin to the point I almost pull it back out.

"Isn't it a bit hot?" I ask, reaching for the facet to blast some cold in.

I know she said she wanted it hot, but fuck. I misjudged the temperature by a mile.

"No," she barks, reaching for my arm to stop me. "Leave it. I need it." The confidence in her tone ensures my hand falls away, and I plunge my other leg into the water.

I might love my coffee steaming hot, but apparently, I'm not as much of a masochist as I thought because I'm getting very little satisfaction from the burn.

But that doesn't stop me from sinking the rest of my body into the scalding water.

The second my balls make contact, all the air rushes from my lungs, but it's still not enough to stop me.

And thank fuck it doesn't because the second I slide my legs on either side of Alana's hips, she leans back into me.

Sliding lower, I wrap my arms around her and take her with me.

The moment we're settled and she's comfortably snuggled on my chest, she breaks.

Her body trembles violently and her loud sobs fill the air.

I've never felt more useless in all my life, but I do the only thing I can, I hold her tighter and hope that it's enough.

REID

I've no idea how long Alana sobs on my chest. All I do know is that I have to let some of the water out and refill the tub to keep it warm and that the sun began to rise behind the trees in the distance.

It has all the makings of the most romantic morning ever. But reality stops that from being the case. I'm not even sure if she notices the sunrise as her tears continue to flood my chest and her soft cries fill the room.

Other than twisting the faucet for hot water, I never let her go.

Eventually, her sobs subside and the trembling ceases.

I start to wonder if she's fallen asleep on my chest. I wouldn't put it past her. She must be exhausted after everything she's been through.

But suddenly she speaks, startling me.

"Who is she?" she whispers.

"Who's—" I begin to ask before realization hits. "Aubrey. She's an acquaintance of mine."

Shifting, she tips her head to look up at me and lifts a brow.

The sight of her bloodshot, red-ringed eyes does things to me.

I've seen so many women cry over the years, but never has one affected me like this one.

I almost miss the silent accusation in her expression as I lose myself in her watery depths and my own regret.

"A friend," I finally add.

She nods, although I can still see her suspicion over my relationship with Aubrey.

"There has never been anything between us. You've nothing to worry about," I assure her.

Her entire body tenses at my words.

"I'm not worried," she mutters quietly. "Just curious."

"Sure you are," I tease lightly. "That's why you wanted to claw her eyes out earlier, because you were curious."

"I did not," she argues, showing me a little bit of her fire. "I just didn't know who she was, and she was here and—"

"She found you, Pet. We wouldn't be here right now if it weren't for her. We owe her everything."

All the air and fight drain out of her.

"I met her a few years ago. She's a honey trap," I explain, giving her the truth. "I paid her to get close to Victor," I confess with a wince.

"I thought you said she was a friend?" she asks, her brows pinching.

"Yeah," I mutter, knowing exactly what she's getting at. "But she's good at her job. And I trust her."

Alana nods, accepting my words.

"Only Reid Harris would send a friend in to fuck his father for intel."

I internally cringe as she lays it out so bluntly.

"You got a better idea, Pet?" I ask, trailing my fingers up her arm before tucking a lock of hair behind her ear.

She doesn't respond. She doesn't need to.

Instead, we fall into another comfortable silence as I continue tracing patterns on her shoulder.

"Why has JD got a bandage on his arm?" she finally asks.

I knew it was coming. He'd crashed on the couch in the master bedroom with it fully on display since he gave Alana his shirt.

While they were all sleeping, I tried to come up with what I'd say if she were to ask me about it before she did him.

But I never did come up with a good answer.

"I fucked up the night you left, Pet," I confess, my voice cracking with regret.

"You did that?" she gasps.

"Not physically, no. I got called to Mexico to meet Luciana Rivera, and I left in the middle of the night."

"Right?" she asks, her brow furrowing as she pieces the puzzle together.

"I left J a note but he never saw it. Instead, he woke up alone. You and Mav had gone, he couldn't find me..." My words trail off as memories of all the blood fill my mind.

"Reid," she whispers, fear laced through her voice.

"Ezra found him. H-he... he nearly—" My words cut off when she presses her face into my chest. "He's okay. Doc fixed him up good."

"I found a notebook he started writing in," I confess.

"I suggested that," she mumbles against my skin. "I thought it might help get out whatever it is that haunts him."

"He told you about that?"

She shakes her head.

"No," she says, shifting around and settling back in my chest. "But I see it."

"He lost someone a few years ago," I explain. It's his story to tell really, but something tells me that he won't mind me giving her just a little bit of the story. "It broke him."

"Loss has a way of doing that," she says sadly, reminding me of something positive I need to tell her.

"Luciana gave me a list of names and locations of the men involved and where some of the girls are."

She sits up so suddenly, water sloshes over the sides, spilling over the tiled floor.

"You found her?" she asks with wide, hopeful eyes.

Reaching for her hand, I twist our fingers together and tug her closer again.

"One step at a time, Pet," I say softly.

She sighs. There's so much pain in it, it cuts me right down to my soul.

"I know. I just... want to try and make it right. Give her the life she always deserved."

When I pull her closer again, she comes happily, falling against my chest and staring up at me.

Some of the fear has vanished from her eyes in favor of hope.

I just pray that I'm not going to have to be the one to shatter it.

"Thank you," she whispers, sliding her hand around my back and holding me as tightly as I am her. "For a moment there, I didn't think you were going to come."

Leaning down, I press a kiss to the top of her head.

The scent of that hangar, the pain they endured still linger.

"Sit up and turn around," I say reluctantly.

Despite the hot water surrounding us, I feel cold the second her skin leaves mine.

Doing as she's told, she turns her back to me.

Reaching for the cup that's sitting on the vanity, I fill it with hot water and instruct her to tip her head back.

A giant blob of shampoo comes next and I begin massaging it into her blonde hair, eliciting a series of quiet whimpers from her.

"You do this often?" she whispers.

"Never."

"Well, you're good at it," she praises, and thank fuck she can't see me because the widest, goofiest smile spreads across my face.

Who knew that something as simple as washing someone's hair could give me the warm fuzzies?

"Tip back," I say, trying to rein myself in.

She does as she's told and cup by cup, I rinse the bubbles from her hair before repeating my previous actions with the conditioner.

Just like before, she quietly moans. She might not be doing them in a sexual way but fuck if those little sounds don't go straight to my dick. And no matter how much I try to convince myself to think of anything but the fact she's sitting before me naked, I still end up hard as fuck for her.

Licking my lips, I remember the moment of weakness I had in my gym with her before I released Mav from the basement.

I've tried to banish it from my thoughts ever since.

Nothing good would have come from obsessing over what could have been if I weren't such a pussy and pulled away. Or from thinking about how badly I want to finish what we started.

She doesn't say another word, instead, just lets me work, and the second I tell her that I'm done, she curls back up on my chest again.

We need to get out. Our skin is pruned, and the water is going cold again, but I can't bring myself to say anything or move.

"It's beautiful here," Alana whispers, staring out the windows as the early morning sun shines into the room.

"Yeah," I agree.

"Where are we?"

"Hazard Grove," I confess.

"Hiding?"

"Laying low," I correct. I refuse to accept that we're hiding from anyone.

We'll return. But not until I'm confident that we can all fight. Fight and win.

Right now, everyone is suffering too much to even think about going into battle with Victor.

"They won't find us here. We can take as long as we need to recuperate and then we make our move."

"You really think we can take them."

"I don't think, Pet. I know."

She nods. I'm not sure if that's because she agrees with me, or just wants to, but I'm happy to assume it's the former.

"I want to be there when it happens. I won't accept being protected from it all, no matter how ugly it gets."

"Pet." I growl.

"I'm serious. I know you want them all dead. And rightly so, you have your own reasons. But they ruined my entire fucking life, Reid. Every single part of me has been tainted by them. I need to see them die. And I need them looking in my eyes as they do so."

It goes against everything I'm feeling to agree with her. I want to wrap her up in cotton and keep her away from those twisted cunts.

Just the thought of her having to be in the same room as them again sends a wave of fire so hot through me I'm surprised the water around us doesn't start boiling.

But at the same time, I can't say no to her.

"I'll make sure you're a part of everything we do from here on out. This is your fight just as much as it is mine."

Twisting around, she sits between my thighs. Her skin is still red from the temperature of the water when we first got in, her hair is dark and hanging limply around her face. Her eyes are bloodshot, the shadows beneath them dark and haunting. Her bruises still more than obvious. But fuck, she's beautiful.

She might think she looks a mess, but she couldn't be more wrong.

My eyes fall to her full breasts, to the pink piercings through her nipples, and my dick jerks beneath the water.

I've wanted a lot of things in my life, but I'm not sure I've ever wanted any of them as much as I want Alana.

My eyes lift to her face, and I quickly discover that I wasn't the only one checking out the view.

It's long seconds before she finds my eyes, and when she does, the most adorable blush colors her cheeks.

A small coy smile plays on her lips, allowing me to see just a hint of the feisty woman I first locked up in my basement.

It might have only been two weeks ago, but it feels like forever. Like she's always been a part of mine and JD's lives. She may as well have been for the impact she's had on both of us.

Something crackles between us, the air charged with

electricity, the pull I've always felt toward her becoming harder and harder to ignore.

She's dropped her guard and let me in. She's allowed me to hold her when she's at her weakest and fuck if that doesn't call to me in a way I never expected.

My heart rate picks up as she leans a little closer, her eyes dropping to my lips momentarily.

There's a little voice in the back of my head that screams for me to stop, to end this before it starts. She's not in the right frame of mind to be making any decision about things like this, and I would be an asshole to take advantage.

Hell, I am an asshole.

Leaning even closer, the scent of her freshly-washed hair fills my nose as her warm palm presses against my chest.

"Pet," I whisper in a pathetic attempt to stop her.

Her eyes flash with excitement, I'm so fucking relieved to see something other than pain and fear that any restraint I did have flies out of the window.

Reaching out, I wrap my hand around the back of her neck, ready to anchor her to me and stop her from changing her mind.

Her fresh minty breath rushes over my face as her lips brush over mine in the gentlest kiss I think I've ever experienced. But as desperate as I am to take more, I hold off, giving her control.

With our eyes locked, she moves again, finally closing the remaining bit of space between us. My heart lurches in my chest and my dick jerks in excitement, but just before we dive in, a roar rips through the room, forcing us to jump apart.

"ALANA? Fuck. ALANA?" JD bellows a few seconds

before the door swings open, crashing back against the wall to allow a distressed looking JD inside. "Oh my God. Fuck. FUCK," he barks, lifting his injured arm to cover his racing heart with this hand. "I thought you'd gone again."

The first thing I think of when I come to is her. Not that it comes as any kind of shock. She's always the first thing I think about.

With her scent in my nose, I reach for her. But when my hand falls, my eyes spring open and everything comes crashing down.

Frantically, I look around, trying to remember where I am.

The phone call from Aubrey.

Meeting her in the clearing and discovering where Alana and Mav were.

The aircraft hangar.

Alana strapped to the table.

Mav's wounds.

I shoot up, my eyes on the bed where I remember her falling asleep last night. I'd wanted her with me, locked in my arms, so I could keep her close, but I was achingly aware that she was in pain and the last thing I wanted to do was make it worse, so after she had a drink, I laid her out beside her husband and allowed her to rest, without being the selfish cunt I really wanted to be.

I sat there for hours watching her. For a while, she slept peacefully, but it didn't take all that long before the nightmares came for her.

It ripped me in two to see her suffering when she was meant to be resting.

As much as it hurt to watch her experience her nightly terrors back at our house, it's worse now knowing that they've been close to her, that they've touched her.

Previously, they were memories of years gone by. But now...

I thought I hated Victor before, but since learning the truth about how they've treated the woman I've fallen for... fuck. I want to skin them alive, making them suffer in every single painful way I've learned over the years.

Even that won't be enough.

Nothing will be enough.

Nothing will take her pain away. Nothing will rid her of the nightmares.

Finding her side of the bed empty makes my stomach bottom out and panic shoots through my veins.

No.

Jumping to my feet, I rip my eyes away from the bed where Mav is still sleeping on his front and scan the room for any hint that she's here.

"ALANA?" I roar, my hands trembling with fear.

A familiar tingle begins in the tips of my fingers, but I can't focus on that.

"Fuck. ALANA?" I shout again before rushing out of the room.

The sun is shining through the huge windows as I run

into the hallway. There are mugs on the table in front of the couch and a plate of crackers. But she's not there.

I pause, desperately trying to listen for voices. But the blood rushing past my ears is too loud.

I know that I shouldn't panic. I know we're meant to be safe here and that she was in no state to run. But that doesn't matter.

Clenching my fists, I will myself to calm down. Nothing good ever happens when I freak the fuck out.

But I can't help it.

"Alana," I whimper desperately, pathetically.

Taking a deep breath, I look around, trying to think rationally.

But then I notice the scent in the air.

My eyes dart toward an ajar door on the other side of the hallway, and I rush forward.

Slamming my hand down on the door, it swings open with ease, crashing back against the wall.

The relief that floods me is overwhelming as I find both Reid and Alana staring at me with wide eyes from the bathtub.

Lifting my trembling hand, I cover my racing heart as the room spins around me. "Oh my God. Fuck. FUCK."

Focusing on Alana's eyes, I beg for the calm to come. And thankfully, after only a second or two, it does.

"I thought you'd gone again," I murmur quietly.

"Julian," she breathes, shifting away from Reid, keeping her attention trained on me. Although, it only takes a few seconds for her eyes to drop to the bandage on my wrist.

Shit.

My heart picks up speed again at the thought of having to confess to what I did. Of explaining just how badly I lost my fucking mind when she disappeared on me. When they all disappeared on me.

But then her brow furrows and sadness washes through her features and reality hits.

"You told her." It's not a question. It doesn't need to be. The answer is written all over Alana's face. And it doesn't get any better when I turn to my best friend.

He looks guilty as fuck.

"J," he starts.

"Did you tell her everything?" I interrupt.

"What? No, of course I didn't. I just... she saw the bandage. I wasn't going to lie to her. There's been enough of that bullshit already."

My eyebrow quirks. "You fucking think? Jesus," I mutter, scrubbing my hand down my face as I look between the two of them. "The whole reason we're here and in this fucking state is because of the secrets and lies."

Neither of them says anything. What is there to say to the harsh truth of the situation?

Changing tactics, I take a step closer, getting a better look at the two of them in the tub.

"What are you two doing, exactly?"

Alana reaches up to tuck a lock of wet hair behind her ear, while Reid swallows thickly.

"Just helping," Reid finally mutters.

"Helping. Sure."

"I'm not in the mood for a cock measuring contest," Alana deadpans. "And the water is cold."

Before either of us can help her stand, she rises from the water.

My mouth runs dry as she reveals her body to me, but the overwhelming hit of desire is squashed the second I take in the dark bruises covering her skin.

She stands there, allowing me to take her in, letting me see everything she's been through.

Anger shoots through my veins and my fists clench as I desperately try to keep my shit together.

When I finally make it back up to her face, she's got her head lowered in shame.

"Fuck that," I bark, reaching behind me for one of the towels that's folded up on a shelf. Clutching it in one hand, I hold my other out to help her from the tub.

The second she's standing in front of me, I wrap her in the fluffy towel and then pull her into my body, holding her tight.

Dipping my lips to her ear, I whisper so that only she can hear, "None of it matters, little dove. All that does is this right now."

She sucks in a shaky breath but doesn't respond.

"Enjoy your bubble bath, bro," I say, shooting Reid a glance before I lead Alana from the room.

I want to take her away and keep her to myself. I want to tell her, show her how those bruises marring her body don't change anything for me. I know she thinks they do, but they don't. But I can't. I can't keep her away from Mav.

Leading her back into the room we all spent the night in, her steps falter when her eyes land on her husband. He hasn't moved an inch since we put him there last night.

"He's going to be okay," I whisper before pressing a kiss on her temple. "Go and sit down, I'll find you something to wear."

She does as she's told, and once I know she's settled, I open the closet and find the bag that Aubrey abandoned in there when she arrived yesterday. Pulling out some underwear, a pair of leggings and a tank, I walk back to my girl.

She stares at the items with her lip curled in disgust.

"Aubrey assured us they'd fit you," I tell her.

"I'm sure they're great," she mutters, holding her hand out for them. "I just prefer your shirts."

I can't help but smile at her confession. "I prefer you in my shirts, too. Or nothing."

Immediately, she averts her gaze from mine.

"Julian."

Reaching out, I cup her cheek, bringing her back to face me.

"Don't hide from me, Dove. You have nothing to hide or be ashamed of."

Her eyes shutter, but she fights it as I hold her eyes steady, begging her to believe my words.

"Let me help you," I whisper. "You're not alone anymore."

A hiccup of emotion bubbles up her throat and her eyes fill with tears.

Leaning forward, I kiss the tip of her nose before dropping to my knees before her.

Finding the panties, I hold them out for her to step into.

I desperately want to rip the towel away and see her, but I don't.

I've no idea what she's just been through, how bad it got. I'm more than willing to give her whatever time she needs to get her head straight.

Resting one hand on my head, she steps into the underwear and I tug them up her legs.

The leggings follow, and then I stand and pull the tank over her head.

Finally, I pull the towel away from her and discard it on the floor.

"Sit," I demand before rushing back to the bag and rummaging around inside.

Once I have what I need, I march back and encourage her to slide to the edge of the couch so I can sit behind her.

With a hairbrush locked in my hand, I begin brushing through her wet locks.

We sit in silence as I work, untangling the knots the last few days caused.

Eventually, a large shadow darkens the doorway a second before Reid appears with a towel wrapped around his waist.

Alana doesn't react to him, but I can tell from the way he sucks in a deep breath that they're looking at each other.

The air crackles between them until it becomes so thick, it's hard to breathe.

I've no idea what happened between them in the bathroom, but clearly, it was intense.

"I could get used to this," Alana finally whispers.

"You'd better. You're ours now. Isn't that right, Big Man?" I tease, using her nickname for Reid.

His shoulders tense, but he doesn't argue with me.

"You hungry?" he asks.

"Yeah," I agree.

He waits for Alana to say something, but when she remains mute, he just nods and disappears from the doorway, although not before he quickly checks on Mav.

Oh yeah, things are definitely changing around here.

With my fingers interlaced with Alana's, we slowly make our way downstairs.

The scent of bacon began wafting up the stairs about ten minutes ago, making my stomach growl so loudly, I finally got to see a smile on my girl's lips.

No words were said between us after I finished her hair, instead, she spun around, wrapped her arms around my neck and refused to let go. It was a really fucking good place to be.

I needed that connection just as much as she did.

But sadly, my need for food put an end to it.

It was only the beginning, I know that. But still, the second she pulled away, I mourned the loss of her touch.

"Hungry, little dove?" I ask as we hit the ground floor.

"I don't know," she confesses quietly. "I'm just... tired, I guess."

Wrapping my arm around her shoulder, I tug her into my side and hold her close.

"Oh wow," she gasps as we step into the kitchen.

I saw the house last night, but I can admit that with my girl by my side, I'm seeing it in a whole new light.

The kitchen is huge. Although, not as big as Reid's—of course. And the view out of the wall of windows is as incredible as upstairs.

There's a large deck fully equipped with furniture and a built-in grill and firepit, and then there is nothing but trees.

My idea of heaven.

I just wish it were cold enough to light a fire.

Reid looks over as we step into the room before lifting the pan from the stove and placing bacon on the plates stacked with pancakes waiting beside him.

"Just in time," he says, before expertly picking up all three and placing them on the table.

Pulling out Alana's chair, I wait for her to take a seat before doing the same, much to Reid's amusement.

"You're such an asshole," he mutters before stuffing a piece of bacon in his mouth.

"Jealous, bro?" I tease, relieved as fuck that we can still joke despite the seriousness of the situation we're in. I'm not sure I'd cope if I couldn't crack a joke.

He scoffs. "You're forgetting which one of us had her naked in the bath this morning."

Alana shakes her head as she pokes at a pancake on her plate.

"Who's the asshole now?"

"What? I took care of you good. Isn't that right, Pet?"

It takes her a second to look up, but when she does, her expression softens as she focuses on Reid.

"You did a great job," she says softly.

He preens at her praise.

"Jesus, when did you hand your balls over to my dove, exactly?"

"Fuck off and eat your breakfast."

I bark out a laugh, loving that we can be unashamedly us right now.

I need it. So. Fucking. Bad.

Cutting off a little pancake with my fork, I reach for Alana's hand under the table.

"You need to eat, baby," I encourage.

When she turns to look at me, I hold my fork out and move it to her lips.

She hesitates, but after a few seconds, her mouth opens and she takes it.

And fuck if it doesn't make my dick jerk. Watching her lick the syrup from her lips doesn't help the situation either.

"Stop looking at me like that," she whispers.

"Like what?" I ask innocently.

"Like you want to eat me for breakfast," she mutters, turning to look back down at her own plate.

I shoot Reid a concerned look before reaching out and dragging her chair closer to me so I can wrap my arm around her.

"Baby, I'll always want to eat you for breakfast. Probably for the best you get used to it. Pretty sure big man over there has had similar thoughts this morning."

She tenses.

"You shouldn't," she says darkly, pushing her plate away. "I'm broken."

The screech of wood on wood rips through the air as she shoves her chair out behind her. Without another word, she takes off toward the doors that will lead her outside.

My heart drops into my stomach and I rush to stand so I can follow her.

"Stop," Reid demands, making my movements falter. "Just give her a minute."

"That's bullshit," I spit, unsure if I'm talking about his demand for me not to follow her, or the words she said before taking off. Quite honestly, it could be both.

"But—"

"I know you want to fix her, J. But it's going to take more than a cuddle and telling her you want to eat her pussy."

Irritation rushes through me, and I throw the fork in my hand across the table.

"I fucking know that," I seethe.

"Good. Now sit down and eat. You need the strength

just as much as she does. She'll still be here when you're done. And maybe then, she'll be willing to talk."

"She didn't talk to you this morning?" I ask, lowering my ass back to the chair like a good little soldier.

"A little. Mostly, she cried," he confesses, sending a wave of jealousy through me. I want to be the one to hold her as she breaks, and I want to be the one who puts her back together. Just like I hope she's going to be able to do for me.

"Fuck. I think that's worse."

"She's strong, J. But even the strongest of people have limits."

"You think... you think they ra—"

"I don't think so," he says in a rush, cutting off my final words before they spill free. "Does it matter if they did?"

"If you're questioning whether it makes me feel differently about her, then no, of course not. If you're asking if it means I want to hurt them more than I already do, then yes, it really fucking matters."

"Good. That's good," he mutters before shoveling another forkful of breakfast into his mouth.

"What's the plan now, then, Boss?"

He glances up at me as he chews.

That one looks says it all.

He hasn't got a fucking clue.

Brilliant.

33

ALANA

The warm fall air blows around me, but it does little to stop the goose bumps that have erupted over my skin.

Staring out at trees, I feel nothing but empty and broken.

Every time I close my eyes, all I see is them. They suck me back into their sick and twisted games and don't stop until I can no longer recognize the woman they've turned me into.

Being in the bath with Reid helped push them aside. So did cuddling with JD. But sitting at that table, doing something as normal as eating breakfast while the two of them bantered was just too much.

I came too close to losing everything...

Birds tweet up in the trees, and the browning leaves rustle as they prepare to fall.

Pulling my legs up, I wrap my arms around them and rest my chin on my knees.

It's so peaceful here. It's probably exactly what I need.

Or it would be if I could push past the nightmares and the fear.

I've no idea how much time passes as I sit here staring out at nothing. But eventually, the sound of a door opening behind me hits my ears and I prepare for company.

It's not that I don't want it. I do.

More than anything, I want to lose myself in their touch, but I'm scared.

Neither of them has shown any signs that they're disgusted by me now that I've been tainted again by those monsters, but I'm struggling to believe they truly feel that way.

Even now, hours after I've been rescued, I feel their touch burning into my skin.

Acid swirls in my stomach, burning up my throat as I think about what they did, what they might have done while I was unconscious.

"Dove?" a soft, welcome voice whispers.

When I look up, I gasp, finding that he's already standing right in front of me.

Lowering his ass to the coffee table, he threads his fingers together as if he needs to do so to stop him from reaching out to touch me.

I hate it. I hate that he's questioning everything.

Why can't he just sweep me off my feet, strip me naked, lay me out, and prove with actions that everything really is okay?

Shaking that fantasy from my head, I remember why he won't do that.

My skin burns again, my need to rip it clean from my body all-consuming.

Maybe they should have just killed me.

"Tell me how to fix this," JD begs, his eyes boring into mine.

A sob rips from my throat without permission.

Years ago, I hardly ever cried. No matter how bad it was, I always held it in. If Kristie saw I'd been crying, she'd have questions. Questions I wasn't willing to answer.

I could hide the cuts and bruises they caused, but I didn't stand a chance in hell of hiding the red-rimmed, bloodshot eyes that I knew would come from releasing all my hurt, anger, and frustration through tears.

Back then, I didn't have anyone to hold me, to ask me how to make things better. Anyone who knew I was broken didn't care about putting me back together. They just wanted to rip more strips off me until there was nothing left.

But now...

Another sob erupts, and this time, JD can't just sit and watch.

Dropping beside me, he lifts me onto his lap, giving me little choice but to straddle him. He holds me close, tucking my face into the crook of his neck.

Now I have people who care.

Men who want to make things better.

Men who don't want me hurting, suffering.

Men who give me everything I've ever wanted.

My sobs get louder as I cling to him, desperately trying to get us even closer, despite knowing that it's impossible.

He buries one hand into my wet hair, holding my head gently while the other—the one with the bandage on—slowly rubs up and down my back.

The only person who's ever held me like he meant it before was Mav, but with the way he held back, it was never this intimate.

I'm pretty sure I've never felt closer to another person as I do right now.

While my own pain might be unbearable, it seems I still have a little space to feel more because JD's is palpable.

"I'm sorry," I whisper into the warmth of his neck.

Unlike before I left, his jaw is covered in more than just a few days' stubble. It's clear that he hasn't been taking care of himself. However, not shaving barely scratches the surface of what he's been through by the sounds of it.

"Little dove," he chokes out, his voice rougher and more emotional than I've ever heard.

I try to lift my head from his neck, but he doesn't let me up.

I want to argue, but also, I'm more than happy to just snuggle here and soak up his warmth.

"You have nothing to apologize for. You haven't done anything wrong."

Sliding my hand from his neck, I move it down the length of his arm until my fingers brush the edge of his bandage.

He sucks in a breath, but when I gently pull his arm from my back and lift my head from his neck, he allows it.

Sitting up, I hold his arm between us, my fingers dancing over the fabric wrapped around his wound.

"Dove," he whispers so quietly, I question as to whether he actually said it or not.

Sucking in a breath, I lift my eyes from the bandage, but it soon rushes from my lungs when I find his eyes and the tear tracks down his cheeks.

"Julian?" I breathe, cupping his rough face in both my hands and leaning closer.

My brow touches his, our noses pressing together.

"I'm sorry," he whispers, his watery eyes holding mine.

Shifting my thumb, I press it against his lips, stopping him.

"Never," I tell him. "Not with me."

He nods but doesn't say anything for the longest time.

We stay exactly as we are, our heads touching, our breath mingling, and our darkness melding. Maybe together we'll be strong enough to fight it.

It's more than obvious that we can't do it alone.

"I warned you," he eventually confesses. "I said that you wouldn't like this side of me."

"Julian," I whisper, rolling my head against his. "There isn't a side of you that I don't like. It's not possible."

He gasps, his lips parting to allow the air in, and I make the most of it.

I've no idea if it's the right thing to do, but losing myself in someone else is the only way I've ever managed to block out all the pain. All I can hope is that I'm able to give him the kind of relief he's offered me in the past few weeks.

The second our lips brush, his hand returns to my back before sliding down to grab my ass.

I gasp, giving him access to plunge his tongue into my mouth.

Every single muscle in my body relaxes the second he deepens the kiss.

Tilting my head exactly how he wants me, he commands the kiss, taking everything he needs, and giving me everything I've been craving.

My time with Mav at the cabin was incredible. It was everything I've always wanted to have with him. But there was always a part of me that was missing. Or more so, a part that had been left behind.

Mav knew it too.

And it's not until this very moment that I discover just

how big a hole JD had left, or how big an effect he'd had on my life in such a short time.

My fingers slide into his short hair, my nails raking across his scalp and making him shiver with need beneath me.

Grinding my hips, I tease both of us as he begins to harden against me.

"Missed you, Dove," he moans into my mouth, "when I woke and you were gone—"

"I didn't leave you, Julian. Not really," I say, opening my eyes so that he can see the sincerity in my eyes.

"I know," he confesses against my lips. "Well, I know that now." His eyes close as a pained breath rushes over my face. "I'm a mess, Dove. You deserve so much more than what I have to offer you."

"Bullshit," I spit, the fierceness in my voice enough to make his eyes pop open again. "You're everything. You've—"

"I love you," he blurts.

It takes a couple of seconds for his words to register. But when they do, my entire body locks up and my eyes widen.

"Oh shit," he hisses. "Fuck. Forget I said that. Fuck, I shouldn't have—"

"Julian, no. Please, don't take it back."

With my eyes locked on his, I beg him not to say that he didn't mean it.

He stares back at me with a whole host of emotions warring behind his eyes.

"I can't take it back," he finally says. "Because it's true."

I shriek when he suddenly moves us, lowering me to my back and wrapping my legs around his waist before diving for my lips again.

There are so many things I should probably say after

that confession, so many things he deserves—needs—to hear after everything he's been through. But he doesn't give me the chance.

He kisses me like it's our first, our last, and all the ones we want to share in the middle all rolled into one.

I don't notice that the sun climbs higher in the sky, or how the temperature increases around us. The only thing I can focus on is him and how his touch, his kisses, his words make me feel.

Without even trying, he banishes all the pain and fear of my past, of what we're going to face in the future, and all I can do is hope that I do the same for him. That I make all the dark thoughts in his head quiet down, all the grief he battles with dissipate, even for just a little while.

Eventually, though, it becomes clear that JD is a little more aware of his surroundings than I am when he pulls away from my lips slightly and growls.

"Enjoying the show, bro?"

My heart lurches and my stomach knots with desire as I look over JD's shoulder to find Reid sitting in one of the single chairs watching us with fire burning in his dark eyes.

"Yeah, not bad." He mutters.

"How long have you been sitting there?" I ask, breathlessly.

"Long enough looking at the tent in his pants. Been like that since your couples' bath, I bet," JD teases.

Heat burns through me. I wasn't in any state to do anything about it at the time, but the fact Reid was hard when we were in the bath together didn't escape my attention.

Reid shakes his head. "Jude's just arrived to check Mav over. Wants to know if that bandage on your arm needs checking out?"

JD pauses before glancing at his arm.

"Get it checked," I whisper.

"And he's brought you meds," Reid adds, making all the air rush from JD's lungs. "And you're going to have to take them.

JD hangs his head.

Reaching out, I cup his cheek.

I'm still mostly in the dark about what happened, but I know enough to know that he needs to be taking whatever that medication is.

We all need him fully present and focused and if that means I need to figure out a way for him to take his meds then I'll make it happen.

"Bro, you know that—" JD starts.

"I do but—"

"We need you," I say softly, searching his eyes. "I need you," I say quieter.

I might not have said those three little words that he did to me, but from the way his eyes widen and his lips part, you'd think I did.

"Fuck, little dove," he breathes, dipping down again and stealing another kiss.

"Okay, that's enough," Reid barks before gripping the back of JD's shirt and dragging him off me.

"Hey, I was busy," JD complains, although he does so with a smirk playing on his lips and heat in his eyes.

"Yeah, well, you've somewhere else you need to be."

"Fucking cockblock," JD mutters, shoving his hand into his boxers.

My eyes drop as he squeezes his dick.

"Rain check, little dove?" He winks, sending a rush of heat between my thighs.

"You should both be resting," Reid points out.

"Relaxed as fuck right now, man," JD argues.

"Get inside and get that arm checked," Reid instructs before shoving JD toward the doors.

He doesn't say anything else until JD has vanished from sight, but his attention never strays from me.

Moving closer, his eyes run down the length of me, reminding me that I'm lying on the couch looking like a desperate whore.

"You okay?" he asks, his voice quiet and unsure.

"Yeah," I say with a smirk.

Lowering his ass to the coffee table, he studies me as if he's afraid I'm about to shatter all over again.

Pushing myself up, I sit in front of him and wait for what he clearly wants to say.

"Alana, you—" he starts but quickly cuts himself off.

"What is it, Big Man? You're not usually one to beat around the bush."

"That," he says, jerking his chin in the direction of where JD was just dry-humping me. "If you're not ready for... You know that he'd stop the second you said so, right? Any of us would."

Rolling my lips between my teeth, I shake my head.

"I know. You're not them, Reid."

"Okay. I just... I don't want you to do anything you're not ready for."

"I'm not made of glass, Big Man. I can handle the hard shit."

"Fucking hell." He groans, scrubbing his hand down his face. "I'm fucking this all up. I don't do this stuff, Alana. I don't care about anyone else's welfare other than trying to keep a leash on JD. I don't know how to—"

"You're doing great. And you might not like this, but I think you care about a lot more people than you realize."

"No one needs me to care about them, Pet."

I smile at him. "If you say so."

"I don't want you to hurt anymore," he confesses quietly. "Me. Us. Them. You've already been hurt enough. It needs to end here."

I consider my words for a moment before I allow them to pass my lips.

"I trust you."

His eyes widen.

"I won't let any of you do anything I'm not happy with. But equally, I trust you to know what I need. I'm fucked up, Reid. Broken beyond belief over and over again. I don't need any of you to wrap me up in cotton. Sometimes—most of the time, to be fair—I'm going to need you all to throw me around and do the exact opposite." He sits back, his chin dropping. "You know. If you're man enough."

His jaw pops at my suggestion that he might not be, and I push to my feet.

I'm still unsteady as hell. Probably due to the fact I haven't eaten anything more than anything else, and the second he sees me wobble, he's on his feet and wrapping his arm around my waist in a heartbeat.

"You really are a big softie, aren't you?" I tease as he leads me inside.

"Only with you, Pet. And if you tell anyone..." he warns, his words trailing off.

"What? Are you going to spank me like a naughty girl?" I tease.

"Fucking hell. I always knew locking you up in my basement was a mistake."

"Oh shush. You loved every second of it."

"Not as much as you did."

34

MAVERICK

Pain is the first thing I feel when my body stirs to life.

No. Pain is the only thing I feel.

It's all-consuming in a way I've never experienced before.

The physical pain is bad, but that's only a small part of it.

The pain in my chest. The pressing weight of the failure I feel is unbearable.

The memories of watching the way they treated Alana. All because I couldn't protect her from them like I'd promised I would always do.

The sharp pain comes again and this time, I can't contain the agony as fire explodes in my back and burns through my body.

A whimper spills free.

I hate myself for it. For showing weakness.

But I can't help myself. All of this is too much to take.

But then...

The most incredible sound in the world fills my ears.

"Mav," a soft, very familiar voice cries before the scent of something so sweet and tempting floods my nose.

"It's okay, babe. You're safe now," she says, sliding her delicate hand beneath mine that is resting on the bed before laying the other on top.

"D-doll?" I force out, desperately trying to rip my eyes open to see her, but my body won't comply. All it knows is pain.

"I'm here. I'm right here. And I'm not going anywhere."

Her grip tightens on my hand as another bolt of pain hits me.

I hiss, barely able to deal with it. But then, thankfully, it subsides.

"Jude is fixing you up."

"Doesn't feel like it." I groan, not even bothering to worry about who the fuck Jude is. If Alana is letting him anywhere near me, then he must be trustworthy.

"Dude, those scars are going to look badass," another voice says from across the room.

"Don't listen to him. Just focus on breathing, yeah."

"Your pain relief will kick in any minute," a deep voice rasps.

"Thank you," Alana whispers, her voice cracking with emotion. It's hearing that that makes my eyes pop open.

My breath catches in my throat as I take her in.

Despite everything, she's still the most beautiful thing in the world.

"Doll," I whisper.

"Fuck, Mav," she chokes out, her eyes filling with tears and her bottom lip trembling. "I thought... for a moment there..."

"You scared us, bro," JD finishes for her.

"I'm sorry. When they came, I knew you'd be safe and

I..." I swallow thickly. My throat is dry, but the pain is nothing compared to that of my back.

"Shush," Alana soothes, her warm palm cupping my cheek. "I'm okay. And you will be too. Then we're going to put an end to all of this, once and for all."

I just about manage to smile at her when I see fire light up her previously dark eyes.

"Okay, I think you're good," the guy—Jude—who I guess was tending to my back announces. "You're going to be out of action for a while yet. But hopefully, it won't be too long until you're able to get back up on your feet."

"Great," I mutter.

"I've stitched up some of the deeper lacerations. Others should heal on their own. But you've got quite a lot of scar tissue back there so—"

"I got it." I grunt, cutting him off. I really don't want Alana to hear any more details than necessary about the first time I was in this mess.

"Okay, well. Looks like it's your turn," he says, the bed dipping as he climbs off.

Ripping my eyes away from Alana, I bite back the pain as I twist around as much as I can to see the man who's fixing me up.

He's an average-looking guy with a thick-rimmed pair of glasses on his face. Honestly, he'd look more at home sitting next to Ellis with a laptop in front of him than tending to my wounds, but whatever.

My brows pinch as he stops in front of JD, who's sitting on the couch. Dropping to his knees, Jude lifts JD's arm, allowing me to see the bandage there.

What the hell?

A frown forms on my brow, but then the mattress dips again and I'm distracted as Alana crawls onto the bed beside me and rests her head on the pillow, leaving only inches between us.

Her warm breath washes over my face, giving me a hit of the woman I've been utterly obsessed with for years.

All I want to do is roll onto my side, pull her into my body, and never let go.

"I love you," I whisper instead, sliding my hand across the mattress so I can tangle our fingers together. It's all I'm going to be getting for now.

"This is healing well," Jude says in the background. "These stitches can probably come out in a few days."

No one responds, making my curiosity burn brighter.

"I'll cover this, but I don't think you need such a big dressing. Just make sure you keep it clean and dry."

The sound of the backing of another bandage being ripped off fills the air before he must press it to JD's wrist.

"And as promised, I have a stash of your meds. I assume you know how you should be taking them."

Silence.

"We're aware," Reid assures him. It's the first time he's made his presence known.

I can't see him from my position, so I can only assume he's standing in the doorway, watching over all of us like the mother hen he pretends not to be.

"Okay, well," Jude says, getting to his feet.

"I'll see you out," Reid says, before their heavy footsteps disappear.

"Fuck," JD breathes, but before either of us can say anything, he stalks over casting us both in his shadow.

"Hey, it's good to see you awake, man," he says, lifting his injured arm to scratch his chin as he looks from my face, to my destroyed back and then to my eyes again.

"You okay?" I ask, attempting to nod toward his own injury.

"Yeah, nothing that our girl here can't fix," he says nonchalantly. "Room for another one, Dove?" he asks. Although he doesn't exactly wait for an answer. He just crawls into the small space behind her and wraps his arm around her waist.

"How are you feeling?" Alana asks, her eyes bouncing between mine.

"Fine."

"Liar," JD coughs, making Alana roll her eyes.

"Mav," she warns. "No more secrets and lies. We've already agreed."

I blow out a long breath. "How long have I been out?"

"Not quite twenty-four hours."

"Shit. What did I miss? Where are we?"

"At some mercenary safe house," JD says, making my eyes widen.

"How the fuck—"

"Reid," Alana says, as if that explains everything. Which, I guess it does.

"Right."

"We're in Hazard Grove. That connection you've got with Kai is solid, right?" JD teases.

"Uh..."

"It's cool. Aubrey has sorted it."

I want to ask, but honestly, I'm too exhausted to get too deep into all of this.

Just as Jude promised, the painkillers are kicking in and I can feel myself starting to drift.

"Never going to let them touch you again, Doll," I whisper, my eyes closing as the darkness comes for me.

"Too fucking right. You're ours now, Dove." Heavy

footsteps pound up the stairs before Reid's dark presence fills the room. "The only men who will touch you again are inside this room," JD promises.

It takes all my effort, but I manage to crack my eyes open just in time to see Alana glance at Reid.

My stomach knots, and my heart aches. But it's nowhere near the reaction I would have had before all of this if I even thought about her being anywhere near him.

"Hey," she says, reaching for my face again. My jaw itches the second she touches me, the beard I'm sporting too long and irritating.

"We're gonna figure all this out," Alana promises quietly.

"I know," I whisper.

Leaning forward, she presses the softest of kisses against my lips.

The next time I wake, the room is in silence and the moment I open my eyes, I realize why.

I'm alone.

With a sigh, I attempt to move.

It hurts like fuck as my back muscles flex and pull, but I can't lie here on my front any longer. I need to move. I need to pee.

By the time I've managed to shift myself into a sitting position, I've got sweat beading my brow and I can barely catch my breath.

"Fuck." I gasp, spotting a bottle of water on the nightstand.

Reaching out, my hand trembles, and the entire thing wobbles and crashes to the floor with a thud.

Hanging my head in defeat, I stare at the offending bottle as it rolls to rest against my foot.

Not two seconds later, a series of feet pound up the stairs.

"Mav," Alana cries before she races into the room, looking utterly terrified with Reid and JD hot on her tail. "Oh my God." She gasps, rushing over to me and picking up the bottle. "You should have called for help," she chastises.

"I had it under control," I mutter as she opens the bottle and passes it over. "Thanks."

Tipping it up, I swallow down mouthful after mouthful of fresh water until I've drained the bottle.

"More?" Alana asks, glancing over at Reid and JD, who are hovering awkwardly just inside the door.

"No, it's okay."

Sitting on her haunches before me, she rests her hands on my thighs and stares up at me with her big blue eyes that always suck me in.

"Tell me what you need, Mav. It's yours."

A smile pulls at my lips.

My back pulls as I reach for her, but I can't not touch her.

Brushing my thumb over her cheek, I revel in its softness, the warmth as her eyes soften.

"I thought it was over," I confess.

She shakes her head. "Never. We've got so much more to give, to experience. This is only the beginning."

"Fuck," I breathe, hardly able to believe how fucking incredible my wife is. "Are you okay? Did they hurt you?"

She smiles at me. "I'm fine, Mav. Just a few bruises. Nothing I can't handle."

I swallow, hating that she has to handle anything.

"Thought you needed a piss, man?" JD asks, stepping forward.

"Y-yeah. Any chance of a shower while I'm in there?"

"Nope," Reid said. There's a smugness in his voice that reminds me of why I used to hate him.

Used to... Yeah, something tells me that those days are long gone.

They could have left me wherever it was they found us. They wanted Alana. She's the one who holds the secrets, the one they want to protect.

But they didn't.

Somehow, they got me out of there, brought me somewhere safe, and got me medical attention.

I tense the second realization hits me. Something that Alana doesn't miss.

"What? What's wrong?"

I close my eyes for a beat, disbelief washing through me.

Pushing my hands against the mattress, I get to my feet, somewhat awkwardly.

"Oh shit. You trying to get the medic back early or something," JD barks, rushing over to my side to help hold me up.

Shuffling forward, Alana takes my other side as I turn to face Reid.

I look at him differently to all the times I have before.

Everything is different.

Sucking in a breath, I hold my hand out for him.

Alana gasps, and my face heats with JD's stare, but I don't look at either of them. My attention remains on the man I've spent my life despising.

Yes, he's Victor's son. But I'm quickly learning that everything else I thought about him was bullshit I told myself. Okay, so he definitely is an arrogant son of a bitch, but then so am I, to a point.

Maybe Alana was right. Maybe we always clashed because we're so similar.

Whatever it was, it's time to put it behind us.

There are bigger things to deal with than our history.

"Thank you," I croak out, my voice is rough as fuck.

Reid's jaw ticks, but it's not with anger. Surprise, maybe.

It takes a moment for him to recover, but when he does, he takes a step forward and slides his hand into mine.

He nods, accepting my words, although he doesn't say any of his own.

"Okay, now I really need to piss."

JD chuckles as I drop my hand and allow him and Alana to help me to the bathroom.

Honestly, I could probably do it alone, but also, I don't want to.

Maybe this teamwork thing won't be so bad after all.

35

ALANA

After JD and I helped Mav to the bathroom, he was on the verge of passing out again, and the second we got him back to bed, he was gone.

Concern for him weighed heavy on my chest, but deep down, I knew he would be okay.

No one said anything about the state of him or what went down between him and Reid, but it was obvious that we were all thinking about it.

Not long after, Reid made his excuses and disappeared while JD and I curled up on the couch and watched over Mav.

I was desperate to continue what we started outside, to get out of my head and focus on something more positive than watching my husband suffer, but neither of us attempted to do so.

So, instead, we just held each other close and absorbed each other's strength.

We both had questions, many questions, but none of them escaped, and eventually, we both fell asleep together.

It's easy to think that Mav is the only one healing,

seeing as he's the one with the worst of the wounds, but we've all been through it recently. We all need to rest, to recover, and to be ready for the battle that waits for us on the other side.

"Shit. Did that hurt?" I ask when Mav hisses in pain as I attempt to give him a wash and clean the dried blood and dirt from his skin.

He wanted a bath, but the three of us point-blank refused. The last thing we need is his back getting infected. So for now, he's going to have to put up with my version of a sponge bath.

"You're fine, Doll. You're the best nurse I've ever had," he says, his eyes rolling down my body, causing tingles to erupt.

The way he looks at me, I might as well be naked.

"I'm not sure about that," I mutter.

"I do. When you were at Reid's, Sheila had to do it. She definitely didn't have your touch," he confesses with a smirk.

"I should hope not." I gasp. "Every time I did that after your fights, all I wanted to do was touch you," I confess, sliding my hand up his thigh, stopping just before I touch anything I shouldn't, given his current condition.

"You've no idea how badly I wanted it."

I can't help but laugh at the pained expression on his face.

"Oh, I knew. I could *see* how badly you wanted it."

"Doll," he warns.

Dropping the washcloth into the sink, I turn to look at him.

"It was worth the wait," I say honestly.

Reaching out, he wraps his hand around my waist and tugs me closer.

"So worth it." He groans, encouraging me to dip lower so I can kiss him.

It starts sweet, a rejoining of souls after everything we've just been through together, but it quickly turns into something more desperate.

Standing between his spread thighs, I hold his head in my hands as I kiss him, pouring every ounce of love I have for him into it.

His groan of pleasure rumbles through me and ends right between my thighs, leaving me hot and desperate.

His hands wander, slipping under the tank JD dressed me in and squeezes my breasts.

"Oh God." I moan into his mouth.

"So fucking sexy." He groans.

This time, though, when the presence of someone else ripples through the room, I'm aware of it.

"You really are quite the voyeur, aren't you, Mr. Harris?"

Mav stills, his hands dropping from my breasts with a hiss of pain as his muscles shift.

"Not my fault you're always doing something you probably shouldn't be when I walk in."

"Pretty sure I'm doing exactly what I'm meant to be doing, Big Man," I say, turning to look at him. "Are you sure you're not just jealous?"

"Doll," Mav warns, knowing me well enough to be able to read my thoughts.

"It's okay, Mav. Reid is just a little cranky because he's the only one I haven't been kissing today."

"Good to know what you and JD were up to when I passed out."

My heart drops, and I turn to look at him. "No, it wasn't like—"

"I'm teasing, babe. I'm glad he was keeping you entertained."

Stepping back up to Mav, I wrap my hand around the back of his neck, keeping my fingers away from the top of his bandage. "I love you," I whisper.

"I'm okay with this," he whispers back. "I think."

"One step at a time," I promise him.

"I made pizza," Reid blurts, still standing in the doorway.

"Nice one, Big Man," I say with a grin, leaving Mav behind for a moment and stepping up to Reid.

Stretching up on my toes, I press my lips to his.

He freezes, and before he gets a chance to think, it's over and I'm moving away.

"The fuck was that?" he mutters as I move back to Mav and wrap his arm around my shoulder so I can help him back to the bedroom.

"Didn't want you to feel left out." I laugh as Mav pushes to his feet and shuffles toward the door, that Reid is still blocking.

He shakes his head, a small smile playing on his lips. It's very un-Reid Harris-like, and I like it. Hell, I more than like it.

"Oh yeah, because that was the same." He scoffs. "Let me," he adds, stepping in to help take Mav's weight.

Leaving the two of them to navigate this new development in their relationship, I turn back into the bathroom to clean up.

"Dove, you coming to join us?" JD calls a few minutes later when I'm rinsing the washcloth.

"Coming," I call back.

"If only." He scoffs. "Ow."

"Behave," Reid chastises.

"Children, children," Mav mutters.

I can't help but smile and my joy only grows when I step out of the bathroom to find the three of them all sitting on the bed with three massive pizzas in the middle of them.

It's a sight I never thought I'd see, but one I'm already obsessed with.

JD surges forward, snagging a slice of pizza before anyone has a chance.

"You're so fucking impatient. Wait for Alana," Reid mutters, ever the host.

"She won't care. She needs me fully fit and energized. Isn't that right, Dove?" he calls as if I'm not standing right here.

"Sure is," I agree, making them all pause and look up.

"Who's the voyeur now?" Reid mutters.

"Just taking in the rare sight."

"Get used to it," JD says around a mouthful of food. "You're not getting rid of us anytime soon."

"Good," I agree before stalking forward and claiming the spot on the bed they left for me.

I grab a slice of pizza and so does Mav, although he doesn't look like he's in total agreement with the idea of eating it.

I get it. I felt the same when Reid put those pancakes in front of me this morning. But we need this. And I don't just mean the food.

"Is there anything you're not good at?" Mav asks after he's finally swallowed a mouthful.

"Fucking," JD pipes up. "All the girls he's ever had run away screaming."

"Fuck off, they do not."

"Do too. I feel it's my duty to let my little dove know exactly what she's getting herself into here."

"I appreciate the warning but what exactly do you think I'm getting myself into here, Julian?" I tease, glancing up at Reid as I do.

He still hasn't taken any pizza, he's too busy sitting back and making sure everyone else is okay.

"Well, from what I walked in on earlier, I don't think you're getting into anything. My man here though, he was having very vivid thoughts about what he wanted to get in."

Mav practically chokes on his next mouthful at JD's words.

"Do you ever think about anything other than sex?" I ask.

"Yep, and it gets me in all kinds of trouble." The movement of his eyes is subtle and brief, but I don't miss the way they drop to his wrist.

"You, trouble? I don't believe it," I say lightly, reaching over to squeeze his hand.

He squeezes my fingers back and gives me one of his panty-melting smiles.

"I feel like I should make a speech or something as we embark on this new stage of our lives together," he teases.

"You're a goofball."

"That is what this is, though, right?" he asks, nervously looking among the three of us. "Because if I'm being honest, I can't think about a future where that might be the case."

"J," Reid starts.

"No, I'm serious. I know we're meant to be hard-ass gangsters who don't talk about feelings and shit, but fuck that. I fucked up last week," he says, lifting his arm just in case any of us had missed it. "I made a massive mistake and nearly hurt those I love." His eyes shift from Reid to me and my heart somersaults as I remember those three little words he said outside on the deck. "And I don't want to do that. I don't want to hurt you. We've got enough people out there wanting to do that. If we're going to do this then we need to pull together in every way we can."

"You're making this sound very serious and official," Mav points out.

"You love her?" JD asks simply.

"More than anything."

"And Reid hasn't killed her. I mean, he made her cookies and he barely does that for me and I'm his boy. And I, well... I'm gone for you, little dove. You fucking sucked me in from that first day I walked into your cell."

"Okay, what fucking meds did that guy give him. Love pills?" Mav asks.

"Julian," I whisper when he stumbles over his words. "We're in this together. None of us know what things are going to look like in the future. All we can do is live for now. And right now, there isn't anywhere else I'd rather be than here with you three," I assure him. "You two with us?"

I ask, looking first at Mav and then Reid.

"'Til death do us part," Mav says, reciting those vows we made that day when I was barely eighteen.

"Yeah," Reid agrees. "I'm in. Although there will be no deaths. Not on my watch."

"Good. Now can we eat?"

Finally, Reid reaches for some pizza. I go to do the same, but JD grabs me and pulls me closer.

"I meant what I said outside," he whispers in my ear, sending goose bumps racing across my skin. "And I might be a selfish fuck, but as long as it's only with those two, I think I can cope with sharing my little dove."

I can't fight the wicked smile that spreads across my face at the image his words conjure up.

"Oh, little dove, I do like your way of thinking," he

teases, able to read my thoughts. "One day, we'll give you the world."

"I don't need that much, J. But I appreciate the offer."

After stealing a kiss, he allows me to finally reach for a slice of Reid's pizza and the four of us sit on the bed and fall into easy conversation. We all avoid the heavy topics that we all know need discussing. There will be time for that, but right now, we just need to enjoy the moment.

We're all here, we're all relatively healthy. And by some miracle, everyone is getting along.

JD's little speech stays with me as the sun sets beyond the windows. Reid has flipped the TV on to watch football highlights—something I was not expecting. And every time I glance around at them, all I can think is that I want it.

This. Us.

A future.

It might be crazy to think that I could embark on some kind of relationship with all three of these men. But I can't deny that there is something here.

Individually, we're powerful.

But together, we're unstoppable.

And that's exactly what we, and our town, need.

Assuming we get the chance to claim it as ours.

36

REID

I left everyone sleeping up in the bedroom a few hours ago.

Mav crashed first. Not unsurprising, considering the strength of the painkillers Jude has him on. But Alana and JD weren't far behind him. The three of them cuddled up on the same bed.

They looked so right. So perfect there. Minus Mav's bandages of course. There is nothing right about them.

They're so effortless together. Like they know exactly the right thing to say that will make her smile.

I guess JD has always been a little like that. He has this way about him that puts people at ease. I just scare the bejesus out of them, even when I'm not meant to.

He was wrong about the women though. Or at least I think he is.

It's been so long since I had one, I've got to wonder if I still know what I'm doing.

Sure, it was fun to start with when all the Hawk whores wanted a piece. I was young, horny and more than happy to take everything they were offering before throwing them away for someone else like a piece of trash.

I thought I had the best life in the world.

But sadly. It got old real fast.

Every interaction was so empty.

I never had a connection with any of them past the fact they were hoping for a permanent position riding my dick. Which they were never going to get.

I might have been missing a connection, but I also wasn't on the hunt for a woman to settle down with.

My life is too unpredictable for that kind of normalcy.

Victor, Razor, and Kurt might be really, really shit examples of how Hawks run their lives, but it's all I've got to go on. And despite them having wives at certain points in their lives, the only purpose they served was to pop out kids, all they've done is cheat on them with any hot piece of ass that so much as breathes in their direction.

But Alana...

"Fuck," I hiss, sitting forward on the couch, resting my elbows on my knees and letting my head hang between them.

I'm exhausted. My body begging for sleep. But every time I shut my eyes, I see her there, strapped to the table and *them* waiting in the wings.

My chest heaves just thinking about it. My fists curl, causing my short nails to dig into my palms.

The potent hatred and the need for vengeance burn through me, making my skin buzz with electricity.

Sitting here waiting for them to heal goes against every natural reaction I have. When someone hurts someone I care about, I react.

I put them in the fucking ground.

But I can't.

Just like everything else I planned that involved my cunt of a father, I need to be patient.

It's just a shame that my patience is coming to an end.

We've all been waiting a long time for this to come to a head. No one more so than Alana.

We need to do it right.

Acting on impulse is going to be the fastest way for the four of us to end up dead.

Falling back on the couch, I let out a long sigh, but before I can lift my eyes to stare up at the ceiling, something else catches my eye.

My heart jumps into my throat as my eyes lock on Alana standing in the darkened doorframe wearing only her tank and panties.

My mouth waters as I take her in from head to toe as memories of having her wrapped in my arms in that bathtub come back to me full force.

She was so broken, so scared.

It's almost impossible to believe that that woman back then and this one standing before me now is the same one.

Her strength and resilience are awe-inspiring.

Reaching out, she curls her fingers around the doorframe, as if she needs it to hold her back. The move lifts the hem of her tank, letting me see just how tiny her underwear is.

I can't help but bite down on my bottom lip as desire washes through me.

In the past few hours, I've walked in on her making out with both JD and Mav. And fuck if she wasn't right earlier when she asked if I was jealous.

I'm not making the move though. There's no fucking way I'm starting anything. Not after—

"Why aren't you sleeping?" she asks, cutting off my dark thoughts.

"Can't," I say simply.

"Aw, come on, Big Man. Even the best papa bears need to rest sometimes."

One side of my mouth kicks up in a smile.

"I—" I swallow, second-guessing myself.

"No secrets or lies, remember," she points out before releasing the doorframe and stalking closer.

The way her hips sway as she moves. Fuck. It's hypnotic.

"I know. I just... shit." Scrubbing my hand down my face, I drop my arm strategically over my crotch, in the hopes of hiding what just her presence alone does to me.

There was a time when I was able to mask any kind of reaction to this woman. But those days are long gone.

Since getting close to her, getting a taste of her, my body reacts long before my brain gets involved.

I've never had such a visceral reaction to anyone before. And as mind-blowing as it is, I don't want it to stop.

She continues moving closer, making my heart pound faster and my temperature soar.

"I... every time I close my eyes, all I see is you on that table."

She stills the second my words register and all the blood drains from her face.

"O-oh."

Lifting her hand to her mouth, she chews on one of her nails before she takes a step back.

"I'll leave you to it."

She's managed to spin around before I find my words.

"No," I bark, my deep voice echoing through the silent house.

She pauses, her small fists curled at her sides.

"I didn't mean it like that, Pet," I explain as I push to my feet and stalk after her.

She's standing in the middle of the huge living room with her shoulders curled in on themselves. I'm not sure I've ever seen her look so small and vulnerable. And that's saying something after all the positions I've put her in over the past couple of weeks.

"I never want you to think that I think any less of you because of the position they put you in." My voice is deep yet quiet as I close in on her.

She startles when the heat of my body hits her back, and she only gets tenser as I reach up and pull her shorter hair away from her slender neck.

"What are you doing?" she whispers.

Without answering her, I dip my head and run my nose up the column of her throat, breathing in her sweet scent.

Goose bumps erupt across her skin as her entire body shudders with desire.

"None of that changes anything. We all have things in our pasts we'd rather forget. In fact, I guarantee that the three of us have many, many more regrets than you do. We made our stupid decisions. You had all yours taken away from you.

"That doesn't make you weak. The fact you're standing here right now with your head held high proves exactly the opposite."

A self-deprecating laugh falls from her.

"I'm standing here right now because I get haunted by everything I've been through every single time I fall asleep. They're invisible. They're not going to hurt me in my nightmares. If I were as strong as you say, then I'd defeat them," she says quietly.

"We will," I promise darkly, letting my lips brush the spot beneath her ear.

She shudders again.

"Reid." She moans, her head falling back to rest on my chest.

"Are Mav and JD sleeping?" I whisper, my hands clamping down on her hips to hold her in place.

She gasps the second she feels how hard I am against her ass.

"Y-yeah."

"Did you come searching for me for a reason?"

"Maybe," she confesses.

When I don't respond, she fills the silence.

"You weren't there and—" She swallows her words as I suck her earlobe into my mouth.

Good work not making the first move, asshole.

"Shit." She gasps when I nip her with my teeth at the same time I drag her harder back against my dick. "W-what are you doing?"

"Thought it was pretty obvious, Pet?"

She sucks in a few greedy breaths before replying.

"I mean, yeah. But..."

"But what? Am I giving mixed signals right now?"

"No, but... before... and—"

Her words cut off when I suddenly spin her around.

Our eyes lock almost instantly and the heat I find darkening hers sends a shot of red-hot lust straight to my dick.

"I know what I did before, Pet. Trust me, I do not need a reminder."

Her eyes search mine. I've no idea what she's trying to find, or if she achieves it by the time she stops.

The air is charged between us as we stand with no more

than an inch between our bodies, our breaths mingling. The room is almost in total darkness, the brightness from the moon outside the huge windows the only source of light.

My body begs me to do something. To shove her back against the wall, to rip her clothes from her body, and to finally take what I've been craving all this time.

Previously, I would, and I hate that I'm now second-guessing my actions.

What I said a moment ago might be true, what she's been through doesn't change my need for her. But apparently, it makes me want to treat her differently.

"I'm starting to wonder if JD was right," she whispers, leaning closer until her breasts brush my chest.

Trailing my fingers up her bare arms, I wrap one hand around the back of her neck, while the other goes back down, bouncing over the goose bumps my touch has caused.

"Right about what, Pet?" I ask. I'm too lost to her to be able to think about him or any comment he's made.

"That you don't know how to please a woman. You have this habit of backing away just as things get good."

A dark chuckle rumbles in my throat. "I can assure you it's not the case."

"Oh really, because from what I can tell, you—"

I steal whatever words are going to come from her lips next when I press mine against them.

"Oh," she mumbles.

Making the most of her reaction, I plunge my tongue into her mouth, searching for hers.

Fuck being a gentleman. If she was interested in one of those, she wouldn't be in a house with us.

The second our tongues collide, any kind of hesitation from either of us flies right out of the window.

Twisting my fingers in her hair, I angle her head exactly as I want it.

My other hand slides around to grab her ass, dragging her against me.

My aching dick presses against her stomach, my balls aching for release.

With her pinned against my body, I begin walking backward, moving us closer to the couch I abandoned in favor of her not so long ago.

Her tiny, warm hands slip under my shirt and a violent shudder tears through me from head to toe.

"More," spills from my lips, without instruction from my brain, before my hand releases her ass for a moment to help her drag my shirt from my body.

The second it passes my head, she drags her nails down my chest and to my stomach. I don't look, I can't. I'm too focused on reclaiming her lips, but something tells me she leaves nice little scratch marks on my skin.

Good. I want her marks on me.

But more than that, I want mine on her.

Spinning us around, my grip on her tightens before I lower her down on the couch.

"Oh God." She whimpers into my mouth as I settle between her thighs.

Wrapping her legs around my waist, she rakes her nails down my back as our kiss deepens, turning filthier by the minute.

37

ALANA

The way he kisses me.

The way he touches me.

It brings tears to my eyes.

I'm not sure if it's because of how long we've waited for this to happen, or if the connection between us is just this potent, but it's everything I hoped it would be.

I want to slow it down and speed it up all at the same time.

The house is in total silence and the only light comes courtesy of the moon.

It's beyond romantic, something I can't imagine Reid planned, or has ever thought about before.

I gasp when his hand slips under the light fabric of my tank. His touch burns, sending heat racing through my limbs.

My own hands roam over his strong, solid body, loving the way his muscles pull and shift as I drag my nails down his back.

My need to mark him, to stake my claim on this enigma

of a man is all-consuming in a way I'm not sure I've ever felt before.

I wanted Mav something fierce after all our years together, but I always knew he was mine.

Reid Harris though... I'm not sure he belongs to anything but Harrow Creek.

But I want to make him mine.

"Oh my God." I whimper when he releases my lips and makes his way to my throat again.

A shudder of desire whips through my body, every sensation he's eliciting in me, ending at my pussy.

My clit throbs with need, but as much as I want to demand he just gets on with it, I also want it to last forever.

Rolling my hips, I grind against his erection.

"Yes." I moan, using him for my own pleasure.

"Fuck." He grunts into the crook of my neck.

"More," I demand. He's called me a whore more times than I can remember, I figure I might as well play the part. "I need more, Reid."

He doesn't respond, although I don't miss the vibrations of his groan against my pulse point.

Just when I think he isn't going to give me what I'm desperate for, his hand slides higher until he's cupping my aching breast.

A loud moan of pleasure spills from my lips before he drags my tank higher, exposing me to him.

"So fucking pretty, he mutters to himself before dipping low and sucking one of my pierced nipples into his mouth.

It stings still, but nowhere near enough to stop him; instead, I arch my back, offering more of myself up for him.

With my fingers twisted in his hair, I revel in everything he gives me, my body vibrating with need as he licks, sucks, and nips at my breasts with no sign of stopping.

He builds me higher and higher just from this alone.

"Boob man, huh?" I gasp as his hot lips switch sides.

Opening his eyes, something crackles loudly between us as he sucks on a spot beneath my nipple, marking me, until it begins to burn.

"Oh God, please," I beg, my panties soaked with the need to feel his lips and tongue down there.

He releases me with a pop, his eye contact still as intense as ever.

"It's funny that you think we ever stood a chance at saying no to you," he mutters, kissing down my belly.

"You sure gave it a good go, Big Man."

"Didn't stop me from wanting you every time I looked at you. Watching you when I should have been doing anything else."

"Oh God." I moan, another rush of heat surging between my legs when he tucks his fingers under the lace of my panties. "Did you get off watching me?" I ask, desperate to know the truth.

He chuckles darkly.

"You fucking love that, don't you?"

I can't help but smile as he relieves me of my underwear. I'm expecting him to immediately spread my thighs, so I'm disappointed when he just sits there on his haunches and stares down at me. Although, the unfiltered heat in his eyes is something I've fantasized about a time or two in the past few weeks.

"Reid?" I whisper, terrified that we've reached that point of retreat we hit in his gym not so long ago.

It takes a second for him to react, but when he does and drags his eyes away from my tits, I get the answer I was hoping for. His eyes aren't just burning with desire. They're alight with it.

My stomach somersaults at the thought of experiencing Reid Harris when he fully loses control.

Fuck. I bet it's beautiful.

I'm ripped from my filthy thoughts as he reaches out and drags my tank over my head, leaving me completely bare for him.

I'm still covered in bruises, but if he cares, then he doesn't show it.

"You need to—"

My words are stolen as he falls over me, stealing every ounce of my attention and claiming my lips.

I want to be disappointed that he hasn't just dived for my pussy, but I can't be. Everything he's giving me right now is too perfect to complain.

He retraces his steps from before after kissing me breathlessly.

I'm a whimpering, desperate mess by the time he grazes his teeth over my hip bones and finally presses his hands against the inside of my thighs and spreads me wide for him.

His eyes widen with delight when he finds the little gem that inspired the matching ones through my nipples.

"How long have you been dreaming about that?" I ask, barely able to catch my breath.

"From the minute I first saw it," he confesses before shifting his big body around and dropping to his stomach, his knees on the floor.

It looks uncomfortable as fuck, but the second his hot breath races over my sensitive skin, I forget all about it.

Reaching out, my fingers find their home in his locks again, and the second he leans forward to lick me, I drag him closer, ensuring he knows exactly what I need from him.

"Oh my fucking God," I cry, my back arching as the sensation of his tongue against my sensitive flesh races through my body.

He moans as my taste floods his mouth and then groans in delight, sending sparks of pleasure shooting through me.

His tongue finds my piercing, circling it, teasing me relentlessly before sucking it into his mouth and tugging harshly.

It's perfect. So fucking perfect, my eyes burn with tears as my release surges forward long before I'm ready.

I try to fight it off as he goes back to proving JD wrong.

He's not shit at this. Not by a long fucking way.

If anything, he could probably give JD and his reputation a run for his money.

It makes me wonder why Reid's skills aren't gossiped about in the same way.

There's no chance of the women he's been with keeping quiet. Those Hawk whores are nothing if not loud about their conquests.

I'm riding the fine edge of release, desperately trying to hold it back, but then his fingers join the party and I lose my mind.

He pushes two inside me, stretching me open in the most delicious way, and I have no choice but to throw myself over the edge.

"REID," I scream as my orgasm takes over every single one of my senses.

My body twitches and convulses as pleasure saturates my muscles and makes my nerve endings dance with delight.

This is it. This is the moment I crave so fucking badly. The moment where everything and everyone vanishes. My bullshit life is nothing. The pain and the nightmares don't exist and I can just be me. Unashamedly me.

I'm flying higher than I possibly ever have before when I finally come back to myself and rip my eyes open, and the second I do, I realize that everything I used to crave, the nothingness, isn't what I want.

Sure, I want the pleasure. But as Reid stares up at me with his impossibly dark and hungry eyes and lips shimmering with my release, I realize that it's not about losing myself.

It's about finding myself.

Reaching for him, I drag him up my body, using only his hair, and the moment I can, I lift up and slam my lips against his.

Our kiss is filthy, messy, and everything I'd always hoped it would be.

We utterly consume each other. There is no strategy or finesse. Just pure unfiltered need.

Shoving my hand between our bodies, I tug at his waistband, desperate to get inside and wrap my hand around his length.

My movements are frantic and useless, and before long, he takes pity on me.

Climbing from the couch, he somehow manages to shove his pants and boxers down his thighs and kick them off without breaking our kiss.

In only seconds, he's back between my thighs and the delicious weight of his hard cock rests against my eager pussy.

"Please." I whimper into his kiss.

The second I reach for him and wrap my fingers around his length, he lets out the most feral growl.

Directing him to my entrance, I try to take matters into

my own hands. But this is Reid Harris I'm dealing with and I should know better than to assume he'll make this easy on me.

Slapping my hand away, he takes over, rubbing the head of his cock over my clit before dropping lower and coating himself in my juices.

"Stop teasing me," I whine.

"Like you've been doing to me?"

"Not my fault you couldn't man up and take what you wanted." I gasp, rolling my hips in the hope of getting him inside me. "Not my fault you held back."

He laughs, the booming sound making my nipples harden painfully.

"Held back, huh?" he mutters. "How's this for holding back?"

My scream is something else when he drops lower and thrusts inside me.

He doesn't even get that deep, but I swear he causes me to shatter into a million pieces from just being inside me.

His grip on my hips tightens as he pulls out. Then he thrusts again, and this time, he fills me so completely, so perfectly that a loud sob erupts from my throat.

"Told myself that I was going to take this gentle." He grunts between thrusts. "But I don't think I can."

"Fuck gentle," I gasp. "Take me. Any way you fucking want me."

And fuck me, does he do just that.

Sliding me farther down the couch so my head is no longer on the armrest, he wraps his free hand around my throat and squeezes the pressure points tighter with every thrust of his hips.

His grip hurts in the best kind of way. A way that Mav was scared to inflict. But I don't have those kinds of worries with Reid. He's more than willing to cause pain in every aspect of his life.

Sweat beads across his brow as he continues to rut into me like a man possessed.

His jaw pops as his teeth grind in his attempt to hold off.

But it's not necessary. From the moment he first pushed inside me, I was ready to fall again.

"Please," I beg, although, with the harsh grip on my throat, no noise breaks free.

"Fuck, Pet. Fuck," he barks, every muscle in his body pulled tight and ready to snap.

Black spots dance in my vision as his grip gets tighter. My pussy reacts, clamping down around him.

And just before I'm convinced I'm about to pass out, the most incredible roar rips from his throat and his cock jerks deep inside me.

My body locks up as my own release crashes into me and the second he senses it, his grip on my throat releases, and I'm able to suck in ready breaths as my body flies.

I stare up at him with wide eyes, watching as he rides out every inch of pleasure. And the second he's done, he collapses on top of me and wraps me up in his arms as if I'm the most precious thing in the world.

38

JD

I knew the moment Alana slipped out of bed last night. I almost reached for her and dragged her back, but one glance around the room told me who was missing, and I decided against being a selfish asshole and let her go.

I didn't know if she was actively seeking him out, or not, but I wasn't going to get in the middle.

I saw the look on Reid's face just as much as she did when I made my little speech earlier.

As much as I was surprised by Mav's agreement, I wasn't shocked by Reid's reluctance to dive in headfirst.

I know that what I was proposing was insane.

Three dangerously possessive men and one unbreakable woman.

Yeah, it could be the worst idea I've ever had. And admittedly, I've had a few. But it also could be the best thing we've ever done.

I'm praying it's the latter because I'm convinced that this is only the beginning for the four of us.

Yes, we've got a lot—and I mean, a lot—of issues to work through and mountains to overcome, but I've got faith in us.

Or more so, I've got faith in Alana to be the glue that holds us all together, even through the bad times.

All we need is for everyone—Reid—to pull their heads out of their asses and be on the same page and we're set.

I lie there listening, waiting to see what was going to happen.

The need to slip out of bed and go and see was all-consuming.

More than anything, I wanted my best friend to put everything aside and just take what he wants for once.

Others might not see it, but he's forever putting everyone else first. It's time he had a little of his own happiness.

I'd almost convinced myself to go down and discover what was happening when the first clue filled the air.

A smile spread across my lips at the same time my dick tented the sheets covering me.

As much as I might have wanted to be the first one to prove to her that what happened back in that aircraft hangar meant nothing to us, deep down, I knew that it needed to come from Reid.

He's been the one holding back all this time. If anyone was going to convince her that she's still the beautiful, sexy woman we first locked up in the basement, then it had to be him.

Once I knew what was happening down there, my need to go and see only multiplied.

With my eyes closed, I tried to imagine what they looked like, what he was doing to her to elicit the kinds of cries and pleas that were spilling from her full lips.

But as much as I wanted it, I forced myself to stay exactly where I was and let them have their moment alone.

Hell knows Reid needed it.

It was hard. Beyond fucking hard. And my dick didn't give a shit that it was currently in bed with another man. All it wanted was her and it was willing to do anything to get it.

By the time they'd finished, it was all I could do to stumble to the bathroom and rub one out with the sound of Alana's cries still echoing in my ears.

After I got some relief, I fell back to sleep shockingly fast.

Mav missed the entire thing, and I'm not sure if that was a good thing or not.

Reid isn't the only one who's going to need a few harsh words with himself because something tells me that Mav isn't going to take to all this as easy as he's making out.

Sharing his wife with his enemy... yeah. Not exactly an everyday occurrence.

My reluctance to give them space has long run out and the second I open my eyes to find the sun shining outside, I swing my legs off the bed and go in search of my dove.

The second I step into the living room and find them curled up on the couch together under a blanket, I can't help but smile.

Moving closer, I lower my ass to the chair closest to them and just watch.

Both are sleeping soundly, their shallow breaths filling the room.

Alana's full lips are parted, her eyelids flickering as she dreams, and all I can do is pray that it's a good one. At least she's got the protection of the baddest motherfucker in Harrow Creek if it isn't.

I can't see him holding her, but I know he is. Something tells me that even in his sleep, his muscles are so taut that no one would be able to steal her from his grasp.

I've no idea how long I sit there watching them, but it's

long enough for the sun to get higher in the sky, changing the shape and size of the shadows across the hardwood floor.

It's so peaceful here. So much so it's almost possible to believe the danger we're in doesn't actually exist.

I'm so lost in thoughts of what's happening outside of these four walls that I don't notice Alana open her eyes.

So when she speaks, I nearly jump out of the fucking chair.

"Should have known you'd be watching," she whispers.

A smile kicks up at the corners of my lips.

"You'd have been proud of me last night though, little dove. I could hear everything, but I didn't move."

She smiles and looks at least a little impressed.

"You enjoy yourself?" I ask, curiosity burning through me.

"It was... intense," she says after a moment.

"Wouldn't expect anything else," I confess, glancing back at my best friend.

A soft smile plays on her lips, but she doesn't say anything else.

"You naked under there, Dove?" I ask, wishing I could see through the blanket.

"You're bad," she teases.

"He's also uninvited," a deep voice rumbles behind her. "Fuck off, J. We're sleeping." He grunts, without bothering to open his eyes.

"Doesn't sound like it to me," I counter. "I was just getting the details of your night from our girl. The bits I didn't hear, anyway."

He moves, the blanket rippling. I don't really think anything of it until Alana gasps, her previously sleepy eyes widening in shock.

A smirk spreads across my lips as my body stirs to life.

"Ready to admit you want her now?" I tease as her moan of pleasure floats through the air.

He laughs but still says nothing.

"From what I can feel, I'd say he does," Alana says lightly.

"You sore, Pet?" Reid growls, his arm still moving suspiciously.

I snort. "As if that'll stop her."

Alana's eyes meet mine, an understanding passing between us.

"Oh God." She gasps.

"I want you to watch JD, Pet. I want you to watch him, as I make you come."

Heat surges through my body. My cock aches behind the confines of my boxers, letting me know that jerking off in the bathroom last night barely took the edge off.

"No fun if I can't see," I mutter.

From the tenting of the blanket, it's more than obvious that Reid has one of her legs hooked back over his, opening her up for him. But imagining it isn't the same as seeing his inked hand moving between her thighs.

Fuck, I bet she's so wet for us right now.

"Reid," she cries, her eyelids threatening to close.

"Eyes, Dove. Don't you dare defy orders," I warn.

She nods, swallowing thickly as I push my hand under the waistband of my boxers, squeezing the base of my dick.

"Show me," she begs.

"When I can't see you. I don't think so. It's tit for tat around here, remember?"

One second they're hidden by the blanket, the next, it's fluttering to the floor, revealing Alana's hot as hell body to me.

Just as I suspected, Reid's inked arm is wrapped around her side, his fingers skilfully playing with that piercing I'm so obsessed with between her thighs.

"Oh God." She moans.

"You like that, Pet?" Reid asks. "You like being the center of attention. Knowing that we're both dying for another taste of you?"

My eyes shoot to Reid, shocked by his openness to confess how badly he wants her. It's unlike him to so obviously do a one-eighty. Although, it was never a surprise to me that he wanted her; it was written all over his face from the first moment I discovered she was our newest inmate.

"Yes." She gasps as he reaches lower and pushes two fingers inside her.

"She wet?" I groan, desperate to hear what I already know.

With my eyes locked back on her pussy, I don't need to look up to know Reid's smirking.

Pulling his fingers free, he holds them up in the sunlight, letting them glisten.

"Fuck." I groan, finally shoving my boxers over my hips and allowing my little dove to get a look at me.

"You want a taste?" Reid asks, making my mouth water for just that.

"You fucking know it." Pushing to my feet, I let my underwear fall to my ankles, and then kick them aside before moving closer.

Shamelessly, my lips part. I'm so desperate for her, I don't give a shit whose fingers I'm sucking her off. But before I get a chance to do anything, he pushes those two lucky fingers into her mouth.

"Dude," I complain, pouting like a pissed-off toddler.

Shaking his head, he pulls his fingers free, leaving her to lick her lips before he shifts behind her.

"Oh shit." She gasps as he pushes inside her from behind.

"What the fuck are you waiting for, bro. I thought we were in this together."

With another look at her stretched pussy, I roll my eyes up her body, taking in the fresh hickeys on her tits and around her throat before I find her lips.

They part before his tongue sneaks out temptingly.

"Julian," she whimpers.

Before my brain registers, my knees hit the hardwood floor with a thud, and I steal her lips, letting the taste of her pussy flood my mouth.

She moans into our kiss, making my dick painfully hard.

Dragging myself away, I look at the two of them again, watching them move together so perfectly. And fuck if I don't want to get in on the action.

Pushing up high on my knees, I grab my length and rub the head across Alana's lips, leaving a trail of glistening precum across them.

She licks it up eagerly, savoring my taste just like I always do hers.

"Fuck, you're a filthy, filthy girl, Dove. I love it."

"Please," she whimpers before opening her mouth wide, inviting me in.

Unable to deny my girl anything, I punch my hips forward and fill her mouth.

"Oh fuck." I grunt as her lips wrap around me, her tongue lapping at the slit, trying to get more. "Look at you, little dove. So fucking perfect. And so fucking ours."

She moans around me as Reid begins fucking her harder.

Her tits bounce and her eyes begin to water, but that's nothing compared to when I reach out and collar her throat.

"Fuck, she just gushed."

"You like this, don't you, Dove? You like being at our mercy.

"Being our filthy little whore."

She nods frantically, or at least tries to when I'm only a second away from fucking her throat.

"You want more?" Reid asks.

"Of course she does. Our girl always wants me. She's perfect like that."

39

MAVERICK

The second I wake, the only thing I can think about is getting up.

My stomach hurts from lying on it for the past... fuck knows how long, and there's a crick in my neck that I'm sure I'm going to be stuck with for a while.

Pushing myself up so I can sit on the edge of the bed is easier than it was the last time I tried, and mostly failed, to do it alone.

The pain is still there, but it's bearable. I'm light-headed, but thanks to Reid's pizza last night, the room doesn't spin quite as badly as it has previously.

It still takes monumental effort to get to my feet, though.

But as hard as it is, I don't back down from the challenge.

With my sights set on the bathroom that holds the promise of relief for my bladder and a toothbrush to fix the state of my mouth, I continue forward.

Now isn't the time for wallowing and drowning.

The other people in this house need me. I need to be an asset, not a hindrance.

I already know that I'm the reason we're hiding here.

If I weren't in such a bad state—if I were able to fight those motherfuckers off instead of being a weak little bitch and falling victim to their torture techniques—then we would be out there right now trying to find those spineless pussies to finally put an end to this, to them.

But as it is, we're the ones in hiding, I'm sure, appearing to be the weak and spineless ones in the situation.

My muscles scream by the time I get inside the bathroom and come to a stop in front of the vanity.

Sucking in a deep breath, I take a moment before looking up.

When I was in here with Alana yesterday, I didn't look.

Just feeling the pain of what they'd done was enough. I wasn't strong enough to look at the evidence as well.

But I can't hide any longer.

Lifting my head, I hold my eyes, wishing that I could see even just a hint of strength in them.

But there is none.

It's been swallowed up by pain and exhaustion, and I hate it.

Turning around, I try to get a look at my back, but it's almost impossible with the number of bandages covering it.

I don't really need to see. I'm more than aware of what it'll look like. I remember it pretty vividly from the last time it happened.

I didn't have a medic or a small yet fierce army to help get me through it then.

I was alone and had to figure out a way to push it all aside so I could return home to my wife.

They wanted to punish me, that was more than obvious

when I followed orders and told Alana I had a job out of town. I was terrified that they were just trying to get me out of the way so that they could get to her. And if I was right, then the longer I was gone, the more chances they had.

Four days I was gone.

Four days hiding in a shitty motel while I waited for the worst of the lacerations to heal enough that I could put on a shirt and move without wincing.

I didn't want her to know what I'd suffered because of our marriage.

She already felt guilty for being a part of my life. No matter how much I told her that I wanted her in it, she never believed me; I could see it in her eyes. The last thing she needed was to see the evidence of how much I was suffering because I made the decision to protect her at all costs.

With a sigh, I reach for the toothbrush Alana gave me yesterday, while I slumped on the closed toilet seat like a broken man as she cleaned me up.

I always used to love her playing nurse. But her cleaning up my knuckles or a busted lip after a fight was a very different experience to what we shared yesterday.

Once I'm feeling fresher, I shuffle over to take a piss.

I stay standing because there's a very real chance that if I sit, I'm never getting back up, and this whole thing has been bad enough, I really don't need anyone to drag me off the toilet.

The second I emerge, my eyes land on the empty bed.

There were three of us in it last night, but I have no memory of Alana or JD getting up. But seeing as the sun sits high in the sky beyond the light curtains, something tells me it might have happened a while ago.

I should get back in it and rest, that isn't news to me, but the thought of lying back down is about as appealing as sticking pins in my eyes.

Now I'm up, I want to stay this way for a while.

I don't want to be the invalid in bed everyone has to bring drinks and food to.

I want to be a part of this team that JD laid out to us all yesterday.

Dragging my hand through my messy, dirty hair, I focus on the stairs I can see through the doorway and I head in that direction.

Blood rushes past my ears as I make my way down. I'm sure I look beyond pathetic, making me even more relieved that I'm doing this alone.

It isn't until I'm almost at the bottom and I can stop concentrating on putting one foot in front of the other quite so hard that reality begins to slip in.

"Fuck, she just gushed." My entire body locks up and Reid's raspy voice fills the air around me.

"You like this, don't you, Dove? You like being at our mercy. Being our filthy little whore."

My grip on the handrail tightens until my fingers begin to cramp.

They're...

"Fuck." I gasp, closing my eyes for a few seconds in an attempt to get it together.

I knew that Alana was fucking JD. I might not have seen them actively fuck, but I've seen everything else. I've even been a part of it.

But knowing that she's doing... whatever she's doing without me.

Jealousy explodes within me. It's so strong my knees almost buckle.

She's my wife.

Mine.

And yet...

"You want more?" Reid asks.

"Of course she does. Our girl always wants me. She's perfect like that."

"Fuck." I hiss.

Forcing my legs to move, I take the last few steps faster than I did the rest. My need to get in there, to see her, to see what they're all doing is all-consuming.

My breath catches when I finally step into the doorway, my eyes landing on the three figures on the couch.

Fire fills my veins as I watch JD fuck her mouth and Reid take her pussy.

They're so lost in the moment, they've no idea that I'm standing here.

And I'm glad.

Experiencing this is intense enough without being in the spotlight.

There's a part of me that wants to leave. That wants to turn my ruined back on them and pretend that I never saw them.

But then there is the bigger part, the more insistent part, that demands that I stay exactly where I am and watch it play out.

My chest begins to heave, my fists clenching at my sides as it becomes obvious that they're all reaching the point of no return.

Ignoring JD's clenching ass, and the inked hand of the man I've hated all my life moving between my Alana's thighs, I focus on my wife.

On the flush of her skin, the way her body moves with them, the more than obvious trembling of her legs as she races toward the end.

She's mesmerizing.

Addictive.

"Our girl." JD's words from a few seconds ago come back to me.

A smirk twitches at the corner of my lips.

I should hate this.

I should be wanting to rip them limb from limb for touching her, for treating her the way they are.

But how can I when she's loving it the way she is?

"Fuck, Dove. Your mouth is insane," JD praises. "That's it. Suck me harder. You want my cum, baby?"

She moans in response, and fuck if my cock isn't as hard as his just thinking about how incredible her lips feel wrapped around it.

"You want me to spill my load down your throat while Reid fills your tight little pussy?"

She moans again, her grip on JD's hip tightening until I'm sure her nails are about to pierce his skin.

"Fuck. Yes. Yes. FUUUUUCK." He groans as his body pulls taut.

I can't see her face, but I know she swallows him down like the good girl she is.

My jealousy surges forward again, but this time, it isn't because they have her, but because I want her too.

I shuffle forward a step, but pause the second JD senses my presence and shoots a smug look over his shoulder.

"That's it, baby," he praises, focusing back on Alana. "Come all over Reid's cock."

He reaches for her breasts and the second he tugs at the bar through her nipple, she screams out her release, her body convulsing between them a beat before Reid groans, falling over the edge with them.

I shouldn't be so enthralled.

But fuck.

I think I love it.

"Oh yeah, you did so good, baby," JD praises. "Don't you think, Mav?" As he asks the question, he steps aside, allowing her to see me loitering like a creep.

Her eyes widen as she sucks in a shocked breath.

"Mav," she breathes, her eyes darkening with a whole host of emotions.

But it's her concern for me that takes precedence.

"You shouldn't be down here," she pants.

"If you didn't want me to watch you with these two, then you should probably be a little more discreet," I say back, my voice deep with desire.

"No, that's not." She stares at me as she fights against Reid's hold.

Finally, he releases her and she swings her legs off the couch.

"I'm worried about you, what if you fell?" she asks, reaching for her abandoned tank and panties that are strewn across the floor.

JD and Reid aren't so concerned about covering up, both of them happy to just let it all hang out.

I'm about to look back at Alana when something on Reid's body catches my eye.

Fuck me. He's pierced too.

"Then you three might not have got the happy ending you were expecting."

"Dove," JD says, scratching his belly as if he's not standing there with his semi on full display. "It's cool. He enjoyed it. Look." The prick nods his head in the direction of the tent in my boxers. "Something tells me that he's feeling more left out than anything else."

Unable to argue with him, I just swallow thickly, keeping my eyes on my wife as she pulls her clothes on.

She steps closer to me hesitantly, before glancing back over her shoulder at the naked assholes.

"Could you two give us a few minutes?" she asks.

"You got it," Reid agrees before pushing to his feet and dragging his boxers up his legs.

"But what if I want to watch," JD pouts.

"Out, Julian," Alana barks, giving him little choice but to agree.

"Pfft. Next time, man," he says, marching closer and holding his fist out for me to bump.

I stare at him in disbelief.

"I'll make us something to eat. Take your time," Reid says before also barking at JD to follow him.

The door closes behind them, and instantly, the air seems to grow thicker around us.

Alana stares at me with rosy cheeks, swollen lips, and a deep frown between her brows.

And all I can think about is how much I want to kiss her.

40

ALANA

I stare up at Mav with my limbs trembling from a mixture of fear and desire.

There probably should be a little regret mixed in there too for allowing that to happen in a place he could so easily walk in and see, but there isn't.

While he might not be overly happy, none of us can deny that JD is right. On some level, Mav really enjoyed seeing that.

The evidence is currently brushing against my stomach with how close together we're standing.

"I-I'm sorry," I whisper, sensing that he needs to hear the words.

His shoulders tense, and I hate that what I've done is causing him pain both mentally and physically. I never want to hurt him.

His jaw ticks as he continues to stare, his nostrils flaring with every deep breath he takes.

A loud gasp rips past my lips when his arm suddenly darts out and he grips my jaw with a force I was not expecting.

"No, you're not," he states darkly.

I fight to swallow, his fingers digging into my jaw as his eyes darken until I'm staring up into two inky pools of black.

The only problem is, I have no idea if it's caused by anger or desire.

I'm fucking praying it's the latter.

"I-I'm sorry you had to see it," I correct, refusing to lie to him. "I'm not sorry I did it."

His lips press into a thin line as he continues to stare at me.

"Is this what you want?" he asks, his voice so deep, the vibrations rumble through me.

I might be standing here with Reid's cum soaking my panties but that doesn't mean my pussy doesn't beg for more.

She always has been a greedy little thing.

Because she was trained that way, a little voice pipes up.

Slamming the door on those dark thoughts, I focus on my husband.

"Yes."

"You want us to treat you like a filthy whore who wants all our dicks any way she can get them?"

His words make my brain short-circuit for a moment and I stare at him dumbfounded.

"Answer me, Doll," he demands.

"Y-Yes. Yes. I want to be your dirty whore."

He blows out a long breath, his entire body relaxing for a beat.

It makes my head spin, but not as much as it does when he drags me closer and slams his lips down on mine.

I barely get a chance to part my lips before he plunges his tongue into my mouth and takes exactly what he wants.

The memory of JD unloading in my mouth not so long ago flickers in my mind. It only makes me hotter.

Our kiss is uncontrolled and filthy.

I can barely breathe through the intensity of it, so the second he pushes me away, I suck in huge greedy lungfuls of air.

My skin tingles with desire as I wait for what's about to happen next.

"Good. Now get on your knees and suck my dick like a good girl."

Shock renders me motionless for a few seconds.

I knew that Mav had this side to him. I've heard the stories of his past, and I saw glimpses of it at the cabin before we were ripped away, but he was mostly holding it back.

Now though...

Seeing what he just did seems to have flipped a switch inside him, and I am fucking here for it.

I land ungracefully on my knees on the hardwood floor as he reaches for the back of the couch to help hold him up.

Really, I should play the role of a good wife and demand he rests.

But that isn't what I'm about to do.

Mav is a big boy—literally and figuratively—and if he thinks he can handle this, then who am I to argue?

Once he's settled, I reach for the waistband of his boxers that are barely holding up against the hard press of his cock and rip them down his thighs, letting him spring free.

The second I catch sight of his glistening tip, my mouth waters with my need to taste him.

Reaching out, I wrap my fingers around his shaft and lean forward, licking at the precum leaking from the tip.

His hips immediately punch forward in his desperation to push past my lips.

"Doll," he warns, "I thought you were going to be a good girl."

His words hit me straight in the clit. My need to please him overwhelms me to the point, I don't even register that I move until the thick head of his cock hits the back of my throat.

"Fuuuuck." He groans quietly, his pleasure spurring me on.

I deep-throat him like I've been doing so all my life. My eyes stream with tears as my need for air becomes almost unbearable. But I refuse to give in.

He's not going to be able to stand for too long, especially after I rock his world, so this needs to be hard and fast.

"Oh fuck," he barks when I reach up and cup his balls, gently squeezing them in a way I learned he likes.

His free hand cups my jaw, his thumb collecting my tears before he lifts it to his mouth and licks them off.

His stomach muscles pull tight, letting me indulge in his impressive six-pack before a surge of saltiness floods my mouth.

A warning for what's to come.

But I'm not the kind of girl who's scared of getting a little dirty.

I hum around his shaft, driving him crazy.

His cock jerks and his hand returns to my head, although this time, his fingers tangle in my hair, holding me exactly where he wants me as he finishes down my throat with a roar.

A roar I'm pretty sure is designed to let the others know exactly what is happening in here.

I don't pull off until he's spent, and when I do, I sit back up on my haunches and look up at him.

I'm a mess. But the best kind of mess from the way he stares down at me like he wants to eat me alive.

Fuck.

If only he could...

His chest heaves, his eyes are completely blown, and if it weren't for the way he uses the couch for support, I'd think this was only the beginning.

Unfortunately, though, despite how much I need him, and how wet I am for him, it's not how it's going to be.

"I think it's time for breakfast," he announces before bending down with a wince to pull his boxers up. "You're not dressed appropriately, though. I'd fix that if I were you," he warns, his eyes locked on my lace-covered cunt before he spins and walks away. He moves slower and with more caution than he probably wants, but I get the message loud and clear.

The second he opens the door, a waft of Reid's cooking floods the room, and my stomach growls loudly. These boys sure have helped me work up an appetite.

I don't get to my feet until Mav has disappeared. I have every intention of heading straight upstairs to change into what I hope will make him happy, but I can't help lingering beside the entrance to the kitchen as he joins Reid and JD.

"Fuck, yeah." JD laughs. "That's the look of a very happy man right there."

"Are you always this much of a prick?"

"A nice morning blowy always gets me in the best of moods, don't you agree?"

"I don't kiss and tell." Mav grunts, making JD bark out a laugh.

"Sure you don't. You just like us to watch instead."

"You haven't seen anything yet."

Silence falls among them as furniture is moved, and I can picture JD putting his teasing aside for a moment to ensure Mav has somewhere to sit comfortably.

"Seriously, though, you good?" JD finally asks, letting his caring side free.

My heart jumps into my throat as I wait to hear his answer.

"Can't say I had plans of starting my day by watching my wife get railed by you two assholes. But I've gotta be honest, I've had worse days."

I breathe a sigh of relief at his confession.

I don't expect Mav to be totally okay with this.

We've spent five years alone. He might have had a couple of friends, but I didn't.

Letting others into our lives was always going to be a challenge, but I never expected it to be Reid and JD, and I never even considered that I'd be letting them into our relationship in the way that we are.

My heart flutters with happiness as I think about the three of them.

"Nah, you fucking loved it. He did, too," JD says, I assume nodding toward Reid. "You should have seen them all cuddled up this morning. So freaking cute."

"I'm not cute." Reid grunts.

"Aw, but you were, bro. It's okay, we won't tell anyone. It can be our little secret that you've handed your balls over to Alana."

"I haven't, I— Fuck," he concedes.

The smile that spreads across my face is beyond

ridiculous as realization hits.

I broke the mighty Reid Harris's resolve. Something he promised me that would never happen.

With my grin still in place, I leave them to their pillow talk and head upstairs to clean up.

As much as I might like to feel the reminder of what we did this morning in the way my pussy aches and the taste of both JD and Mav lingers on my tongue, I really don't need to spend the rest of the day with Reid's cum running down my thighs.

If I ever needed evidence that the guys' ribbing him about how long it had been since he saw any action, then the amount of jizz he unloaded inside me in the past few hours is all I need.

I throw myself into the shower, hating that I wash their scent off me before I brush my teeth, fix the mess that is my hair and then step into the closet totally naked.

There isn't much in here, just what Aubrey brought with her.

Scanning my options, I reach for the only one that makes sense.

A white tank with wide arm holes and nothing else.

A smirk pulls at my lips as I take in just how much side boob it exposes.

Oh yeah, this is definitely what Mav was imagining.

With my hair up in a messy bun, or the best I can do now I've lost a lot of inches, I make my way back down.

The banter is still going strong when I step into the doorway, so much so that they don't notice me as Reid plates up four breakfasts and JD and Mav stare at the food as if they haven't eaten for a week. Which he pretty much hasn't.

Clearing my throat, I successfully pull all their eyes in

my direction.

JD's chin drops only a beat before Reid literally drops the pan in his hand.

"Shit," he hisses, quickly collecting the two sausages that jumped out while Mav watches me with approval in his eyes.

"Good girl," he praises as I push from the doorframe and stalk closer.

I don't stop until I'm right beside him.

He's sitting backward on a dining chair so he doesn't risk hurting his back. Threading my fingers into his hair, I lower down and kiss him like I used to dream of doing every single morning back at our house.

Another throat clearing drags my lips from Mav's and I glance up at JD through my lashes.

"Damn, Dove. You know how to stretch a guy's patience."

Dropping a kiss on Mav's nose, I move toward JD. I have every intention of just kissing him too, but the second I'm within reaching distance, his hands wrap around my waist, and I'm hauled into his lap, straddling him.

Sliding his hand under the tank, he exposes my bare ass to the room, not that the room is complaining.

"Fuck, Dove. Your pussy is fucking scorching. Didn't your husband return the favor earlier?"

Mav chuckles. "Figured making her wait would be more fun."

"Oh, sadist. I like it," JD teases. "What do you say, Big Man? You up for some fun?"

Looking over at Reid, I watch as his Adam's apple bobs with a thick swallow.

What the hell have you gotten yourself into here, Alana Murray?

41

ALANA

JD's plans didn't exactly play out because after we'd all stuffed our faces with Reid's incredible breakfast, the burner phone Aubrey gave him started ringing and he disappeared from the kitchen and locked himself in a room I was yet to explore.

Something told me it was an office. An office filled with books, maybe.

I'm yet to get to the bottom of his out-of-character collection in his own library, but I'm confident that I'll get there.

All of us still have a lot to learn about each other, but there is time. Or at least, I hope there is.

I guess that all really depends on how all of this ends.

All we can do is hope that it plays out as we want and that the Hawks who are currently living out their last few days aren't the ones under this roof.

With Reid occupied, I forced Mav to go and find somewhere to rest. He was adamant that he wasn't returning to the bedroom until it was actually time to sleep, so he shuffled off toward the living room.

Just seeing him in there made my blood heat as memories assaulted my brain.

And while he rested, JD and I cleaned up.

Okay, so when I say cleaned up, I mostly mean that we made more of a mess than we started with.

By the time we joined Mav, who was blankly staring at the TV while the news channel played, my tank was soaked and see-through, and JD still had bubbles clinging to his chest.

JD tucked himself on to the end of the couch where Mav had stretched out, keeping his back away from the cushions and I snuggled myself in front of him.

I was barely on the couch, but with Mav's arm around my waist, I was confident that I wasn't going to hit the floor anytime soon.

Unsurprisingly, it didn't take long for Mav to fall asleep. He might like to try to pretend that everything is okay, but we can all see that he's struggling. Hell, I'm struggling and I didn't go through half of what he did.

Before long, the excitement of the events around the world ensures that all three of us drift off to sleep.

While it might be frustrating that we're out of action, I can also appreciate that we needed this time away from home to figure everything out.

I've no idea how long I'm out for, but when I come to, it's to the sensation of someone drawing patterns on my ankle.

Blinking to clear my vision, I find JD at the end of the couch where he fell asleep, staring down at my feet as if they hold the answers to all the world's problems.

"Hey," I whisper, letting him know that I'm awake. "You okay?"

Sucking in a breath, he glances up. First at me and then Mav, who's sleeping peacefully behind me.

"Yeah," he lies.

Panic hits me like a truck.

"Did you take your meds?" I blurt, chastising myself for not checking sooner.

A sad laugh falls from his lips.

"Don't worry, little dove. Big Man wouldn't let me forget. He's like a dog with a bone."

"Good," I state, relieved that one of us has managed to keep their head in all this. I guess there is a reason he's the boss after all.

Letting his eyes drop again, my heart aches for the pain that radiates from him.

"Do you want to talk about it?" I offer.

I may have pieced a few things together about what happened, but I don't know any details. Reid kept those to himself, and rightly so. But I'm desperate to know whatever JD will allow me and to try and help in any way I can.

He lets out a long, pained breath and lets his head fall back against the couch.

Closing his eyes, his grip on my ankle tightens, but his lips never move.

I start to think he isn't going to talk, and I'm about to ask another, less painful question when he suddenly speaks quietly.

"I woke up, and you'd gone, Dove. I thought you'd slipped out of my bed in the middle of the night to be with Mav. But when I went searching, it was obvious that you hadn't been there either.

"The house was deserted. I had no one to turn to or any idea what was going on."

He falls silent, and I want more than anything to

comfort him, but I don't want to disrupt his thoughts or wake Mav. Something tells me that he wouldn't be so forthcoming with this if Mav was listening too.

"I was already struggling a little. You knew that. You saw that."

I have to bite down on the inside of my lip not to respond. I had seen that, and I just wish he would have talked that day on the swing. Maybe it would have helped.

Maybe...

My heart sinks. What's the point in maybes?

I need to think about now, about the future, not concern myself with things we could have all done differently in the past.

"All day I waited to find out what was going on, but no one came back. Reid's cell wouldn't take a call, and I found both of yours in his safe.

"Fuck," he hisses. "Do you have any idea how many photos of you Mav has in his camera roll, Dove?"

My lips part to say no, but the word never breaks free.

"He loves you something fierce." JD's voice cracks with emotion. "I already knew it. I saw it in the way he looked at you, the way he touched you. But fuck. Knowing he had you. That I had no idea where you were and had been left behind. It killed me, Dove. Fucking killed me."

Pain cuts through my chest. Deep down, I know that I didn't do this. I would never intentionally hurt him. But just knowing that I had a hand in it, cuts me so fucking deep.

My eyes burn with tears, as I think about him home alone without any answers.

I keep my eyes on him, grateful that he's got his closed and can't see how much this is hurting me just to hear.

I want to be this for him, I want to be his sounding

board when he needs to get things off his chest, I want to be his voice of reason when things are chaotic in his head.

I want to be everything for him. What I don't want to be is the reason he's hurting or second-guessing himself.

"I took your advice," he says suddenly. "I found an old notebook and pen and along with my bottle of vodka, I started writing shit down. Shit that I've never laid out on paper before."

I'm pretty sure I stop breathing as I wait for what comes next.

"I started writing about you," he confesses. "Writing about how I knew right from day one that having you in our basement was going to end in disaster."

I suck in a breath, willing my body not to react to his words, no matter how much they affect me.

"I'm pretty sure I started falling for you the first time I came down and found you strapped to Reid's chair."

"Fuck. You were so fucking beautiful, Dove. I'd been watching you, telling myself that I was going to keep my distance, but I couldn't."

"And then that first time I touched you, felt the softness of your skin under my fingers, saw your reaction to me. Fuck. I was gone."

"But for me... falling comes with consequences. Consequences I'd only experienced once, but ones I knew were going to come back to haunt me at some point in the near future."

I want to assure him that I never wanted to hurt him. But honestly, in those first days, hell, even in the ones that came after, I probably would have willingly hurt him if it meant breaking free and getting back to Mav.

"Maya," he says simply.

I may not know who she is. But the sound of another

woman's name rolling off his tongue makes my stomach knot.

It's wrong. I'm married. In love with another man. Yet him just saying a name causes a wave of jealousy so strong to hit me that I've no idea how I remain still.

"I assume you don't know her?" he asks, finally dragging his eyes open and turning to look at me.

His eyes bounce between mine as he reads whatever is he can see in my blue depths. Thankfully, whatever is there doesn't scare him off.

Shaking my head, I mouth, '*no.*'

He nods, accepting my words.

"She was a girl I met at a group home I attended. She was... fuck." He gasps, dragging his hand down his face. "She was a fucking whirlwind.

"From the first moment I saw her looking like she'd been dragged into the building by her ankles, I was gone for her.

"She was feisty and honest and blunt. Fuck me, was she blunt. There was never a doubt about how she felt about something. She didn't like you; she'd step right up to your face and tell you.

"I was in awe of her. She took life by the balls and didn't give a shit what anyone thought."

"Reid and Knox aside, she was the best person I had ever met in my life. She was everything I was missing and about a million more things I had no idea I needed."

"She had issues. I knew that, and I wasn't afraid of them because every day she fought against the shit hand life had dealt her. She wanted better, more. She wanted to take that shit hand and shove it up everyone's ass."

He chuckles. "We got in so much trouble together," he confesses.

"Why doesn't that surprise me," I whisper with a smile, liking this girl despite my initial reaction.

"I fell so fucking hard for her. We did everything together. Every-fucking-thing. She was my first. My everything. Until..."

My entire body locks up as his words trail off.

I knew what was coming the second he put her in the past tense. That and the little information Reid gave me and I knew this has a very, very painful ending.

"Things got bad. To this day, I don't know what triggered it. But she started to lose control."

"She was always wild and out of control, but she was never reckless. Careless."

"Until one day she took it too far." He sucks in a shaky breath and I can't get up and crawl into his lap fast enough.

"She left me behind," he confesses quietly. "I loved her so fucking much and she left me. I wanted to go with her. I wanted it so badly and I—"

"Shush, it's okay." I soothe when he starts to lose it. "I've got you."

"I tried, Dove. I took the knife that Reid had given me for my birthday and I took it to my wrist, praying that it would take me to her."

I cling onto his shoulders, holding him tighter than I ever have before, as our tears—our pain—collide and meld together as one.

"The next thing I knew, I woke up in the hospital with Reid sitting right by my side and this massive fucking black hole in my heart."

"When you left, Dove, I—"

Pulling my face from his, I take his cheeks in my hands and wipe his tears away with my thumbs.

"She sounds incredible," I say honestly.

He nods, his jaw popping against my palms as he swallows.

"I won't leave you, Julian," I promise him. "If I disappear, I promise you that I will come back. I will always come back to you."

Pressing my lips to his, I close my eyes and just hold him, letting him feel the weight of my promise.

Neither of us moves to deepen the kiss, we don't need to. It's already intense enough and full of promises.

Rolling my head up, I press my brow against his and stare into his watery eyes.

"I love you too, Julian," I whisper.

42

MAVERICK

L istening to them cry killed me, but I didn't let them know that I was awake.

They needed that moment.

He needed to finally get his truth off his chest and she needed to feel the weight of his trust in her to hear it.

Our lives didn't collide very often. I'm older than Reid and JD and I'd already finished school and embarked on a life as a fully-fledged member of the Hawks when JD lost Maya. But that didn't mean that I didn't know about it.

Victor tried to keep it on the down low, but gangsters were gossipers, just like the old wives of the town, and rumors spread fast. Hell, for a few hours, I was under the impression that JD had succeeded in following his girl to the other side.

I remember being relieved he hadn't achieved it. He might have been Reid and Knox's friend, not mine, but even I could admit that he was a good guy, and had a promising future as a Hawk.

If only I knew then what I knew now. Maybe we all could have handled everything differently.

While he was fighting for his life, I was embarking on mine with Alana in it. I didn't have much time to be concerned about anyone but her back then.

Maybe if I'd have looked a little further outside our little bubble, I wouldn't have the understanding of JD's loss that I do now.

With a sigh that's full of regrets and my own loss, I push myself up and sit on the edge of the couch as I think about what they're probably doing wherever they disappeared to.

Movement outside the door catches my attention, and when I look up, I find Reid loitering.

"You okay?" he asks, making me give him a double-take. It's going to take me a little while to get used to him not hurling abuse at me every chance he gets.

"Y-yeah. We all had a nap and then Alana and JD—"

"Left you to have their own fun," he adds with a smirk.

"He told her about Maya. They thought I was still asleep."

"Shit," Reid breathes, reaching up to rub the back of his neck.

"So I guess that explains the bandage on his wrist then."

Stalking into the room, Reid falls into the chair opposite me and drops his head into his hands.

"I had no idea he was that close to the edge. If I knew then I wouldn't have gone to Mexico like I did." Regret comes off him in waves.

"I believe you."

He stills and glances up, pain filling his eyes.

"And he won't hold it against you. He'd want you to get answers for Alana above all else."

"I'd prefer if he was here to see us end this, though," he mutters.

"He will be. It's going to happen. Any updates?" I ask,

noticing the time and just how long he could have been on the phone for.

He shakes his head. "Still no sign of them. They're working on it, though."

"What happens if they don't find them? We can't hide here forever."

"We won't. Once you're back on your feet properly, we'll go home."

"Home," I muse.

"My home. Our home," he corrects.

"Right," I breathe, thinking of the home Alana and I created over the last five years.

Is that it? Are we just meant to walk away from it now that we're... what the hell ever we are now? Or am I expected to go back there and leave my wife with them? I can tell them right fucking now that that isn't happening.

"I'm not running scared from them. I'm happy to take some time to heal, but that's all they're getting."

"They can hide all they like, but we will find them, and we will take them down."

"And what if they find us first?" I ask, voicing my biggest concern right now.

"Exactly why we need to get home as soon as possible."

"You don't trust this place?"

"I trust Aubrey. She wouldn't knowingly put us in danger. But our lives are the epitome of danger."

"Don't we fucking know it," I mutter.

"You hungry?"

"Do you do anything but cook?" I ask, raising a brow at how fast he can flip the switch between thinking about ending his father's life and cooking lunch.

"Yeah. I torture and kill people, too."

"Brilliant."

"You want to go and see if the love birds have worked up an appetite? Or are the stairs too much for you to handle?" he taunts.

"I've got it. Thanks for your concern."

His shoulders shake with laughter as he leaves the room, heading for what seems to be his favorite place in the house.

Shaking my head, I set about embarking on the mammoth climb that is the stairs and finding what will ultimately be my wife in bed with another man.

Why is it that thought gets me hotter than it should?

I spent years wanting to make her mine, and now... how I get her, I have to share her. And I'm not hating it.

Fucking mind-blowing.

I'm panting like I've run a marathon by the time I hit the top of the stairs.

But surprisingly, everything is quiet. There's no moaning or screaming of JD's name.

I hate to admit it, even if it is to myself, but a little disappointment drips through my veins.

Silently, I shuffle closer to the door to what I can only assume is the master bedroom that we've all been sleeping in.

As I get closer, voices finally hit my ears, but they're not full of passion, just whispered words meant for just the two of them.

Coming to a stop in the doorway, I find both of them under the covers, their noses barely an inch from each other's. It's almost as if the rest of the world doesn't exist.

My heart thumps against my rib cage as dejection tries to make itself known.

But deep down, I know she's not choosing JD over me.

This whole thing isn't one of us over the other. It's all of us.

I shake my head, trying to stop it from spinning with that crazy thought.

The movement is enough to catch the attention of the two people in bed.

"Hey," Alana says, a smile lighting up her face at the sight of me.

"Feeling left out, man?" JD asks as I move deeper into the room.

"Reid wants to know if you're hungry," I say as an explanation for my presence.

"Stupid question," JD mutters with a laugh. "So you didn't just come up here to steal my spot."

"I mean, if it's on offer, there's no way I'm passing up the chance."

"How about you take my place," Alana offers. "I need to go and clean up."

Throwing the covers off, both of us zero in on her bare body as she pushes to stand and not another word is said between us until she's closed herself in the bathroom and we've managed to remember how to connect our brains to our mouths.

I study JD, searching for signs of the pain I heard in his voice while he was talking to Alana downstairs.

"What?" he asks as he pulls himself up so he's sitting, leaving the sheets to pool around his waist, hiding his metal-filled cock.

"Nothing," I say, unconvincingly.

"I think we're all too close now to cover shit up. Out with it."

When I hesitate, he realizes what I'm failing to say.

"You were awake, weren't you?"

"J," I start. "I didn't listen on purpose, but I also didn't want to stop you because—"

"It's okay," he says. "It's better that everyone knows my... issues."

I shake my head.

"I'm not going to pretend it's anywhere near the same, but Alana and me, we do understand. She lost her best friend, her sister. And I lost Ivy a few years ago. I didn't love her, not like you did Maya, but it still felt like I lost a part of myself."

"Death sucks, huh?" he mutters, keeping his head lowered.

A bitter laugh spills from my lips. "If it's the good ones, yeah. Don't give so much of a shit about the bad ones."

"Good thing, I guess. We've put a few in the ground between us."

"Yeah," I agree, wondering briefly like I often do about the families of those we end.

They might be monsters, but even the worst of the worst have families and people they love.

Victor and Kurt's faces pop into my head.

Or maybe they don't.

Maybe not everyone out there has a redeemable quality.

"I just want you to know that Alana isn't the only one who'll listen, should you need it. We're... we're a team, right?"

He blows out a breath, visibly relaxing.

"Yeah, bro. We are. Definitely a team if you're tapping the same pussy."

A soft groan comes from behind me. "He has such a way with words, doesn't he?"

"Wonderful," I say sarcastically.

"True though, right?"

"Get your lazy ass out of bed, we don't want to keep Big Man waiting," Alana teases.

"Lazy ass?" he asks, his eyes wide in shock. "Do I need to remind you just how hard this 'lazy ass' made you come not so long ago?"

Alana's cheeks heat and an adorable smile plays on her lips.

"We didn't hear anything downstairs; it couldn't have been that good," I taunt.

"Oh," JD starts, puffing his chest out as he throws the cover back without a care in the world. "It was that good. Isn't that right, little dove?"

"I'm not getting involved in this pissing contest," she says, pulling her hair into a band to get it away from her face.

"I think we all know that I can make her scream like no other. There's no shame in coming second."

"Second?" a third male voice barks. "I don't fucking think so."

"Oh Jesus," Alana mutters as she marches toward Reid and places her hand on his chest and tries pushing him back out of the room. "Can we not do this now?"

"When would you like to do it, Dove? You've had a go on all of us now, of course our male egos want to know who's the best."

"Okay, we are not doing this," Alana announces, giving up on trying to move the forcefield that is Reid Harris and instead slips around him and out into the hallway. "What's for lunch, Boss? Smells amazing."

"Not as good as my fingers," JD counters, making both Reid and me groan. "What? You're both jealous as fuck and you know it."

"Christ," I mutter, stalking closer to Reid, who also looks ready to bolt. "He's your friend," I point out.

"Sometimes I can't help but wonder why," he says under his breath.

"Fuck off, you both love me and you know it. And one way or another, we are going to figure out which one of us makes Alana come harder."

"Hardly a fair test when you two are full of fucking accessories."

"Nothing wrong with enhancements, bro. Especially if they help make her claw at your back like a savage."

"We're not all about drawing blood." I scoff.

"Oh, bro, you can't take that fucking line with us. We know all about your antics before you got yourself hitched. You were a dirty motherfucker, am I right?" JD looks from me to Reid.

"I'm with her, I'm out of this."

Reid takes off, and I quickly follow behind him, more interested in knowing what he's made us to eat than I am in diving into ancient history and the women who let me unleash all kinds of kinky shit on them. The only woman I want to unleash those things on now is my wife, and she's currently waiting downstairs.

"You're just too scared to get yours pierced," JD calls after me.

"Is he always this much of a pain in the ass?" I ask as we descend the stairs.

Laughter follows my question and I quickly shoot back, "Don't bother answering that."

Knowing that everyone around me knew what I was going through made me feel lighter.

I was worried that they'd all start watching me as if I was going to break at any moment—I wasn't, I had my dove back, I was feeling pretty fucking great—but they didn't treat me any differently to before my confession.

Obviously, I knew that Ivy and Mav were close and that she died a few years ago, not long after having Daisy, but I was too selfish to really put too much thought into how that affected him.

But seeing a familiar grief in his eyes helped settle something inside me.

We'd already formed some kind of brotherly bond, probably because I forced his hand into getting Alana to bounce around on his dick, but knowing that we had another shared experience, shared pain, helped to solidify our friendships.

The rest of the day was calm. It was... nice.

Just like I'd announced, we were becoming some kind of

fucked-up team and it was getting easier and easier to be around each other.

Most of the time, it's been Alana, Mav and me hanging out in the living room or enjoying the warm fall rays out on the deck while Reid has been locked away in the room he's claimed as his office, chatting on the phone to fuck knows who.

He's given us basic updates about what's going on, but he hasn't gone into detail. There's a part of me that loves being naïve to what is happening outside this safe house. I mean, why would I give a shit when I've got everything I need inside these four walls? But there is another part, and a newly revived part, that is itching to get on with this fight and come out victorious on the other side.

I just have to trust that when Reid has intel that's really worth sharing, he will. He's never done me wrong before.

The slam of a door rips through the air, causing Mav to pause the movie the three of us are watching before a familiar voice calls, "You have ten seconds to put all genitals away."

"You're funny," Reid barks back from the kitchen where he's busy cooking. It's pretty much the only thing he's done aside from being on the phone these past few days. Oh, that and stealing Alana away from us in the middle of the night when he doesn't think we notice.

"There are some things I just can't unsee, Harris," Aubrey calls back.

She pauses in the doorway to the living room with arms full of grocery bags to greet us before she continues to find the boss, Jude trailing after her like a good little pup, carrying even more supplies.

In a heartbeat, Alana is on her feet and staring back at both of us.

"What?" Mav asks.

"Are you two really just going to sit there?"

"Uh..."

"She might have something important to say," Alana argues.

Glancing over at me, I see a familiar expression on his face.

Contentment.

It's a good fucking feeling. One I'm not sure I've ever truly felt before.

But as good as this little bubble we've found ourselves in is, it's going to have to burst eventually.

"Yeah," Mav agrees, sliding to the edge of the couch.

He's moving much easier now, but it's obvious that he's still struggling. And until that improves, we're not going to be going anywhere.

"I guess the medic is here for me anyway."

Throwing his arm around Alana, they make their way toward the kitchen with me hot on their tail.

"This is bullshit," Reid spits venomously at whatever Aubrey just said to him.

They're standing on either side of the island with all the bags between them.

"It doesn't matter right now. You're not ready," she soothes.

"That's not the fucking point. He shouldn't be able to give us the slip like this. We're fucking better than he is."

"We are," Aubrey agrees. "And we will find him and we will win."

"He hasn't called you at all?" I ask, more than aware that Reid set her up to be his father's little fuck toy.

Gross.

"No."

"You think he's on to you?" I ask with concern.

If that's the case then...

"There is a chance, but I highly doubt it. I'm just not important enough to him to risk his location."

"Prick always thinks with his dick, I highly doubt that." I scoff.

If Aubrey is disgusted about what she's had to do with Victor, she doesn't show it.

Just another day at the office for her, I guess.

"You spoken to Luciana yet?" she asks, turning back to Reid.

"Yeah, I was finally allowed ten minutes of her time," he mutters, clearly unimpressed with how protected Luciana is.

"And what did she say?" Aubrey prompts.

"Not much. She's only got a small team working on this. She's not going to be a lot of help."

"Well, that's nice." Aubrey scoffs, rolling her eyes.

"If we need her, she promised me that she'll be here. But what can she do right now? You two want coffee?" he asks, turning toward the machine.

"You know it."

We all fall into a tense silence as the reality of our situation presses down on our shoulders. It's easy to forget when we're relaxing, but the second Aubrey comes knocking—or storming in—so does reality.

"Mav, shall we go and check out your back?" Jude says, breaking the silence.

"Been looking forward to it," Mav deadpans before kissing Alana on the head and stalking out of the room with the medic hot on his heels.

"Give us some good news, Aubs," Reid begs as he passes her a mug.

She thinks for a moment. "They haven't found you yet."

An unamused laugh tumbles from Reid's lips. "Yet? That the best you got?"

"Give me a couple of those cookies over there and I'll see if I can come up with something better," she teases, nodding to his most recent batch.

"Pain in the ass," Reid mutters as he does as he's told. It's bizarre watching him follow orders, and when I glance over at Alana, I find a similar kind of amusement on her face.

"Maybe, but where would you be without me right now?"

"Have those two really never fucked?" Alana whispers in my ear, making all my hairs stand on end.

Looking down at her, I search her eyes for a moment. She's trying to look strong and self-assured, but I see the jealousy swirling within her. She's practically oozing green.

"No, they've never bumped uglies."

"But they're so—" she swallows, cutting off her words, "I dunno, close, I guess."

"I think he sees her more like a sister than anything else. You've nothing to worry about with Aubs, Dove."

Her brows pinch harshly. "What? I'm not worried."

"Sure, you're not," I tease, glancing over at Reid and Aubrey to make sure they're distracted before I reach out and cup her face. "I promise you, I have never seen him act the way he does with you with anyone else. You're one of a kind, baby."

The most incredible smile curls at her lips.

"So are you, Julian," she whispers before reaching up on her toes and kissing me a little too deeply, considering we have an audience.

"So how is all this working exactly?" Aubrey asks loudly, clearly not distracted at all.

"Do we really need to go there?" Reid asks quietly.

"It's pretty easy really, Aubs. We're all just trying our best to make this one happy," I say, making Alana shriek when I suddenly pull her into my body and drop into one of the chairs.

She thinks for a moment, seemingly too interested in what is happening here. "So do you have some kind of schedule or something? And does Mav get first dibs seeing as she's wearing his ring?"

"Oh, hell no," I bark, tightening my arms around my Dove. "All's fair in love and war, ain't that right, Harris?"

Reid glares at me from his position resting against the kitchen counter.

"So are we talking one at a time here or an every hole is a goal situation?"

Reid snorts in shock at her words. I'm pretty sure coffee actually squirts out of his nose.

"Aubs."

"What? I'm intrigued."

"Well, the other morning, your boy here was behind my dove with his—"

Alana's hand claps over my mouth, stopping me from explaining that epic situation.

"Julian," she hisses.

"What?" I mutter around her hand before licking up her palm.

Wrinkling her nose, she pulls it away

"It's not like Aubs is going to judge. I bet she's been involved in some far more fucked-up situations over the years."

"Truth," the woman in question mutters before focusing

her attention on Alana. "I think me and you need to talk, girl."

"And here I was thinking this couldn't get any worse," Reid complains.

"It could totally get worse. What are all your little brothers up to these days?" Aubrey asks, wiggling her brows suggestively.

"Stay the fuck away from my brothers."

"Oh, come on. It's not like I'd corrupt them. I've done a job in Maddison County; I know exactly what the baby Harris's get up to."

Reid scrubs his hand down his face before the burner in his pocket begins ringing.

Pulling it free, he stares down at the screen.

"J, you're with me. Let's leave the girls to talk about dick."

A grin curls at my lips. "My girl can talk about my dick all day long if she wants," I offer. "Jacob's ladder, Aubs. Fucking epic. Right, Dove."

"Now, J," Reid barks like the impatient motherfucker that he is.

I expect him to march toward his newly-claimed office, so I'm confused when he heads for the stairs.

Jude and Mav are deep in conversation as we climb the stairs, although it ends abruptly when we step into the room.

"How's it looking?" Reid asks.

"Great. Healing really well. He'll be back to full working order in no time."

"Alana will be thrilled," I deadpan, earning more than a couple of glares.

"Great. Can we have a moment?" Reid asks.

Jude hesitates before packing up his stuff and scurrying out of the room.

"It's okay, he was finished," Mav murmurs, when Reid props himself up against the dresser and hits the speaker button on his phone.

"Malakai Saint," he says in greeting but also to clue us in as to who we're talking to.

"Harris. Rumor has it that you've been trying to hunt me down," he says smugly.

"Well, couldn't get hold of the organ grinder so thought I'd turn my attention to the monkey," Reid snarks.

"Takes one to know one."

Malakai Saint is the stepson of Hazard Grove's infamous leader Sidney Hyde.

Reid and I haven't had a lot to do with him. He's always been one of Victor's associates, and he's been one of the hardest for Reid to break with his plan to bring Victor down. And Malakai—or Kai to those who actually know him—hasn't been all that much easier to get in contact with.

Until Mav crashed into our lives.

"We need to talk, Saint. We've got some issues right now, and we need—"

"Well, fuck me sideways," he taunts. "Is the great and mighty Reid Harris actually asking me for a favor?"

Reid's teeth grind. There's no fucking way he'd reach out like this if it weren't absolutely necessary.

"I'll owe you one, Saint. That's for fucking sure."

"And my old man isn't interested in this... arrangement?"

Reid sucks in a deep breath, his nostrils flaring.

He's going out on a limb here. I might not know too many details about what's going on, but I do know that Reid is taking a massive fucking risk here.

And if he's wrong...

"I'm hoping that we could do this, heir to heir and all that."

Silence.

My heart rate picks up, and when I meet Mav's eyes, he doesn't look all that much more confident about how this is going to go, even though he's the one who brought this possible intel to the table.

If he's wrong, or worse, fucks us over... well. We don't need to think about what would happen next.

Curling my fists, I wait for Malakai to say something.

Anything.

Finally, when he does, everyone in the room lets out a sigh of relief.

"Okay, Harris. Let's talk. Heir to heir."

44

ALANA

I study Aubrey as she lowers herself into the chair opposite to me. Her dark locks blow gently in the wind, the sun making her golden skin glow in a way that I'm sure only makes me look pale and gaunt.

She really isn't good for my self-confidence, even if I have been spending my days with three of the most desired men in Harrow Creek.

I take her in, a frown marring my face as I try to figure her out.

She's friends with Reid and has been for a long time by the sounds of it. There shouldn't be a question about her being trustworthy. But I can't accept her that easily.

Not when she's one of the only people who knows where we are right now. She holds the key to destroy the men I care about.

"You do know that you're living every female's wildest fantasy right now, don't you?" she asks, appearing to be unfazed by my scrutiny.

"I don't care what every other woman out there wants. The men inside this house are mine," I state protectively.

The words float between us, and I wait to see how she's going to react.

But then a smile spreads across her face and she relaxes back in the chair, crossing one leg over the other.

"Okay, mama bear, I'm not after your cubs," she jokes.

"You and Reid," I start unable to let this go. If she's going to be a part of our lives, even just briefly, I need to know the truth.

"Girl, Reid and I would end up killing each other if we went there. We're far too pig-headed to be compatible in any way."

"So you've never—"

She shakes her head, although it's not in a patronizing way. "No, we've never. Not even come close. I'm not your competition, Alana. Those boys are all yours to play with."

Her words are spoken with nothing but honesty, and I see it shining in her eyes as well, making me sink back into the cushions.

"Now tell me about that," she demands. "I want all the ins and outs," she teases.

I stare at her in shock.

I've never had a girlfriend. I've never done... this.

Kristie was too young, not that I ever had any boy gossip that I could tell her. She had a few tales about boys she fancied at school, but it was nothing more than a crush.

And then I had Mav.

I've seen plenty of girl talk on the TV and I was always jealous of those easy relationships, where you can be completely open and talk about everything, but I was aware that I never stood a chance of ever having one.

Firstly, the fewer people I talked to the better, and also, who the hell would ever understand me, what I've been through?

But as I stare into Aubrey's dark eyes, I can't help but wonder if I've found someone who might just embrace the darkness of my past. Hell knows she must have enough of her own to do the job she does.

"There isn't much to tell really," I say lightly.

"Oh bullshit," she barks happily. "You're hooking up with not one but three Hawks. You've got all the ins and outs going on."

She raises a brow pointedly and I can't help but laugh.

"Okay, yeah. There have been a few."

"All three at once?" she asks, leaning forward with interest.

I smirk. "Not yet."

"Oh, but you want it, don't you?"

I shrug, trying to play it cool.

Do I want to know what it would feel like to have the full attention of all three of them? To have their hands all over me, their lips? To have them fill me so completely? Oh hell yes, I do.

"Dirty, dirty girl," Aubrey teases. "I can see it in your eyes."

"They're hot and I have needs. Sue me," I concede.

"Damn, I need to find myself a setup like this," she muses.

"Fucking old corrupt gangsters not doing it for you?"

She pauses and I regret the question instantly.

"Shit. I'm sorry, you don't have to answer that."

"No, it's fine. I can't expect details from you and not spill. Although I'm not sure you actually want details."

A shudder rips through me as I think about the man she's been tasked to play.

"No, I really don't. Reid was an asshole to ask you to get involved with him," I say fiercely.

"It's my job," she explains. "And I probably don't need to tell you that he's paying me handsomely for my support."

"I should hope so. I know what those men are capable of and—"

"But do you know what I'm capable of?" she counters, cutting me off.

"Uh…"

"I know what I'm doing, Alana. Reid asked me to help because he trusts me and he knows that I'm good at my job. I need you to trust me too. We will bring these motherfuckers down."

I suck in a deep, calming breath.

"I know. And I do trust you. All of you."

"You just have to be patient."

"Yeah, I'm struggling with that, if I'm honest. Being here with the guys twenty-four seven is great, don't get me wrong. But being so locked away from the outside world and having no idea what they're up to is unnerving as fuck," I explain.

"They're going to come for us sooner or later and I'm worried we won't know it's coming."

"We'll know," Aubrey assures me. "I have guys stationed ready for intel and so does Reid. They'll fuck up sooner or later. They're too fucking arrogant not to."

I can't argue with that. Victor, Razor, Dad, they all think the sun shines out of their asses. But is it enough?

Fuck. I hope so. I really fucking hope so.

Talking to Aubrey about… well, everything really, comes so easily that when the guys emerge from the house, I don't realize how much time has passed. The sun has sunk low in the sky, and it isn't until JD drops down beside me and pulls me into his lap that I discover just how cold it's gotten.

"You two look like you're getting on," he murmurs.

"Were you watching us, Julian?" I accuse.

"Maybe. I like seeing you laugh, Dove. So fucking beautiful."

He leans in to steal a kiss, and Aubrey announces, "And that's my cue to leave."

I just about manage to wave goodbye before JD steals every ounce of my attention and lays me out on the couch, kissing me until the sun finally sets.

I've no idea where Reid and Mav are, or if they're watching, but I'm confident that they're not too far away.

"Missed you, little dove." JD groans in my ear as he rocks against me, driving me higher and higher despite the layers of clothing between us.

"I haven't been anywhere."

"You were out here, and we were in there. Too far." He hums, kissing down my neck.

"You're a goof."

"I'm yours, you mean."

"I don't know," I tease. "Might need reminding."

"Oh, Dove. You're asking for it now."

Before I know what's happening, his weight has vanished and I'm being lifted from the cushions.

"Julian," I gasp, "what are you— Oh," I breathe when he expertly twists me around, leaving me with my knees on the seat, looking back at the house.

Gripping the back of my neck, he forces me to bend over, leaving my panty-covered ass sticking up for him.

"Beautiful," he muses a second before he tucks his fingers under the lace and drags them down. "Can you see them, little dove?"

I blink heavily, focusing on the two more than obvious

figures standing on the other side of the floor-to-ceiling windows that cover this entire side of the building.

"Yes," I confess.

"Good. I want you to keep your eyes on them the whole time. "You're going to watch them as they watch me fuck you."

"Oh God." I whimper, heat surging between my legs.

"You think they can watch without getting involved?"

Fuck. I really hope not.

"Mav hasn't watched anyone properly take you yet, has he?"

I shake my head, holding my husband's eyes.

My heart rate picks up, and my stomach knots at the thought of him being unable to handle this.

My lips part to say something, but then Mav moves. It's so subtle that I wouldn't see it if I weren't so focused on him. But he nods.

I've no idea if it's directed at me, letting me know that it's okay, or at JD to tell him to continue.

Crack.

The slap is so unexpected that I cry out into the night, my voice echoing through the trees. It's eerie as fuck.

Defying orders, I look over my shoulder at the darkness of the woods behind us.

I'm assaulted by images of me running through it, twigs snapping underfoot as my body trembles and my heart races. But it's not like my nightmares. I don't have monsters chasing me. Well... not the same kind of monsters.

Crack.

"I told you to watch them, Dove," JD barks, his fingers twisting in my hair to drag my head back into place.

I find Reid's dark eyes first. They burn with unfiltered desire. But it's Mav's eyes that make my breath catch. He holds mine for a beat before he looks behind me at the exact spot I was just staring at.

He knows.

After our conversation in the cabin, he knows what I want from him. From them.

My thoughts and dangerous fantasies are stolen from me when JD suddenly plunges two fingers inside me.

"That's it, baby. Good girls get rewarded."

I gush around his fingers, and he mutters a curse under his breath.

"Fucking perfect, Dove. You've no idea."

"Please," I beg, rocking back against him, desperate for more.

"You want my cock, baby?"

"So bad. Please, Julian."

"You want my dick while Reid and Mav watch?"

"Yes, yes," I cry, already on the verge of losing my goddamn mind from his fingers alone.

"I bet they're so hard for you right now."

My mouth waters as I think about them, hard, beautiful, desperate. Desperate for me.

"They're going to be so fucking jealous of me."

I cry out when he pulls his fingers from my pussy, leaving me empty and my muscles clenching around nothing.

"Look at you, such a filthy girl. Your pussy is just begging to be stretched open, Dove."

"Please," I beg.

His grip on my hair tightens, forcing my head up and my back to arch for him.

"Ready?" he asks.

"So ready." I whimper impatiently.

"I wasn't asking you, Dove. I know you're ready. I can see it glistening down your thighs."

Relief floods me when he presses the head of his dick against my entrance, coating himself in my juices.

"Look at them, Dove. Look how badly they want to be me right now."

Mav has his hand in his sweats, not bothering to cover what's happening beneath them. Reid, on the other hand, is standing firm. Only his eyes give away how he's feeling right now.

JD's hand tightens on my hip, and the next thing I know, he's surging inside me, filling me so deep, it's all I can do not to combust right there and then.

He fucks me like a demon, putting on a show for our spectators.

Just before I'm about to fall over the edge, he pauses and drags me up from the couch so my back is pressed to his front.

A rush of cool evening air glides over my chest as he drags my tank up and exposes me to them.

With one hand on my breast, tugging at my piercing and driving me crazy, the other descends for my clit.

Both Reid and Mav's eyes follow, their focus completely on me.

It's mind-blowing.

I love it.

I love their attention.

I love seeing the burning desire in their eyes.

The only thing that would be better would be if they emerged from behind the glass.

"You're thinking about them, aren't you, Dove?"

"Yes." I gasp as he pinches my clit.

"You want them to join and make you an even filthier whore?"

"So bad." I whimper, barely able to hold it together as images of the four of us locked together fill my head.

"One day, Dove. One day, we'll fulfil every single one of your fantasies. But for now, you're mine. It's my cum I want to watch spilling out of your pussy in a few minutes' time."

"Oh God, please."

"You want it, Dove. It's." Thrust. "All." Thrust. "Fucking." Thrust. "Yours." Thrust.

That final punch of his hips sends us both crashing over the edge.

Everything goes dark as pleasure assaults me.

Long seconds pass as I ride it out, taking everything JD offers me and hoping that I give him the same in return.

And when I come to, I quickly discover that we're no longer alone.

Instead, my husband stands before me with his hard dick in his hand, impatiently waiting for his turn.

"That's it, little dove," JD encourages, bending me over again as Mav moves closer. "Suck your husband's dick while I'm still balls deep in your pussy."

45

REID

I f you'd have asked me who I thought would bail on the scene playing out before us in the yard, then I'd have put money on it being Mav.

That poor motherfucker spent five long years pining after a woman—his wife—who he wouldn't let himself have.

I'd have thought standing there watching her be taken by someone else—by my best friend—would break him.

But clearly, I'd have lost a lot of money because he was more than getting off on it.

I guess I shouldn't be that surprised. He had a rep for getting up to all kinds of filthy things back in the day. But it's easy to forget that side of him when it hasn't been seen for so long.

Hell, sometimes we went weeks, if not even longer, between seeing him at the clubhouse.

To begin with, we had no idea it was because he secretly had Alana living with him. It soon became obvious why he was so absent when their surprising union was announced. Then we all thought he was too busy at home fucking her. Until the truth of that came out.

Do I feel like a pussy for bailing? Yeah, I guess. I find it hard to care, though.

I might have agreed to embark on this, but it'll still take a long time for me to get fully onboard and open up. For them to really understand what goes through my head and what makes me tick.

I shared Alana with JD without an issue the other morning. I've watched her with both of them from the shadows many, many times. But doing so while standing shoulder to shoulder with her husband was different. And I'm not even sure if I can explain why.

He was into it. Alana and JD were certainly into it.

Hell, so was I. I'd be lying through my teeth if I tried to convince anyone that I wasn't hard as fuck watching her get railed by my best friend.

But still... I couldn't stay there.

Maybe it's the pressure of what's happening on the outside. The reality check that came from talking to Aubrey and Malakai.

Fuck knows, but I was out of there the second she closed her eyes.

I might have left, but there was no way I was allowing her to watch me do it.

And it also didn't stop me from going straight to the window in the bedroom to continue watching.

Alone and shrouded in darkness.

A place where I'm most at home.

Ripping open my fly, I push my hand into my pants just as JD shoves Alana forward, allowing her access to Mav, who has finally joined them.

"Fuck." I hiss, squeezing the base of my dick.

Pressing my free hand against the window, I peer down at them, happier than I was before being an invisible voyeur.

JD never moves away from behind her. Something tells me he's waiting for round two, and to be honest, from the way she's deep-throating Mav, it won't be long until he's recovered and ready to go again.

And just to prove me right, not two minutes later, he starts thrusting into her.

I stand there unmoving as they all work together to find their almost simultaneous releases.

All the while, I do nothing but hold my aching dick like a loser.

But I don't want to stand here and jerk off over the little alfresco porno they're making.

I want more than that.

I want her.

My fist clenches against the window as I fight with my own desire. The second they're done, I step away, falling even deeper into the shadows.

With my head tipped toward the ceiling, I suck in a deep breath and try to rein myself in.

The temptation to run back downstairs and take what I so desperately need is strong. But I'm better than that. I'm stronger than that.

Giving into temptation left and right isn't how I've gotten myself in the position I'm in.

Everything I do is well-planned and calculated.

I've never experienced anything—my younger brothers aside—that is so wild and uncontrollable as Alana and the effect she has on all of us.

With a loud, pained sigh, I march toward the bathroom and flip the light on.

After standing in darkness for so long, it burns my eyes, but I don't let it slow me. Instead, I turn the shower on and then strip out of my clothes.

My dick stands hard and proud from my body, the tip glistening with precum, taunting me over what could have been.

With my head tipped back, I let the water rain down on me, sucking in deep and steady breaths, trying not to imagine what they're doing outside.

Is it over? Or were they just getting started?

Mav is getting stronger every day, his ability to move getting easier.

Has he got bored of waiting and finally getting what I'm sure he's been dreaming about?

Is he balls deep inside her right now?

My fists clench at the thought of it being him instead of me.

A loud, irritated growl bubbles up my throat, but it never breaks free because the crash of the door against the bathroom wall rips through the air.

"What the—" My words die when I find Alana standing there naked, staring at me as if she wants me to be her next meal.

The air turns heavy, sparks crackling between us as we do nothing but stare.

"You left," she says, nothing but disappointment in her voice.

Unable to explain why, I just shrug.

"You were enjoying yourself so much, didn't think you'd notice."

Her eyes narrow in suspicion.

"I think most people would notice when you leave a room, Harris," she taunts. "But no one more than me."

She takes a step closer, and my dick jerks in excitement.

Running my eyes down her body, I take in the hickeys on her neck, the fullness of her breasts, and the pink diamonds speared through her nipples. The dip of her waist and then the curve of her hips. I bet if she were to turn around, she'd have JD's handprint glowing on her ass.

I swallow, my mouth watering so fast I'm not sure how I don't end up drooling all over the tiles.

"You missed out on all the fun, Big Man," she continues, moving closer still.

"I watched."

"Of course you did," she teases. "Did you watch me suck off Mav? JD come inside me again?"

I swallow, my Adam's apple bobbing, the only answer she gets.

She already knows the truth. She can see it in the way my cock aches for her.

"And now you're standing here on your own. You trying to punish yourself for something?"

"N-no, I—" I stutter like an idiot as she finally steps into the walk-in shower, her body getting covered in light spray.

She smirks, reading everything I'm not saying in my eyes.

"Masochist," she mutters before suddenly dropping to the floor.

"Oh fuck." I grunt as she wraps her hand around my length and sucks me into her hot mouth. "Fuck."

She stares up at me with her big blue eyes, and all the fight, all the desire to keep tight control of every aspect of my life, just falls away.

Reaching out, I thread my fingers through her now-damp hair and pull her closer, using her for exactly what I need. And just like I predicted, she takes it.

All of it.

Her eyes flood with tears as I cut off her air supply, but she doesn't so much as falter.

"Fuck. Your mouth is insane."

Why the fuck wasn't I doing this sooner?

In record time, a familiar tingle erupts in my spine as my balls begin to draw up. But as much as I want it—need it—I'm not finishing in her throat.

It's just not fucking happening.

Reaching down, I tuck my hand under her arms and drag her off my cock.

"Hey," she complains the second she realizes what's happening, but there is nothing she can say that will make me change my mind about how this ends.

Lifting her, I slam her back against the tiled wall, making her gasp in shock before wrapping her legs around my waist and crashing my lips to hers.

Without missing a beat, her tongue pushes out to meet mine and we embark on a filthy, all-consuming kiss as our bodies grind and shift, desperate for more.

Reaching between us, I grab my cock and line up against her entrance.

I don't bother teasing her, we both know that she's already dripping for it. And if she weren't, JD will have unloaded enough in her to do the job.

She screams in delight the second I thrust into her.

Grabbing her jaw, I drag her mouth back to mine and swallow every single one of her cries and pleas for more as I fuck her into the wall.

My orgasm is right there. Hell, it has been since the moment I saw her on her knees for me. A position I've wanted her since that first moment I locked her up in my basement.

I've wanted to watch tears flood her cheeks as I choked her on my dick. And fuck if my imagination paled in comparison to the real thing.

Her nails claw at my back, probably opening up the scratch wounds from the first time we were together on the couch, but I don't give a fuck. I'll wear her mark proudly.

My fingers dig into her ass as we both approach the end, but it's not enough. She needs more.

Lifting one hand, I hold a finger up to her lips.

"Suck," I demand before plunging it into her mouth.

My eyes cross when she laps at my digit, just like she did my dick not so long ago, making it even harder to stave off my release.

The second I'm happy, I return to her ass, only this time, I run my fingers between her cheeks, finding her puckered hole.

"Oh God." She gasps the moment she realizes my intentions. "Reid. Oh fuck. Yes."

I push against her ring of muscle as she continues to cry out, her body trembling in my arms as her release approaches.

"Relax, Pet. Let me in," I instruct before kissing her again.

The second she falls into the kiss, her body sags, and I push forward, stretching her open.

She screams, her eyes wide, as I continue to kiss her, fuck her, consume her.

One more thrust of my hips, and she falls, tumbling into the most beautiful release I've ever seen.

And the second her pussy clamps down on my dick, I throw myself right over the edge with her.

"Oh my God." She gasps, resting her forehead against my shoulder, her heaving breaths racing over my skin as she comes down from her high. "Think I might sleep for a week after that."

"You'll be lucky." I laugh, utterly blissed out on this woman. "I'm pretty sure you're going to be hounded for repeats of that from all of us."

"Here's hoping. Just in case there was any doubt, JD was wrong. You are really, really good at that."

I can't help the cocky smirk that twitches at my lips.

"Glad to hear it, Pet."

"But next time," she starts, making me wonder where she's going. "It's your dick I want in my ass."

All the air rushes from my lungs.

There isn't much that shocks me, but it seems that Alana is the exception to the rule because she's surprised me more than I'd like to admit to over the past few weeks.

"And maybe one of the others in the pussy too."

I glance down just as she opens her eyes and peeks up at me.

"We get through this in one piece, and I'll give you the fucking world, Pet."

"Just you, Reid. And them. Us," she says sleepily, her body getting heavier in my arms.

"Yeah," I agree. It doesn't actually sound so bad.

46

ALANA

I wake like I have done every morning since we've been here with the sun streaming in through the light curtains and a hot man on each side.

Since Reid experienced me freak out in the dark that first morning we were here, I haven't missed that we've never been totally in the dark.

It's a pretty great place to be.

Lifting my head from the pillow, I glance over one hot, inked chest to find the fourth member of our team. As suspected, Reid is laid out on the couch, although he's not asleep like the two on the bed with me. Honestly, I'm not sure he ever actually sleeps. Instead, he's staring up at a phone with his brows pinched together and a concerned expression written all over his face.

"Is everything okay?" I whisper.

It's barely loud enough to be heard, or at least I don't think it is, but that doesn't stop it from startling him to the point he drops the cell right on his face.

I just manage to catch my barking laugh before it breaks free.

He rubs his nose and collects the offending device before glaring at me. It falls short, though, because the time of me being even slightly scared by the infamous almost-gang leader is long gone.

I see him for who he really is now, the big, soft teddy bear who bakes cookies and takes care of those he cares about in a way I'm not sure he's even aware of.

Honestly, he's pretty incredible. Not that I'm going to tell him that. His head is big enough already.

"What's wrong?" I ask a little stronger this time.

"Other than a suspected broken nose?" he mutters.

"Don't be a baby," I tease.

"It hurt. Hit me harder than Mav's fists ever have."

"Liar." Mav growls from behind me.

"How would you know? Ever punched yourself in the face?" Reid shoots back.

"It's too early for this," I complain, falling onto my back and staring up at the ceiling.

Honestly, I love their banter.

There was a time not so long ago where I questioned whether they'd be able to get past their hatred of each other. But it seems that having a mutual, bigger enemy might just have bonded them in a way the entire town thought would be impossible.

I can't help but wonder what their fathers would think —if their sons weren't actively trying to kill them, of course. It was what they always wanted when they were kids. Their sons to work together to continue their corrupt legacy.

Well, they might now be working together, but the only thing they want to do with their fathers' legacy is ruin it.

There's movement on the other side of the room as Reid gets up. Snuggling deeper between two of my men, I let out a contented sigh. Things might be up in the air, and I might not fully relax until our fathers are dead, but this right now is pretty damn good.

A shriek rips from my lips when suddenly two large, warm hands wrap around my ankles under the covers and I'm hauled down the bed.

"What the hell are you doing, Harris?" I squeal as the sheets are ripped away from all three of us.

It leaves Mav in just a pair of boxers, me in a man's tank —standard—and unsurprisingly, JD is naked. And when I stop moving, I find myself in the perfect position.

As if it knows I'm staring, JD's dick jerks as I lick my lips.

"What's going— Oh," JD rasps, when he sees the situation that's unfolding before him.

On his knees at the end of the bed, Reid spreads my thighs and stares at my pussy as if he wants to eat it for breakfast, which I guess he might be about to do.

The bed shifts and when I look back, both JD and Mav are watching with interest.

"What the fuck are you waiting for, bro? It isn't going to come to you."

"It might if he makes me wait long enough," I counter.

Reid's eyes flash with heat before he dives for me.

After the way he retreated the other night while I was with JD, and then JD and Mav in the yard, I was worried we'd pushed him too far.

It's funny because I never would have thought he'd be the one who'd have the issue with this sharing thing we've got going on. But there we go, I guess stranger things have happened—like Mav being okay with it.

"Oh fuck." I gasp as he licks up the length of my pussy before focusing on my piercing.

"Christ, that's hot," JD mutters, his dick growing harder before my eyes.

Reaching out, I thread my fingers of one hand into Reid's hair, holding him in place, not that I think he needs all that much encouragement. The other encircles JD's cock, making him grunt in pleasure.

"Now that's what I'm talking about," he says happily, moving to get a better view.

The bed shifts again as Mav tries to find a comfortable position. His back is healing nicely and he can almost function normally but lying down is going to be an issue for a while.

"Oh," I gasp when his shadow falls over me.

Looking up, I find him on his knees, looming over me with fire burning in his eyes and his cock tenting his boxers.

"Arms up, babe," he demands, forcing me to remove my touch from Reid and JD briefly.

He rips my tank from my body in one swift move, exposing me to all of them.

"That's better," he murmurs as JD reaches for my hand and puts it back on his dick.

"No, that is better," he muses as I begin stroking him at the same speed Reid licks me.

Gazing back up at Mav, I open my mouth, inviting him to join the party.

"Fuck, I love you." He grunts, shoving his boxers around his hips, freeing his cock.

My mouth waters, but he doesn't give me a chance to lick my lips. Instead, he shimmies forward and pushes the head past them.

I suck eagerly, desperate to have his taste coating my tongue.

"Look at you, little dove. So fucking beautiful."

"Perfect." Mav grunts as I take him deeper.

Reid groans, I assume in agreement, but he doesn't remove his mouth from my pussy, so I can't be totally sure.

He works me perfectly, alternating between teasing my clit and plunging his tongue inside me.

It's good. Incredible.

And when he knows I'm close, he gets his fingers in on the action to find my G-spot.

I moan around Mav's shaft as my release approaches and begin working JD faster.

"Oh shit, I'm not going to last."

Ripping my eyes from watching Reid eat me, I stare up at him, silently telling him that it's okay. That he can let go. I am here for it.

But before he gets the chance, Reid pushes me over the edge.

Mav slips free of my mouth as I lose control of my body.

Reid works me until I'm spent and it's not until I open my eyes a few seconds later that I find all of them looming over me, dicks in hand.

"Fuck me." I gasp, totally overwhelmed by the sight of the three of them.

JD falls first, his deep groan filling the room before hot jets of cum cover my chest. Mav is next, muttering my name as he follows suit. And finally, Reid crawls on the edge of the bed between my thighs and shoots his load all over my stomach, officially marking me as theirs.

My chest heaves and my heart aches in the best kind of way as the significance of the moment washes over me.

Theirs.

I'm theirs.

And more than that, they're mine.

"**A** girl could get used to this," I say as JD fills my wine glass and Reid places a plateful of delicious-smelling pasta in front of me.

"You should," Mav says from beside me.

He's still on light duties around our temporary home, but I can see that he's desperate to get in on the action and do more than lounge around waiting to heal.

Each day he's getting stronger and each day the knot in my stomach gets tighter.

With him almost ready to fight, it means reality is just around the corner. And I'm not sure I'm ready for it.

Being here in our little bubble has been everything I could have ever wished for. The four of us have bonded, our relationships growing every day. But I'm not ready to have them tested.

It doesn't feel right yet.

We've only just found this... this ease between us all and there is every chance it's about to be ripped away.

"For real?" JD groans when the front door slams and Aubrey shouts, "Honey, I'm home."

Multiple sets of footsteps thump through the hallway, making my heart jump into my throat.

"I come with a gift," she announces as she emerges in the kitchen. "And just in time I see," she says happily, her eyes locking on the food Reid is dishing up.

She looks up at him and smiles, but unlike before, I don't feel even a stirring of jealousy. Those few hours we spent chatting on the deck the other day helped to banish all of it.

One glance at the size of the pan in Reid's hand and reality hits.

He was expecting her. Or them, it seems as Jude and then an older man I don't recognize steps into the room.

"Griff," JD announces with a wide smile before he walks over and gives him a friendly man-hug that involves a lot of back-thumping.

Mav's hot breath rushes over my ear before he whispers, "Reid's uncle."

"Ah."

I study the man with new eyes, and suddenly, I wonder how I missed the resemblance. Their eyes, they're almost identical. Although Griff's have a few more lines around them.

"He's from Seattle. Ever heard of Kingston, or the Kings?"

"Err... should I?"

"No, I guess not. He's part of them." When my brows pinch in confusion, he continues, "On his mom's side. We don't have a brothers-in-rival-gangs situation."

"Right. Good. That's... good?"

"Yeah, babe. It's good."

"Griff, this is Maverick and his—" Reid clears his throat as he realizes what he was about to say. "And this is Alana."

"Ah, I've heard a lot about both of you," he rasps, moving closer to shake our hands.

Confusion covers Reid's face, making it more than obvious that whatever he's heard hasn't been from us.

Interesting.

"So, is that Bolognese for dinner, kid?"

"Take a seat," Reid says, and he quickly follows orders, Aubrey and Jude not far behind.

I watch as everyone pulls out a chair and takes a seat.

"You okay?" Mav whispers in my ear, his attention burning the side of my face.

"Y-yeah," I stutter, looking around at all the faces before me in disbelief. "I've just... I've never had this," I confess.

JD drops into the chair beside me and reaches beneath the table to squeeze my thigh.

"A family," I add, feeling so much warmth and love from both of them.

"It's pretty fuck awesome, huh?" JD mutters. "I get it, though, after a lifetime of not having it, it can be overwhelming as fuck."

Laying my hand on his, I give him a supportive squeeze back.

"Shit, this smells good," he then announces before diving for his pasta as if we didn't just have a little moment.

Mav chuckles and leans in to kiss my temple.

"It might be unexpected, but there are worse places to be."

"You've got that right," I say before reaching for my fork and twirling up some spaghetti. "Oh my God," I mumble as the flavors explode on my tongue. I shouldn't be surprised, every single thing Reid has cooked has been incredible, but wow.

"My boy can cook," Griff announces with a wide grin as he dives in for more.

Silence falls around the table as everyone enjoys Reid's meal, and it's not until the bowls are empty that chatter resumes.

The important conversations are pushed aside as uncle and nephew—and JD—reconnect. I sit and listen to everything, soaking up every bit of information I can.

I had no idea how desperate I was to learn everything there is to know about the enigma that is Reid Harris. But I'm like a freaking sponge sucking it all up.

Eventually, though, the conversation takes a turn

toward our current situation. And as much as I want to know about what's coming next, I don't listen with nearly as much enthusiasm.

And apparently, I'm not the only one who notices.

"Shall we leave them to it?" Aubrey asks from across the table. "I came on my bike and a little birdy"—she flashes a look at Mav—"Told me that you're a bit of an adrenaline junkie."

A wide smile spreads across my face.

"Hell yes."

"Whoa, we get to watch, right?" JD asks, doing a total one-eighty on the other conversation happening around us.

"Such a dog, Julian," Aubrey chastises.

"Takes one to know one," he banters back.

"You boys go and talk business. Us girls are going out to play." Pushing her chair back, Aubrey waits for me to give both Mav and JD a kiss before joining her, a move that drags every set of eyes around the table to me, despite them all knowing what's happening here. I guess knowing and seeing are two very different things.

My eyes collide with Reid, and my chest compresses as I debate whether I should walk around the table and give him one too.

But in the end, he takes that decision out of my hands when he shoots me a panty-melting grin and says, "Have fun. Don't do anything I wouldn't do."

"Pfft, fat chance of that, Harris," Aubrey snarks. "Come on, girl. I brought you a spare jacket."

Together, we disappear down the hall, leaving the boys behind.

Excitement bubbles in my belly at both the prospect of getting on the back of a bike but also, leaving the house.

If I were going with anyone but my men or Aubrey, I

might be nervous, but I'm a long way from feeling that way as she leads me out.

"And this is my baby," she says, waving her hand out to the completely black Kawasaki.

"She's beautiful," I say, moving closer and taking in her sleek lines.

I wasn't a fan of motorbikes until the day Mav handed me a set of leathers and a helmet—to hide my identity as we rode through the streets of Harrow Creek—and took me out for my first ride.

It's something I didn't realize I was missing until this very moment.

"Hell yeah, she is. A better ride than any man I've ever met too."

"I'll let you know my opinion on that when you bring her to a stop."

Laughter falls from my lips as I take the jacket Aubrey offers me and quickly throw it around my body, more than eager to get on and feel the wind in my hair.

"We don't all have three stallions to ride whenever the desire takes us," Aubrey sulks, a pout on her full lips.

"Never say never. Who knows what's around the corner."

She thinks for a moment, something darkening her eyes. But I don't give her time to linger on it.

"Come on then. Give me a thrill, baby."

Forgetting whatever just sent her to a dark place, she happily agrees and throws her leg over the bike. She waits for me to join her before she brings the engine to life.

"Woohoo," I cry as the vibrations of the beast rock through me.

Laughing, Aubrey kicks the stand away and then shoots

off, making me shriek with delight as she heads for the tree line.

"Oh my God," I scream as she barely slows before we disappear into the darkness.

Holding her tighter, I duck my head. No idea why, the trees are well above us, but it just feels right as we bounce over the rough terrain as if we're on a motocross track.

"You're fucking crazy," I bellow over the rumble of the engine and the air whooshing past my ears.

"Woooo," she screams as we hit a bump and leave the ground.

My stomach drops into my feet, but I fucking love it.

My heart pounds like a bass drum, and my lips tingle with adrenaline as she continues up a bank.

Once we're at a clearing at the top, she stops the bike and kills the engine.

The house with my men inside is right beneath us. It's the first time I've seen it from the outside, and it's every bit as breathtaking as the inside.

"Wow, it's beautiful up here." The view of Hazard Grove in the distance isn't all that different from the view of Harrow Creek from Reid's house.

"Yeah, it's something," Aubrey says, but something in her voice drags my eyes away from the town laid out before us in favor of focusing on her.

"What's wrong?" I ask, studying her as if I'll get the answer from her eyes alone.

Lifting her arm, she glances at her watch.

"There's something I need to tell you," she says.

Panic assaults me. Something is wrong here.

Very. Very wrong.

"What? What is it?"

She hesitates, and just as her lips part to say more, the

most almighty bang rips through the air, rocking the ground beneath us.

Spinning around, I stare in horror as a series of windows shatter, glass flying through the air.

My heart jumps into my throat as smoke begins billowing from the building before bright flames begin licking up the side of the building.

My lips part to scream but I'm motionless. Frozen in place as my worst fear plays out before me.

Another loud explosion echoes into the silence around us before the house is engulfed in a massive fireball.

My entire world falls from beneath me.

No.

No.

My feet move without instruction from my brain. My need to be down there with my men is too much, and I take off.

But before I get anywhere, a hand wraps around my upper arm, holding me back.

"NOOOOOO," I scream, desperately trying to fight it off.

But it's pointless. She's too strong.

And even if she weren't.

It's too late.

Want to know what happens next? ONE-CLICK your copy of Fearless, the final book in the Harrow Creek Hawks series!

Keep reading for a sneak peek of The Revenge You Seek.

THE REVENGE YOU SEEK
SNEAK PEEK

Chapter One

Letty

I sit on my bed, staring down at the fabric in my hands.

This wasn't how it was supposed to happen.

This wasn't part of my plan.

I let out a sigh, squeezing my eyes tight, willing the tears away.

I've cried enough. I thought I'd have run out by now.

A commotion on the other side of the door has me looking up in a panic, but just like yesterday, no one comes knocking.

I think I proved that I don't want to hang with my new roommates the first time someone knocked and asked if I wanted to go for breakfast with them.

I don't.

I don't even want to be here.

I just want to hide.

And that thought makes it all a million times worse.

I'm not a hider. I'm a fighter. I'm a fucking Hunter.

But this is what I've been reduced to.

This pathetic, weak mess.

And all because of *him.*

He shouldn't have this power over me. But even now, he does.

The dorm falls silent once again, and I pray that they've all headed off for their first class of the semester so I can slip out unnoticed.

I know it's ridiculous. I know I should just go out there with my head held high and dig up the confidence I know I do possess.

But I can't.

I figure that I'll just get through today—my first day—and everything will be alright.

I can somewhat pick up where I left off, almost as if the last eighteen months never happened.

Wishful thinking.

I glance down at the hoodie in my hands once more.

Mom bought them for Zayn, my younger brother, and me.

The navy fabric is soft between my fingers, but the text staring back at me doesn't feel right.

Maddison Kings University.

A knot twists my stomach and I swear my whole body sags with my new reality.

I was at my dream school. I beat the odds and I got into Columbia. And everything was good. No, everything was fucking fantastic.

Until it wasn't.

Now here I am. Sitting in a dorm at what was always my backup plan school having to start over.

Throwing the hoodie onto my bed, I angrily push to my feet.

I'm fed up with myself.

I should be better than this, stronger than this.

But I'm just... I'm broken.

And as much as I want to see the positives in this situation. I'm struggling.

Shoving my feet into my Vans, I swing my purse over my shoulder and scoop up the couple of books on my desk for the two classes I have today.

My heart drops when I step out into the communal kitchen and find a slim blonde-haired girl hunched over a mug and a textbook.

The scent of coffee fills my nose and my mouth waters.

My shoes squeak against the floor and she immediately looks up.

"Sorry, I didn't mean to disrupt you."

"Are you kidding?" she says excitedly, her southern accent making a smile twitch at my lips.

Her smile lights up her pretty face and for some reason, something settles inside me.

I knew hiding was wrong. It's just been my coping method for... quite a while.

"We wondered when our new roommate was going to show her face. The guys have been having bets on you being an alien or something."

A laugh falls from my lips. "No, no alien. Just..." I sigh, not really knowing what to say.

"You transferred in, right? From Columbia?"

"Ugh... yeah. How'd you know—"

"Girl, I know everything." She winks at me, but it

doesn't make me feel any better. "West and Brax are on the team, they spent the summer with your brother."

A rush of air passes my lips in relief. Although I'm not overly thrilled that my brother has been gossiping about me.

"So, what classes do you have today?" she asks when I stand there gaping at her.

"Umm... American lit and psychology."

"I've got psych later too. Professor Collins?"

"Uh..." I drag my schedule from my purse and stare down at it. "Y-yes."

"Awesome. We can sit together."

"S-sure," I stutter, sounding unsure, but the smile I give her is totally genuine. "I'm Letty, by the way." Although I'm pretty sure she already knows that.

"Ella."

"Okay, I'll... uh... see you later."

"Sure. Have a great morning."

She smiles at me and I wonder why I was so scared to come out and meet my new roommates.

I'd wanted Mom to organize an apartment for me so that I could be alone, but—probably wisely—she refused. She knew that I'd use it to hide in and the point of me restarting college is to try to put everything behind me and start fresh.

After swiping an apple from the bowl in the middle of the table, I hug my books tighter to my chest and head out, ready to embark on my new life.

The morning sun burns my eyes and the scent of freshly cut grass fills my nose as I step out of our building. The summer heat hits my skin, and it makes everything feel that little bit better.

So what if I'm starting over. I managed to transfer the

credits I earned from Columbia, and MKU is a good school. I'll still get a good degree and be able to make something of my life.

Things could be worse.

It could be this time last year...

I shake the thought from my head and force my feet to keep moving.

I pass students meeting up with their friends for the start of the new semester as they excitedly tell them all about their summers and the incredible things they did, or they compare schedules.

My lungs grow tight as I drag in the air I need. I think of the friends I left behind in Columbia. We didn't have all that much time together, but we'd bonded before my life imploded on me.

Glancing around, I find myself searching for familiar faces. I know there are plenty of people here who know me. A couple of my closest friends came here after high school.

Mom tried to convince me to reach out over the summer, but my anxiety kept me from doing so. I don't want anyone to look at me like I'm a failure. That I got into one of the best schools in the country, fucked it up and ended up crawling back to Rosewood. I'm not sure what's worse, them assuming I couldn't cope or the truth.

Focusing on where I'm going, I put my head down and ignore the excited chatter around me as I head for the coffee shop, desperately in need of my daily fix before I even consider walking into a lecture.

I find the Westerfield Building where my first class of the day is and thank the girl who holds the heavy door open for me before following her toward the elevator.

"Holy fucking shit," a voice booms as I turn the corner, following the signs to the room on my schedule.

Before I know what's happening, my coffee is falling from my hand and my feet are leaving the floor.

"What the—" The second I get a look at the guy standing behind the one who has me in his arms, I know exactly who I've just walked into.

Forgetting about the coffee that's now a puddle on the floor, I release my books and wrap my arms around my old friend.

His familiar woodsy scent flows through me, and suddenly, I feel like me again. Like the past two years haven't existed.

"What the hell are you doing here?" Luca asks, a huge smile on his face when he pulls back and studies me.

His brows draw together when he runs his eyes down my body, and I know why. I've been working on it over the summer, but I know I'm still way skinnier than I ever have been in my life.

"I transferred," I admit, forcing the words out past the lump in my throat.

His smile widens more before he pulls me into his body again.

"It's so good to see you."

I relax into his hold, squeezing him tight, absorbing his strength. And that's one thing that Luca Dunn has in spades. He's a rock, always has been and I didn't realize how much I needed that right now.

Mom was right. I should have reached out.

"You too," I whisper honestly, trying to keep the tears at bay that are threatening just from seeing him—them.

"Hey, it's good to see you," Leon says, slightly more subdued than his twin brother as he hands me my discarded books.

"Thank you."

I look between the two of them, noticing all the things that have changed since I last saw them in person. I keep up with them on Instagram and TikTok, sure, but nothing is quite like standing before the two of them.

Both of them are bigger than I ever remember, showing just how hard their coach is working them now they're both first string for the Panthers. And if it's possible, they're both hotter than they were in high school, which is really saying something because they'd turn even the most confident of girls into quivering wrecks with one look back then. I can only imagine the kind of rep they have around here.

The sound of a door opening behind us and the shuffling of feet cuts off our little reunion.

"You in Professor Whitman's American lit class?" Luca asks, his eyes dropping from mine to the book in my hands.

"Yeah. Are you?"

"We are. Walk you to class?" A smirk appears on his lips that I remember all too well. A flutter of the butterflies he used to give me threaten to take flight as he watches me intently.

Luca was one of my best friends in high school, and I spent almost all our time together with the biggest crush on him. It seems that maybe the teenage girl inside me still thinks that he could be it for me.

"I'd love you to."

"Come on then, Princess," Leon says and my entire body jolts at hearing that pet name for me. He's never called me that before and I really hope he's not about to start now.

Clearly not noticing my reaction, he once again takes my books from me and threads his arm through mine as the pair of them lead me into the lecture hall.

I glance at both of them, a smile pulling at my lips and hope building inside me.

Maybe this was where I was meant to be this whole time.

Maybe Columbia and I were never meant to be.

More than a few heads turn our way as we climb the stairs to find some free seats. Mostly it's the females in the huge space and I can't help but inwardly laugh at their reaction.

I get it.

The Dunn twins are two of the Kings around here and I'm currently sandwiched between them. It's a place that nearly every female in this college, hell, this state, would kill to be in.

"Dude, shift the fuck over," Luca barks at another guy when he pulls to a stop a few rows from the back.

The guy who's got dark hair and even darker eyes immediately picks up his bag, books, and pen and moves over a space.

"This is Colt," Luca explains, nodding to the guy who's studying me with interest.

"Hey," I squeak, feeling a little intimidated.

"Hey." His low, deep voice licks over me. "Ow, what the fuck, man?" he barks, rubbing at the back of his head where Luca just slapped him.

"Letty's off-limits. Get your fucking eyes off her."

"Dude, I was just saying hi."

"Yeah, and we all know what that usually leads to," Leon growls behind me.

The three of us take our seats and just about manage to pull our books out before our professor begins explaining the syllabus for the semester.

"Sorry about the coffee," Luca whispers after a few minutes. "Here." He places a bottle of water on my desk. "I know it's not exactly a replacement, but it's the best I can do."

The reminder of the mess I left out in the hallway hits me.

"I should go and—"

"Chill," he says, placing his hand on my thigh. His touch instantly relaxes me as much as it sends a shock through my body. "I'll get you a replacement after class. Might even treat you to a cupcake."

I smile up at him, swooning at the fact he remembers my favorite treat.

Why did I ever think coming here was a bad idea?

Chapter Two
Letty

My hand aches by the time Professor Whitman finishes talking. It feels like a lifetime ago that I spent this long taking notes.

"You okay?" Luca asks me with a laugh as I stretch out my fingers.

"Yeah, it's been a while."

"I'm sure these boys can assist you with that, beautiful," bursts from Colt's lips, earning him another slap to the head.

"Ignore him. He's been hit in the head with a ball one too many times," Leon says from beside me but I'm too enthralled with the way Luca is looking at me right now to reply.

Our friendship wasn't a conventional one back in high school. He was the star quarterback, and I wasn't a cheerleader or ever really that sporty. But we were paired up as lab partners during my first week at Rosewood High and we kinda never separated.

I watched as he took the team to new heights, as he met with college scouts, I even went to a few places with him so he didn't have to go alone.

He was the one who allowed me to cry on his shoulder as I struggled to come to terms with the loss of another who left a huge hole in my heart and he never, not once, overstepped the mark while I clung to him and soaked up his support.

I was also there while he hooked up with every member of the cheer squad along with any other girl who looked at him just so. Each one stung a little more than the last as my poor teenage heart was getting battered left, right, and center.

With each day, week, month that passed, I craved him more but he never, not once, looked at me that way.

I was even his prom date, yet he ended up spending the night with someone else.

It hurt, of course it did. But it wasn't his fault and I refuse to hold it against him.

Maybe I should have told him. Been honest with him about my feelings and what I wanted. But I was so terrified I'd lose my best friend that I never confessed, and I took that secret all the way to Columbia with me.

As I stare at him now, those familiar butterflies still set flight in my belly, but they're not as strong as I remember. I'm not sure if that's because my feelings for him have lessened over time, or if I'm just so numb and broken right now that I don't feel anything but pain.

It really could go either way.

I smile at him, so grateful to have run into him this morning.

He always knew when I needed him and even without knowing of my presence here, there he was like some guardian fucking angel.

If guardian angels had sexy dark bed hair, mesmerizing green eyes and a body built for sin then yeah, that's what he is.

I laugh to myself, yeah, maybe that irritating crush has gone nowhere.

"What have you got next?" Leon asks, dragging my attention away from his twin.

Leon has always been the quieter, broodier one of the duo. He's as devastatingly handsome and as popular with the female population but he doesn't wear his heart on his sleeve like Luca. Leon takes a little time to warm to people, to let them in. It was hard work getting there, but I soon realized that once he dropped his walls a little for me, it was hella worth it.

He's more serious, more contemplative, he's deeper. I always suspected that there was a reason they were so different. I know twins don't have to be the same and like the same things, but there was always something niggling at me that there was a very good reason that Leon closed himself down. From listening to their mom talk over the years, they were so identical in their mannerisms, likes, and dislikes when they were growing up, that it seems hard to believe they became so different.

"Psychology but not for an hour. I'm—"

"I'm taking her for coffee," Luca butts in. A flicker of anger passes through Leon's eyes but it's gone so fast that I begin to wonder if I imagined it.

"I could use another coffee before econ," Leon chips in.

"Great. Let's go," Luca forces out through clenched teeth.

He wanted me alone. Interesting.

The reason I never told him about my mega crush is the fact he friend-zoned me in our first few weeks of friendship by telling me how refreshing it was to have a girl wanting to be his friend and not using it as a ploy to get more.

We were only sophomores at the time but even then, Luca was up to all sorts and the girls around us were all more than willing to bend to his needs.

From that moment on, I couldn't tell him how I really felt. It was bad enough I even felt it when he thought our friendship was just that.

I smile at both of them, hoping to shatter the sudden tension between the twins.

"Be careful with these two," Colt announces from behind us as we make our way out of the lecture hall with all the others. "The stories I've heard."

"Colt," Luca warns, turning to face him and walking backward for a few steps.

"Don't worry," I shoot over my shoulder. "I know how to handle the Dunn twins." I wink at him as he howls with laughter.

"You two are in so much trouble," he muses as he turns left out of the room and we go right.

Leon takes my books from me once more and Luca threads his fingers through mine. I still for a beat. While the move isn't unusual, Luca has always been very affectionate. It only takes a second for his warmth to race up my arm and to settle the last bit of unease that's still knotting my stomach.

"Two Americanos and a skinny vanilla latte with an extra shot. Three cupcakes with the sprinkles on top."

I swoon at the fact Luca remembers my order. "How'd you—"

He turns to me, his wide smile and the sparkle in his eyes making my words trail off. The familiarity of his face, the feeling of comfort and safety he brings me causes a lump to form in my throat.

"I didn't forget anything about my best girl." He throws his arm around my shoulder and pulls me close.

Burying my nose in his hard chest, I breathe him in. His woodsy scent mixes with his laundry detergent and it settles me in a way I didn't know I needed.

Leon's stare burns into my back as I snuggle with his brother and I force myself to pull away so he doesn't feel like the third wheel.

"Dunn," the server calls, and Leon rushes ahead to grab our order while Luca leads me to a booth at the back of the coffee shop.

As we walk past each table, I become more and more aware of the attention on the twins. I know their reps, they've had their football god status since before I moved to Rosewood and met them in high school, but I had forgotten just how hero-worshiped they were, and this right now is off the charts.

Girls openly stare, their eyes shamelessly dropping down the guys' bodies as they mentally strip them naked. Guys jealousy shines through their expressions, especially those who are here with their girlfriends who are now paying them zero attention. Then there are the girls whose attention is firmly on me. I can almost read their thoughts— hell, I heard enough of them back in high school.

What do they see in her?

She's not even that pretty.

They're too good for her.

The only difference here from high school is that no one knows I'm just trailer park trash seeing as I moved from the hellhole that is Harrow Creek before meeting the boys.

Tipping my chin up, I straighten my spine and plaster on as much confidence as I can find.

They can all think what they like about me, they can come up with whatever bitchy comments they want. It's no skin off my back.

"Good to see you've lost your appeal," I mutter, dropping into the bench opposite both of them and wrapping my hands around my warm mug when Leon passes it over.

"We walk around practically unnoticed," Luca deadpans.

"You thought high school was bad," Leon mutters, he was always the one who hated the attention whereas Luca used it to his advantage to get whatever he wanted. "It was nothing."

"So I see. So, how's things? Catch me up on everything," I say, needing to dive into their celebrity status lifestyles rather than thinking about my train wreck of a life.

"Really?" Luca asks, raising a brow and causing my stomach to drop into my feet. "I think the bigger question is how come you're here and why we had no idea about it?"

Releasing my mug, I wrap my arms around myself and drop my eyes to the table.

"T-things just didn't work out at Columbia," I mutter, really not wanting to talk about it.

"The last time we talked, you said it was everything you expected it to be and more. What happened?"

Kane fucking Legend happened.

I shake that thought from my head like I do every time he pops up.

He's had his time ruining my life. It's over.

"I just..." I sigh. "I lost my way a bit, ended up dropping out and finally had to fess up and come clean to Mom."

Leon laughs sadly. "I bet that went down well."

The Dunn twins are well aware of what it's like to live with a pushy parent. One of the things that bonded the three of us over the years.

"Like a lead balloon. Even worse because I dropped out months before I finally showed my face."

"Why hide?" Leon's brows draw together as Luca stares at me with concern darkening his eyes.

"I had some health issues. It's nothing."

"Shit, are you okay?"

Fucking hell, Letty. Stop making this worse for yourself.

"Yeah, yeah. Everything is good. Honestly. I'm here and I'm ready to start over and make the best of it."

They both smile at me, and I reach for my coffee once more, bringing the mug to my lips and taking a sip.

"Enough about me, tell me all about the lives of two of the hottest Kings of Maddison."

"**O**kay... how'd you do that?" Ella whispers after both Luca and Leon walk me to my psych class after our coffee break.

"Do what?" I ask, following her into the room and finding ourselves seats about halfway back.

"It's your first day and the Dunn twins just walked you to class. You got a diamond-encrusted vag or something?"

I snort a laugh as a few others pause on their way to their seats at her words.

"Shush," I chastise.

"Girl, if it's true, you know all these guys need to know about it."

I pull out my books and a couple of pens as Professor Collins sets up at the front before turning to her.

"No, I don't have diamonds anywhere but my necklace. I've been friends with them for years."

"Girl, I knew there was a reason we should be friends." She winks at me. "I've been trying to get West and Brax to hook me up but they're useless."

"You want to be friends so I can set you up with one of the Dunns?"

"Or both." She shrugs, her face deadly serious before she leans in. "I've heard that they tag team sometimes. Can you imagine? Both of their undivided attention." She fans herself as she obviously pictures herself in the middle of a Dunn sandwich. "Oh and, I think you're pretty cool too."

"Of course you do." I laugh.

It's weird, I might have only met her very briefly this morning but that was enough.

"We're all going out for dinner tonight to welcome you to the dorm. The others are dying to meet you." She smiles at me, proving that there's no bitterness behind her words.

"I'm sorry for ignoring you all."

"Girl, don't sweat it. We got ya back, don't worry."

"Thank you," I mouth as the professor demands everyone's attention to begin the class.

The time flies as I scribble my notes down as fast as I can, my hand aching all over again and before I know it, he's finished explaining our first assignment and bringing his class to a close.

"Jesus, this semester is going to be hard," Ella muses as we both pack up.

"At least we've got each other."

"I like the way you think. You done for the day?"

"Yep, I'm gonna head to the store, grab some supplies then get started on this assignment, I think."

"I've got a couple of hours. You want company?"

After dumping our stuff in our rooms, Ella takes me to her favorite store, and I stock up on everything I'm going to need before we head back so she can go to class.

I make myself some lunch before being brave and setting up my laptop at the kitchen table to get started on my assignments. My time for hiding is over, it's time to get back to life and once again become a fully immersed college student.

"Holy shit, she is alive. I thought Zayn was lying about his beautiful older sister," a deep rumbling voice says, dragging me from my research a few hours later.

I spin and look at the two guys who have joined me.

"Zayn would never have called me beautiful," I say as a greeting.

"That's true. I think his actual words were: messy, pain in the ass, and my personal favorite, I'm glad I don't have to live with her again," he says, mimicking my brother's voice.

"Now that is more like it. Hey, I'm Letty. Sorry about—"

"You're all good. We're just glad you emerged. I'm West, this ugly motherfucker is Braxton—"

"Brax, please," he begs. "Only my mother calls me by my full name and you are way too hot to be her."

My cheeks heat as he runs his eyes over my curves.

"T-thanks, I think."

"Ignore him. He hasn't gotten laid for weeeeks."

"Okay, do we really need to go there right now?"

"Always, bro. Our girl here needs to know you get pissy when you don't get the pussy."

I laugh at their easy banter, closing down my laptop and

resting forward on my elbows as they move toward the fridge.

"Ella says we're going out," Brax says, pulling out two bottles of water and throwing one to West.

"Apparently so."

"She'll be here in a bit. Violet and Micah too. They were all in the same class."

"So," West says, sliding into the chair next to me. "What do we need to know that your brother hasn't already told us about you?"

My heart races at all the things that not even my brother would share about my life before I drag my thoughts away from my past.

"Uhhh..."

"How about the Dunns love her," Ella announces as she appears in the doorway flanked by two others. Violet and Micah, I assume.

"Um... how didn't we know this?" Brax asks.

"Because you're not cool enough to spend any time with them, asshole," Violet barks, walking around Ella. "Ignore these assholes, they think they're something special because they're on the team but what they don't tell you is that they have no chance of making first string or talking to the likes of the Dunns."

"Vi, girl. That stings," West says, holding his hand over his heart.

"Yeah, get over it. Truth hurts." She smiles up at him as he pulls her into his chest and kisses the top of her head.

"Whatever, Titch."

"Right, well. Are we ready to go? I need tacos like... yesterday."

"Yes. Let's go."

"You've never had tacos like these, Letty. You are in for a world of pleasure," Brax says excitedly.

"More than she would be if she were in your bed, that's for sure," West deadpans.

"Lies and we all know it."

"Whatever." Violet pushes him toward the door.

"Hey, I'm Micah," the third guy says when I catch up to him.

"Hey, Letty."

"You need a sensible conversation, I'm your boy."

"Good to know."

Micah and I trail behind the others and with each step I take, my smile gets wider.

Things really are going to be okay.

DOWNLOAD NOW TO KEEP READING

ABOUT THE AUTHOR

Tracy Lorraine is a *USA Today* and *Wall Street Journal* bestselling new adult and contemporary romance author. Tracy has recently turned thirty and lives in a cute Cotswold village in England with her husband, baby girl and lovable but slightly crazy dog. Having always been a bookaholic with her head stuck in her Kindle, Tracy decided to try her hand at a story idea she dreamt up and hasn't looked back since.

Be the first to find out about new releases and offers. Sign up to my newsletter here.

If you want to know what I'm up to and see teasers and snippets of what I'm working on, then you need to be in my Facebook group. Join Tracy's Angels here.

Keep up to date with Tracy's books at
www.tracylorraine.com

ALSO BY TRACY LORRAINE

Wicked Knight #1 (Stella & Seb)

Wicked Princess #2 (Stella & Seb)

Wicked Empire #3 (Stella & Seb)

Deviant Knight #4 (Emmie & Theo)

Deviant Princess #5 (Emmie & Theo

Deviant Reign #6 (Emmie & Theo)

One Reckless Knight (Jodie & Toby)

Reckless Knight #7 (Jodie & Toby)

Reckless Princess #8 (Jodie & Toby)

Reckless Dynasty #9 (Jodie & Toby)

Dark Halloween Knight (Calli & Batman)

Dark Knight #10 (Calli & Batman)

Dark Princess #11 (Calli & Batman)

Dark Legacy #12 (Calli & Batman)

Corrupt Valentine Knight (Nico & Siren)

Corrupt Knight #13 (Nico & Siren)

Corrupt Princess #14 (Nico & Siren)

Corrupt Union #15 (Nico & Siren)

Sinful Wild Knight (Alex & Vixen)

Sinful Stolen Knight: Prequel (Alex & Vixen)

Sinful Knight #16 (Alex & Vixen)

Sinful Princess #17 (Alex & Vixen)

Sinful Kingdom #18 (Alex & Vixen)

Knight's Ridge Destiny: Epilogue

Harrow Creek Hawks Series

Merciless #1

Relentless #2

Lawless #3

Ruined Series

Ruined Plans #1

Ruined by Lies #2

Ruined Promises #3

Never Forget Series

Never Forget Him #1

Never Forget Us #2

Everywhere & Nowhere #3

Chasing Series

Chasing Logan

The Cocktail Girls

His Manhattan

Her Kensington

Made in the USA
Middletown, DE
03 August 2024

58431390R00265